MW01128640

TOM & CHRISTOPHER
AND THEIR KIND

A Novel

ANTHONY MCDONALD

Anchor Mill Publishing

Anthony McDonald

Anchor Mill Publishing
4/04 Anchor Mill
Paisley PA1 1JR
SCOTLAND
anchormillpublishing@gmail.com

Cover illustration: *Lovers of the Sun* by Henry Scott Tuke. Cover design by Barry Creasy.

Tom & Christopher And Their Kind

In memory of Tony Linford.
And for Steve Gee, Nigel Fothergill, and Thomas
McGlone

Acknowledgements

I am grateful to John Newberry, Andi Rivett and Yves Le Juen for their expert input in areas of knowledge into which I could only dip a cautious toe.

The title of this book pays affectionate tribute to Christopher Isherwood.

Anthony McDonald

Colloque sentimental

Paul Verlaine

Dans le vieux parc solitaire et glace
Deux formes ont tout à l'heure passé.

Leurs yeux sont morts et leurs lèvres sont molles,
Et l'on entend à peine leurs paroles.

Dans le vieux parc solitaire et glace
Deux spectres ont évoqué le passé.

- Te souvient-il de notre extase ancienne?
- Pourquoi voulez-vous donc qu'il m'en souvienne?

- Ton coeur bat-il toujours à mon seul nom?
Toujours vois-tu mon âme en rêve? - Non.

Ah ! les beaux jours de bonheur indicible
Où nous joignions nos bouches ! - C'est possible.

- Qu'il était bleu, le ciel, et grand, l'espoir!
- L'espoir a fui, vaincu, vers le ciel noir.

Tels ils marchaient dans les avoines folles,
Et la nuit seule entendit leurs paroles.

(Tom's translation)

In the old park, frozen, lonely, Two figures walk, two figures only.

Their eyes are dead, their slack lips mutter. We strain to hear the words they utter.

In the old park, frozen, lonely, The past comes back to two ghosts only.

'Do you remember our ancient rapture?' 'Why do you want me to recapture...?'

'Your heart still beats at the thought of my name? Is my soul in your dreams?' 'It's not the same.'

'Beyond words was our joy that day When our lips first met.' 'If that's what you say...'

'The sky was so blue, our hopes were so high...' 'Hope has fled, vanquished, along the night sky.'

So saying, they walk through the wild oat-grass. While the night alone hears them as they pass.

Anthony McDonald

Part One

1962

Anthony McDonald

ONE

Climbing that hill. It felt more like climbing a wall. They were soaked to the skin and freezing cold. Even their suitcases were wet. They hadn't opened them to inspect the damage wrought by the sea.

They came at last to the familiar door on the corner where the Rue Faidherbe and the Rue Hamy met. Tom pressed the bell. There was a minute's silence. Like an Armistice Day silence it spoke of eternity. Then the door opened and Michel stood framed in it. He wore his usual garb of bib-and-brace dungarees with – they had always presumed – nothing underneath. *'Merde,'* Michel said. Then he spread his arms wide and placed a hand on the shoulder of both the woe-faced young Englishmen who stood before him. 'Come in,' he said. 'You're soaking wet.'

He dragged them inside and shut the door. *'Zut!* What's happened to you? No. That can wait.' In the tiny space at the foot of the stairs he snatched their suitcases from them and started to stagger up the steep and narrow flight that is familiar to anyone who has ever lived above a shop. 'We'll get you into some warm clothing. Come on up.' They followed, mute.

1

In the easel-crowded, canvas-crowded, space of the artist's studio above, Armand leapt naked and impressive out of the single bed. 'What's happened?' he asked.

'Get towels and some clothes,' Michel told him. He turned to Tom and Christopher. 'Take your wet clothes off.'

They had to. There was no arguing with that. They had never stripped naked in front of Michel and Armand before. Why would they have? But they had just been treated to the sight of Armand leaping out of bed in all his morning glory, even if he was now already stuffing himself into underpants. Tom was conscious of making a poor showing of himself: his dick a tiny pepper-pot, his ball-sac walnut-sized. After all, he'd just been drenched by the chilly sea. Glancing at Christopher he saw that his young friend's adornments were in a similarly shrivelled state: his penis peeping childishly above half-retracted balls. He found himself feeling as though that circumstance was his, Tom's, fault. While the two French boys tried hard not to notice what their English friends looked like below the waist, or pretended not to, perhaps. Then Armand remembered what he had been asked to do; he turned and rummaged in a drawer and threw Tom and Christopher a pair of corduroy trousers and a sweater each.

Michel looked down at the two damp suitcases that filled the remainder of the cluttered floor-space. He may have bitten back the first question that rose to his lips. The obvious question. At any rate, he didn't ask it. He went ahead two moves and said, 'You can stay as long as you like.' Tom and Christopher looked around them. Michel could hardly have meant here, in this tiny space, where the two young Frenchmen shared a single bed.

Armand said, 'Have you been ship-wrecked? Were people lost? Hurt?'

'Not as bad as that,' said Tom. 'We came over on a small sailing boat. Our friends' fishing smack. Took a pounding from the waves. Our friends have gone back across.'

Michel frowned. 'Tell us what this is all about.'

'We had to leave England,' said Christopher. 'Had to escape.'

'Because…?'

'Because of sex,' Christopher said.

Neither Michel nor Armand showed any sign of surprise that two English boys should have had to flee their home country because of sex.

All of a sudden Christopher, still standing naked, began quietly to cry. Tom put his arms around him and held him close. Over Christopher's shoulder he said to the others, 'I think he's still in shock.'

'My mother has a washing-machine,' Michel said matter-of-factly. 'We'll go up there later and get your clothes washed and dried.' The word mother triggered a further explosion of tears in Christopher. Tom clasped him tight.

'Our birthdays were just three days ago,' said Tom. 'Don't know if you knew we shared the same birth date. Three years apart but both June the twenty-first.' Tom had just turned twenty-two, which was Michel's age; Christopher was now nineteen, an age that Armand would attain in a few more weeks.

They were sitting in the sunshine outside a café in the Rue Hamy, a few doors from the studio flat. Below them the brown and red roofs of Boulogne were spread out like a patchwork picnic cloth. Gulls danced in the blue above. Christopher said, 'That was the day it all went wrong.'

Tom gave the details. 'Two of the boys, just thirteen, were found in bed together and were expelled for it.

3

Chris tried to comfort one of them, and told him that we were lovers, sleeping together and having sex. But apparently the kid passed that information on to his father, thinking it would be treated as a mitigating circumstance. It wasn't, of course. The father is a barrister or judge or something, and he hit the roof. He threatened to expose the school as a hotbed of vice and called the police. We got warned in advance by the assistant headmaster and told to disappear at once.'

'So we did just that,' said Christopher. 'But we had nowhere to disappear to. All we could do was come to France. To be safe.'

'Your English laws are shit,' said Armand.

'I thought no-one called Christopher Chris,' Michel said.

'He lets me now,' said Tom gravely. 'Has done for the last hour and a half.'

There was silence for a bit. Michel broke it. 'Tell us about last night.'

Michel and Armand already knew about the two older Englishmen, Roger and Malcolm, who ran a pub on the cliff-top near the school where Tom and Christopher had taught. Now Tom told the French pair how they'd run to their friends just twenty-four hours ago in their extremity of fear and distress; how they'd lain low for the whole of yesterday, then sailed after darkness fell and when the tide was right.

'The sea was calm at first,' said Christopher, 'but then it grew rough.' His voice still bore the scars of the terror he'd felt last night.

'It was off Cap Gris Nez that we all got drenched,' said Tom. He was finding that even now, with his feet planted firmly on the pavement beneath a café table, his body continued to experience the sensations of the night: the heaving rise and fall of the swell; the invisible waves that reared in front of them, their white crests becoming discernible only at the last moment, high up, coming out of the terrifying blackness... Tom wrestled his mind away from the memory. 'We're still alive at least.' He realised that he could do something here that would have been impossible in England in a similar place. He put an arm around Christopher's shoulder, drew his head towards him and kissed the side of it. 'Are you all right now?'

'Not quite yet,' Christopher said.

Above them, from the crown of the hill, the bells of the domed cathedral began to ring out. Today was Sunday. Christopher pulled his head away from Tom's embrace and turned to look at him. 'I suppose we ought to go to Mass,' he said.

Tom's heart sank. The words, *You go if you want to, but for God's sake count me out,* rose inside him but he choked them back. 'I thought we'd done with all that,' he said instead. 'After all that's happened I don't think we owe much to the Catholic Church.'

Christopher said uncomfortably, 'It's just that we survived last night: we didn't die. Perhaps we ought to give thanks.'

Tom looked at Michel. 'You don't do the church thing, I suppose?'

'No,' said Michel. 'My mother still does, though I don't think she'd still call herself a believer. She'll be in the cathedral for Mass.'

Armand said, 'Look, if Christopher wants to go to Mass I don't blame him after the night he's had. And we could all go along. Support him. But not up there...' He pointed up the hill towards the sound of the cathedral bell, still tolling. 'We could go down to St Nicolas in the Place Dalton. We won't run into our parents there. Afterwards we can go across the square to lunch Chez Alfred.'

The church of St Nicolas was the oldest of Boulogne's churches. Parts of the moth-grey building dated back to the thirteenth century, though much of the exterior had been added much later than that. It also boasted a feature that would have been unusual in England: a male toilet, open to the sky, attached to the southern side of it. The four friends made use of it before trooping inside for Mass.

'Introibo ad altare Dei,' the service began, as it would have done at that time in England, Spain or Italy. Or America or Japan. The sermon was in French of course. 'This Sunday,' began the small, rotund and grey-haired priest, 'coincides with the midsummer feast of St John. Many people assume that this midsummer feast celebrates St John the Apostle, the disciple whom Jesus loved.' He paused and smiled coldly. 'I regret to have to disillusion them. Today we commemorate the life of John the Baptist, the cousin of our Lord Jesus Christ. Now, what do we know of this John, this John the Baptist? That he turned his back on the world, that he walked out into the desert and – yes, we have all read the story – lived on wild honey and locusts. Then, on the bank of the Jordan he found himself baptising his own cousin Jesus. "One is to come among you," he had said, "the straps of whose sandals I am not worthy to unloose." It is from the moment of Christ's baptism by John in the river Jordan that we date the beginning of his ministry on earth…'

Christ's ministry on earth, Christopher thought. Three years it had lasted, just three years, before the man was hunted down and killed. Yet it was still going on, wasn't it? With the likes of Father Louis and Father Matthew back in England, preaching and teaching, just like this rotund little man in green vestments in the pulpit here at St Nicolas. It was still going on… Or was it? Was the whole thing a mass delusion, as Tom believed it was?

Yet here was a whole big church packed with believers. Worldwide there were millions, perhaps billions of them. Christopher didn't have the numbers at his fingertips. Surely such numbers couldn't all be wrong… Christopher found this was all too much to think about. Especially this morning. He looked along the pew. At Tom beside him, slimly muscular, honey-blond, supportive. At tall handsome Michel, with his mop of dark brown curls, dark-lashed blue eyes and, even in church, clad in overalls that revealed his bare hips at the sides… Armand, the sloe-eyed beauty with straight hair that was shiny black. Armand, petite as Christopher was himself. None of his three handsome companions believed in what was going on at the altar in front of them. But here they all were, wanting to take care of him in the aftermath of his crisis. His crisis? Tom's crisis also. He mustn't forget that. Suddenly tears were pouring down his cheeks again. Tom must have seen them, for his arm was around Chris's shoulder at once. That was wonderful, Christopher thought. The more wonderful for the fact that they were in a church. The priest's words cut suddenly in on his reverie. *'Avec la tête sur un plateau.'* With his head on a plate.

It was little more than a month since they had all eaten together 'Chez Alfred'. Now Christopher felt giddy with the strangeness of this déjà vu experience. They sat in the same chairs, amidst the same old-fashioned plain décor – yellowing paintwork and brown-painted wood. The menu was the same. The waiters recognised them and, as before, chatted easily with Michel and Armand. But life had changed so much in the meantime – almost literally overnight – that they were no longer the same people. Life was no longer the same life. The last time they'd dined here they had been two young teachers enjoying a cross-Channel weekend trip. This time they were fugitives, on the run from the British police. Things could hardly have changed more, Christopher thought, if they'd died and come back reincarnated as otters or bats.

They had mussels *à la marinière*. The mussels were tiny and cheap. Inside most of them was a minute orange crab the size of half a grain of rice. Tom and Christopher both looked a bit anxiously at these and wondered if they were supposed to be there. But Michel and Armand were slurping their mussels down without taking any notice of the stowaways that lurked inside them, so the English lads followed the French example and swallowed manfully. It wasn't as though you could taste the little objects or even feel them in the mouth.

The mussels were followed by uncomplicated steaks and chips. Tom and Christopher had ordered theirs medium *(au point)* but found when they arrived that they were quite alarmingly red inside. Though when they tasted them they found the flavour and texture a distinct improvement on the steaks they were used to. They weren't sure they'd ever want to go as far as Michel and Armand, though. When those two cut into their steaks the flesh inside was purple-crimson, and liquid of the same colour swam out onto their plates. Not for nothing, thought Christopher, did the French request a rare steak with the word for bleeding: *'saignant'*.

'You can have my room at my mother's.' Michel reintroduced that subject in a very matter-of-fact tone of voice.

'Gosh,' said Tom. 'Are you sure she'd be OK with that?' The offer sounded more than generous.

'Of course she will. Anyway, it's my room, *n'est-ce pas?'*

'We wouldn't want there to be any awkwardness…'

'There won't be any,' Michel reassured him. 'You've met her. You know how much she likes you both. And how supportive of Armand and me she is.'

Christopher nodded his head at that. A mother who was more than happy with her son's openly homosexual relationship was something he would never have believed existed had he not encountered such a one in the person of Michel's mother Sabine. 'It all seems too good to be true,' he said.

Michel said, 'We'll be going up there for supper. I'll telephone presently and say there'll be four of us. Explain what's happened. Tell her we need to use the washing-machine, and that I'm lending you my room for as long as you need or want it.'

When they had paid the bill and left the restaurant Michel made for the telephone call-box in the square. He came out of it a few minutes later with a beaming smile and announced that all was fixed. Supper, use of washing-machine, accommodation, the lot.

They went to the beach after that. It was quite a lengthy walk. It took them along the quayside at which they had disembarked just seven hours before. How strange it was to revisit the spot in different company. They walked past the window of the café at which they'd had early morning coffee with Roger and Malcolm. They didn't stop there or point the place out.

How like a dream this all was, Tom thought. The escape by night. The arrival on a foreign shore. The welcome they'd been given by Michel and Armand, which was better than they'd dared to hope. Starting a new life… Thinking about that made Tom frown a bit. The future was going to be tough. He with Christopher… He couldn't guess how, or even if, that relationship was going to work out. He willed himself to enjoy the present moment. Enjoy the sunshine, the walk by the harbour wall on the way to the beach. This moment of June, as Virginia Woolf wrote. Tom seized the moment and hugged it to himself.

Boulogne harbour is long and narrow, formed in the mouth of the river that runs through the town. Where the river meets the sea the quays metamorphose into two breakwaters that divide the deep current of the river from the beach shallows on either side. As the youths reached this point the view opened out ahead of them. There the English Channel lay, sunning itself in the lazy afternoon warmth. How different it was from the many-headed monster that had roared and reared at them in the small hours of last night; that had tried to engulf and swallow them and take them to the bottom of its deep bed.

Along one section of the far horizon, thirty miles distant, lay the coast of England. It was slender as a piece of worn white shoelace. Like the sea it looked peaceful and innocent, fragile almost. Yet like the sea it was hostile towards them: a place of menace to which they could not return without courting grave risk.

Cautiously Tom looked sideways at Christopher's face, alert to the possibility that a new wave of tears and emotion would be triggered by the sight of the distant cliffs. But that didn't seem about to happen. Instead Christopher spoke.

'I wonder if Malcolm and Roger are home yet.' He peered at the sea as if trying to spot the tiny shape of the Orca with its tan-coloured sails, tacking its way northward in the lee of the English coast.

'Let's hope so,' said Tom. He was pleased to find Christopher voicing concern for other people: a sure sign, Tom reckoned, that he was on the mend himself. All the same he didn't want Christopher's thoughts to dwell too lovingly on Roger or – especially – Malcolm. Red-haired, brown-eyed Malcolm had had quite a thing for Christopher and Christopher had returned the compliment. Last night, at the moment of his greatest terror, under the onslaught of a wave that was breaking over them both, Christopher had thrown himself round

Malcolm and begged him to take him home with him. Malcolm had behaved quite wonderfully, Tom now thought. He had reminded Christopher that it was Tom he was in love with, and had returned the boy to him. Yes, Malcolm had behaved like the perfect gentleman, but Tom would not want either himself or Christopher to be reminded too often of the incident.

They climbed down from the breakwater onto the beach and went down the golden incline to an un-peopled spot, where they threw themselves onto the sand. 'We haven't got towels or trunks,' said Armand. 'Though probably a swim is the last thing Tom and Christopher would want at the moment.'

'Here goes, anyway,' said Michel. He kicked off the moccasin slippers that clad his feet and then slipped the straps of his famous blue dungarees off his shoulders, let the garment fall the length of his body and stepped out of it, revealing his nakedness like a butterfly emerging from a chrysalis.

Tom was more than impressed. But he wasn't going to be outdone. He promptly took off the sweater Armand had lent him, and his shoes, and then the corduroy trousers. Just as in Michel's case there was nothing underneath. Then Christopher and Armand had to follow suit. Christopher too had nothing on except sweater and trousers. Armand was the only one of them with anything underneath. He stood for a moment in indecision and his underpants. Michel made the decision for him. He lunged playfully at Armand and, laughing, pulled the underpants off.

'You're sure we can't be arrested for this?' Tom asked, only half joking.

Michel peered around them. 'Everyone's hundreds of metres away,' he said. 'Anyway, who'd bother to come and arrest us?'

Armand had guessed rightly when he'd supposed that Tom and Christopher wouldn't want to go swimming this afternoon. Perhaps out of an unconscious desire to show solidarity with them the French pair made no move towards the water either. They lay on the sand together, half dozing, close enough together for quiet conversation but without touching one another.

They were aroused from their group reverie by the passing of a shadow across their faces and naked forms. *'Michel et Armand!'* the shadow's owner greeted them in a strong male voice. They all sat up.

A man of about fifty stood looking down at them. He had iron-grey hair, and a grin on his face. Although he wore long trousers his shirt was off and tied around his waist. His top half was bare except for a white-spotted red neckerchief. He looked at Tom and Christopher. *'Messieurs,* I don't think I've had the pleasure…'

Michel spoke. 'Gérard, these are our two English friends, Tom and Christopher. Newly arrived in France.' He turned towards them. 'Gérard is a rather famous painter; he has a studio in Paris.' He turned back to Gérard. 'What are you doing in Boulogne?'

Gérard nodded slowly. The grin remained on his face, although it had grown more thoughtful. He said, 'I'm looking for something to paint. Something or someone. Or a group of people perhaps. At least, I was looking for that.' He gave the four nude men an appraising stare that had nothing unpleasant in it. 'Maybe I've just found it.'

Michel was the only member of the quartet to retain the power of speech. 'Are you saying that you'd like to paint the four of us?'

'Maybe,' Gérard looked searchingly into all their faces. 'And for a fee of course. If you – or any of you – want to discuss the possibility you'll find me in Le Chat qui Pêche at ten o'clock.'

'Tonight?' checked Armand.

'Tonight,' said Gérard and strode off.

Armand said, 'I need a piss. Does anyone mind?' Nobody answered that. Armand scooped a rabbit burrow in the sand with one hand and then lay front-down on top of it. He then did what he needed to – that was apparent to the others only from the contractions of the muscles of his flanks – then back-filled the hole and rolled round again onto his back. Christopher had found the scene rather charming and mildly arousing. He decided that he would copy Armand's example should the need arise while they were still out on the beach. Then he said, 'Michel, we're meeting your mother this evening. I'm really looking forward to that. But I need to contact my own mother. Tell her I'm all right.' Tom peered anxiously at Christopher's face; there were no signs of tears there yet. Christopher went on. 'I need to let her know I'm alive at least.' He paused, and the others waited in silence for him to go on. Which he eventually did. 'I don't know how to. I could never explain everything in a letter. If I tried to phone…' He stopped before his voice could break.

Tom reached out a hand and laid it on Christopher's hot tummy. 'I know,' he said. 'I understand. I know all about it.' Tom was in the same predicament as Christopher. He too had parents who would soon wonder what was happening. But this was not the moment to share that. Only one person's distress can be dealt with at a particular moment. Tom said, 'You can phone your mother this evening. Just say you're alive but that things are complicated. Do it from a call-box. International call. We'll pass the hat round for the cash. Your mother will understand when the money runs out. It's the best you can hope to achieve today.'

As if raising a bid Michel offered, 'You can phone your parents from my mother's. Free. Talk as long as you like. Have a long chat…'

Armand put a hand on his lover's wrist and stopped him in his tracks. 'I don't think a long chat is what Christopher, or his mother, wants at this point. He should send a telegram. Everybody knows they're expensive and are used only for important messages. *Alive. Well. In France. Will write soon.* That's all that needs to be said.'

'I can't do that today,' said Christopher and for the first time in several hours started to well up.

'Do it in the morning,' said Armand sweetly. He reached out and stroked Christopher's face. 'As soon as the Post Office opens.' He smiled into Christopher's eyes. 'Trust me. Your mother won't die overnight.'

TWO

They sat in Sabine's elegant salon chairs that were Second Empire, with gilded scrolled arms and red-upholstered seats. The chairs were far from comfortable but you knew they were worth an absolute fortune and that made it all right. They were drinking an aperitif of Dubonnet with ice and a curl of lemon zest.

'We must find jobs for you both,' said Sabine calmly, as if playing hostess to shipwrecked sailors who had landed without future or fortune was something she did every day of the week. 'Meanwhile, Sunday supper is just Sunday supper: no more than that. There's beetroot with mayonnaise, then cold chicken with sautée potatoes and watercress, cherry clafoutis and cheese to follow. Will that be enough?'

They would have said yes even if they'd thought it wouldn't be. But they were honest and still said yes.

Michel said, 'Gérard wants to paint the four of us.'

'Very nice,' said his mother. 'Pocket money for all of you. It doesn't amount to Tom and Christopher having a job.'

'If it amounts to pocket money that's still better than nothing,' said Michel.

'I'm thinking about the shop,' said Sabine. 'Wondering if we could take on two extra staff.' She looked expectantly at Tom.

Tom's brow crowded with worry lines. How could anyone serve behind the counter in a French ironmonger's when their grasp of the language was as fragile as his and Christopher's was? Even in English he would be struggling with the vocabulary: hasps and clasps, angle-brackets and Y-plates; Rawl-plugs and 9-amp plugs; counter-sink drill bits; different colours and brands of paint... 'I don't know...' he said.

Christopher, who had behind him the experience of serving behind the counter of his father's builders' merchant store in his school holidays, was struggling with something bigger than that: the situation in which he found himself. He was safely ensconced in a bourgeois French *salon*, being fed and cosseted by someone else's mother, while his own mother must be beside herself with worry on the other side of the sea. And what a sea lay between them! A sea that tossed and writhed in the night, that reared and plunged like a mustang that wanted to shake you off its back. His body's memory of last night's experience was still so powerful, so overwhelming, that he felt it in every nerve of his body. Even his eyes still saw the room around him quake, pitch and roll from time to time. It would steady itself for a moment and Christopher would breathe an easy breath, thinking he'd at last done with it, but then it would start up again.

Could all these worlds be real? he asked himself. The home he'd known with his parents back in England – a home he might never see again, he now thought, with a clenching of his gut and throat. The cosy apartment in Boulogne in which he now found himself, being looked after by someone else. The awful terror of the watery world between the two, among whose vertical gleaming slabs he had thought he would be crushed to death last night. It couldn't all be real. Some of it must be an illusion. He feared, as he looked around the warm room and smelt the comforting aroma of frying potatoes, that this was the illusion – this and his parental home – and that the real world was the one of black towering waves and unforgiving night-time depths: a reality from whose jaws he had been snatched only as a temporary measure in the darkest of the dark small hours.

'It might be easier,' Armand was saying, 'for the two of you to work in a bar. The names of the goods are easier to grasp. Wine is wine and beer is beer. The names of the dishes are written on the menu. You don't have customers coming in and asking for bicycle-chain links or plumber's force-cups.'

'Then think of a bar that's short of staff,' said Michel.

'We'll find one,' Armand said very firmly. So firmly that Michel was stopped in his tracks and Tom and Christopher were startled by his apparent confidence.

'They don't need jobs tomorrow,' Sabine reminded her son and Armand gently. 'A few days' rest are probably in order.' She looked at Tom and Christopher. 'You are here as our guests.' Then she looked back at her son. 'Michel, I don't want crimson hands in the morning. You are a painter so it doesn't matter. Will you go and slice the beetroot?'

They arrived in the Chat qui Pêche at ten o'clock. With its dark-painted walls, cushions on the floor and candles in coloured jars it seemed comfortingly familiar. Gérard was already there, his shirt on now, seated at a table with two younger men. He beckoned the four of them over. The two men who were sitting with Gérard took this as their cue to depart. They slid up off their seats without quite standing up, then slipped away around the edge of the room towards the bar like mice.

Dragging two extra chairs from a nearby table that was unoccupied, the new arrivals sat down around Gérard in a disciple-ish sort of group. Gérard beckoned to the man behind the bar and as soon as he arrived to take the order commanded five glasses of Pastis without asking anyone whether that was what they wanted or not.

'What are you all doing tomorrow?' he asked. Michel said that he had to work at the shop in the morning. He could get away by three, he thought. Armand was free all day; the café where he worked was closed on Mondays. While as things currently stood Tom and

Christopher had no diary appointments for the rest of their lives. 'Then may I spend the day painting the three of you?' Gérard said. 'Michel to join us as soon as possible after three o'clock?' He explained that he had it in mind to paint them all lazing naked in a boat and in the water around it, just off the beach...

'That's going to get a bit of unwanted attention, I'd think,' Michel said.

Gérard looked at him with fond amusement. 'It would if we did it on the public beach here,' he said. 'But I plan to go to Audresselles.' He turned to Christopher and Tom. 'Audresselles is a fishing village a few miles from here, towards Gris Nez.'

'Nice spot,' said Michel. Then a look of concern came over his face. 'Though I'm not sure...' Now he turned to Tom and Christopher. 'How do you feel about the sea and boats...?'

Tom took it upon himself to speak for them both. 'Chris'll be fine by tomorrow.' He put a hand on his friend's knee as if to convince him of this fact. 'And I won't have a problem with it.'

Gérard frowned at them. 'You might have had a problem with boats? I don't quite...'

'They recently had a bad experience,' Michel said. Then he found he had to explain what he meant. It all came out, like a pile of tangled-together sheets from a laundry basket. The previous night's adventure. The escape from England. The reasons for this. The last time Tom and Christopher had been painted together... It meant there were no gaps in the conversation for the following hour at least.

Gérard's imagination was clearly stirred by the story of their being painted as David and Jonathan. He chuckled at the innocence of Molly O'Deere, painting them naked to the waist in the first place, then entering the painting in a county exhibition... 'But was it actually a good painting?' he asked.

'We thought so,' said Tom. 'Molly may have been simply a school teacher but she's a real artist. The judges of the exhibition decided her painting of us was the star exhibit. A London art critic praised it highly. "Audacious and technically assured," he wrote.' He paused and blew into his cheeks before letting the air out with his next remark. 'He also piped the whistle as far as we were concerned. His review was headed, "Libido in the Cathedral." That was the beginning of the end for us.'

'It's why we're here now,' Christopher added.

'I see,' said Gérard. He looked thoughtful for a moment then said, 'I think I'd like to see this picture. Is the exhibition still on? And you said it's where?'

'In Canterbury cathedral,' Christopher said. 'In the chapter house.'

'I think the exhibition continues right on into July,' said Tom. 'Though Molly might have decided to withdraw her painting by now.'

'Because of what it led to?' Gérard nodded comprehendingly. 'But Canterbury isn't far to go. Ferry to Folkestone, then… I suppose there'd be a train? We could all make a day of it. Maybe next weekend…'

'Gérard,' Michel interrupted his flow. 'Tom and Christopher have only just got here. They're not going to want to go back just yet.'

'It's not just about not wanting,' said Tom. 'I don't think we dare. We'd probably be arrested as soon as we got to passport control.'

'Of course, I see,' said Gérard. 'I hadn't thought it through.'

'Nothing to stop you going on your own, though, Gérard,' Michel teased him.

'Or taking you two.' He jabbed a finger towards Armand and Michel.

'I'll walk up with you,' Michel said.
'You needn't,' Christopher and Tom said together.
'But he will anyway,' Armand said. 'And I'm coming too.' They had already climbed half a mile up the town's steep hill from the Chat qui Pêche to where the two French lads lived above the shop. Continuing on up the hill to Michel's mother's house took them almost as far again. This late at night their route seemed almost vertical
'Just this once, you understand,' said Michel, sounding very serious about it. But then he giggled, unable to keep the pretence up. Together the four of them climbed through the lamplight of Boulogne's night-time streets.

Sabine was already in her bedroom when they entered the house. Light shone from under the door, though, and Michel spoke to his mother through the crack at the side. Then they all trooped into the room that was really Michel's but was to be Tom's and Christopher's for the foreseeable future. They had seen it earlier and dumped their luggage in it. They had also been given Michel's key to the house. Now Michel and Armand withdrew and left them to it. Not without a parting goodnight kiss between everyone, which by now seemed as natural as anything in the world.

Then the door was shut and Tom and Christopher were alone on the inside of it. The silence of the room beat suddenly at their ears. The light of it, provided by a single bulb that hung from the ceiling inside an elaborate shade, seemed buttercup yellow. It had a colour and a quality – was the electricity here yellow? – that was inseparable from the idea of France.

The bed was single. Michel had left the bedroom of his childhood to go and share a single bed with Armand in a much less comfortable room than this one: his studio above the family shop. Perhaps it was less than ideal to have glorious sex with your boyfriend in the room next to your mother's, Tom thought. It was something very remote from his own experience. How would it be, though, to have glorious sex just a wall away from someone else's mother? They would have to see.

'It's home,' Christopher said suddenly. 'This is our very first home together, Tom.'

Tom felt the sting of tears suddenly, though none fell. He turned and took his lover in his arms, lifted him half an inch off the floor and swung him half a turn around the little room. 'It is, Chris,' he said as he let his feet land on the floor again. 'Yes it is.'

Gérard drove a Renault 4L that was pillar-box red and nearly new. It was not difficult to spot, perched on a pavement edge in the Place Dalton that next morning at nine. Gérard wound the window down as Tom, Christopher and Armand came up. Armand leaned in and said, 'Can we go to the post office first? Christopher needs to send a telegram. I know it's in the opposite direction from Audresselles...'

Gérard gave Armand a grin. 'Jump in. The post office is...?'

'The other side of the harbour. Rue du Biez. I'll navigate.' Which meant, naturally, that Armand hopped into the front seat while Tom and Christopher bundled themselves into the back.

It seemed a labyrinth to Christopher. A one-way system, a river bridge... He had a heavy feeling in the pit of his stomach; his mouth was dry and every time he thought about the precise wording of the telegram he was going to send his temples throbbed. They climbed a hill, Armand pointed to a building and Gérard pulled up outside. Christopher noticed that the car's handbrake was simply a bent metal rod, its gear-lever a knob-handled walking-stick that protruded from the dashboard. He had never seen a car that was fitted out like this.

'The other thing is…' Armand was saying.

'I know,' Gérard said. 'You need money for the telegram.' He leaned over to the boys in the back. 'My jacket's there. Wallet's in an inside pocket. Just give me the wallet.'

Tom got out of the car with Christopher. It was a moment when Christopher needed his support. They went together into the post office. Christopher spoke to the counter clerk in a mixture of French and English, then wrote his words down on the form he was given. Still without speaking he showed Tom what he'd written. He'd used Armand's suggestion of the previous day exactly. *Alive. Well. In France. Will write soon. Christopher.*

'You forgot one thing,' Tom said.

'Hmm?' queried Christopher.

'Love,' said Tom.

Christopher added it.

It was after they had paid, taken the receipt and turned towards the door that Christopher noticed it: his steps were propelling him high into the air, as if he were walking in a world with no gravity. He was ridiculously afraid he would bang his head on the lintel of the door as they walked out through it. Then they were outside – in the fresh coastal air and the late June sunshine. 'Feel better now?' Tom asked. Christopher could only nod and grin.

They drove back down the hill, across the river bridge, and then towards the coast road that started by the beach. From the edge of the town the road climbed up among the cliffs. On a large green expanse at the top a small crowd of men were playing cricket, all dressed in white shirts, white trousers and white boots. 'What is that?' Armand asked in astonishment. 'Crocket?'

'Cricket,' Tom corrected. He was as astonished as the rest of them. Nobody played cricket in France.

'They must be English holidaymakers,' Gérard said. 'Cricket on French soil! Whatever next?' He laughed to show that had been a joke.

Across the water to their left the cliffs of Kent gleamed in the morning sun like a necklace of white teeth or bone.

Their short route took them along the high street of Wimereux, past the village of Ambleteuse and then, leaving the main road to take itself on to Calais, turned down a lane to the place called Audresselles, where a little river wound its way into the sea and fishing boats lay hauled up on the sandy banks.

They parked, if that as the right word for what they did: running a Renault securely into the edge of a sand-dune and stopping it. Gérard opened the tail gate and hauled his equipment out of it. Easel, folding stool, stretched canvasses and cloth bag filled with palette and paints. Another bag with water bottles in it. Tom thought about the work he had come here to do and about the equipment that he required in order to do it. In contrast to Gérard, who had to lug cumbersome stuff around with him, Tom wore his equipment beneath his clothes. For better or worse he had come to work with no brief-case, no books, no tool-bag. He had brought only his nakedness.

Christopher, thinking along the same lines, remembered a limerick…

A Puritan, fuming and oathing,
Regarded all women with loathing.
It made him feel mad
That no matter how clad,

They were all naked under their clothing.

There was a first time for everything, though, Christopher thought. And Gérard had already seen him and Tom naked. They had been auditioned, had not been found wanting, and had got the parts. He hoped the wind wouldn't be too chafing. At least he'd got that telegram off to his parents. He could park his burden of guilt and anxiety – until the reply came back.

Still fully clothed the three young men followed Gérard along a sandy path among the fishing boats They came to a row of shacks against which iodine-smelling nets were piled up in tangles and lumps. Gérard knocked at the door of one of the shacks. He didn't wait for an answer but pushed the door open. 'We want to borrow the boat,' he said, without any preliminary greeting, to whoever was inside in the darkness. There was just time for the others' eyes to pick out the forms of three white-haired men who were sitting mending nets and who were nodding their silent consent to Gérard's request, before Gérard backed out from the shack, forcing the others into a rapid reverse behind him. Gérard closed the door as he came out.

Borrowing the boat was not quite what the words might immediately conjure up. The boat was a small rowing boat – though it had a little mast rigged amidships – that had a large hole stoven in the bottom of it. It was at this point that they all had to take their clothes off, leaving them on the sand a prudent height above the tide-line. All of them including Gérard.

They dragged the damaged boat down the bank, then through a channel of water about six feet wide and four feet deep. This began easily enough but became an awkward and arduous task as the small hull filled up. Gérard knew where he was going, though. A small sandbank lay just below the water's surface and they hauled their prop up onto this and perched it there, returning to the shore to pick up a number of rocks with which to weight it. It gave a very passable impression of being afloat.

It was only after their strenuous exercise was finished and they were admiring the illusion they had created that Tom and Christopher gave a thought to the fact that they were all naked. They were both surprised to realise they'd quite forgotten that.

Once the boat was in position Gérard pulled his trousers back on, though nothing else. Separated from the others by the narrow water channel he set up his easel, perched himself on his folding stool and, calling instructions to his young models, began to sketch and paint.

There were times when Gérard seemed to be sketching in some detail on canvas, at other moments quickly dashing off a pencil impression on a cartridge block. And then he had his paints out and was applying oil boldly to the canvas. Afer a while Christopher lost interest in even looking at Gérard's activity. He simply heard his orders and, as if falling deeper and deeper into a trance, carried them out. All around him were water and light. He was asked to immerse himself in the shallow channel, or to swim a couple of strokes. He did that. The light shone into his eyes from where the water reflected it just inches from his face. The sun warmed his skin like a candle held too close. Or he was asked to sprawl across the gunwale of the boat, legs trailing in the water. Sometimes Tom's body was up close to him, sometimes Armand's was. He felt the aromas of their sun-warmed skins like freshly shelled hazel nuts. From time to time he'd steal a look at both the others' penises and at his own. None of them had grown entirely hard at any point, but all were burgeoning, lolly fatly, and just managing to avoid a state of full erection by a hair's breadth in everyone's case. Had one of them suddenly hardened there was no doubting that everyone else's would have risen in sympathy before anyone could say knife.

Suddenly there was Michel striding towards them, a tall silhouette cresting the dunes before dropping down towards them by the water's edge. It could hardly be much past noon... Tom called to Gérard: asked him what the time was. He was astonished to be told it was four o'clock.

True, they'd had to move the boat twice as the tide retreated, finding new shallows for it to rest on a little further out. And they'd swigged water from the bottles that Gérard had brought. But they'd had nothing else to drink, and nothing to eat. They watched Michel as he took his clothes off – his bib overalls were all he was wearing – and as he splashed through the water to join them. 'I got here on the bus,' he said.

'You did well,' Armand said, and gave his lover a kiss.

The sitting – if that was the right word – went on for another hour and a half. By that time there was almost no water in the little estuary, and the boys were floundering in sand and mud. Gérard put the tops back on his paint tubes and said that it was time to stop. The four youths ran out into deeper water to splash themselves clean of mud and then ran back, pulling their clothes on bracingly while their bodies were still wet.

Gérard drove them all the way to the top of the town, and dropped them off right outside the door of Michel's mother's house. 'I'll be in the Chat qui Pêche later,' he said. 'With cash.' He waved as he drove off.

The four of them trooped indoors. They had breakfasted here together early, before Michel had had to go to work and Armand had walked down with the others to the Place Dalton. Sabine had made them coffee and spread butter and jam on *biscottes*, crisp rounds of 'toast' from a packet. That was the last meal they had had. Sabine greeted them now. She held an envelope in her hand. She held it out to Christopher. *'Pour toi,'* she said. *'Une telegramme.'* She knew better than to smile as she said it.

THREE

The telegram read: *Will await letter. Your disappearance in newspaper. Whatever have you done? Mummy.* Christopher showed it to Tom. 'Signed without love,' he said coldly.

'Don't read too much into that,' Tom said. 'Love is an expensive word. You've bought yourself some time anyway. They know you're safe. You can take your time over the letter you write.' He put an arm around Christopher's shoulder for a second and looked carefully into his face. He was relieved to see that he showed no inclination to cry.

They showed the telegram to the others. Sabine said to Christopher, 'It could have been worse,' and smiled gently. Then she looked at Tom. 'If it's in the papers then you need to write to your parents too, you know. A telegram in the morning at least.' She sounded quite stern as she said this. Tom found himself not minding that Michel's mother appeared to have adopted Christopher and him as two additional sons, much as she seemed already to have adopted Armand. He was surprised at himself for not minding Sabine's talking to him in this way. Then he wondered if the aroma of a casserole wafting out of the kitchen might have something to do with this.

Gérard handed the cash he had promised to the four lads at once. The other two boys who had been with him the previous evening were once again at his table in the Chat qui Pêche but this time they didn't slink away. They stayed and were introduced. They were Benoît and René. They had been at school together, they now worked on the ferries as stewards, and saw themselves as a couple. They too had occasionally sat as models for Gérard – without their parents' knowledge. Benoît had the look of a Botticelli angel, while René, who was equally attractive, had a craftier, more worldly-wise look about his eyes. An angel presumably would not need to be worldly wise.

Gérard announced his intention of doing some more painting the next day and asked who among the six young men would be free. Tom and Christopher only, it appeared. Gérard immediately hired them and arranged to pick them up as before. Tom asked if they could make a detour to go by way of the post office again. He had a telegram to send.

'In that case,' said Gérard, 'why don't I pick you up in the car-park of my hotel? It's on the way.' He named the hotel. It was the one in the Rue de Faidherbe in which Tom and Christopher had stayed just a month before. It was run by another pair of men: Thierry and Robert, two more friends of Armand and Michel. The town seemed full of people like themselves, Christopher thought. Admittedly, their social life here centred on a bar that catered almost exclusively for a homosexual clientele, but even so. Christopher had never come across anything like this in England. Perhaps in London? He wondered for a moment about that. But London was not a place he knew well. Perhaps he would never know it now.

As the hour in the Chat qui Pêche passed Christopher began to feel a bit uncomfortable physically. A light-headed dizzy feeling began to come over him and occasional lightning bolts of headache flashed around his skull. He felt his shoulders and legs begin to heat up as though someone had lit a fire around him. He thought about this. He'd had one glass of red wine with Sabine's flavoursome beef casserole and was now on his second small glass of Pastis. It was a quantity of alcohol he could handle easily by now. At last the obvious struck him. 'Tom,' he said, 'I think I've had a bit too much sun.'

'Get him some water, iced. Lots of it,' advised Gérard.

'My mother's got some lotion in the bathroom cupboard,' said Michel. 'Rub him with that when you get home.'

'All over,' said René. 'If he's been posing naked on the beach all day. Don't miss out any part of him. You'll both enjoy that anyway.'

The iced water came as soon as it was asked for. A whole big jug-full. The others made Christopher drink the lot. 'Are you sure you'll be all right for tomorrow?' Gérard asked.

'Of course I will,' said Christopher. A deep-rooted survival instinct told him he needed to share the next day with Tom. If Gérard were to spend the whole day alone with a naked Tom... Or else Gérard might ask some other gilded youth along... He repeated with emphasis, 'I'll be fine.'

He wasn't fine in the night, though. He had certainly enjoyed the experience of being rubbed all over by Tom with a milky pink lotion before getting into bed, and so had Tom, but he woke up in the small hours and was sick. Luckily he made it to the bathroom and was able to leave everything clean afterwards. Luckily too, Christopher thought, Tom slept through the episode. He wouldn't have liked Tom to see him in the state he was in: he wasn't as sure of him as that. As he was drifting back to sleep afterwards he found himself resolving once again that when morning came he would go out with Tom to be painted no matter how ill he was.

But in the morning he didn't feel ill. Only sore. Tom awoke a few seconds after Christopher. 'How are you doing?' he asked.

'Fine now. Just a bit sore. I threw up in the night.'

That news wrung Tom's heart. 'Oh Chris, I didn't know. You should have woken me up.'

'You couldn't have stopped me being sick,' Christopher said.

'That's not the point. It's better not to be alone, that's all. When I'm here.' Tom stopped. 'Someone who loves you.'

The L-word hit Christopher like a cricket bat. It hadn't been used between them since they'd arrived in France. Not even in the four weeks before that. Thinking about it… It had only been used by each of them once. Christopher said, 'You really mean that? After all that's happened…'

'Of course I do.' Tom made a move to clasp Christopher tightly in the small bed but stopped himself. 'Oops. Got to be careful while your skin's tender.' He made do with a light caress of Christopher's shoulder, flank and arm.

'Tom, I wasn't sure you still…'

'Of course I do.' Tom's distress was in his face. 'Of course I do. How could I not? Why else would I be here?'

Christopher wrapped his own arms around Tom, though cautiously. Less cautiously he said, 'I love you too.'

'Then there's nothing much wrong with the world,' Tom said.

Christopher considered that statement as they got up and breakfasted with Sabine. Their situation was so extraordinary that he could hardly begin to make sense of it. Forced to leave their home country – or so they thought – jobless, penniless and with Christopher's place at Oxford now probably lost, they had seemed just two mornings ago to be in the most miserable state imaginable. Yet unimaginable things had happened. They had been welcomed as old friends by Michel and Armand – whom they had actually only met a month ago and spent only a couple of evenings in their company then; they had been given a room in a well-appointed house; meals had been cooked for them... Sabine had treated them like prodigal sons and waved away their offers to pay her for any of this. They had done a day's work already and had received payment for it in cash; today they were going to earn more. The work was congenial, hardly work at all, even if it had played havoc with Christopher's skin. Yes, there remained the awkward fact that he, and Tom too, would have to deal with his parents at some point soon – must write that letter tonight – but on balance, especially now that Tom had said he still loved him, things were not looking so bad. Christopher's positive view of the state of things was only slightly darkened when they arrived in the car park of Gérard's hotel and saw that Benoît and René were already with him in the car.

'We thought you were sailing the seas today,' Tom said to them when the doors were opened.

'The early morning sailing got cancelled,' Benoît said. 'We thought we'd tag along.' He smiled sweetly at Tom and Christopher and said to René in French, 'Budge up.'

They had to make more than one stop before leaving the town for Audresselles. There was Tom's telegram to his parents to be dealt with. Standing at the counter in the post office shoulder to shoulder with Christopher exactly as he had done yesterday, Tom thought hard about the wording he would choose. In the end he felt he could do no better than Christopher had, using the formula supplied so promptly by Armand: *Alive. Well. In France. Will write soon. Love, Tom.* Next they stopped by a *pharmacie* to buy two bottles of the pink lotion: one to replace the bottle in Sabine's bathroom cupboard, the other for rubbing over Christopher in the course of today. And then they halted on the road beside the beach at a news-stand.

British newspapers arrived in France one day in arrears. Even in Boulogne, which was a mere ninety minutes away by ferry and from where, on a clear day, you could obtain a clear view of Dover Castle and the nearby imposing wireless masts. Today was Tuesday. The cataclysm hadn't occurred till mid-Saturday morning, so reports of it were unlikely to have made the Sundays. They took a chance and bought Monday's Daily Telegraph: it was the paper that Christopher's parents took. They paid what all of them thought an exorbitant price.

They were hardly front-page news. They had almost given up looking when their eyes were caught by a small headline in a cul-de-sac of a column on a very inside page.

Prep School in Crisis
The Star of the Sea Roman Catholic preparatory school in East Kent was this weekend buffeted by waves of supposition when Queen's Counsel Mr Stephen Dexter alerted the police to homosexual activity that he alleged had taken place there. The events that he reported involved both pupils and members of staff. When officers from the local constabulary arrived to investigate, two members of the teaching staff, Mr Thomas Sanders and Mr Christopher McGing were found to have disappeared. There is as yet no trace of their whereabouts. Another member of staff, deputy headmaster Dom Matthew Harding, a priest and monk of the Benedictine order, was taken in for questioning but then released. No comment was forthcoming from the school, or from its governing body, the Roman Catholic Abbey of St Aidan in the nearby town of *******.

That was all. Enough to appal Christopher's parents, though, and Tom's too. 'You notice they write Roman Catholic twice,' said Tom. 'Why do they always have to do that? They wouldn't write Anglican twice if that was the case.'

'And why are we named?' asked Christopher with unusual heat in his voce. 'No-one accuses us of anything. Yet it's written quite deliberately so as to allow people to think we had sex with kids.'

Tom sighed. 'As far as the laws of England are concerned, Chris, you still are a kid. They'll accuse me of seducing and abducting you when they run out of alternatives.'

'Qu'est-ce qu'il y a?' Benoît wanted to know, and Tom and Christopher were obliged, for the benefit of the others, to translate the report into halting French. Then at last they drove off. When, fifteen minutes later, they arrived at Audresselles, parked in the sand dune, got out of the car and took their clothes off, both Christopher and Tom felt – although they knew this could only be temporary – a disproportionate sense of relief.

Christopher found some relief in something else. Although Benoît and René both looked very pretty when they were naked, their genitals were a size smaller than his own were and two sizes smaller than Tom's. There seemed no logical reason why such a thing should matter, yet somehow it did, and Christopher found himself feeling less threatened by the existence of the two new French boys than he'd done when he'd been squeezed up with them both in the back seat of the Renault while Tom had ridden in the passenger seat in front.

'I've borrowed sun-umbrellas from the hotel,' Gérard announced as he unpacked the boot. 'We don't want anyone else to get sunburnt. There's a new rule as from today. Nobody to stay in the full sun unnecessarily when they're not being painted. Especially Christopher.' He shot him a mock-severe glance. 'I'll call you as and when I need you. Oh, by the way, I told the two chaps in the hotel you were in town. Thierry and Robert. They remembered you both from a month ago, and hope to catch you in the Chat qui Pêche one night soon.'

No boat was involved today. Just rocks and eddying tidal pools, with the estuary and a lfar-off line of fishing boats and cottages forming the distant, framing view.

It was different from yesterday. Christopher missed the fun of splashing in shallow water, of hauling himself in and out of the boat, and rolling naked from time to time, accidentally on purpose, like one of a litter of puppies, with Tom, Michel and Armand. Today it was more like a cricket game at school. Christopher remembered the situation fondly. He remembered how, when you were waiting to go in to bat, or had been got out, you would lie on the grass with a friend, looking up together at the blue sky; he remembered how private and intimate those conversations could become. Sometimes it seemed this was the only time you could talk to people in this deep and serious way, the only time at boarding school you weren't in public with a front to keep up: the front that you needed, to guard you from the spite of the world.

So it was now as they took turns to sit under the sunshades, sometimes alone, sometimes in twos, sometimes as a group of three, watching a painting take shape in front of them, watching Gérard painting it (he had a sunshade of his own today) and watching the others pose. Although the conversations formed a rather tangled thicket of intertwined English and French it seemed that the fact of all being naked together was an additional stimulus to the baring of souls.

'So you are together how long exactly?' René asked Christopher when it was their turn to sit, just the two of them together, in the shade.

'Since the beginning of term,' Christopher said. 'Two months... Nearly three.' It seemed a very short time, he thought, now that he was actually putting it in words.

'Hein. For us, for Benoît and me, it is years and years. Ever since...' He broke off, then shrugged. 'Since longer than either of us can remember. Our parents were always friends. Even by the age of six or seven we were already...'

'I see,' said Christopher, getting the picture fairly clearly. 'And you have been together ever since?' He thought this rather encouraging.

René said, 'Yes, in the main.' He went on, 'You and Tom... I suppose for you it is very new. You are still ... how to say? ... I mean, is it always just the two of you?'

Christopher thought he could see where this was going. 'Of course it is,' he said a bit primly. 'We don't need anyone else – or want anyone else – to share sex with us.' But even as he said this he could see a movement, a slight swelling of something between his legs that indicated that whatever he felt and thought his body had other ideas. And though he tried not to look too keenly he couldn't help noticing that René's physical self took a similar view.

'That is like Michel and Armand are,' René said calmly. 'They like to tease a little, to flirt, to lead others along, but they are only for each other and themselves.' He shrugged. 'I say good luck to them if that is what they want. But with Benoît and me...' He grinned slyly. 'We are very sure of each other. And since a long time. So... Well, we like to play the field. Sometimes separately, sometimes together.'

This was a way of behaving that Christopher found he deplored with every fibre of the being that he had been brought up to be. And yet a tingle of excitement ran through him like an electric current: all down his arms, his legs ... and of course elsewhere. Perhaps it was as well that at that moment Gérard called to him and asked if he would move into the picture that was being created. He stood up and walked towards Tom, who was seated on a rock from which he had been gazing for half an hour at Benoît, who had been lying on his front on the sand and looking up at him. Now Benoît was finished for the time being and Christopher and he walked past each other as if Benoît had been bowled out and Christopher was taking his place at the wicket. As they passed each other Benoît smiled mischievously, glancing down for an instant to below Christopher's waist, and then gave his bare shoulder a glancing rub with his hand as he walked on.

A little time later Tom found himself sharing the shade of the sun umbrellas with the naked Benoît. Benoît kept gazing sideways with undisguised admiration at Tom's dick. While Tom's glances at what lay in Benoît's lap were more guilt-infused and circumspect. 'Gérard pays very well,' Tom said, introducing one of the few subjects that can take people's minds off thoughts of sex. 'Four of us yesterday, four of us today. Unless he sells like Picasso, how does he manage to afford all this?'

'He has a partenaire who lives with him in Paris. The partenaire works for a merchant bank and is *assez riche*.' A good phrase, Tom thought. It translated easily as *rich enough*. 'It is the partenaire whose money pays for Gérard's painting. He is some years older than Gérard, of course.' A worried look crossed Benoît's angel face. 'I don't mean to say that Gérard makes no money. He is well thought of in Paris and his work is exposed in the galleries of the Rue de Seine. His pictures fetch good prices… Though perhaps not quite enough to pay a lot of people like us.'

'Let's be thankful for partners then,' Tom said. He found himself suddenly looking years ahead, into a future that was impossible even to imagine. Would there come a time when his own riches (acquired God knew how) would be supporting a fifty-year-old Christopher? Or even more mind-boggling, might Christopher become amazingly successful at something and subsidise an older lover, Tom, in his dotage? It was like looking through someone else's horribly strong spectacles. He found it dizzying and almost painful to try to peer so far ahead. He took the metaphorical lenses off and returned to a more manageable, shorter-term view of what might lie in store. 'Do you think Gérard will give us a break for lunch today? Yesterday he got so carried away with things that he didn't.'

The minds of both of them went back to Saturday morning letter copy at Star of the Sea. There they had each supervised their own class while the Sunday morning letter home was written in laborious draft. Now they were themselves drafting their letters home, Christopher sitting at Sabine's dining-table, Tom at her elegant writing-desk in the *salon*. Sabine herself was tactfully out.

Both had had to steel themselves for this major task. Even their purchase of blue air-mail letters, postage pre-paid, on the walk back from Gérard's hotel had something of an epic quality, a no-going-back-now feeling about it. Later they were going to have something to eat at the café where Armand worked, before meeting back up with the others at the Chat qui Pêche. That later part of this evening – gratification deferred – was to be their reward for the emotional and mental stress of the letter-writing task. While they wrote they could see each other through the open door that connected *salle à manger* and *salon*. Though only occasionally did they actually look up and catch each other's eye, so engrossed were they in the task in hand. At last, after about an hour – and surprisingly with only a few seconds between them – they came to the end of their letters and put the caps back on their pens.

Tom looked through the doorway into the salon and at Christopher. 'I'll show you mine if you show me yours,' he said, and laughed.

Christopher did manage a smile at that but he said, 'I'm not sure…'

'Well, as you like,' Tom said. 'You can read mine anyway, though, if you want.'

Christopher got up and walked towards Tom. They handed each other their letters, then sat down in two of Sabine's gilded chairs that were next to each other and read in silence. Tom had written this.

Dear Mum and Dad,

I hope you are both well and not paying too much attention to the newspapers. You will have had my telegram by now, so will know my whereabouts. Specifically I am in Boulogne with my friend Christopher, who taught with me at Star of the Sea this term. We are staying in the house of the mother of another friend of ours, a French chap called Michel, who we met when we came over here together at half term. They are a prosperous family and may be able to find work for both of us. In fact we have already done two days of paid work since we arrived on Sunday, assisting a rather famous painter from Paris.

What happened at Star of the Sea was that two of the boys were expelled for getting a bit too intimate with each other. Despite what the newspapers may have hinted none of the staff were in any way involved in this. However the father of one of the expelled boys levelled an accusation at the two of us – I mean Christopher and myself – which, though he could never prove it, would have been impossible for us to disprove. For this reason we decided to cross the Channel, and are staying here as a matter of prudence, until things have blown over in England.

I think it would be difficult for me to return to see you in England in the very near future. On the other hand you are most welcome to come and see me here in Boulogne. There is a good and inexpensive hotel in the Rue Faidherbe which is run by other friends of ours, or it may be that our hostess here, Michel's mother, Sabine, would be able to put you both up.

Whatever you do, don't worry about me. I shall be all right.

With Love,
Thomas

Christopher's letter read thus.

Dear Mummy and Daddy,

I will try to explain what has happened and why I am here in France, though it will not be easy to write my thoughts clearly. It may not be easy for you to read this either. I can only ask you to be understanding.

You say you've seen the newspapers. So have I. There was a slur in the report which I read in yesterday's Telegraph (Monday June 25th). It implies that Thomas Sanders and I were involved in sex with boys at Star of the Sea. Nothing could be further from the truth.

On the other hand something else is true, and as I would not be able to deny it if you asked me face to face, I may as well tell you now in this letter so that the matter is out in the open. I am in love with Tom Sanders and he is in love with me. It is as simple as that. However, the police would have made all sorts of things out of that, and that is why the two of us decided to escape to France in the middle of the night.

We are safe here, and are being looked after by sympathetic friends. We are looking for work in France and friends are helping us search.

I am missing you both terribly. I hope I will be able to see you soon. It might be difficult for me to come to England but it would be lovely if you could come to France.

Looking forward to a letter from you soon.
With Lots and Lots of Love
Christopher

Tom looked up at Christopher after he'd finished reading that. He reached an arm around Christopher's neck. 'Hmm,' he said thoughtfully. Then he said, 'I think it's time I took you out and bought you a drink. We can post these on the way down the hill, before you have second thoughts.' And then he leaned across from his chair to the one that Christopher sat in and gave him a peck on the cheek.

FOUR

Le Chat qui Pêche was not vast and on a Tuesday night it was not particularly crowded. Nevertheless it was a surprise to Christopher and Tom to find that the small group of people already there consisted almost entirely of people they knew. They arrived with Michel and Armand – they had all eaten together in the café where Armand worked as a waiter. But now here were Gérard and Benoît and René, and also two figures they hadn't seen since their first visit to Boulogne: the stocky, soldierly-looking Thierry and his other half, the willowy, slightly camp Robert. (Though camp was not a word that Tom or Christopher had come across at that stage of their lives.) They were the managers – or owners? Tom and Christopher hadn't liked to ask – of the hotel in the Rue Faidherbe.

Thierry stood up and came to greet them with a handshake and a broad grin. 'Gérard told us you were back in town,' he said. 'You haven't looked in, so…' He chuckled. 'Sometimes Mohammed must go to the mountain.'

'Sorry for not calling in. It's been a bit of a whirl…'

Christopher said, 'But you two out together? Who's looking after the hotel?'

'We left it in the capable claws of the mynah bird,' said Robert.

The mynah bird. They had forgotten the bird. It was quite a character, with its habit of punctuating other people's conversations with a throat-wrenching smoker's cough or a remark in its deep baritone voice that was sometimes all too apposite. It probably was capable of running a hotel…

'Seriously,' said Thierry, 'We've got a young lad now who helps out from time to time. There's nothing to do at this time of evening. Just let guests in through the door and give them their keys.'

'Well, if you find you need two more young lads…' Tom said, 'As from tomorrow we're free for the rest of our lives.'

'You certainly don't let the grass grow,' said Thierry, and laughed. 'But we'll bear that in mind. Of course, your employer of the last two days leaves for Paris in the morning.'

René had now left his chair and arrived among them. He put an arm around Thierry's shoulder. 'Have you seen these two without their clothes on?' he asked him. Thierry laughed and said no. 'Well it's not a sight to be missed. They're both very splendidly endowed.'

Gérard called from the table just two yards away. 'René! Heel, boy. Sit down!'

They were too many for any of the small tables, so they arranged themselves on and among the scatter-cushions on the floor and the waiter bent down towards each of them in turn when he arrived with their tray of drinks.

'You should see the place we live one day soon,' said Benoît to Christopher, huddling close to him. 'High up in the mansard – we live like dormice in the roof – but with a view down to the sea, and very cosy.'

'Especially cosy as they only have a single bed,' said Robert, arching his eyebrows as he leant across. Christopher found himself wondering how Robert knew about their new friends' sleeping arrangements and coming very quickly to a supposition that might or might not have been correct.

Gérard was in more serious mode. He asked Tom, 'What are you going to do for work now you find yourselves locked out of your home country? I mean, in the long term.' He was sitting with his arms clasped around his knees rather self-consciously, as older people

43

tend to do when obliged to sit on the floor among a younger crowd.

'I suppose we shall end up teaching English,' Tom said. 'Most people in our situation do.'

'You don't sound too cheerful about the prospect,' Gérard told him.

'Yes and no,' said Tom. 'When we were here at half term we met someone else who'd had to leave his school in England in awkward circumstances. Much, much older than us. He was trailing round with a woman in tow. Drunk the whole time, and not enjoying life much by the look of him. He was teaching English here and there. He didn't seem a very happy example to model ourselves on.'

'You don't have to end up drunk and unhappy just because he did,' Gérard said. He unhooked one hand from around his knees and took a sip of Pastis. 'You don't need me to tell you that life is what you make it. You say he had a woman in tow. Well, you've got the most gorgeous, sweet-natured boy imaginable. Some people would say you were the luckiest man alive.' Gérard gave him a very penetrating look. 'I wonder...'

A few seconds passed. There was no sign that Gérard was going to finish his sentence. 'Wonder what?' Tom politely asked.

'Just thinking out loud. What about moving on from here to Paris when autumn comes? When the schools and colleges go back. What's called the *rentrée*. You could do some modelling for me there. Now, that wouldn't be a full-time job or anything like one. But the art schools are always on the look-out for people who are unselfconscious enough to pose for the life classes. People who – well, to be honest, people who look really good whether clothed or naked. People like yourselves. It might be something that would keep you going until the teaching fell into place. In any case Paris is much fuller of opportunities, of whatever sort, than Boulogne. That's a very obvious thing to say. Might you be interested? If you were I could introduce you to one or two people who might be able to help.'

'Whoa, whoa, that's all going a bit quickly,' said Tom. 'Paris...We'd need somewhere to live. It'd be expensive...'

'Whereas you have a room in Boulogne, courtesy of Michel's mother, for free. But I imagine you might not be able to count on that for the rest of your lives...'

'No, obviously not,' Tom said, then stopped. He felt wrong-footed. 'I'm sorry. I should have said thank you for your offer of help... Maybe, maybe... I'll need to think about it. I mean we'll need to think about it. I have to talk to Christopher.'

'Of course, of course,' said Gérard. 'Why not now?'

'Chris,' Tom called to him across the cushions. Robert and René seemed to be on the point of climbing onto Chris's lap from opposite sides and colliding when they got there. 'Chris, come here a minute.' Tom thought his summons had been a timely one.

Even before they had said goodnight to Armand and Michel halfway up the hill they were finding it impossible to keep their hands off each other. They had spent two days now romping on a beach with naked young men – two different pairs of them – and had spent an evening on the receiving end of suggestive banter and innuendo-laden jokes. The previous night Christopher's skin had been too sore with sunburn for them to enjoy anything in the way of sex when they got to bed. By now their fully wound sex-drives were straining against the brakes. Once they had let themselves in to Sabine's house they practically raced each other up the stairs and into a state of undress.

Though Christopher's skin remained blotched with pink it was no longer too hot or too painful to handle. Each of them tried to get the other into a position in which he could be fucked, both having an identical urge to penetrate the other but not explaining or requesting this. Their efforts turned into something more like a fight in the narrow bed, and it was only brought to a halt by their fear of falling onto the floor with loud thumps that would disturb Sabine in the room next door. It was Christopher who gave in and spoke first. 'OK,' he said. 'You can do me tonight. Tomorrow, my turn. Promise? And so, high on the company they'd been keeping, and on thoughts of a possibly lucrative move to Paris, they had their first, very pleasurable, fuck since their arrival in France.

They were up late that next morning and got their own breakfast in Sabine's kitchen. Sabine had already gone out. They had given very little thought to what they might do that day, Wednesday, the middle of the week, with Gérard returned to Paris, and all their other new friends at work. It was a sunny end of June morning, though, and they decided they should simply spend the day lazing on the beach. There was a little hiatus before they could set out. Christopher took up his pen again and wrote to the Oxford college that had offered him a place in the autumn, explaining that for personal reasons he would be unable to take the offer up this year and could they defer it.

On their way down the hill they posted the letter, then called in at the ironmonger's. It would have been unthinkable simply to walk past the place where their best friend worked. As they pushed open the door and went down a step they realised that although they knew the studio upstairs well enough they had never before set foot inside the shop.

From deep inside a cave of splendours – chisels, hammers. garden hose, electric plugs and cable, step-ladders and paraffin lamps – Michel greeted them with a smile over the shoulder of the customer he was serving. The smile said very economically, *Good to see you; I'll be with you in a moment.* Then their eyes were caught by a small wave of greeting, glimpsed through a half-open door. Beyond it, in a cubby-hole of an office, Sabine sat at a small desk which was strewn with account books.

A few minutes later Michel was giving them an intimate tour of the shop and its inventory. 'Maman has been saying that she might want one of you to give her a hand with the book-keeping through July and August. Staff will have their holidays. She too...' He shrugged his shoulders. 'Even I might manage a few days off with Armand. Who knows? Book-keeping. Has either of you ever done that?'

Christopher was trying to take in an awful lot. That *bouilloire* did not mean kettle, as he had always thought it did. They didn't do kettles in France; They heated water for tea and coffee in saucepans instead. That a plasterer's trowel was a *truelle,* a gardener's one was a *deplantoir,* and a *citerne à eau de pluie* was a water-butt... 'I've seen the books at my father's place. It's a builders' merchant store. But I'm not fantastic at figures.'

Tom said, 'I've never worked in any kind of shop but I can add up. I was JCR treasurer in my Oxford college.' In case this sounded boastful he added, 'Just in my final year, of course.'

'Well, you can think about it together,' Michel said. 'It's not going to happen this week, if it does.'

Sabine had come out from her cubby-hole and joined them. 'If you want to take these two out into the sunshine for a coffee,' she told her son, 'I'll mind the shop for ten minutes.'

They sat at the same pavement table at which they'd had coffee on Sunday, just after they'd arrived and got out of their wet clothes. Just three days ago…

Christopher frowned intensely at his espresso while vigorously stirring sugar into it. Then, 'Michel,' he said suddenly, 'Benoît and René seemed to be saying that you and Armand were the only couple among their homosexual friends who are faithful to each other. That all the rest are…' He couldn't find the word.

Tom supplied it. 'Promiscuous.'

Christopher didn't acknowledge the vocabulary gift. 'Is that how it is?'

Michel looked at Tom, who caught his eye in return, twenty-two-year-old to twenty-two-year-old. Then he looked back at the younger Christopher. 'It is and it isn't,' he said. He smiled at Christopher serenely. 'I think that perhaps there are different ways of being alive, of being young, of being in love, and of having sex. What suits us, Armand and me, is what suits us at the moment. Yes, it's true that we don't do anything with anybody else, because that's the way we want it. In ten years?' He shrugged. 'Who knows where we will all be then. It seems to me…' he paused to collect his thoughts and process them into something that made verbal sense, 'that everyone has to make his own accommodation with sex and the relationship he has. What works for one couple may not work for another. You and Tom will have to make your own decisions about how you want things to go, in that way. But you can be sure of one thing. That just because Benoît and René enjoy sex with other people also, that doesn't mean they love each other any less. Did you know…?' He paused a second and smiled at both of them in turn. '…That they have been in love together since they were six?'

They did spend the day on the beach. That day became a holiday from thought and strife. All their letters were posted: nothing more could happen on those fronts until replies came back, which might easily take a fortnight; there was no point in even speculating what those replies might say. There was a possibility of work in Paris, but they would hear nothing until Gérard returned from there at the weekend; nothing further could be done for now. The same went for the offer of work at the ironmonger's, starting the following week. Tom had offered to buy provisions and cook a meal for them all that evening; Sabine had accepted graciously, but asked if it could happen the following day. She already had a chicken ready for this evening, which she planned to joint and sauté… So the day became one in which they needed to do nothing, needed to plan nothing: a pause in the ongoing struggle of life. They already knew that, in a whole lifetime, those days were rare.

From time to time a ferry would set sail from the out-of-sight port. It would appear behind the harbour mole as if walking along it, then emerge onto the flat expanse of the sea, crawling across it like a snail crossing a paving slab before vanishing into the distant haze. On one of the ferries Benoît and René would be at work, serving drinks to passengers, waiting tables. They hadn't yet asked for the name of the ferry on which they worked, or indeed whether it was the same one every day, so they waved at each ferry that passed them just in case. The sea on which the ships sailed so proudly was navy blue during the morning, with an occasional white fleck far out. But as the sun swung round it turned turquoise and began to spark and flash. Later its entire surface became silver and then the first of the ferries they had seen leaving the harbour in the morning came back out of the distant mist and grew larger as they watched. It had gone to England and back in just five hours, returning like a ghost from another world. It had done the one thing they could not do. Neither of them voiced those thoughts, but their hands found each other's as they watched the ship make its unhurried way into the sheltered water behind the breakwater and with that simple contact they knew they were thinking the same thing.

At last the sun began to squint into their eyes and told them it was time to leave the sea and head inland. They had taken nothing with them to the beach except bottles of water (and Christopher's pink lotion) and had eaten nothing since their buttered *biscottes* at breakfast time. They would be ready for Sabine's chicken sauté.

'You know,' said Tom as they climbed the homeward hill, 'there's something we should do. Make contact with Roger and Malcolm and tell them we're OK.'

'You're right,' Christopher said. 'A letter, you mean?'

'I was thinking we might phone.'

'That'll cost a lot. We'd need a lot of coins.'

'Change a note at the shop.' Tom pointed with his head; they were approaching the ironmonger's now. The shop was just closing when they walked in. Michel was stuffing notes and cheques from the till into a cloth bag. *'Ah bon,'* he said when he saw them. 'Good that you've come in. I have a message for you...' He started to scoop coins into plastic bags.

'Before you tidy the money away,' Tom interrupted, 'we wanted to ask for change for the phone.'

'You don't need it. You can phone Gérard from my mother's.'

'It's not Gérard we need to phone...'

'Oh, I think you do.'

'No,' said Christopher. 'We need to contact our friends Malcolm and Roger, the ones who brought us over on their boat...'

Tom said, 'You say we need to phone Gérard?'

'Yes,' said Michel, leaving his coin bags and turning all his attention to Christopher and Tom. 'He phoned this afternoon. Can you go to Paris tomorrow? There's someone who would like to meet you.'

They phoned the Admiral Digby from the call-box in the Place Dalton. Tom held the receiver and spoke when their ring was answered, while Christopher was in charge of dropping the bag-full of coins into the slot one by one. Through the long distance crackle Tom could make out that Roger – it was he who answered – was very pleased to have news from their end. 'And you got back home safely on Sunday?' Tom asked, though the very fact that Roger was there on the end of the phone line had answered the question before it was put.

'Yes, fine,' Roger said cheerfully through the crackle. Then, 'I'm going to take this upstairs.' There came a seemingly endless pause during which Christopher's coins followed each other into the slot at an amazing rate. Then at last, 'Sorry about that. But the bar is walled with ears. Yes, back safely. No big waves, the tide was good, we moored in the river mid-afternoon, and had time for a nap before opening the pub for the evening at seven.'

It sounded wonderfully familiar. Normal. Nice. Tom could picture it all. A wrenching feeling near his diaphragm told him he missed it all. 'It's been in the papers,' Roger was saying. Tom told him they knew that. 'The school's clammed up of course. Pulled up the drawbridge as it were.'

'But you,' Tom asked. 'Have the police, the press, been on to you?'

'Neither of those. Don't worry. Nobody seems to know of our connection. But that's why I came upstairs.'

'Of course,' said Tom. Very quickly he told Roger of their good luck in finding a billet with Sabine, about their job prospects, about Paris in the morning...'

'Don't spend all your hard-earned wages on a phone-call,' Roger told him. 'Write to us when you can. Give our love to Christopher.'

'And ours to Malcolm too...' The call ended. Tom found it strange to be bandying the word love around with two friends of the same sex as them, even though they were all homosexual. But perhaps, keeping the company that he did now he was in Boulogne, he would be getting used to it pretty soon.

A massive black steam engine stood at the head of the train they boarded that next morning at the harbour station. Platforms here were low compared to England so that not only did the engine – so curiously different in aesthetic design from its British counterparts – display the full majesty of its connecting-rods and driving-wheels between intermittent clouds of blown-off steam, but you climbed aboard the carriages by way of integral steps as steep as a ladder. Christopher wondered what would happen if you were a small old lady travelling with a massive suitcase. Perhaps you wouldn't be travelling alone. The train whistled and they set off through the streets of the town – a bit of a novelty in itself – before joining the main line. The windows were open because of the heat of the day and the smoke blew in from time to time. Halfway to Paris the cathedral of Amiens presented its immense self for inspection among the slag heaps of Picardie, and then at last they were nosing along beneath the beetling east slope of Montmartre before snaking to a stop beneath the glass roof of the Gare du Nord.

Gérard had come to meet them and stood patiently beyond the barrier, on the far side of a small sea of embraces, and luggage passing from hand to hand. Tom wondered if he would have put himself to that trouble if they were twenty years older, less fair of face and form or, heaven forbid, of the female sex.

'On va manger,' he said in the matter-of-fact way that French people have; with the unspoken assumption that going for something to eat is not just one option among others as it might be in Britain but an immutable priority. 'Across the road. We go to the Hotel Terminus Nord.' And he led them out of the concourse – the hall of lost footsteps as it was more poetically known here – and across the wide spread of tarmac where the buses and taxis honked and parked.

Amid the Baroque splendours of the hotel's brasserie they tasted a salmon mousse with chives, breaded escalopes of veal, an assortment of cheeses garnered from the four corners of the map of France and a frothy dessert of meringue and cream. Even though they stuck to a prudent single glass of white wine each, it was not the kind of preparation for a job interview that they would have considered a good idea back at home. But things worked differently here. They were ready to accept that. To embrace it even. If you didn't accept things like this, they both thought, you had come to the wrong place. After they had finished eating Gérard paid the bill with a wave of his wallet and a flourish of notes.

Gérard hailed a taxi outside. 'Ecole des Beaux-Arts,' he told the driver when they got inside. 'Rue Bonaparte. 6ième.' Two little twists brought them onto the Boulevard Sebastopol which ran arrow-straight two full kilometres towards the river through set after set of traffic lights. As they neared the Seine the spire of the Sainte Chapelle appeared framed at the end of the street.

'Is that Notre Dame?' Tom asked, then wished he'd kept his ignorance to himself when Gérard told him that they'd see the cathedral in a few minutes. Only a glimpse of it, though, as the taxi threaded its way across one bridge onto the Ile de la Cité then across another bridge that took them off it. A moment later they had turned off the Quai Malaquais and were set down at the entrance gate of a grandiose building that was framed around courtyards like an Oxbridge college. 'Hmm,' said Tom, inspecting it. 'This takes me back.' Again he wished he hadn't spoken. Christopher was having to forego his place at Oxford. He hoped Christopher hadn't registered the allusion to his own time there.

Gérard led them into the presence of a small black-haired woman who had bright dark eyes like those of a mouse. They were interviewed, not in her office but in the large bare hall in which the life classes took place. 'It can be cold in winter,' the woman said with the ghost of a smile. 'If you last that long, that is.' In a very easy, conversational way she got from them the details that she needed: background, current address, what had brought them to France. Then after a little pause that was just long enough to register as a pause she said, 'I have to ask you a question you may find indelicate. Could you spend a long time naked among a group of female students without becoming sexually aroused?'

Before either of them could find an answer Gérard spoke. 'I don't think that'll be an issue in the case of these two. Even a group of young men... I've painted them both naked in the company of other boys in a similar state of undress and there were no problems of that sort.' He smiled at the woman. 'My dear Madame Blétry, I would not have recommended them to you if I hadn't been extremely sure of their quality in all departments. You'll find them punctual and with a responsible attitude to work.'

Madame Blétry gave another chilly smile. 'Then I think we can safely say there will be work for them in September.' She turned back to Tom and Christopher and told them the hours and the fees they could expect. The terms did not amount to an *abondandance de richesses*, Madame Blétry told them, but it would be enough to enable them to pay a modest rent and to eat.

'Then all that remains is for me to find them a room to live in at an affordable price,' said Gérard. He pulled a mock-grimace. 'And that may prove the harder part.'

Tom and Christopher thought it nothing short of miraculous that Gérard would trouble himself with their domestic arrangements at all.

FIVE

It was dark when they got back to Boulogne; they walked directly from the harbour station to the Chat qui Pêche. Of the people they knew only Michel and Armand were there and they both found themselves rather pleased about that. Part of the pleasure of sharing good news depends on which other people are the first to hear it.

But there was news for Tom and Christopher too. There would definitely be a part-time job for Tom, book-keeping at the shop, starting on Monday. He could work either mornings or afternoons, or a mixture of both. There was also something for Christopher. This too would involve covering for people who were on their summer breaks: in the café where Armand worked. Part-time again, but with both of them working... (And with no rent to pay, thought Tom. At least for the moment...) If Christopher was interested could he call in and see the *patron* tomorrow morning at eleven o'clock. 'There's an expression in English,' said Tom. 'Having all your treats in one week.' The word treat reminded him. He called to the barman, while making a circular motion with his forefinger around their little group. *'Prochaine tournée: c'est pour moi.'* His French was daily growing more idiomatic and confident.

Having very few appointments in your diary was no proof, it seemed, against the inherent tendency of appointments to clash. The next day was the feast of Saints Peter and Paul in the Christian calendar: for observant Catholics the world over a Holy Day of Obligation, a day on which they were bound to go to Mass. The main Mass of the morning was at eleven o'clock, both in the cathedral and at St Nicholas. Exactly the time of Christopher's appointment with Armand's boss. True, there was an evening Mass in both churches, for the benefit of those who were out all day at work, but that would probably clash with the time at which Sabine usually served the evening meal.

And there lay a further complication. Tom had promised to cook for them all the previous day, but then had come the summons to Paris. Tom could reasonably have cooked the following day but, as well as its being St Peter and Paul it would be Friday, a day on which Catholics in those days were not supposed to eat meat. Tom had been planning to make a shepherd's pie: it was a dish he was confident with. His repertoire did not extend to fish. Even when life was at its simplest, when you had three nearly empty days stretching ahead of you, it still managed to tie itself up in knots. Sabine, to whom they put all this the next morning at breakfast, told them what the French equivalent of Murphy's Law was. *'C'est la loi du pain beurré,'* she said. The law of buttered bread. Even in France, it appeared, if you dropped a buttered slice by accident you could be sure which way round it would land on the carpet.

But it was Sabine who proposed the simple solution. If Christopher wanted to go to Mass then she herself would go with him in the evening at seven o'clock. Fish was quick and easy to cook. They would have supper all together when they got back. As for Tom's shepherd's pie, that could wait. Any day in the coming week would be fine for that.

It crossed Tom's mind to say that since Christopher only half believed in God and the teachings of the Catholic Church he was only half obliged to go to Mass. He decided not to say it. He needed to be careful with Christopher's sensitivities these days. The more so in the light of what he'd read of Christopher's state of mind in that letter to his parents.

Christopher's interview with the proprietor of the Café La Chope turned into nothing more threatening than a friendly chat. They had met each other on their earlier visit to Boulogne and seen each other again on Tuesday night. Could Christopher start on Tuesday with the breakfast shift? It meant coming to work at seven o'clock. Christopher thought of the delicious thing he was getting used to – waking up slowly in bed with Tom and not having to get up for a bit – and said yes, he could manage that. The *patron*, his new boss, gave him a tour of the kitchen – it was no bigger than the galley in a submarine – and of the bar with its bottle rack and optics, and a lesson in how the Gaggia espresso machine worked. Then he was released back into the sunshine, where Tom awaited him, drinking an unhurried coffee out on the pavement, and they spent another lazy afternoon on the sunlit, sea-lit beach.

Tom found that his sensitivity towards Christopher's residual religious feelings did not extend as far as actually accompanying him to Mass. When Christopher and Sabine set off towards the cathedral a few minutes before seven Tom ensconced himself in a chair in Sabine's tiny garden, finding a last lingering chink of sunlight, and began to dip into Sabine's many French recipe books.

Sabine's house was near the top of the town, just a hundred metres from where the cathedral – or more correctly the basilica – was perched beside the castle on the very top. They didn't talk of anything very serious on the short outbound journey and of course they were respectfully silent, except for Amens and occasional other responses in Latin, during the service itself. But on the two minute walk back Sabine asked, 'Have your parents phoned in response to the letter you sent?'

'No,' Christopher said. 'I didn't give them your phone number. Do you think I should have?'

Sabine pursed her lips. 'That was entirely your choice. You don't need my advice on that and, in any case, advice given after the event is quite worthless. *Tu aurais du…* You should have… It's one of the more useless forms of words on earth.'

'I just thought that a reply from them by letter might be easier to deal with.'

'Perhaps you're right,' Sabine said. 'Only, when it comes … *oh, la,* here I am, giving you advice … a warning at least … perhaps you should be ready for bad news. I mean, try not to hope for too much.'

'It'll be the same for Tom,' said Christopher stoutly. 'We both have the same thing to face.'

'I wonder,' said Sabine thoughtfully, almost to herself. Then, 'Tell me, is either of you an only child?'

'No,' said Christopher. 'I have two older brothers and a little sister, Tom an elder brother.'

'I think that's good on both counts,' said Sabine. 'Michel is an only child. And – perhaps you know this already – so is Armand.'

You wanted to have more children, Christopher thought with a sudden, unusual flash of insight. That's why you love Armand so much. That's why you've taken to – and taken into your home – the two of us.

They were at Sabine's front door now. Michel and Armand arrived from the other direction at the same moment, and they all went in together.

'I've learned so much about cooking,' said Tom, greeting them. 'Looking through your books. Even the words I didn't know became somehow transparent and I could guess their meaning.'

Michel had bought skate wings on the quayside. Sabine poached them lightly, and served them with melted butter that had been heated just enough to turn it amber, without burning it, and strewing parsley, a drop of vinegar and pickled capers on top.

It was Michel who showed Tom around the ledgers and other books when he started work at the beginning of the next week. Tom had assumed that Sabine would be his Monday morning mentor and was surprised to find his young friend assuming the role himself. Somehow he hadn't expected to be learning book-keeping from an accomplished painter in oils and water-colour. But it was a lazy piece of thinking, he realized. It was the same thinking that made school-kids imagine their physics teacher had no opinions about Shakespeare, or that their English master had never been forced to recite the theorem of Pythagoras. People, all of them, were a whole bundle of different accomplishments and knowledge-sets. They had to be, in order to get through life.

'When you come to the end of a page,' Michel told him, 'whatever page of whatever it is, you have to add the totals crossways as well as downwards. The total in the right-hand column must be the same as the total of the bottom line going across. If there's a discrepancy you have to go through the whole thing, again and again if necessary, and find it. There's no short cut.' He stopped for a second. 'Well, there is one short cut,' he said. 'If your discrepancy is a multiple of nine – which means the digits add up to it – seventy-two or sixty-three, say – then you've probably copied down two digits the wrong way round, so you can go through and look first for that.' Tom was grateful to Michel for this piece of information. In the weeks to come he would save himself hours of work and frustration by knowing it.

Christopher would not be starting work till the following morning: the café was closed all day Mondays. Instead he spent the morning buying the ingredients for Tom's shepherd's pie. Though strictly speaking it would be a cottage pie, as it was to be made with minced beef. Sabine told him where to buy it. 'Don't use the *boucheries chevalines,*' she warned him, 'unless you particularly want to make it with horse.' Actually the *boucheries chevalines* were fairly unmistakeable. They all had gold-painted, life-size busts of a horse's head over the door. Christopher could find no moral objection to eating horse anywhere inside himself; at the same time he discovered a squeamish disinclination to try it.

Having obtained his pound of minced flesh he bought onions and garlic at a greengrocer's. Tom and he had discussed the question of the garlic. Neither of them would have used it at home; their parents didn't, and it wasn't even to be seen in the shops except in dried form in little tubs, flaked and mixed with salt. Here it was all around them; there were bulbs of it in the shops; it turned up in Sabine's own cooking, and they found they liked it. So garlic had joined the list of ingredients. Then Christopher made another discovery in the greengrocer's. You could buy a flavouring bundle: a small carrot, a bay leaf and a sprig of thyme were pressed into the concave side of a short piece of celery stick and tied together with thread. As Tom wasn't there to be consulted, Christopher took an executive decision and added one of these to his purchases.

While they were preparing the dish in the afternoon Tom had a moment of panic when it dawned on him that there would be no Bisto powder to make the gravy with. But he had profited almost without knowing it from leafing through Sabine's cookery books and also from occasionally seeing Sabine herself at work in the kitchen. When he had given the meat and vegetables their preliminary frying he added a squirt from a sort of toothpaste tube that contained tomato concentrate – something he had never seen before in his life – added a splash of read wine – Christopher had bought a litre of Nicolas's Vieux Ceps to be drunk with the meal – and set aside the liquid that drained off the pie filling when it was spooned into the oven dish, to be heated and served as a separate sauce.

The pie having taken the best part of a day to prepare, it was eventually despatched in under twenty minutes. Tom and Christopher were relieved and delighted to see Michel and Armand wolfing it down. Even Sabine, who ate at a more sedate pace, appeared to enjoy it. At any rate she said she did.

Christopher found it was a wrench to have to get up at six, leaving Tom behind, all warm and snug and naked in bed. It felt like having to get out of a nice hot bath before you were ready to. However, all over the world people were doing the same, getting up to go to work. It was good that they both had jobs, he thought. Good for their pockets and good for their self-respect. Christopher found himself looking forward to the day when they would be able to offer Sabine some rent.

He was glad he had been given a lesson on how to work the espresso machine. He spent his first two hours doing nothing except make cups of coffee endlessly while people queued and rapped coins on the zinc. His new boss carried the cups to outlying tables and later collected money which went into a bag at his waist. Armand wasn't there: he would be doing a later shift.

Other things that sold at that time of the morning were croissants – they lived in a basket on the counter and were handed out in exchange for immediate cash – and hard-boiled eggs, which had been cooked first thing that morning and were now perched, still in their shells, in a wire Christmas-tree-like arrangement that you had to be careful not to send flying when handing cups of coffee across the counter. Hand in hand with the dispensing of coffee came, once the first ten minutes had gone by, a constant stream of washing up. Christopher served his first glass of draught lager, *pression* they called it, a few minutes before nine o'clock.

Then, to his great astonishment he found himself, at just past eleven, serving a glass of wine to a customer who turned out to be Gérard. He was wearing a knapsack and carrying a raincoat. 'What are you doing here?' Christopher asked.

'I might have asked you the same question,' answered Gérard. 'I was expecting to see Armand. But it's good to see you gainfully occupied... I have to say, you do get about.'

Christopher grinned at him. 'And Tom's working in Michel's shop,' he said tail-waggingly. 'Doing the accounts.'

'As I said...' said Gérard. 'But to answer your question, I'm taking the ferry to Folkestone shortly. Then the train to Canterbury where I shall most probably spend the night. I have a burning curiosity, I find, to see this painting of you and Tom as David and Jonathan by your Miss Who Dare.'

'Miss O'Deere,' corrected Christopher, though he was startled to hear of Gérard's plans. He had said something about wanting to see the picture once before, but he hadn't sounded too serious.

'You wouldn't be free to come with me, I suppose?' Gérard said.

'I wish I could,' said Christopher, trying to hide the confusion of feelings that welled up in response to being asked. 'But I have to work again tomorrow – this is only my first day in this job – and besides, I'm pretty sure I'd ... that Tom and I'd be arrested if we so much as set foot on British soil just at the moment.'

'Ah well,' said Gérard. 'I just thought I'd ask. Perhaps I'll find Benoît and René on the boat. Though I don't imagine their schedules would allow them a night on shore with me in Kent.'

'I hope you'll look in on your way back,' said Christopher. 'We'd be more than interested to know what's happened with the painting. Plus any news at all of Molly O'Deere herself.'

'You shall see me on my return,' said Gérard. A tiny mischievous smile curled at the corners of his mouth. 'Either here or in the Chat qui Pêche .'

After he had finished his wine Gérard took his leave and walked straight across the bridge to the ferry port. He had his passport in his pocket, some notes in sterling in his wallet and a couple of travellers' cheques just in case. He bought his ticket at the little office, was nodded through the control points and a few minutes later was climbing the steep stairway up onto his ship. He stood out on deck as the ferry set sail, experiencing that moment of exhilaration that is experienced by everyone who sets out on an international journey just for the fun of it. Looking astern over the white-painted rail, he watched the town of Boulogne swing sideways as the ferry negotiated the harbour entrance. It was a view he ought to paint, he thought, full of colour, sea and interest. He wondered, though, if he would ever manage it; ships leaving port with timetables to keep didn't hang about.

Eventually, once the ship had gained speed and left the shelter of the outer breakwater, the gathering strength of the wind forced him inside. But a new pleasure awaited him in the café-bar. There was Benoît on duty behind the counter. René was on board too, his friend explained, working a different bar on another deck.

'I don't suppose the two of you would be free to come to Canterbury with me,' Gérard said boldly. 'Come and see this picture the two English boys are always on about. Stay the night. Change your shifts…'

Benoît laughed at him. 'Ever the optimist you are, Gérard. You won't be surprised to know we can't change shifts just like that.'

'Always worth asking on the off-chance,' Gérard said. He ordered a small beer for himself, and Benoît drew it up through the pressure pump.

'On the other hand,' said Benoît, looking carefully at the blonde beer he was pulling rather than at Gérard, 'our shifts are a bit different today. We're not due to come back till tomorrow. This ship needs something doing to it. They're doing it at Folkestone for once. We're supposed to be sleeping on board. I could ask, I suppose, if we'd be free to go to Canterbury instead…'

There wasn't a direct train from Folkestone to Canterbury. They had to change at Dover. It wasn't difficult: all three of them had serviceable English. Once they arrived in Canterbury they quickly found a hotel just a short walk from the east station. It was housed in a very ancient-looking building; it had already become apparent as they looked along the streets nearby that almost everything in Canterbury was antique.

'Have you a room large enough for three of us?' Gérard asked as they arrived at the reception desk.

The woman behind the desk looked at them a bit beadily. 'And you are…?' she said.

'I am the well known painter Gérard De Martinville,' said Gérard with a flourish. 'Presenting my two nephews, René and Benoît. From Paris.'

'I'll see what we can do,' the woman said.

It was a walk of only a few minutes through sunlit afternoon streets. The houses that lined the pavements were either handsome or pretty – or simply quaint. Then the cathedral stood in front of them. They approached it through a massive gate.

'We look for the exhibition of fine art,' Gérard said to the first person who came within earshot once they had entered the nave's echoing space. His tone suggested that, if the exhibition had got lost or had strayed somewhere the person he was addressing would be expected to join in the search. The exhibition was still on, the stranger told them. The principal exhibits were in the chapter house.

They walked a little way round the cloister, where a vast number of small canvasses were displayed, and turned in through the high doorway. And there they were. In pride of place, on the wall right opposite: David and Jonathan, alias Tom and Christopher, in cricket trousers, Tom holding a maroon cricket ball, both endearingly part stripped to the waist.

'Oh là, oh là,' said Gérard. *'Pas mal. pas mal.'* Not bad. It was about the highest praise one artist might bestow on another's efforts.

The David and Jonathan was a big picture, occupying about eight square feet of wall space. It had been painted with impressive confidence and, quite apart from anything else, had wonderfully captured the characters and likeness of the two young men who had posed for it. Both of them stared forward from the canvas, while Christopher's bare arm was laid lightly around Tom's shoulder. They might have been brothers, only the biblical characters were not, and Tom and Christopher were not. In a way that had been the problem.

Gérard found a woman at a desk who looked as though she might be in charge of the exhibition, for this afternoon at least. 'I would like to know,' he said, 'if the David and Jonathan is for sale. If it is, then I would be interested to buy it.'

The woman gave the three of them a startled look. 'It is not for sale,' she said. She teetered on the brink of saying the next bit for a second, and then she said it. 'To be honest with you the picture has caused some trouble. The lady who painted it is, I'm told, extremely upset about it.'

'Tell us the story,' said Gérard, and a look of wry amusement flickered across his face.

'The painting was done, I believe, in a spirit of complete innocence. But some very clever critics from London thought they saw homosexual undertones in it, and said so in the national press. The dean and chapter were very disturbed by this. They felt that a painting so controversial should not be hanging in a Christian church and asked the Kent Arts Society to remove it from the exhibition. Well…' She lowered her voice to a conspiratorial pitch and went on. 'The Society didn't take this lying down. If the picture had to go, then they would remove the whole exhibition to another venue, telling the press of their decision and the reason for it.' Now she looked around her. In a whisper she added, 'The chapter backed down and so it's still here. Meanwhile, the lady who painted it also asked to have the painting withdrawn but the Society pointed to something in the small print of their contract and said she couldn't have it back till the exhibition closed next month.'

'Ah,' said Gérard. 'It is good when artistic organisms show strength of character, is it not? But perhaps I can contact the lady painter after the end of the exhibition and offer to buy it from her at that point. Very few things are not-for-sale when the offer is high enough. Do you have her address?'

'No,' said the woman firmly. 'I can not give you that. But you may give me yours and I shall make sure that she gets it.'

'In that case may I have some paper and a pen and write her a short note?'

Pen and paper were found after a few minutes' anxious bustle. Gérard wrote his little note in French. He knew what he was doing. He was pretty sure he remembered Tom or Christopher telling him that Miss O'Deere taught French as well as art.

'You needn't worry, Gérard,' Benoît said to him in their own language. 'Tom and Christopher lived in the same building as the painter lady. They know the address.'

'That is good too, of course,' said Gérard. 'It means we have two separate ways to make the approach.'

After another searching examination of the painting Gérard and the others toured the vast cathedral itself, and then took another saunter through the town's streets, pausing in front of some of the town's other tourist sites. By then it was time to eat something, they all thought, and turned their wander around the old city into a serious hunt for a restaurant that could offer something French.

The following evening all three of them were back in Boulogne and at the Chat qui Pêche. They recounted to Tom and Christopher – and to Armand and Michel – the main events of their trip to England. They omitted the details of their sleeping arrangements. But Tom and Christopher were able to hazard a fairly accurate guess.

SIX

Gérard was returning to Paris early the next morning and so he left the Chat qui Pêche for his hotel around ten o'clock. The other four set off up the hill at the same time: they all had work to do in the morning. 'It puzzles me,' said Tom as they walked, 'why he should be so interested in that painting. I mean, to want to see it might be one thing, but to travel all the way from Paris to Canterbury to see it… And then to want to buy it when he gets there…'

'That's Gérard for you,' said Michel. 'His character in a nutshell. Impulsive. He sees something. He likes it. He wants to own it. However odd a whim it might appear to others.'

Armand added, 'Of course it helps no end that he has a filthy rich boyfriend. In his situation he can do impulsive things like that. I suppose he's simply got used to doing it.'

Michel went on, 'It does tell us one thing, though. There can't be any doubt about the quality of Miss Astaire's work. He wouldn't be offering money if it wasn't a first class painting.'

'Miss O'Deere,' said Christopher automatically. 'You're thinking of the American dancer.'

'I wonder how she is, though,' said Tom. 'Gérard said she was upset by the whole thing. Which I'm not surprised about. She was in quite a bad way when we last saw her. She's now had nearly a fortnight for it to hit home.'

'Home,' said Christopher thoughtfully. 'Term will be almost at an end. Molly will go home then, I suppose. Or does she live at the school all through the holidays like the priests do? I never thought of her as having a home. Never asked her.'

'She wrote letters to her family in Ireland,' said Tom. 'So did Miss Coyle.'

'They were just teachers we worked with,' said Christopher. 'We never got to know them at all…'

'Well here we are,' said Michel, taking a key from the pocket of his dungarees. They had reached the corner of the Rue Hamy. Michel unlocked the door next to the shop while they said their goodnights, then Armand and he disappeared inside, to make their way up the steep stairs to their bedroom-cum-artist's studio. Tom and Christopher were left alone together on the pavement They carried on up the hill.

'And thinking of Molly,' said Christopher, 'What about the boys who got expelled? Angelo Dexter, Simon Rickman. I can't imagine how their summer holidays are going to be.' It was as though Gérard's visit to England had reopened a door that they had closed and locked behind them. They were once again conscious now of half-glimpsed things going on behind it.

'And poor John Moyse,' said Tom. 'While we're on the subject. All his certainties and self-confidence blown away just as he gets made house captain for the last few weeks of his last term.' He gave a snort. 'With only his diary to sustain him. The diary you encouraged him to keep.'

'It's something, I suppose,' said Christopher doubtfully. 'But writing's small comfort when you've lost your friends.' He thought back to his time at Star of the Sea. He'd only been there a couple of months. But so much had happened in that time, so many very important things – having anal sex for the first time, falling in love, being accused of heaven knows what, losing a first job – that in his memory it seemed a very solid place: the people he'd known there, especially John and Angelo, like major players in the drama of his life to date.

When they got home Sabine was still up. 'There's a letter for you Tom,' she said.

'A letter? At ten o'clock at night?' There hadn't been one when they'd had dinner with Sabine at seven, nor earlier in the day.

'It was wrongly delivered to next-door,' Sabine said. 'Madame Deschaumes brought it round after you'd gone out.'

'Better see what it is, then,' said Tom, feeling a clenching in his stomach and bracing himself. He didn't have to wait to see the writing on the outside of the blue air-letter to know who it was from. Sabine handed him a paper-knife so promptly that she must have made sure in advance that it was to hand. Tom, still standing in the kitchen, slit the paper and read it silently. Then he handed it to Christopher.

Darling Tom

Whatever happens to you in this life be assured of our love. That will never ever go away.

Yes, we read the awful stories in the newspapers. But so much in the papers is a mix of truth and half-truth and just plain lies. We thought about phoning the school but then decided not to. We preferred to wait till we had heard from you. Anything more you want to tell us we will listen to gladly, and where there are things you don't want to share with us, we will not pry.

Of course we were worried for a few days when we didn't hear from you, but we didn't go out of our minds. We knew you'd get in touch when you could or when you were ready to.

Daddy and I would love to come to Boulogne for a weekend very soon. You didn't put a phone number in your letter so we can't contact you to arrange this easily. If you want to call us though, make a reverse-charge call and we will pay.

Daddy has a bad back at the moment. It lets him get out of all sorts of jobs at home. Meanwhile the garden is doing well and the runner beans are already halfway up their poles.

With love from your father and me,
Your ever-loving
Mummy

PS We are looking forward to meeting Christopher, your friend.

Tom had remained dry-eyed when reading the letter. He watched intently now while Christopher read it. Christopher finished reading and handed the letter back. And it was his eyes, not Tom's, that sprang with tears.

'I have had no reply either to the note I wrote to Miss Who Dare in the cathedral, or to the letter I posted to her direct,' said Gérard. 'Though I must thank you boys once again for giving me the address you had.'

'It's early days,' Tom told him. 'Letters between France and England take ages.' Over a week had passed since Tom had received his letter from his parents. His lover had as yet had no reply from his.

They were sitting on the narrow sloping pavement outside Chez Alfred, having Sunday lunch. The slope was so steep that their table had to be chocked up with wedges at its lower end to prevent the wine tipping over and everything else sliding off. The chairs were left to their own devices and the people sitting on them managed as best they could. The lunch was appetising as well as substantial; it was mid-July now and the sun was brilliant and hot.

'I've been looking for a place for the two of you when September comes,' Gérard said. They were quite a crowd around the table – Michel and Armand, René, Benoît, Thierry and Robert had joined them – but Gérard was addressing just Christopher and Tom. 'I haven't had much luck. It isn't that there is nowhere to rent in Paris; far from it; it's the question of an affordable price.' Tom and Christopher nodded. That wasn't the case only in Paris: they both knew that. Gérard bit off a piece of baguette and chewed it thoughtfully for a moment. Then he said, 'I've been talking about this to Henri, my partenaire. If you'll permit me I will give you the benefit of his thoughts.'

A thrill ran through Christopher at that moment. It was a thrill of deep dismay at one level, yet of excitement in some other, till now hidden, depth. Extraordinarily he knew exactly what Gérard was going to offer them; he didn't know how he knew it, and the discovery surprised him, but he had no doubt at all as to what it was.

'Henri and I own a quite large apartment on the west slope of Montmartre. It is not very far from the Gare du Nord where I met you the other week…'

'Come on, Gérard,' René ribbed him gently, 'Henri owns the apartment. Everyone knows that. Henri and I!' He rolled his narrow eyes: it looked rather odd.

'All right,' said Gérard. 'We *have* an apartment, then. It's large and a bit rambling. Some young impecunious artists use some of the spare rooms. We don't charge them rent. The rooms are fairly basic. One is coming vacant in a few weeks' time. Henri and I have talked this over and we'd like to offer it to you.' He held up his hand. 'Before you say anything, anything at all, I need to tell you something that may make you pause in your thoughts. The fact is, and I have to be honest with you about this, that in this household we have a fairly relaxed attitude to certain things.' He peered sharply into their eyes to see what they were picking up: how far they had got. 'I'm talking about attitudes towards sex. I don't mean that everyone says yes to everything everybody else wants all the time...'

'They did when we were there last year,' René put in impudently.

'Don't be cheeky now,' Gérard admonished him in a rather arch way. It was a way of speaking that Tom and Christopher were beginning to associate with a certain kind of homosexual man. It only emerged, they had noticed, when the speaker felt himself in a safe place among like-minded friends. 'I'm talking seriously,' Gérard said.

He returned his attention to Christopher and Tom. 'I mention this because such a way of living might not suit you. Until very recently you were both teachers at a very religious school. I have the utmost respect for any scruples you may have, whether based on religious principles or based on anything else.' Gérard took a sip of wine. He gave his two newest protégés another searching look. 'We wouldn't want to invite into our slightly unconventional ménage anyone, any pair of boys, who wouldn't feel comfortable with such relaxed arrangements. And it would work both ways.' He shrugged. 'In first, they, the new arrivals, would feel uncomfortable with the set-up. In second, we who already live there would quite naturally feel uncomfortable at having them in our midst...' He took another swallow of wine. Tom and Christopher copied him, and looked at him, mute as sheep. Gérard continued. 'I'm putting this on the table fairly and squarely so that you are in possession of the main facts when you decide whether to accept our offer or not. And...' he held up his hand again, 'I'll just finish by saying that you will not have to decide anything today. If your answer is no it won't affect my friendly feelings towards you both, nor the offer of work you've had from Madame Blétry, nor my willingness to hire you as models in the course of my own work.'

Tom jumped in before Christopher had a chance to scupper everything with a single word. 'It's a very generous offer, Gérard,' he said. He felt his body trembling all over and hoped the others, especially Christopher, couldn't see. 'We'll need to think about it, Christopher and I, as you've already realised.' He smiled disarmingly, first at Gérard, then at Christopher. 'It's something we'll need to talk about privately.' He gave Christopher an encouraging nod and was relieved when Christopher picked up the cue and nodded back at him and then at Gérard too.

They didn't get a chance to discuss Gérard's proposition out of earshot of the others for some hours: a wait they both found difficult. French Sunday lunches were long, pleasurable affairs, they were discovering. Unlike in England there wasn't really a period that you could refer to as "after lunch". But when they did find themselves moments of privacy, walking through the streets towards the Chat qui Pêche, for example, they found the subject too difficult to broach. They didn't really feel comfortable about raising it between them until they got to bed that night and were reassuringly wrapped in each other's arms.

'Gérard's offer...' began Tom.

'Mmmm?' said Christopher.

'Difficult, isn't it?'

'Yep.'

'What do you think?' Tom asked, making sure of Christopher by giving him a momentarily tighter squeeze.

'I don't know,' said Christopher. 'What do you?'

'It's hugely tempting. Living in Paris rent free, like we do here...'

'Which reminds me,' Christopher said, 'we must give Sabine some money now that we're getting paid each week.'

'Mmmm,' said Tom.

'The thing is,' said Christopher, 'we're two people in love. It feels natural to keep the sex just for ourselves. It's also ... sorry to keep harking back to the Catholic thing ... the way we're supposed to behave. Monogamy. Like in a marriage. Just because we can never actually be married doesn't mean we shouldn't respect marriage's rules.'

'I'd go along with that,' said Tom. 'The first part of it more especially. I wouldn't feel right with another person in bed with us right now. Let alone a different person instead of you.' He felt Christopher's body flinch minutely in response to those last few words: it was as if he'd had a small electric shock.

'If we don't go along with it...'

'I know,' said Tom. 'How would we ever find a place we can afford? If Gérard, with all his inside knowledge and contacts in Paris hasn't been able to...'

'That is, if he's actually tried.'

'You're getting smarter by the day,' Tom said.

They had learned to synchronise their working hours, more or less. If Christopher had a morning shift at the café then Tom would catch up with the shop's paperwork in the morning. If Christopher's shift was later in the day, then Tom did his flexible hours in the afternoon. That way they were able to spend nearly all their free time together. That was what they wanted. By now they were deeply in love.

The morning after their pillow conversation about Gérard's offer – a conversation that had ended inconclusively – they were both free. By common accord they made straight for the shop when they left the house in the mid-morning and asked Michel if he was free to join them for a coffee outside.

'Yes,' Michel said, and smiled. 'Or if it's something very private you want to discuss we could go up to the studio and have coffee there.'

They hadn't been inside Michel's studio for a week or more. It was Michel's and Armand's bedroom after all, and when it came to regular contact, well, they routinely dined all together with Sabine, while Tom and Michel worked together in the shop for part of almost every day. There was no need to repair to the bedroom for routine catch-ups. Now as they glanced around it the studio appeared unchanged since their last visit. The same paintings were stacked against the walls and the same unfinished canvas stood on the easel as had been there when they'd arrived the previous month.

'Not done much painting lately?' Tom asked conversationally. He and Christopher sat down on the bed together. Michel, having put a saucepan of water on the gas-ring, took the chair.

'When have I had time?' Michel answered. 'Now that you two are here.'

That gave both of them a jolt. They weren't sure what interpretation to place on the remark.

Tom said quickly, 'You mustn't let us hold you up, I mean, stop you painting.'

'Yes,' Christopher chipped in. 'You don't have to look after us all the time. Make some time for yourself. For painting. Time with Armand too.'

'Don't worry about that,' Michel said. 'We spend every night in bed together after all.' Christopher fidgeted slightly at the mention of bed. It was the one he was sitting on. 'Don't feel guilty,' Michel went on. 'I like spending my time with you. The same goes for Armand. When you leave for Paris … if you leave for Paris … how shall I say this? You'll leave a big hole.'

'Well it's about Paris we wanted to talk to you,' Tom said. The conversation needed to get back on track, he thought. The agenda was complicated enough without considering how much Michel and Armand would miss them when they went away. And how much they would miss Armand and Michel …

'It's about Gérard's offer,' Christopher said, equally quickly.

'Of course,' said Michel. 'I knew.'

'If it was you and Armand the offer had been made to,' Christopher said, 'would you take it? What would you do?'

Michel looked uncomfortable for a moment and let out a long breath before he spoke. 'This is very difficult to say. I knew that you would ask me, or ask Armand, exactly that. We stayed awake quite a long time last night discussing it if you want to know.'

'So did we,' said Christopher.

Michel grinned. 'You hardly needed to tell me that.' He paused, but only for a second. 'It's impossible for anyone to say what they'd do in someone else's situation. Nobody can be in the same situation as anybody else. They can be in similar ones but that's as far as it goes; so as for giving advice based on that… Well, it doesn't work at all. However… For what it's worth I can tell you I'm pretty sure what Benoît and René would do. They would accept. I know this because they did it once before. For a short time last year.'

'Right.' Said Tom. 'I see.'

'The thing is,' Michel said, 'it didn't seem to do their own relationship any harm at all. Having a free-for-all among that household, I mean.'

'Well, that's something I suppose,' said Tom. 'I mean, we've seen them together and they still seem like young boys in love.' A thought struck him. Actually it had struck him before, but he only decided to mention it now. 'This partner of Gérard's, Henri. Have you met him? How old is he?'

'He says he's fifty-nine,' said Michel. 'But he also said that last year. Yes, I've met him a couple of times. He comes to Boulogne sometimes with Gérard when he's on one of his weekends. To see what Gérard's getting up to, I suppose. He's actually quite young for his age. In looks, I mean. He's lean and fit, like Gérard is.'

'Well, that's something,' said Tom. He sounded marginally relieved. 'It shouldn't be a consideration, I know…'

'But of course it is,' said Michel. 'Obviously. Anyway…' He grinned naughtily and his head went on one side a little. 'Am I allowed to ask what your thoughts are at this moment. Are you thinking you might accept the proposal?'

'We'd need to talk about it a bit more,' said Tom. Christopher had gone very silent, he'd noticed. 'What you said about the love between René and Benoît not being affected was quite…' He almost said, 'encouraging,' but quickly thought again and said, 'interesting,' instead.

'On the other hand,' said Michel with a note of warning in his voice, 'we thought – Amand and I thought – that if we'd been asked, we'd have probably said no. Yes, everybody's different, and if the offer had been made to us instead of you we might have decided differently. However, we don't need to go to Paris: we have everything here for us in Boulogne. My father's business and all that… But in the end we thought that, if we were in your position, and if we accepted an offer of that kind, we'd be worried that… How shall I say this? We'd be worried that our relationship might not survive it.'

'Really,' said Tom thoughtfully. Michel had surprised him. 'I've always thought you have a wonderfully secure relationship.' Memories of the hugs that he and Christopher had had with Michel separately, and of their painful consequences, came uncomfortably back.

'Thank you for your honesty, Michel,' Christopher said.

Tom said, 'I think the water's boiling for the coffee.' Michel turned and looked into the corner of the room where the gas-ring was. It was filling nicely with a cloud of steam.

They went back up to Sabine's house after they'd had their coffee with Michel, intending to while away the time in her garden looking at recipe books in French – it was something they were both now getting keen on – for the hour or two that remained before they went to work. The post had arrived in their absence. It was lying in a small heap inside the hall, just inside the door: evidently Sabine had not come in and found it. Among the envelopes they saw one light blue one, with a give-away edging of red and darker blue. Christopher bent down and picked it out from the pile. 'I'll get the opener,' said Tom. 'Wait.'

But Christopher hadn't waited. He'd scrabbled at it with his fingernails, then slit it roughly, tearing it, with his middle finger. He read,

Dear son,

It was good to have news of you. We are both pleased that you are well. But I have things to say that will not please you.

You say that you love a man. I have to correct you. The emotions that you feel towards this man, and he to you, are not love. They are something else which, to spare your feelings, I will not name.

The Church teaches us that love is a holy thing between a man and a woman. It is a wonderful thing

whose purpose is to bind those who marry and, if possible, have children. It is not to be talked of lightly, and especially not in connection with a male friend. When David talked of his love for Jonathan (now you know I'm thinking about that terrible picture, which your father and I have been to see) he did not mean the thing you are thinking of. I am sorry to say that you are in a state of <u>grave error</u>.

I'm also sorry to have to tell you we shan't be coming to France to see you. We feel that would be to condone things which we cannot condone. I'm sorry if this news hurts you. It is the way we have been taught and brought up, and we can do no other. Perhaps the worst thing for us is that it was the way you were taught and brought up too.

You will be welcome here at home, of course, but only when you have come to see the error of your ways and renounced the evil influence of your friend Thomas. Until that time, I am afraid, we can not, in all conscience open our door or our hearts to you.

But when the great day comes – when you have seen the right path once more – you can be assured of a homecoming like the Prodigal Son's. For there is no love in the world that compares to the love of parents for their daughters and sons. We look forward to, and will pray night and day for, that wonderful dawn.

Mummy and Daddy

'You'd better read it,' said Christopher in a chill voice, and handed it to Tom.

They continued to stand in the hallway while Tom read. While he did this, line after line, he wondered that Christopher had not already dissolved in tears. Perhaps he was in shock. When Tom finished the letter he didn't speak but put his arms around Christopher, holding him tight like a vice, and nuzzling him, cheek to cheek. He felt a rage well up in him suddenly. A rage such as he'd never felt before. It was as though he'd become a sentient volcano, in which lava was rising from unimaginable depths, ready to explode upwards with a force that was beyond measure. Christopher stood still and rock-like in his arms, while it was Tom who burst into a fury of tears.

SEVEN

'It's meaningless,' Christopher said. 'My mother's religion. The Church's view. The whole bloody lot.'

They were sitting in Sabine's charmed tiny garden, in which a plum tree and a pear tree grew. They hadn't brought cookery books out with them; they had more than enough to keep them occupied. For the most part Tom said nothing, but sat alongside Christopher on the bench beneath the wall, hip against hip, thigh against thigh, clasping Christopher's hand while Christopher said the things he had to say.

The words, like fish-bones, came choking out. 'You can't say anything worse to another human being than to say that the love he bears another doesn't count: that it's something less than the love that you experience yourself...' Christopher groped around inside his vocabulary store and found the words he needed were not there. The word disrespect had not been turned into a verb back in 1962. It might have been helpful if it had been, for Christopher could have done with it at that point.

'What she means, and what the Church thinks, clearly, is that there's no difference between my loving you – and, OK, expressing that in a sexual way – and the two of us buggering every man in Paris, day after day, year after year, till the end of our lives...'

'Or till we run out of men,' said Tom, and gave Christopher's hand an extra-specially supportive squeeze.

'You might as well murder someone,' Christopher went on (after returning the squeeze). 'When you deni... Is it denigrate I mean...? When you denigrate someone's love like that you deny their humanity just like you do when you kill them. You take it away completely. I think love is what we're made of. I think our love is what we are.'

Tom thought that a cynic could have countered the assertion with other suggestions about what people are made of. Slugs and snails and puppy-dogs' tails would be some of the more innocent ingredients. But he was in no mood to be cynical just then. 'That's a beautiful thing to say,' he said instead, and just saying it made him get quite choked up.

'That being the case,' Christopher went on, '…I mean about what our bloody religion says, and what my mother clearly thinks, I don't see why we shouldn't go to Paris and live with Gérard and Henri on the terms they suggest. If it didn't damage René and Benoît's relationship, then ours ought to be all right.'

Tom was startled. His surprise was palpable to Christopher, transmitted thigh to thigh. 'Are you sure?' he said. 'You want to tie all this in with the decision about Paris? Anyway, this isn't the moment to decide something like that. We need to sleep on it again at least. See how we feel in a day or two.'

'Well, I've decided anyway,' said Christopher. 'If you want to overrule me in a day or two… Well, I'd accept that. Give and take, in any relationship. Sometimes I'll have to accept being overruled by you.'

'And vice versa too,' said Tom, 'as you well know, but were too polite to say.'

'There is one thing, though,' said Christopher. He seemed to have decided that the trauma he'd suffered on reading his mother's letter had earned him the right to steer the conversation entirely his way, like the right to extra rations in a warship's sick-bay.

'What's that?' asked Tom.

'If we're going to be having sex with other people we'll need to be together when we do it. I wouldn't want either of us to be going off and doing it separately, you with one chap and me with another.'

'Right,' said Tom, reeling after yet another whack of surprise from Christopher. 'I'll try and remember that.'

Just a few days later Tom told Gérard that they would accept his kind offer of a room; that they'd discussed the free and easy attitude towards sex that prevailed in the household and decided that they had no problem with it. And a few days after that they went to Paris at Gérard's invitation and inspected their future residence. To say the house impressed them would be an understatement. It was old, large and ramshackle, situated in the very attractive rue St Vincent, a stone's-throw from the Sacré Coeur Basilica. It even had an overgrown garden, with big trees in it, falling down the hillside behind the house, from which you could get glimpses of central Paris. Inside the house they were shown the room that would be theirs, and were introduced to two of the house's young occupants, who were called Marcel and Alain. 'Can't wait to move in,' said Tom to Christopher. 'Ditto,' said Christopher.

Tom's parents paid their promised visit over the last weekend in July. Tom met them in the arrivals area of the ferry port and escorted them proudly across the railway tracks and the river bridge to the hotel in the Rue Faidherbe, carrying his mother's small suitcase. Inside the hotel Tom introduced Thierry and Robert as good friends of Christopher and himself and then, from its cage in the centre of the hall, the mynah bird claimed their attention with a guttural croak of, *'Faites comme chez vous,'* which Tom explained meant, make yourselves at home. That astonished them somewhat. 'Was it taught to speak by a man with a throat problem?' his mother asked.

'By a very heavy smoker, I imagine,' Tom said. 'You wait till you hear him cough.'

After they had seen their room Tom took them along the street to La Chope, where Christopher was coming to the end of a shift. Both Tom and Christopher had been a bit calculating: engineering that first meeting in the neutral surroundings of the place where Christopher worked and was actually at work at the time.

So Tom's parents were introduced to the handsome, thistledown-blond waiter who brought them their coffee with practised aplomb, and then were able to collect their thoughts about the elfin beauty who had come into their son's life so unexpectedly, while he bustled away to serve someone else. Watching his retreating rear end (a thing he always enjoyed) Tom thought with admiration that Christopher, who had been waiting tables a mere month, gave the impression of having done it all his life, so confident and agile was he in the role.

Later, after Christopher's shift came to an end, the four of them explored the town together. They saw the castle, or what was left of it, a stone's throw from Sabine's house and the cathedral, and sat in the walled garden that surrounded it in what had once been the moat. Day-flying hawk moths hovered over the valerian that grew from cracks in the walls and, although the season of birdsong was well over, one or two blackbirds consented to sing for their entertainment as they sat enjoying the peaceful space and its flowers.

In the evening there was a welcome dinner party hosted by Sabine in her dining-room. Christopher and Tom, Tom's parents, Armand and Michel were all there and the cooking was shared by Sabine and Tom. Tom's first month in France had dramatically transformed his culinary skills. There were artichoke hearts in vinaigrette. Then breaded veal cutlets, cheeses from

Normandy, just a department away, and a tart of mirabelle plums.

Tom's parents managed to seem quite at ease. They chatted with Sabine and the boys in a mixture of English and French. Christopher was very conscious of the importance for them of Sabine's presence. Like a reassuring beacon ahead of them she presented the image of a very normal, intelligent middle-class French woman, who went to church regularly and who happened to have a homosexual only son. She was a mother who made her son's boyfriend unequivocally welcome in her home and treated him as a second son. Christopher thought that a better example of how to behave in the circumstances could not have been found anywhere. He blessed their luck that, through meeting Michel, they had tumbled into her household at this crucial point in their lives. Tom's relationship with his parents would reap untold benefits from this happy accident. Then Christopher thought about his own parents and a yawning pit seemed to open up inside him. If only they could be here this evening. If only they too could meet Sabine and be guided by her example as Tom's parents, he hoped, would be.

The next day, Sunday, even Tom consented to go to Mass. They walked the short distance up to the cathedral in quite a big phalanx. Tom, Christopher, Tom's parents, Sabine... And out of solidarity Michel and Armand had joined the party too. They filled a whole pew when they got there. 'Everyone calls it the cathedral,' Tom told his parents as they peered admiringly around the light and graceful building. 'But there's no bishopric here. No bishop's chair. Strictly speaking it's a basilica.' And he went on to explain in a whisper how the pleasing classical structure had been designed not by an architect but by a local canon, on the back of an envelope in the early nineteenth century.

Sight-seeing bus tours ran up the coast from Boulogne to Cap Gris Nez and Cap Blanc Nez, with a stop for lunch in Calais. Tom had booked four seats on one of them: for his parents, Christopher and himself. By now Christopher felt delightedly, warmly, part of Tom's family, and sat happily chatting to Mrs Sanders, wedged against her on the narrow coach seat while Tom, just in front, talked with his father. Christopher liked families, he decided. Having lost his own very recently in a fit of frankness, he needed to be part of other people's. He was starting a collection, it seemed. He'd started with Michel's mother; now he'd notched up Tom's parents too.

They had lunch in one of a row of sea-food restaurants that lined the beach at Calais. Ferries with different names and colours from the ones they knew at Boulogne came and went across the glassy sea along the Dover route. The ships sailed along beside the beach in a dredged channel through the shallows for several miles, before turning out into the deeper waters and heading across to the other side.

Cap Blanc Nez involved a panting climb up a grassy slope from the coach park to the viewing platform at the top of the vertiginous chalk. Tom was afraid his mother might give up before she got there, but she didn't. Getting to the top brought the reward of plunging views downwards on three sides, and a very clear view of Dover's ten-mile line of white cliffs – and its massive castle that drew the eye up to the skyline. Christopher thought of banished noblemen in medieval history who would have stood here looking at that sight, unchanged through the centuries, and vowing to return with armies, defeat the king who had banished them and make the kingdom theirs.

Cap Gris Nez, though even closer to England, offered a slightly less impressive panorama, as it was only half as high above the sea as the white cape was. At least the walk from the coach park was on the flat this time. They stood by the lighthouse in the sunshine and Christopher thought about the last time they'd seen it – flashes of light that reared and stumbled, disappearing among the high waves in the midnight darkness. Lord save us, or we perish. Now the lighthouse seemed so solid, so unmoving in the sun, and the sea so calm and silent. Christopher found it hard to believe that what had happened to them that night had happened. He gained in that moment a bitter piece of adult knowledge: that so would all the big moments of his life, past, present and future, disappear behind him, becoming insubstantial and dreamlike.

Passing the village of Audresselles on the way back, and the turn-off to the little beach where the river came out, Christopher made no mention to Tom's mother that a month earlier they had both been painted there naked. He guessed that neither would Tom mention it to his father.

They had another visit a few weeks later, towards the end of August. At their invitation Roger and Malcolm sailed over on the Orca. They arrived on a calm sea at the end of the afternoon. Tom and Christopher were waiting for them, on the lookout for them on the beach, and when the rust-red sails came into sight they moved to the harbour quay, ready to help them tie up when they came in. It was a stirring moment for them both: seeing the Orca again. Stirring too to see Roger and Malcolm again: Roger two decades older than them, Malcolm just ten years. Only two months had passed since they'd last been together, but life had changed so utterly for Christopher and Tom that they were almost like two couples meeting for the first time. Christopher remembered the feeling he'd had when reunited with parents after his first term at boarding school: he'd lived so much that they didn't seem the same people any more. Malcolm's red hair had been cut scrubbing-brush short at some point in June. Now it was thick and curly again. Christopher thought it looked nicer this way. He guessed that Roger thought so too.

They stayed two nights. They were taken to Le Chat qui Pêche, and met Tom and Christopher's friends there. They also dined Chez Alfred, and slept at Sabine's house, on Tom and Christopher's bedroom floor.

Before their arrival Tom had said to Christopher, 'We'll tell them about our move to Paris, of course, but perhaps not that we're likely to end up in bed with the whole household when we get there. They might not like the idea. They're a pretty monogamous pair.' He stopped, remembered a couple of incidents suddenly: Malcolm once kissing Christopher aboard the Orca; Christopher throwing himself at Malcolm when frightened on the night-time sea. 'Well, I've always supposed they're a monogamous pair. But even if they're not, the same thing applies. It might lead to complications, with all four of us sleeping in the same room.' Christopher agreed to follow Tom's suggestion, although a bit reluctantly. He had a fond memory of Malcolm once placing a hand on his bare thigh when they were alone together in a car. Nothing had happened beyond that. Except that Christopher had placed his own hand on the warm and red-furred surface of Malcolm's thigh too. He didn't tell Tom this now.

During their short stay they took Tom and Christopher out for a sail. 'We'll be gentle with Christopher this time,' Malcolm said when Christopher told him he hadn't been at sea since the last traumatic time. In the event his fears proved groundless. The wind was light and the sea calm, sparkling like champagne, and the whole experience was a happy one. Both Christopher and Tom took the helm at different times; the atmosphere was one of close and comfortable friendship; there were no upsetting or disturbing moments, either emotionally or nautically.

In the evening, back on shore at Boulogne Roger made an announcement to them. In the Chat qui Pêche, appropriately. 'We have a move on the horizon too.'

'What?' said Christopher, jumping in a bit too soon. 'You're not leaving the Admiral Digby? Giving up the pub?'

'Rather the opposite,' said Roger, a self-satisfied expression stealing over his face. 'Malcolm is moving in with me permanently.'

'Gosh,' said Christopher, looking at Malcolm. Malcolm's expression remained unchanged. He always looked self-satisfied.

'That's wonderful,' said Tom.

'What do your parents think?' Christopher put the question to both of them. It would concern Malcolm's parents more immediately. Aged thirty he still shared their living-space, their house in Sandwich. And he was their only son.

'They're happy with it,' Malcolm said airily. He gave no further details.

'Mine too,' said Roger. 'Not that they're really involved.

Christopher sighed. 'You're lucky with your parents. All three of you. I just wish I was so lucky with mine.'

The following morning Roger and Malcolm sailed away. For the second time in two months Tom and Christopher watched the tan sails fade from sight as the Orca rode the light swell, and it felt like saying goodbye to England all over again.

A few days later came September, and with it came the rains. And it was time to move to Paris as they'd agreed.

If waving goodbye to Malcolm and Roger had been painful, leaving England all over again, well now it turned out that saying goodbye to Boulogne was painful too. They'd grown very attached to Sabine, and to Michel and Armand. Even parting from Benoît and René, and Robert and Thierry wasn't the easiest thing in the world. The drive down the hill to the station in a taxi, in the back their two small suitcases that contained everything they owned between them, was almost silent. But they cheered up on the train journey; this was the third time they had made it, and it was becoming familiar.

Gérard cooked a welcome dinner in their honour, and served it in the biggest room in the house, which was the kitchen. Despite the comfort of the surroundings, and the intimacy of the little group, there was an atmosphere about the occasion that reminded them awkwardly of the first night of a new term at boarding school. Gérard's partner Henri took the head of the table while Gérard himself sat at the bottom. Clustered around them were the two young men they had met on their first visit, Marcel and Alain, who were in their early twenties and clearly a couple, and a slightly older man called Charles.

'I hope you like the beautiful food of France,' was Alain's conversational opener. It was a cliché that Christopher and Tom were already used to. Christopher studied Alain's face carefully as he came out with it, noting the smile that was both sweet and roguish: a synthesis, perhaps, of Benoît's and René's. Moments such as this one – like those start-of-term suppers at boarding-school – heightened the senses. 'Of course we like French food,' said Tom simply. 'Who could fail to?' The cliché had been replied to with the correct antiphonal answer. The right answering cliché. It did the trick. The lock clicked open; the ice was broken. A starter of tomato salad was served; red wine was poured into the glasses.

'So, you two love-birds, how long have you been together?' Charles, who was sitting next to Christopher, asked them.

The answer turned into quite a long story, which included their departure from England and its circumstances, as well as an account of what they'd been doing in Boulogne over the summer. Did they paint? The others asked them. No, they didn't. They'd come to Paris to do some modelling. They hoped eventually to move into English teaching.

'It's a shame you don't paint,' said Marcel. 'We'd know so much more about you if you did.' At that point Christopher felt Marcel's hand alight on his knee under the table.

One of the attic rooms in the house had been turned into a big studio, and after dinner they were shown round it. It had big mansard windows that looked towards the northern suburbs: narrow wedges of northern suburb could actually be glimpsed between the buildings on the other side of the street. The studio's interior looked like Michel's, but four times as big. Three easels were set up in it, and it was the more spacious for not also containing cooking facilities or a bed. The young artists were all eager to show off their recent work, snatching canvasses almost at random from the stacks that leant against the walls, and competing for the attention of Christopher and Tom. There were representational works, which Tom and Christopher were comfortable with, and were relieved to be able to praise them: in their relatively untutored eyes they did indeed look good. Other things were dismayingly abstract. What could you say, by way of praise or informed comment, of a small square canvas whose surface had been covered, at some expense, with squirts of different hues of red oil paint, straight from the tube and unmolested by any brush or knife? It looked like a section of the floor of a pigeon loft during the red fruit season, but they were hardly going to say that.

'Are all of you up here full time, then?' Christopher asked.

'Not all day, every day,' said Alain. 'Charles…' he gestured towards the slightly older man '…is the only one of us who has enough money to let him do that. 'We two,' he meant his partner Marcel and himself, 'have to earn a bit by other means. I work part-time in a café and Marcel works in an ironmonger's shop.' Tom started to laugh. 'What's funny about that?' asked Alain, looking taken aback.

'Nothing,' said Christopher. 'It's just that that's exactly what we did for two months. Me in a café and Tom at an ironmonger's.' The tension vanished in a snicker of laughter than ran through the group.

Marcel and Alain wanted to head out to a bar after that and they asked Tom and Christopher to join them. But the new arrivals said they were tired – moving from one home to a new one had been emotionally draining as well as physically strenuous – and they were pretty well ready for bed. Another time, though. Tomorrow, after they'd done their first sessions in the life class, it would be nice…

They took possession of their new bedroom. It was bigger than the bedroom of Michel's childhood that they'd had at Sabine's and furthermore, luxury of luxuries, it was furnished with a double bed. A large mirror stood on the mantelpiece opposite the bottom end of the bed. Tom and Christopher undressed each other slowly, ritually, like priests disrobing after Mass, then they stood together on the bed, arms around each other's shoulders (as well as being a loving gesture this was a practical necessity given the springy terrain on which they stood) and admired each other's and their own naked reflections in the big glass. Unsurprisingly their dicks began to rise bobbingly as they watched. 'Better get used to this,' said Tom. 'From tomorrow morning this is going to be our job.'

'I worry about this,' said Christopher, tapping the side of his appendage. 'I mean about getting stiff in the class.'

'You won't,' said Tom, though he said this only to reassure his lover. He was worried about the same thing himself.

The door opened suddenly. No-one had knocked on it. The door was in the corner of the room just to the left of the mirror and Tom and Christopher nearly toppled over as they instinctively twisted their frames towards it. There was no time, and they didn't have enough hands available, or big enough ones, to hide their cocks.

Charles stood in the doorway, fully dressed. 'What a beautiful vision,' he said. 'I came to wish you both goodnight. He used the formal old-fashioned phrase: *Je vous souhaite la bonne nuit.* 'I think you'll be comfortable in that bed. I know it well. Perhaps I can join you in it sometime? If you'll allow me, that is. Though perhaps not tonight, I think.' A very thoughtful smile spread over his face as he watched the speechless pair a further second before shutting the door and disappearing behind it.

Tom and Christopher then half fell, half dragged each other, backwards onto the bed. 'Do you think there's a keyhole in the door?' Tom asked, as they sprawled, their mute astonishment slowly giving way to laughter.

'Don't know,' said Christopher. 'I know Charles is a bit older than us but don't you think – when he's smiling like he did just then – he has a rather handsome face?'

EIGHT

In the morning they threaded their way through the streets and vennels of Montmartre to the nearest metro stop, which was Lamarck-Caulincourt. They were armed already with season tickets – Gérard had sent them out the previous evening to familiarise themselves with the walk to the underground station, get their photos taken in a booth and a buy a monthly coupon. Not having to do all this now at eight a.m. saved precious time.

The train made alien noises, quite unlike the sound of the London tubes. The doors were not automatic, you lifted a little catch yourself to open them, and they closed, following a deep parp of warning from the driver, with a whoosh and a clunk. The names of the stations were not called out. They read them on the station walls, tried pronouncing them in their heads and wondered if they were getting them right. Abbesses, Pigalle, Notre Dame de Lorette, St Lazare, Concorde. They exited there and walked across the big square to the river, then walked alongside it. To their left lay the gardens of the Tuileries, to their right the view across the water to the great buildings of the French state on the other side. They were walking along the busiest nocturnal haunt of unattached homosexual men in Paris, though they didn't know this at the time. At last the classical front of the Ecole des Beaux Arts appeared on the opposite bank and they crossed towards it by the nearest bridge, the Pont du Carousel. Starting a new job in Paris was the same as starting one anywhere else, they were discovering. You got that familiar sinking of the stomach as you walked through the entrance door everywhere in the world.

They found their way to the big room where the life classes were held. Students were already arriving and jostling for space and a good view of the dais where the models would sit. Painters were placing easels while in front of them those who would simply be sketching positioned the low wooden trestle-seats called donkeys. Madame Blétry appeared from nowhere. She greeted them with something that was almost a smile. 'Welcome,' she said, 'and make yourselves at home here. Christophe, you will be in here. Tom, this week you are next door. Normally you will be required till five, but as today is the first day of term you should both be finished by around two.' She showed them the cubicle in which they could both disrobe and put on the dressing-gowns and slippers that they'd brought with them in a bag. The cubicle was occupied, they discovered when Madame Blétry pulled open the curtain, by a completely naked girl. They were both taken aback by that but pretended not to be. The girl unhurriedly wrapped a dressing-gown around herself and they all said *bonjour* and shook hands, exchanging names. The girl's was Diane. She came out of the cubicle and Madame Blétry walked away.

'You won't find yourselves doing this for long,' said Diane.

'Why?' asked Tom.

'Nobody does. It's the most boring job in the world. People, boys especially, get fed up very quickly and move on.'

'I see,' said Tom. 'We've been booked for four weeks, then a gap of four weeks when we'll need to look for something else. We've been booked here again for the last four weeks of term. And you've been doing this how long?'

'I started the second half of last term,' said Diane. 'I'm supposed to be doing some fashion modelling soon. I've only come back this term to fill the time before they want me. They're going to give me a call soon.' She tossed her head and a long mane of chestnut hair that had been partially trapped by the collar of her dressing-gown sprang free. She was very beautiful, Tom thought, and wondered whether, when he and Christopher were alone again together, he would share this thought with him. He wondered if Christopher found her attractive too.

A stocky, bearded man walked into the room and summoned Diane. 'Looks like I'm on,' she said. 'In room three. See you two later, maybe.' Then she followed the man out of the room, her walk full of elegance and poise.

'Hmm,' said Christopher, and Tom said, 'Hmm,' too. Then they squeezed into the small cubicle together, undressed, put on their dressing-gowns and emerged again, Tom to be led away to the small room two, while Christopher climbed onto the platform that awaited him

Although he had sat naked for Gérard on two occasions, and enjoyed the company of other boys who were similarly unclad, Christopher was new to the experience of sitting naked in front of a group of fifteen or more, all painting or sketching him from a slightly different angle, and some of whom were female. He peeled off his dressing gown and it was taken from him by Madame Blétry, the slippers likewise, and then adopted the pose – sitting on a box thoughtfully, chin on left hand, left elbow propped on left knee, right hand spread on right knee – that the drawing master, Professor Blum – required. Madame Blétry then marked the positions of Christopher's feet on the wooden floor, so that he could return to his pose exactly after each break – there would be a short one of these after forty minutes or so and a longer one at mid-morning coffee time. Then Madame Blétry pulled electric heating panels into position around Christopher. They were mounted on tall stands and could be moved around at Christopher's request, Madame Blétry told him, as and when his various extremities grew cold.

Christopher had never got an erection in the presence of a woman: that he knew. But he had never sat naked in the presence of a group of them before. He needn't have worried, he soon discovered. He'd managed to romp naked with Michel and Armand, then Benoit and Rene, in the cause of art and had only got a little bit hard. Sitting in front of a number of clothed people of both sexes who were seriously trying to draw him to the best of their ability and who wore intent, not to say worried looks on their faces had no impact on his intimate hydraulics at all. He tried to find things to think about as he sat there doing nothing at all. He wondered if he should take a leaf out of John Moyse's book – take the advice that he had himself given the boy – and keep a diary while he was here. Parisian Diary, it would be called. Or Parisian Journal. Wasn't journal the name that John had given to his? He could Frenchify the title perhaps. *Journal Parisien.* When he'd got tired of thinking about this he started to wonder how Tom was getting on next door.

The atmosphere in the room was intense. Only the voice of the professor was ever heard. He would comment loudly on the different students' work, while their peers listened in. During the short breaks Christopher would put his dressing-gown on. He was invited to walk down and look at the different students' attempts to draw or paint parts of him. Some of the students engaged him in conversation and timidly he tried to be encouraging about the work he saw.

There was no sign of Diane in the dressing cubicle when Christopher returned to it to put his street clothes on when he finished at around two. But a second later the curtain opened and Tom walked in, looking a bit overwhelmed. 'Did you have any problems?' Christopher asked him.

'Like what?' Tom asked.

'I mean, did you get hard?'

'No, not at all,' said Tom. He looked into Christopher's face very searchingly. 'Why? Did you?'

They were free for the rest of the day. They sauntered westward along the quays as far as the Place St Michel, and there they stopped at a brasserie, sitting down at a table on the pavement outside. Across the water lay the Ile de la Cité, and a view of the west front and southern side of Notre Dame – towers, spire, rose window and gargoyles – as well as the Palais de Justice, the police headquarters and the graceful Sainte Chapelle. They had a beer each and a croque-monsieur. The price was a bit eye-watering, but they reckoned they deserved a treat after their first day's work in the capital. And anyway, they were paying for the view.

They didn't go the whole way home by metro train afterwards but got off one stop before theirs, at Abbesses, at the bottom of Montmartre hill. It seemed a bit perverse to give themselves a massive slope to climb when they could have continued on up in the train to Lamarck-Caulincourt, but it was early afternoon, they had nothing particular to do when they got back to the house they had just moved into, and besides, they had been sitting down all day.

The route up from Abbesses to the Place du Tertre was composed of alternating flights of steps and streets that, viewed from below, looked nearly vertical, although the journey was picturesque in the extreme. 'Do you think that, wherever we find ourselves living, it's always going be up some massive hill?' Christopher asked Tom.

'Isn't the whole of life just one big business of climbing uphill?' Tom replied. Secretly he was awed by Christopher's innocent assumption, at the age of nineteen, that the two of them would be in harness together for the rest of their lives. It was something that Tom devoutly wished for but, at the ripe age of twenty-two, doubted could possibly come true.

'Do you remember what Father Louis used to say about mortal sin?' Christopher said suddenly as, hands grabbing at cold iron railings, they tackled yet another flight of outdoor stairs.

'No,' said Tom, startled. 'You tell me.'

'He called it a terrible perishing, and the death of the soul. He said that mortal sin was terrible, and felt awful, because it was a separation of the soul from God. A terrible emptiness inside.'

Tom stopped and looked at him, full of concern. 'You don't feel like that, do you?'

'Yes,' said Christopher, his voice a whisper. 'But it's not separation from God I'm thinking of. It's losing the love of my parents. It leaves a dizzying void, a bottomless pit inside. It's the most awful feeling in the world.'

'My poor, poor Chris,' Tom said and, heedless of the panting climbers around them, took him in his arms as they stood on the steps, halfway up, so neither up nor down. Tears sprang to his eyes. He wondered if the same feeling would be his to experience were he to lose Christopher, as he was sure would inevitably happen, one day.

They climbed the hill and made their way through the Place du Tertre, where a hundred artists were doing lightning sketches of a thousand tourists. Every street was enticing in the afternoon sun, speared with shadows and wreathed with the smoke of a hundred Gitanes. But they could explore Montmartre another time. They were tired suddenly; the emotional expenditure of their first half day in their new job, as well as Christopher's baring of his soul on the steps had weakened them and they wanted nothing more than to get back inside the house in the Rue Vincent and collapse together, cuddling, on their double bed.

When they got in they found the house empty except for Charles. He was sitting alone in the big kitchen with a rather elegant tumbler in front of him and a bottle of Vieux Ceps by his side. (Vieux Ceps was an eminently quaffable blend of the wines of southern France and the until-last-month colony of Algeria. No bottle of wine was ever labelled *Vin Ordinaire*.)

Nobody spends, or has ever spent, their entre day painting. Probably not even Michelangelo. Charles, who painted beautifully, nevertheless spent much of his day slouching in armchairs in the company of curvaceous bottles of Nicolas's unpretentious red wine. He looked up as they came into the kitchen and smiled an uncomplicated smile. 'Well, hallo my two beauties,' he said. 'How was the first day at school?'

They were in France, in Paris, in Montmartre. When Charles asked them to bring two fresh glasses from the cupboard and help him enjoy the litre of Vieux Ceps they didn't think of saying no. 'I always thought red wine was kept in dark bottles to preserve its colour,' Christopher said. He had noticed some time ago that the bottles of red *vin ordinaire* were of clear glass, but hadn't thought to question it before.

'That's true of fine wines,' Charles answered seriously. 'Sunlight can damage a wine over time. But this is bottled one day, sold the next and drunk the third. The sun doesn't spoil it in such a space of time.' He spread his legs wide suddenly and very deliberately pawed his genitals through his corduroy trousers. 'So what are you two thinking of doing with the rest of your day?'

'Thinking of going to bed quite shortly,' said Christopher calmly, to Tom's astonishment.

'That'll be nice,' said Charles. 'Having seen the two of you together last night… Well, I can easily imagine how nice that will be.' He stroked his crotch again meditatively, but aiming the gesture at the two of them full-square.

Christopher turned towards Tom. 'Shall we let him join us?' he asked.

Tom was startled, but he was also torn. He wanted to keep Christopher all to himself, but he did find Charles attractive in his way. Also, he was rather thrilled to hear his young lover talking in this man-of-the-world kind of way: it was an aspect of Christopher he was only just getting to know. And then, Christopher was in a state of deep distress about his parents' reaction to his news. Tom would do anything that Christopher wanted, at this juncture, to make his life more bearable. Tom shrugged. 'Why not?' he said.

Charles rose from his chair, stepped round to where Tom and Christopher sat and reached a hand down onto each of their trouser waistbands. Grasping these he made as if to lift them out of their chairs. They got the point and helped him by standing up of their own accords. Standing close together they began to grope one another through their trousers, though no-one at this point risked a kiss. Then Charles took one hand away from Christopher's private region and laid a finger on his nose. 'Bedroom,' he said and laughed into Christopher's, then Tom's, eyes.

They trooped around the corridor to Tom and Christopher's room and went in. Standing together again, this time they did begin to kiss one another, trying to time their hesitant peckings without crashing into one another's skulls. Then they started to undress one another but this too became confusing and difficult – Tom's hands and Charles's seemed to have lives of their own, competing for Christopher's nipples and shirt buttons – and they ended up completing the task themselves. Charles had already had the pleasure of inspecting Tom and Christopher in their naked state the night before. Now it was their turn to get a look at Charles. He was Tom's height but a little stockier. His drinking hadn't yet had time to interfere with his youthful sleekness and he cut an impressive figure standing with them, fully erect now, just as Tom and Christopher both were.

They didn't stay standing for long. Charles toppled himself backwards onto the bed and pulled the others down on top of him. It took a little time to establish who was going to do what to whom. Charles eventually made it clear that he wanted to be fucked by Christopher. He may have decided this would be an easier option than taking Tom, whose penis was a size or two larger than the elfin Christopher's. He let Christopher enter him from behind, then rolled onto his side, taking Christopher with him. Tom was able to wriggle round, his figure 6 becoming a 9, taking Charles's modest-sized but impressively rigid cock into his mouth while Charles took his. As a formula for pleasing everyone it worked out reasonably well.

It did feel rather weird to Tom: tasting the salty sourness of a stranger's cock while the man he loved was burying himself in the same unfamiliar person just inches away; he and the man he loved sharing the body of someone they didn't love between them; his mouth occasionally plucking by accident an unfamiliar coarse dark hair.

Because of the novelty of the situation for the two younger men, they climaxed rather quickly. First Christopher inside Charles's rear entrance, then Tom in Charles's warm mouth, then Charles himself. While Charles was happy to drink Tom greedily, Tom pulled his head away smartly at the first taste of Charles's own ejaculate and finished him with his hand. They wriggled apart from each other and wiped themselves with towels. 'That was nice,' was Charles's verdict. 'Anyone fancy another glass of wine?

Everything was new about today, Christopher thought, accepting the invitation with a *'Pourquoi pas?'* Why not? And it was another new experience to drink that glass of wine, still naked with Tom and Charles in the kitchen, in slanting autumn sunshine, and to not turn a hair when Marcel and Alain came into the room in their outdoor clothes, laughing the collusive laughter of friends.

They put their clothes back on shortly afterwards. It was time to prepare dinner, and tonight it was Charles's turn. He managed this splendidly, despite whatever quantity of wine he might have drunk during the day, producing a salad of eggs and mayonnaise, then pork escalopes, before falling back on fruit and cheese. Gérard and Henri were not at dinner; they had gone out somewhere.

After dinner Charles retired to his bedroom – to collapse, Tom and Christopher assumed. As they had done the previous night Marcel and Alain asked them if they'd like to go out for a nightcap with them in a bar, and this time they said yes. They found themselves on a tour of the top of Montmartre hill: *la Butte,* their guides called it. At the corner of their own street, where it crossed the Rue des Saules, Marcel pointed out the pink painted cabaret bar, Au Lapin Agile. 'We'll go there one night,' he said. 'But you have to book and unless you're pushy you only get one drink all night. It's become very touristy now.' Alain told them how it had been a favourite drinking haunt of Toulouse-Lautrec and, more recently, Picasso. Edith Piaf had sung there regularly in her early days. Both boys seemed to be enjoying their role as tourist guides.

They passed on through the lamplight-shadowed streets, were shown the empty horse pond at the end of the Rue de L'Abreuvoir, and the Moulin de la Galette at the top of Rue Lepic. Alain chilled them with the tale of the nineteenth-century miller, defending his property against invading Cossacks in 1814, who had been killed and butchered, his quartered body nailed to all four of the famous mill's sails. *'Pour décourager les autres,'* said Tom.

'It didn't discourage his son,' Marcel told him, his serious face reproving Tom's levity. 'It was he who turned the place into the world-famous dance venue.' They walked a little way down the Rue Lepic and went into a bar.

'It's a little irony of Montmartre,' said Alain. 'We live right on top of the most famous bars in Paris, but we don't go into them. We have to go a little way down the hill to find something less expensive, less full of tourists.'

'I understand,' said Christopher, for whom this was a new concept. He wondered what Alain and Marcel, who had seen him naked with Tom just a few hours earlier, would look like when in the same state themselves. He wondered what the four of them would do in bed when, as it surely would, the time came.

The time didn't come that night. Over one or two beers Marcel and Alain told the story of how they had met at art school, where Gérard had taught them. How Gérard had taken them into his house when they were penniless a year before and had housed them ever since. 'In return for the usual favours, of course,' Marcel added, and gave an it-can't-be-helped sort of shrug. A little more conversation later all four realised how tired they were and how ready for sleep. 'Back up the hill again,' said Christopher as they wandered out into the steep street.

Back at their new home Tom and Christopher said a chaste goodnight to the others and climbed into bed, falling asleep almost immediately in each other's arms. Nobody came to their room that night, not even just to have a look at them, and they slept undisturbed till dawn.

'A letter addressed to both of us?' queried Tom. It was morning. They had been living at Henri and Gérard's house for a week. Tom took the envelope from Gérard's hand. It had been addressed in an unformed hand to the Star of the Sea preparatory school in England, with the words *Please forward* written above. Another hand had written their current address in the Rue Vincent alongside. Tom called to Christopher who was just then coming into the kitchen and they opened it standing side by side.

'But who re-addressed it?' Christopher said. 'Nobody there can know where we are.'

'One person could have guessed, just possibly.'

'Who?' asked Christopher, still not getting there.

'Molly?' suggested Tom. 'Our dear Miss O'Deere?'

The letter insider the envelope was not from Molly O'Deere, though. It was from John Moyse.

It bore the address of the Roman Catholic public school for which the boy had been destined after he left Star of the Sea.

Dear Christopher and Tom,

I hope I may call you that now instead of Mr. McGing and Mr Sanders. Term started here just a few days ago It is a big change for me. After being a prefect, and briefly a house captain, to be a junior boy again. I am trying to make new friends but that is never easy at first. You don't have a clear idea about who or what new people really are.

That was true enough, Tom and Christopher both thought.

Angelo Dexter is here too. I didn't think they'd let him come but they did. It was very nice to find him here. Not so good is that he's in a different house which means a different dorm. So we can not see as much of each other as we would like. He says he has heard nothing from Simon all through the holidays and he is sad about that. He is going to try writing to him at the public school he was supposed to be going to and see if he has got there.

The rugger season is upon us. I'm scrum half again, which I always used to be; there is nothing new under the sun. (Notice my use of the semi-colon; I hope you'll be proud of me.)

I don't know if you'll get this letter. I imagine you must be in France, but I can't easily imagine where – or what you are doing there. I just hope very much that you are together, as Angelo and Simon sadly can not be. I'm sending this letter care of the Star of the Sea, hoping that someone there will have an address for you.

You will think me silly but I am actually a bit homesick here. I miss the bedtime chats with Christopher.

Best wishes
From
John (Moyse)

'Gosh,' said Christopher.

'I know,' said Tom. 'It's like walking along a beach and finding a bottle with a letter in it, then finding the letter is addressed to you.'

'We'll write back of course,' said Christopher eagerly. Inside his head he was already framing sentences.

'Are you sure that's a good idea?' Tom cautioned him. 'Writing a letter to a child? A letter coming from us, I mean. With our address at the top.'

'For God's sake, Tom! Address or no address, the English police can't do anything to us here. We're not going to write anything improper. Nothing lewd.'

Tom laughed. 'I suppose you're right. I hadn't thought straight. I was only thinking it might count against us if we went back one day.'

'We'll tell him not to show the letter to anyone…'

Tom lifted his hands in the air expressively. 'Now what's that going to look like…?'

Christopher sighed. He shook his head. 'Why does life have to do these things to us?'

Tom kissed the side of his cheek tenderly. 'Because it does. Because life is life. Because it does these things to everyone.'

NINE

Christopher had three goes at drafting a letter to John Moyse. It would have been easier perhaps if the letter had not been going to be signed by Tom as well as by him. As it was, Tom kept intervening and wanting Christopher to change things. Christopher could well have said to Tom, 'All right, you do it,' but he thought that Tom might then be even more uncertain what to write and never get round to it. At last a version took shape that they were both reasonably happy with. They headed it with their Rue St-Vincent address.

Dear John

Your letter did well to find us. We think Miss O'Deere must have forwarded it to us, having guessed correctly at our address because by happy accident a French artist wrote to her from here, offering to buy the David and Jonathan picture. From her silence on the subject it would seem that she has refused the offer.

But perhaps we should go back a bit. We left England not because we had done anything wrong but because Angelo's father had told the police that we were same-sex lovers, and had then told Father Matthew. It was Fr Matthew who told us we needed to leave.

We think you knew that we had friends with a fishing smack. They helped us escape to Boulogne, where we have other friends (as Angelo noticed one day!) We feel safe in France because the law interferes less in the private love lives of citizens than is the case in England. Our friends in Boulogne found us somewhere to stay, and jobs for the summer. Tom worked as an accounts clerk in our friend's shop, and Christopher in a bar.

Now we have moved to Paris where another friend, the artist Gérard de Martinville, is letting us live in his big house here in Montmartre along with other young artists. We are earning some money as models, sitting for students to paint us in the Life Classes at one of the big art schools here while we look for jobs as teachers of English.

You know now where we are. If you find yourself in Paris come and see us. Please tell Angelo that the same invitation applies to him. We hope you will share this letter with him, and let him know we are happy he got into his new school alongside you, and wish him well.

On the other hand, it might be an idea not to show this letter or talk about it to too many other people. You (and Angelo) are old enough and wise enough to understand why.

It's normal to feel homesick for a bit in any new place. The same feeling affects us sometimes even here.

We hope you won't feel we have been more frank with you than you would wish us to be, or that we have shared information that you would have preferred us to keep to ourselves. However we both believe that it is best to be honest and open with other people, as far as that is possible and reasonable.

With fondest regards (they had spent ages agonising about exactly what phrase should go here)

Christopher and Tom

Once they had written this, crossing a very particular Rubicon in the process, they found they wanted to write to other English friends – school-friends of Christopher's, Oxford friends of Tom's – to let them know their recent history and where they were. As in the case of the letters they'd sent to their parents there would be a wait of a couple of weeks before anything came back – if anything ever did. The time-scale was akin to the one they were familiar with when sowing seeds.

Gérard exhibited his work twice yearly, in one of the galleries in the Rue de Seine – it was usually the Gallerie Laval – just a block away from the Ecole des Beaux Arts. His autumn exhibition this year opened less than a fortnight after Tom and Christopher's arrival in Paris and it involved them most intimately since, among many other works, the whole series of paintings that Gérard had done at Audresselles was on display. There were Tom and Christopher in canvas after canvas, variously with Michel, Armand, René and Benoît, often with their genitals in full view. With a stroke of irony that pleased everyone, Gérard employed the two English boys as porters during the setting-up of the exhibition, so that they found themselves sometimes actually carrying and hanging those pictures of themselves. Taking the irony one step further, Gérard also gave them some pocket money to act as waiters on the evening of the initial private view – here in France it was called *le vernissage*, the varnishing – so that they were handing round glasses of champagne and canapés to people who were almost heedless of their physical presence in the room while engrossed in, and heartily praising, their painted images on the walls just feet away. Only once or twice in the course of that evening during which large sums of money changed hands, did a wealthy patron of the arts look into the eyes of the boy who recharged his or her wine glass and exclaim, *'Bon dieu! C'est vous!'*

It was evident from his behaviour that Gérard's "partenaire" Henri was a major presence at these events. This evening he played the role of host, and patron of his talented discovery and protégé, the younger Gérard, with a theatrical flourish and great aplomb. This was a side of Henri that Tom and Christopher hadn't seen before. At home he was self-effacing, allowing Gérard to strut the conversational stage at dinner and often meekly doing the washing-up afterwards. Presumably his mental energy was more than taken up on a normal day with the numerical tightrope-walking of his job in merchant banking. They had half imagined that Gérard's initial warning about the sexual mores prevailing at Rue St-Vincent hinted at the likelihood of Henri knocking on their bedtime door, and they had braced themselves in readiness. But that hadn't happened in the ten days since they had arrived. Only Charles had turned up at their door till now. Charles had made up for any slowness on the parts of the others, though. Since that first threesome just over a week ago the experiment had been repeated two more times.

The *vernissage* was a long and triumphant evening. By the end of it there seemed almost as many red stickers attached to Gérard's paintings as there were paintings attached to the walls. But not all the red dots were stuck to Gérard's work. Henri had been generous to Gérard throughout his life and Gérard had turned out to be a good pupil. His own generosity to his young friends did not stop at free accommodation in the house he shared with Henri. A section of the exhibition at the Gallerie Laval was given over to work by Gérard's protégés, so that a small number of paintings by Charles, Alain and Marcel were hanging alongside Gérard's this evening. An exhibition in the Rue de Seine was a showcase to which they could not have had easy access on their own. Yet thanks to Gérard here they were.

There were Montmartre street scenes by Charles, some abstracts and a moody portrait of Alain by Marcel, and a series of depictions of building construction sites in central Paris by Alain. You knew they were of central Paris, as either the Eiffel Tower or the Sacré Coeur Basilica was placed helpfully in the background to each one. Enough red stickers had been accumulated by the three younger artists to keep them all in red wine – Tom did the rough calculation – for about a year.

It was late when they went to eat. They drove off in a fleet of taxis to Chartier's in the Rue Faubourg Montmartre. It was roughly halfway between the left-bank gallery and home. So many people came along. There were people Tom and Christopher knew – their housemates – and people they didn't. There were people in between: people they knew but hadn't expected to be dining with this evening. Mme Blétry was one, another was their fellow life-class model Diane.

Chartier's had been going for some seventy years. It was a tall engine-shed of a building with vast mirror windows and globe lights hanging overhead. Bow-tied waiters, all pencil-thin, competed to balance the largest possible number of plates of food up their arms. Service was swift; simplicity of orders appreciated. They ordered a vast tureen of snails with garlic butter to share, then steaks and chips, all steaks to be seriously rare.

Tom found himself seated next to Henri. They had never had anything approaching a private chat together in the ten days since Tom had come to live in Henri's house. He remembered, with some awkwardness, the time he'd had breakfast with the headmaster at the Star of the Sea. As he had done on that occasion, Tom let the older man take the conversational lead.

'You're a strikingly beautiful young man,' was Henri's opening remark. 'It's a pleasure to have you living with us.' He smiled a smile that was almost too big for his face.

'Thank you.' said Tom, chasing a snail around his plate with a bite-sized piece of baguette. If he managed to capture it, which was by no means a certainty, it would be his first snail. 'Your generosity has rather saved our lives.'

'It seems to me,' said Henri, who was already on his third snail, 'that you are a very happy couple: Christophe and you. A very blessed couple and a very lucky one.'

'Not luckier than you, surely? You and Gérard.' He smiled very fulsomely at Henri. He had had a number of glasses of champagne in the course of the evening, in between serving them to other people. That and the sight of dozens of people admiring his naked form, depicted multiple times on canvas, was making him bold.

'No,' said Henri, 'You are right, of course you are. I was indeed lucky. Gérard too, if he cares to admit it.' A look came into Henri's eyes just then and it was a look that Tom recognised. It was nevertheless a shock to see that look there. It struck him with the force of a big wave: the discovery that a man of sixty could be powerfully attracted to a fifty-year-old – and to a fifty-year-old with whom he had already lived for many years..

Winded by this discovery, Tom asked, 'How long have you been together with Gérard?'

The answer came swiftly. 'Twenty-eight years, four months, five days.'

Tom screwed up his nose. 'You do the calculation every day?'

'Bof,' said Henri. 'Interest rates, currency conversion rates changing from day to day, stock exchange latest…' He made an expansive gesture on the table top with his hands, for a moment forgetting the snails. 'Those things… It's the job I do. So how would I forget the intimate statistics of more important matters?' Henri relaxed and returned his attention to his snails. Once he had downed two more of them he looked back at Tom with a different expression in his eye. 'Charles says you have an impressively big *bite*. How to say in English? I forget.'

'Cock,' said Tom. 'Or dick.'

'Of course,' said Henri. 'Charles says yours is impressively big. Is that true?'

'It's nice of him to say so,' said Tom, smiling in spite of himself. 'But everything is relative.'

'Oui,' agreed Henri, nodding as he chased the last of his snails around the plate. *'Tout est relatif.'*

When the meal was finished the big party drifted out into the street. Some people looked for taxis, others headed for the metro stop, another group, including the Rue St-Vincent contingent, simply walked. Strolling up the Rue du Faubourg-Montmartre they lost a few people on the way as those branched aside on their different homeward routes. By the time they reached the church of Notre Dame de Lorette and were still only a third of their way home Christopher found his bladder telling him it wouldn't wait for him to walk another mile and a half before emptying itself. He turned off the main road – by now they were walking up the Rue des Martyrs – into a dark side street, the Rue Chorot, and did what he had to in a nook between two dustbins.

But he wasn't alone in his nook for more than a second or two. Alain had had the same need, apparently, and had followed Christopher into the side street. Side by side they pissed companionably. It was Alain who spoke. 'It's a very nice cock you've got,' he said. 'Ten days I've been waiting to see that. It's certainly been worth the wait.'

Christopher looked across at Alain. He wasn't at all offended. Rather the reverse. 'It's not as big as yours is,' he said banally.

'There are other qualities besides size,' said Alain. He giggled, then reached out a hand and gave Christopher's dick a cautious tweak. Cautious only because he didn't want to get his hand wet. Christopher returned the compliment.

'Come on, we'd better catch the others up,' said Alain, his voice not hiding his regret. They buttoned themselves up and returned to the main street. The other five hadn't got far ahead, they were still in sight, and it wasn't difficult to catch them up. Perhaps some of them had also had to make a comfort stop. Tom turned and smiled at Christopher and Alain when they came up, but he was in conversation with Marcel and they continued to walk side by side up the city's gentle slope towards Abbesses. Ahead of them walked Henri, Charles and Gérard, from time to time throwing arms affectionately round one another's shoulders. Christopher and Alain brought up the rear. Before long they saw Marcel place an arm round Tom's shoulder and leave it there, and Tom make no attempt to shake it off. A moment later Christopher felt Alain's arm land confidently around his own shoulder and neither did he try to shake it off.

It was a warm evening and nobody seemed to be minding the long walk. Christopher didn't know what Tom and Marcel were talking about as they walked arms linked. Though he was able to make a shrewd guess. If it was the same as what Christopher and Alain were talking about it was sex.

Alain had a lot of questions for Christopher. When had he first done something with another boy? Had he tried it with girls also? No, Christopher said. *'Moi pareil,'* said Alain: Same here. When had Christopher first noticed his attraction to his own sex? What did he like doing in bed? This was a bit difficult, as Christopher's French vocabulary in this area was non-existent and Alain was similarly bereft of the words in English. Alain gave Christopher some choice new words to learn, explaining their meanings with gestures of hand, tongue, hips and lips. Christopher found even this quite titillating, especially as while Alain was explaining things he didn't keep those organs of his to himself. At one moment Tom turned round, alerted by the boisterous giggling coming from just behind him. 'Behave yourselves,' he remonstrated with them, but he couldn't help grinning broadly as he said it. From what Christopher could see a moment later, it seemed that Tom was receiving a similar vocabulary lesson himself.

At Abbesses they left the Rue des Martyrs and wound their way steeply up to the Place du Tertre, which was eerily deserted for once. A few minutes more and Gérard was unlocking the front door at the house in the Rue St-Vincent. In the kitchen they sat briefly over coffee and Armagnac, even though more alcohol was hardly needed by any of them, and what was going to happen was already in train, not needing further drink to fuel it.

Charles would be sharing a bed with Henri and Gérard tonight, that was very apparent. As for the other four... 'You haven't seen our room yet, have you?' Marcel asked Christopher and Tom rhetorically. 'Want to come and see it?'

The room was slightly smaller than Tom and Christopher's was but it had an equally big bed in it, and an equally big mirror above the mantelpiece. The situation in which they now found themselves was far beyond any sexual experiences that either of them had had, together or separately, to date. Sensibly they let Marcel and Alain take charge of things. Which they did.

Alain had claimed Christopher earlier, it seemed, when they had pissed alongside each other in the Rue Chorot. He still had eyes only for him and started to undress him in front of the mirror as they stood at the end of the bed. Right beside them, no more than a wrist's brush away, Marcel was bestowing the same attention on Tom. An attention that Tom returned in kind. Similarly Christopher started to take Alain's clothes off. It looked as though they were going to be two separate pairs for whatever happened next. Perhaps it was simpler that way, Christopher thought with something like relief.

A minute later Christopher ended up on the bed, on his back, with Alain looking into his eyes. Alain's own eyes were filled with soft laughter-light and when Alain asked politely if Christopher would let him fuck him there and then Christopher said yes.

Next to them, touching them with shoulders, hips and flailing feet, an identical scene was playing out. Only here it was Tom the English boy on top, with Marcel on his back, legs spread, underneath. As he pleasantly plumbed the depths of his Frenchman for the night Tom found himself looking diagonally down at Christopher. He was enjoying the novelty of the experience, certainly, but couldn't help wishing he had Christopher's familiar body beneath him, and that his cock was inside Christopher's familiar anus rather than in Marcel's, charming and attractive as the young Frenchman was. Then too, a part of him, a part that stayed aloof from sexual excitements and brief experience, found itself asking how it had come about that all this had happened: how could Christopher and he have got to this point so quickly, within just a few weeks of falling in love?

Afterwards the four of them drifted off to sleep between the wet-patched covers of the same bed. It wasn't possible to make a night of this, though. They were like fledgling birds that uncomfortably overflowed the nest. Christopher and Tom, soon awake again, just as Alain and Marcel were, explained that – nothing personal – they would head back to their own room for the rest of the night. They made no attempt to sort their clothes out from the tangled pile on the floor but, explaining that they would be back for them in the morning, left the room and scampered back around the corridor to their own – suddenly very welcome – bed as naked as they were for most of their days at work. Back in their own bed they held each other tightly. 'It's good to be home,' said Tom.

'Hmm,' said Christopher.

Tom worried a little, unsure how to interpret the *hmm*. Was it a murmur of agreement or of uncertainty? But he didn't worry about it for very long. Soon they were both fast asleep.

In theory an air-letter could travel between France and England in a matter of hours – the Paris-London flight was a matter of forty-five minutes only – and the reply could return at the same speed. It rarely happened. As it was with the sowing of lettuces, the result of your effort showed itself after some twelve or fourteen days. Just occasionally, though, there was a whirlwind exception. So it was that, just five days after Tom and Christopher had penned their laboursome and thoughtful missive to John Moyse a letter arrived, addressed to Christopher, in a handwriting that was not that of John Moyse.

My dear friend Christopher

How happy I am to hear from you. John showed me the letter from you and Tom. I know the letter was from both of you but the handwriting which I looked at and it matched your signature was yours.

You saved my life that aweful morning and I think you know you did. You gave me the strenth to face my father and my mother which was even worse.

I thought this was going to be a very long letter because my heart is so full of things I want to say. But now I'm writing it I don't know what to say. You don't want to hear about rugby games and wins and draws.

Christopher you are so special to me. I miss you more than anything. Christopher I love you.

Think what you like of me. I don't care. I just had to say it anyway and you are two hundred miles away.

I shall find a way to come and see you in Paris I don't know how but I shall. You did invite me after all.

With all my love
Angelo

Christopher felt himself go hot and cold as he read this, standing next to Tom. He felt that his face had become a chameleon's, changing colour second by second with every shot of adrenalin that pumped into its bloodstream. For a moment he thought that he wouldn't show Tom the letter but crumple it in his hand and throw it into the fire like someone in a film. But there wasn't a fire. All he could have done with the crumpled page would have been to stuff it in his pocket (swallowing it whole was not a realistic option) and then Tom would have had to ask him why. He showed Tom the letter instead.

'Wow,' said Tom after he'd read it. He looked seriously shocked. 'You certainly made an impact on the boy.'

'You knew everything that happened,' Christopher said, trying to grasp at something solid in his head, like an iron railing to hold. 'You know what happened and what did not. And every word that was said on both sides. I just tried to help him. Nothing more. And it's true what he says in the letter. We did invite him over. But it was a sort of polite courtesy, wasn't it? He wasn't supposed to read anything big into it.'

Tom took Christopher in his arms. 'It's OK.' (OK was American and lower class. They weren't supposed to say it. This was the first time Tom had ever used the expression in talking to Christopher.) 'It's OK. The boy's got a crush on you. He'll grow out of it. Don't worry. In the meantime, take it as a compliment.' He pulled his face just far enough away from Christopher's to be able to smile into it. 'I would. Lighten up, my darling. It's all OK. If the boy wants to come over here to see you that's fine by me too. Wanting something is one thing and doing it quite another. He's only thirteen. Hardly the age for travelling to France on his own with a one-way ticket. I think you're probably safe from finding him suddenly on the doorstep. As I say, it's something he's going through. He'll get over it.'

TEN

Christopher had no idea what he could say in reply to Angelo's letter. He couldn't ignore it. If someone tells you they are in love with you, you need to find some sort of answer within yourself and then tell them it. Even if the answer has to be hurtful it can not hurt as much as silence would. Christopher was aware that Angelo had taken a problem that had been entirely his own and chucked it fair and square at Christopher, making it Christopher's problem now. Perhaps that wasn't very fair of Angelo, Christopher thought, but then, what was ever fair about love? All's fair in love and war…There was a good case for making the old saw read the opposite. Christopher was anything but cruel, though. He would shoulder his new burden manfully and find something to say to Angelo. One day soon. One thing in his favour was that Angelo's letter had arrived just a couple of days after he had written it. He was part Italian; he had aunts in Tuscany: he would know how long letters took to come and go between England and the continent. He wouldn't expect Christopher to receive his letter until a few more days had passed. This gave Christopher a bit of a respite. With luck some inspiration for what he might write back to Angelo would come to him as the days went by. For the moment, though, he had the luxury of being able to push the matter to the back of his mind.

There was plenty else going on in his life anyway. A lot of it involved sex. Sex with Tom and Charles, sex with Tom and Marcel and Alain. Once with Gérard and Henri, and that actually turned out to be much more fun than either Tom or Christopher had imagined in advance. It was always sex including Tom, though. They had stuck to the rule they'd agreed before even coming to Paris. If they were going to have sex with other people they were both going to be involved in it. Even though they found they liked it that way and wouldn't have wished things otherwise they were still proud of themselves for having stuck to their principle.

They made the discovery that having more sex, and more adventurous sex, did not satisfy their appetites for it. Instead their appetites grew with eating and they wanted more and more. In Christopher's case particularly. Evidence for this emerged one day in the life class, when something happened that he had dreaded since day one.

A new student had joined the class the previous day. He was an elf-like boy with wire-rimmed spectacles. He was Christopher's age and size, pale-skinned and blue-eyed. Christopher found him heart-hurtingly attractive. He seemed shy and nervous – understandable things in a newcomer to an established group – and Christopher's heart went out to him. He had a job trying not to look at him directly while he was posing – it would have been 'coming out of pose' as well as being blatantly obvious. But he managed to talk with him during the breaks, chatting briefly, saying a few encouraging words about the embryo painting that was developing on his easel. He had to be sparing with his minutes, and share some of them with other students. Not to do so... Again his interest in the other boy would have been blindingly, embarrassingly obvious.

That night thoughts of the slim young man kept slipping into his consciousness as he was embracing Tom in bed – it was one of those nights when, as in old and less complicated times, they were sleeping alone together. Then in the morning, as he sat nude on his dais just a few feet from the new student, he found he couldn't keep his thoughts off him. All too easily he could imagine him sitting where Christopher sat, with all his clothes off... And then the inevitable happened.

Christopher didn't notice it at first. He was aware only of a frisson in the room, as if breaths were being drawn in silently. Then he noticed the looks he was getting, saw faces that were making an effort to try and remain serious. Then he saw it out of the corner of his eye: the un-noticed, un-commented-on member that had been lying in his lap innocuously was no longer lying in his lap but standing in it.

The drawing-master was regarding him beadily. He cleared his throat. *'Ah, bon,'* he said. 'Time for a ten-minute break perhaps.'

Within seconds Christopher's erection had subsided. In a show of bravura that was perhaps ill-judged he sauntered around the room, talking to the students, without putting his dressing-gown on as he usually (though not always) did, defying anyone to mention the untoward incident, defying his cock to give a repeat performance. He wanted to make a statement of the fact that everything was going on as normal. The tactic seemed to work at first, and he took a particular delight in standing close to his new favourite and chatting insouciantly in French about the painting he was making. He noticed that neither he nor any other student had attempted to capture and set in paint his momentary tumescence.

Then Madame Blétry appeared. She seemed to flutter like a mother partridge as she hurried towards Christopher. She carried his dressing-gown in front of her and held it out to him. 'Put this on, Christophe,' she scolded him. 'Immediately! Whatever were you thinking of?!'

Christopher wasn't sure whether to share this tale of minor humiliation with Tom when he saw him next. In the end he did share it. Tom looked at him sternly for a moment, then his expression melted into a grin that was a bit sheepish. 'The same thing happened to me yesterday,' he said. 'A bit embarrassing. Mme Blétry making a fuss and all. I wasn't going to tell you.'

A letter arrived from John Moyse. He was really happy to hear their news, relieved that they were doing all right, and thanked them for their understanding words about being homesick. He was getting used to his new school as the weeks passed, feeling less homesick. Then came some details of Rugby matches and rehearsals of a play that he'd been cast in. At the piano he was getting used to his new teacher and quite liked him. He was being stretched, physically as well as musically, he said, by being given Beethoven's Appassionata sonata to learn. Then John came to the subject of his friend Angelo.

I showed Angelo your letter and we talked about it. We agreed not to show it to anyone else. He seemed a bit adgitated. I asked him if we would send a reply from both of us. He said he would rather write seperately. I don't know if he has done this. Anyway, he is thinking about you both and very happy to have your news.
With my best wishes
John

It was not a letter that required an immediate reply. But it was a reminder that someone else's letter very definitely did. Christopher was still in an agony about what to write to Angelo. Tom sat down with him in the kitchen in the Rue St-Vincent later that afternoon when everyone else was out and said, 'We'll do it together.' For some reason those words went to the deepest place in Christopher's heart.

In the end, although it was Christopher who put pen to paper, most of the words were Tom's suggestions –

though they were suggestions that Christopher accepted eagerly.

Dear Angelo

Do not be worried that I might have a problem with the things you said in your letter. It was lovely to hear from you, and better than any account of Rugby scores.

Love is a big word and a big thing. Perhaps you already know that it is also a very painful thing. It hurts everyone who ever gives it, and it hurts everyone who is lucky enough to receive it.

I'm very honoured by what you've said to me. Though I've done nothing to deserve it. My difficulty is that I'm not in a position to return your feelings. You know by now that I love Tom and have given my heart to him. It also means, to be frank, that we're faithful sexually.

This was less perfectly true than it had been a month ago, and Tom and Christopher were uncomfortably conscious of the fact as they wrote the sentence. But this was not a moment for muddying the waters with the messy stuff of adult relationships.

Although this, my thing with Tom, is my first experience of being in love, for Tom it is the second or third. He says that we may all fall in love more than once in a long lifetime and I'm not experienced enough to contradict him.

What I mean is simply, who knows what the future holds – for any of us.

The invitation to Paris – although it was meant seriously of course, we feel it's unlikely you'd be able to get here under your own steam, and we're not in a position to actually help you to do this. If you did find yourself here, of course you'd get a warm welcome. But it may not be possible. I'm sure we'll meet again one day, though, if not here and if not yet, then perhaps in the years ahead in England.

That paragraph was a terrible muddle. It was, however, a true and accurate account of Christopher's confused feelings. It seemed best to let it go as it was. Then they had to struggle with the valediction. Would Angelo appreciate the difference between love with a small L and love with a big one? If he didn't, they weren't going to draw his attention to it. They settled for:

With love and best wishes
Christopher

When their initial four weeks of modelling at the Ecole des Beaux Arts came to an end Tom and Christopher got another block of work in a smaller art school, in the Rue des Norvins, on the slopes of Montmartre and just around two street corners from where they lived. Again the work came to them thanks to Gérard; he had recommended them to his contacts at the school. They were engaged for four weeks, at the end of which time they would return to the Beaux Arts for their second block of work. They had done nothing up to now about looking for English teaching work. Although they were not getting rich they were making enough money to pay for their daily needs and even save a bit, thanks to Henri and Gérard, who were still allowing them to live at their Rue St-Vincent house without paying a single centime in rent. Life was easy, life was comfortable. They were more than happy to do without the stress and effort of teaching English to the French.

Their new place of work, the Atelier des Norvins, was a chummier place than the grand Ecole des Beaux Arts, if only because it was barely a quarter of the size of the more famous establishment. They would have friendly chats with the students and the drawing masters, and go for a drink with them sometimes when work was done, listening to stories about the old and famous artists who had inhabited Montmartre over the years. In particular they enjoyed the story of the donkey who, in 1910, painted a famous picture with its tail.

The donkey was owned by the then *patron* of the Lapin Agile. This gentleman, le père Frédé, was persuaded to lend the animal to a group of his customers who had in mind a practical joke. Those customers had included a couple of young artists who wanted to cock a snook at a new style of painting that people were beginning to call Impressionism. A paintbrush was tied to the donkey's tail, while a few carrots at the front end did the rest. The painting, bold strokes of bright blues and reds, was exhibited with the title, Sunset over the Adriatic, while the name of the artist was given as Boronali, an anagram of the donkey's name – Aliboron. Not until it had been reviewed favourably and sums in excess of four hundred francs offered for it was the painting revealed for the hoax it was.

'Shades of David and Jonathan,' said Tom to Christopher as, walking home a few minutes after hearing the story, they talked about it.

'Except that was hardly a hoax,' said Christopher. They rarely talked about the picture these days. Gérard had never heard anything in reply to his letters to Molly O'Deere, and by now he seemed to have stopped thinking about it.

Tom and Christopher let themselves into the house in the Rue St-Vincent and walked into the kitchen. Where they were mightily surprised, but very happily so, to see Michel and Armand sitting at the table, in conversation with Gérard and Charles and with glasses of wine in front of them. It became a moment of delighted reunion, of smacking kisses and hearty hugs.

Michel was in Paris, they discovered, to discuss with Gérard the arrangements for a forthcoming exhibition in the Rue de Seine gallery: an exhibition devoted entirely to Michel's own work. It would be his first Paris exhibition: a very big moment in his life and a giant stride away from his day-to-day business of running the ironmonger's shop he had inherited. Armand had come along just to be with his lover and to have a day out in Paris.

The exhibition was scheduled to open immediately after Christmas... After Christmas! This was a piece of the future that hadn't yet been mentioned between Tom and Christopher. Nor had Christmas itself. It was an idea so difficult this particular year that they had blocked it out of their thoughts. But now it had been mentioned and now suddenly it was Michel who brought up the idea of Tom and Christopher's Christmas and smartly tackled it. Looking at them both across the table he said, 'Christmas will be difficult for you, I realise. Especially for you.' He looked at Christopher. 'Not reconciled with your parents. My mother was talking about this. She's asked me to invite you both to spend the Christmas holiday with us. If you'd like that. There may be a little bit of work in the café and at the shop.' He shrugged and mugged a grin. 'Of course you may have other plans...'

'We've no plans at all,' said Tom very seriously. 'Your invitation's wonderful. It would be perfect.' Christopher nodded silently. Tom had already said the words he might have used.

'Good,' said Armand. 'A good day all round. Everything's sorting itself out.'

It went on being a good day all round. The whole household dined out at a small and cosy restaurant in the Rue de Caulincourt, and Armand and Michel only just caught the last train back to Boulogne that night by the skin of their teeth.

The next morning a letter came from England. It was addressed to Christopher, in a hand that, since they had re-read this letter's precursor some hundred times between them, there was no mistaking.

Dear Christopher
Your letter to me was very kind and lovely. Thank you
for writing the way you did.
I have found a way I can come and see you in Paris.
One of the teachers here, our French teacher in fact is
collecting names of boys who will go on a school trip to
Paris at the end of term for two days if their parents give
permission and will spend the money. I will join the trip.
Then when we are in Paris I will give the teacher the
slip, dodge out of the day's planned activitys and come
and see you instead...

The letter went on a little longer, then ended, *I do love*
you Christopher.
With all my Love
Angelo

Christopher and Tom read the letter together, standing
side by side in the kitchen. They looked at each other.
Tom sighed. 'If this actually comes to pass...' He shook
his head involuntarily. 'We could get into the most
dreadful trouble as a result.'

Christopher said, 'We're in the most dreadful trouble
already, Tom. Largely because of Angelo. I don't see
how it could get any worse.' He wasn't looking very
cheerful as he said it.

Towards the end of November they returned to the
Ecole des Beaux Arts for their second four-week spell of
work. The Atelier des Norvins wished them well and
assured them there would be more work for them after
Christmas if they wanted it. In the weeks that followed
Angelo's plans – arriving by letter, and each letter
signed, *with all my Love* – were firming up. The trip
would be over a weekend; the boys would arrive in Paris

on the Friday night. They would be staying at a Catholic boarding school on the Avenue de Clichy which, Angelo had been told, was only a ten-minute walk from the foot of the Butte de Montmartre. All being well he would come and find Christopher (*and Tom*, he added in brackets) at their home in the course of the Saturday morning. Could Christopher draw a little map for him that would show the best way to walk from the Avenue de Clichy to the Rue St-Vincent? With a heavy feeling in the pit of his stomach and feeling very irresponsible, Christopher drew the map and sent it back to Angelo by return of post.

The weekend of Angelo's planned visit was the one before Tom and Christopher would travel back to Boulogne for Christmas and that Saturday morning found them busy sorting out the things they would pack and take with them. It was a good activity to be engaged in when you were full of nerves and apprehension. 'He won't turn up,' Tom told Christopher several times in the course of the morning. 'Kids plan these things, like they all plan running away from school, but they don't carry them out.'

'Well yes,' said Christopher. There was an edge to his voice. 'As a general rule that's true: they don't. But there's always the odd exception. Boys do sometimes run away from school. I'm sure we've both known cases.'

'Christopher…' Tom stopped folding pairs of trousers and turned and looked straight at his lover. 'What are you hoping? Hoping that he'll turn up? Or hoping that he won't.'

'I…' began Christopher uncertainly. But he got no further with the thought because at that moment the doorbell rang.

Angelo had once seen Tom giving Michel a hug in the street – in Boulogne, outside the ironmonger's shop. He probably had that scene in mind now, for as soon as the front door was opened to him he threw his arms around Christopher with great confidence and kissed him on the lips. Then he did the same to Tom, though this time the kiss was only on Tom's cheek.

'You'd better come in and have a coffee,' said Christopher in a shaky voice.

It would have been easier in many ways to have had that coffee at a nearby café, out on the pavement even in December as it was mild this week, but Christopher was terrified that Angelo's school party and the teacher supervising it would walk past and... His stomach nearly turned a somersault as he thought, and tried not to think, about the awful consequences of that. The knowledge that Angelo's father was one of the leading barristers in England didn't help.

They had the kitchen to themselves. They were relieved about that. And their relief deepened when Angelo, instead of making histrionic speeches about undying and unrequited love, behaved like any normal fourteen-year-old who was excited at finding himself out on his own in Paris. 'We were allowed out in groups of four,' he told them. 'Though we have to be back for lunch. Well, my group's turned into a group of three. The others are sworn to secrecy on pain of death.'

'The others?' Tom wanted to know. 'Will they be swarming around Montmartre?'

'I doubt it,' said Angelo. 'We're doing Montmartre tomorrow as a group. Coming up to the Sacré Coeur for Mass. This afternoon it's Notre Dame and the Latin Quarter. The Eiffel tower tomorrow afternoon before travelling home.' Angelo got up from his chair at that point and walked round the table to where Christopher sat. He wrapped his arms around Christopher and nuzzled his warm face into the angle of Christopher's neck. Christopher made no attempt to push him off. A hot flood of emotion spilled inside him and wordlessly he hugged Angelo back.

A lot of things happen when one person hugs another. The people concerned are scarcely aware of them at the time, let alone in a position to analyse or make sense of what is going on. So it was now with Christopher. He liked Angelo. They'd known each other for six months. There was a history of mild flirtation on Angelo's side which Christopher had dealt with as professionally as he knew how, politely keeping Angelo at arm's length without being rude to him. Though, yes, he had sat with his arm round the boy on that morning of crisis when Angelo had been expelled and was alone in a room in floods of tears. Angelo needed this hug now; he'd as good as crossed the Channel for it, and Christopher was unable to deny it to him. But then, once he had his arms round Angelo Christopher knew he was drawing pleasure from the moment. The pleasure itself then made him uneasy, for he feared it was a transgressive one. He needed to let Angelo go but for the moment couldn't quite manage it. A whole world of moral complexity and turbulent emotion then, lay packed inside that simple phrase: he hugged Angelo back.

After a few seconds Tom cleared his throat. He said, in a measured tone, 'Perhaps it'd be a good idea to take a walk around Montmartre. See a little of the streets?'

Christopher saw the point of this, if Angelo did not, and was about to unwrap himself. But he didn't have time to complete the action before the door opened from the inside corridor and Charles walked in wearing just a dressing-gown and carrying his last night's empty wineglass. *'Oh là,'* he said. 'Who have we here? How very nice.'

Christopher and Angelo extricated themselves very quickly from their embrace and sprang apart. Tom said, 'Morning, Charles,' and stood up very purposefully.

'We're just going for a walk around Montmartre.' He turned to Christopher and Angelo, and said, 'Come on, chaps,' in a rather steely voice.

Armed with their recently acquired knowledge, and as residents of the Montmartre slopes, they were able to give Angelo an impressive guided tour of the Butte. They pointed out the Lapin Agile... 'Actually, it's a play on words,' Tom, reverting to schoolmaster mode, told Angelo. 'As well as meaning the agile rabbit, it also means Gill's rabbit. *Le lapin a Gill.* Gill being the name of the artist who painted the original sign...'

'That's quite funny,' said Angelo. 'Maybe you could take me there tonight, and then I could stay the night with you.' He gave Christopher's upper arm an intimate squeeze as he said this. It was impossible to tell whether he was joking or not.

''Fraid you're not invited,' said Tom, trying not to sound unfriendly about it. 'If only because you'd be missed at the place you're staying at; then the police would be called and Chris and I would be in terrible trouble.' He smiled at Angelo. 'As you know full well.'

'Hmm,' said Angelo. Then, 'Chris... Can I call him Chris?'

'Yes,' said Christopher.

They pointed out the old Château des Brouillards in its big wild garden, where Renoir had painted and the poet Nerval had laid down his lines. They saw the defunct horse pond in the Rue de l'Abreuvoir. The Moulin de la Galette. The Place du Tertre. Then suddenly it was time for Angelo to go back and have his lunch.

'I'll come back tomorrow morning,' he said. 'I'll slip out of Mass and come and find you. You're only just round the corner from the Sacré Coeur.'

'Don't get into trouble,' Christopher cautioned him. 'You'll get us into trouble too. You know that.'

'Such a pity you won't let me stay the night,' Angelo said.

'Enough of that,' Tom cautioned him. 'It was nice to see you. Hope we'll meet again, but…' he looked at his watch. 'Time you went and got your lunch.' They were standing at the top of the Calvary Steps, which run down the steep side of the Butte, alongside the funicular railway from the Sacré Coeur at the top to the boulevard at the foot. They were the steps on which Tom and Christopher had stopped, months ago, and Christopher had held onto the railings and talked about mortal sin. Memories of the public cuddle that Tom had then given him coincided now with Angelo's saying, 'Give me a cuddle at least, before I go.'

Christopher didn't want to, and yet he did. He hesitated a second, then, like someone bowing to the dictates of fate and unable to exercise his will fell in with Angelo's request. No words came from him. He just let Angelo hold him, while he held Angelo in his arms, a little less tightly than the boy was holding him. Tom stood patiently for the minute or so that it took for Angelo's need to subside, then accepted a quick hug from him after he'd detached himself from Christopher. Then Angelo turned and started down the steep steps. He hadn't gone far before he turned, waved back up at them and called, 'See you tomorrow.' They waved back at him but made no reply. Then they watched him till he was out of sight, making for the busy boulevard far below. Beyond, above the rooftops, the whole of central Paris lay spread out for inspection: its railway termini, its opera house, its old royal palaces and its church spires.

Christopher was the first of them to speak. 'Sorry about that,' he said.

'Well, yes,' said Tom. 'I have to hope he doesn't turn up again tomorrow. For both your sakes. Too much emotion building up, and nowhere for it to go. Dangerous, Chris.' He put an arm on Christopher's shoulder and turned him away from the empty steps and the infinite view. 'Let's get some lunch somewhere.'

They slept late the next morning, and were hardly aware what the time was when they awoke in broad daylight with a strange sense of unease. They'd been woken by an exchange of voices in the kitchen, they thought, or people talking on the stairs. An opening, then shutting door…

Christopher bounded out of bed. His heart was thumping; he didn't know why. Still naked he ran downstairs. The ground floor was deserted. He ran back up the stairs. On an impulse that came from God knew where, he turned the handle of Charles's bedroom door and barged into the room.

Beside the bed a naked, stiff-cocked Charles stood, starting to undress Angelo who stood with his arms loosely around Charles. Both faces turned abruptly towards Christopher, expressions of shock only just finding time to appear on them before Christopher, who hadn't thrown a punch since he was in the fifth form, sent his right fist flying towards Charles with a speed he didn't know it was capable of. The fist connected with Charles's cheek and the impact sent Charles sprawling onto the unmade bed.

'Chris, what are you…?' began Angelo, as Christopher threw himself down on top of Charles and started to pummel his head and shoulders with flailing fists. But only for a second. Tom was in the room, pulling hard at Christopher. He was stronger than Christopher was and quickly pried him away from Charles who bounced back up from the bed and came towards the pair. There was blood on his face. This time it was Tom who hit him, aiming for the blood splash, before Charles could punch Christopher. Charles went down again.

Then Gérard and Henri were in the room, in silk dressing-gowns. 'Come out, all of you,' said Henri, almost shouting the words. 'Not in my house. We don't do this here.' He got himself in between Charles and his uninvited guests and pushed Tom and Christopher towards Gérard who then bundled them out of the door. Angelo followed, minus his shirt and very subdued.

In the corridor Tom said to Angelo very firmly, 'You're supposed to be at Mass in the Sacré Coeur. I think you should go back there now. We'll ask Gérard to go in and collect your shirt and tie.'

Christopher turned to Angelo, 'Why the fuck did you let him…?'

'Because you wouldn't play,' said Angelo and suddenly crumpled into noisy tears.

'Come on,' Gérard said to Angelo and took the boy into his own arms to comfort him before either Tom or Christopher could make the matter worse by doing so themselves.

Tom caught hold of Christopher. 'And what were you thinking of? Punching fucking Charles.'

'Don't know,' Christopher muttered.

'I think you do,' said Tom. 'Charles was only going to do what you wanted to do yourself. You lost your temper because Charles got there first.' He gave his lover a look that was as painful as the punch that Chris had given Charles.

Part Two
1967

ELEVEN

They were typical long-term British expats in that they missed Marmite, and listened to the news on the BBC Home Service as often as they could. And the news grew interesting for them during that summer of '67. Harold Wilson's Labour government, and a substantial section of the Conservative opposition were supporting a Private Member's Bill that sought to overturn the law that had made homosexual acts a criminal offence since 1533.

'Not that they're going far enough,' said Tom. 'Between consenting adults in private sounds fair enough. Till you look at the small print. Adult means not below the age of twenty-one, although you can get married or die for your country years before you get to that age... And *in private* doesn't count as private if there's any other person in the house at the time, even if they're asleep in another room.'

'But if they're in another room they wouldn't need to know,' said Christopher.

'And that's the way it is at the moment,' said Tom, leaning forward seriously. 'It doesn't change very much.'

'We have to think of it as a start,' said Christopher. 'A step in the right direction. A step on a long road...'

The voice from the transistor radio cut in. '...Against the bill. Against it tooth and nail, against it hook, line and sinker, against it warts and all.'

'Who was that?' asked Christopher.

'Missed it,' said Tom. 'Whoever he was, at least we know where he stands.'

'Is that good?' asked Christopher absently.

The newsreader, effortlessly suave, went on, 'The Home Secretary, Mr Roy Jenkins, speaking in support of the Bill, said, "Those who suffer from this disability carry a great weight of shame all their lives."'

'Disability?' Tom's brow furrowed. 'It doesn't feel like a disability. Does it to you?'

'No,' said Christopher, although there was a *but* in his voice. 'Not like a physical disability... I'll try to explain... I don't have sex with women and I don't miss that. I suppose people who don't like chocolate don't feel they're missing anything. Provided they like other things instead. But we've been handicapped if you like by the law. Not able to work in the country where we were born.'

'Hmm,' said Tom. 'I sometimes wonder if we fool ourselves. We like it here in Paris. We're teaching here; we'd be teaching if we were back there. Same difference.'

'That's ungrammatical,' objected Christopher. 'You mean same thing.'

'It's an expression,' said Tom. 'Just an idiom. Anyway, I'm only using it, not teaching it.'

'Same difference,' said Christopher, and laughed.

Tom half rose from his seat at the table, leaned across their partly eaten meal and playfully cuffed Christopher on the side of his head. Sitting down again he resumed, 'And did we really need to come all this way to escape the law in the first place? I sometimes ask myself that in the small hours. We could have laid low at Roger and Malcolm's place till things blew over. No-one accused us of anything more than telling someone else that we were lovers. The police wouldn't have hunted us down just over that. They'd have made a couple more enquiries at Star of the Sea and then given up the search. They've better things to do.'

'It's lain low,' said Christopher. 'Not laid low.' He put a neat forkful of chicken into his mouth and chewed it.

A fortnight later they had exchanged Paris for Boulogne. The sky was a cloudless blue and all around them the sea sparked at intervals while it rose and fell gently as a sleeper's chest. The breeze swung back and forth lightly, bringing them alternate wafts of harvest fields and stinging salt. 'It makes me smile,' said Armand. 'The thought of your elegant Queen Elizabeth signing a paper that says you may have sex together in the privacy of your own bedroom.'

'It makes me smile,' said Roger who was the skipper this morning, 'to watch you holding onto the backstay for dear life with one hand while holding a champagne flute with the other.' They all laughed, including Armand, who was concentrating hard on trying to spill neither his bubbly nor himself.

It was a good moment. They were a mile or two out of Boulogne harbour in the Orca. There were Roger and Malcolm, on their annual sailing visit to their friends across the sea. Tom and Christopher, spending their summer here as usual, were out with them. Michel and Armand too. It had become a tradition by now. The bottle of champagne was new, though. Other years there had been cans of beer. But on this particular day they were celebrating the passage of the Bill – there had been a late night vote in the Commons just ten hours ago, the Royal Assent had been given this morning – that made law-abiding citizens of Roger and Malcolm, provided they restricted their physical expressions of affection to the private space of the pub they owned, after the customers had gone and the staff returned home. The law had been passed that removed any remaining excuse for Tom and Christopher to claim they were obliged to live in France for the remainder of their lives.

Michel leaned forward from his seat on the gunwale. 'So will you be going back?' Among their little group of friends it was usually he who asked what everyone else wanted to ask yet somehow couldn't. It was Michel who would say the difficult things; over the years it had been he who would name the elephants in the room.

'Don't know,' said Christopher. 'Going back... Maybe.'

'I do know,' said Tom. 'He has a place at Oxford waiting for him. He's written and they've confirmed it's still open. I'm not going to let him forgo that. He might be prepared to pass it up. I won't let him, though.'

'He's written already?' Roger asked.

Christopher nodded awkwardly. 'Yes.'

'I made him,' said Tom. 'Stood over him while he did it. As soon as we knew the Bill was liable to become law. It's not something he can throw away.'

The wind banged in the red sails, sunlit overhead.

'But you?' Michel asked. 'While Christopher's studying. What would you do?'

'Go back to university myself? OK, I've got a degree. But that's not considered enough to teach with these days. They want you to have a PGCE as well.'

'Which is what exactly?' Armand wanted to know.

'Post-graduate certificate of education,' said Roger. He'd been a teacher himself some years before and knew. 'It means an extra year at college.'

'Can you do that at Oxford?' Michel asked Tom.

Tom shrugged cautiously. He too was trying hard not to spill his champagne as they rode the gentle swell with an occasional lurch. 'I can try.'

Christopher said, 'Well, if not this year, well, next maybe.'

'Why wait?' said Armand. 'Either you want to do something or you don't. And if you do, then now's the time.'

'Hmm,' said Christopher. He sighed, looked around at the sea and the comforting rural coast nearby. 'It won't be easy to give up all this. Summers here by the sea. Our teaching jobs in Paris. Our flat there...' He frowned. 'It's more than that. It's all this. Friendship.' He looked at Armand, then at Michel. 'You two.' He might have made an expansive gesture with his hands but prudently did not. He too had a glass to hang onto; he too was trying not to fall into the sea.

'You'd come back often,' said Armand sweetly. 'Roger and Malcolm do. You'd see us as often as you do living in Paris.'

Tom smiled quietly. That was just what he had been going to say. Armand had saved him the trouble, and drawn Christopher's fire.

Tom tried always to lead where Christopher was concerned. He was the senior partner and they were both acutely conscious of that difference in age of three years. Christopher needed his guidance and support: he was a tender and sensitive character; a degree of vulnerability went with that. All the same Tom tried to be careful not to bully him. Not a day had passed during the past five years during which Tom hadn't thought through the terrible scenario: the one in which Christopher turned to him, perhaps on waking one morning, perhaps after a goodnight kiss, perhaps on a bus or in a train, and said, smiling through a shared pain, 'It's been wonderful, Tom, all these years. I wouldn't have missed a minute of it. But it's time to say it's over. I need to move on.' The thought of this made Tom shudder some dozen times every day, as when a cold cloud casts its shadow under the sun. So it was good when sometimes there was someone else to say the difficult things to Christopher and it not have to fall every time to Tom. Tom looked across at Armand, perched on the gunwale, and smiled. Then, for good measure, he smiled at Malcolm too.

Approaching forty now, Malcolm looked more than ever like a well-fed, contented cat. A ginger Tom. 'What about we sail up to Gris Nez and back?' he suggested now. No-one was going to say no. They did this every year without fail. Apart from the attractiveness of the route itself this little annual jaunt served the purpose of little by little laying the ghost of the great wave that had so frightened Christopher all those years ago. Rounding the tip of the cape, passing the lighthouse, seeing the white cliffs of Cap Blanc Nez coming into view across a pussy-cat friendly sea… Each year this experience in the summer sunshine served to push Christopher's nightmare further down the tunnel of perspective that was memory: memory of incident, memory of fear.

They re-set the sails and tacked slowly northwards in the fickle, changing, little breeze. Northward. Towards England in effect. Today the white cliffs of Dover weren't visible; they lay hidden and enfolded in the skirts of a sunshine and water haze. But there they stood, ahead of them: invisible or not, there stood the forbidding walls and gateways of what had once been their home and now might be their home again some time before not too long.

'Should you decide you want to go back…' Roger's words cut in on the others' various reveries. 'In August, September… Don't know when university terms start these days… We'd come and get you. Malcolm and I. If you decided you wanted to travel that way.' He looked at them with questioning eyes. He had ten years on his lover. He was going grey, but his dark brown eyes still shone, like lighthouses, Tom had once thought.

'Gosh,' said Christopher, and Tom said, 'Many thanks.' Neither of them had thought as far ahead as actual travel plans.

'It might be nice,' said Tom after a few seconds of searching thought. 'Not least because we arrived here without showing passports on either side. Officially we've never left the UK's shores – as far as the authorities are concerned. The sudden return of two people who'd never left England in the first place might cause questions to be asked. Might… I only say might. I don't know how the systems work.'

'Neither do I,' said Roger, sitting at the helm, easing the tiller an inch or two. 'The fact that we don't know their systems helps them to keep control.'

'They,' said Malcolm. 'And who are they?'

'They, in the end,' said Armand with a smile, 'amount to your charming Elizabeth: *Sa Majesté Britannique*. Just like here. In France *they*, every time, turn out to be De Gaulle.'

Tom and Christopher were still in Boulogne a fortnight later, still havering indecisively, still arguing politely the pros and cons of going back or not, when a letter arrived, forwarded by their concierge in the Rue de Turin in Paris. It was from John Moyse.

Dear Christopher and Tom

I am sure you will be pleased by the passage of the Sexual Offences Act. I imagine it would make it easier for you to return to Blighty if that, at some point in the future, is what you want to do.

Meanwhile I have some news of my own too. I think you know I had a conditional offer of a place at Wadham College, Oxford. Well, for some reason known only to themselves – though I am not complaining in the slightest – the powers that be at Wadham have transformed their offer from conditional to unconditional. It means I'm definitely Going Up (as I've learned to say) in October.

I remember that Christopher had an offer from an Oxford college that couldn't be taken up five years ago. I wonder if it is still open. It would be fun if you (Christopher) could take it up this year. We could all be Oxford students together. What a gas!!!

When I say all – well, I know that, Tom, you have already been to Oxford. But I'm sure you could get a job there doing something like lay dinner tables or sweep floors (only jesting)... By all of us I mean that Angelo has got a place at Oxford too. He may be too lazy or too busy (haha) to write and tell you so himself so I'm taking it upon myself to do so. (So to do? Which, in your eminent opinions, both of you, is the better literary style?) Anyway, he's going to be at Worcester College which – Tom, you'll know this anyway, but Christopher may not – competes with Wadham to have the prettiest college gardens at Oxford...

There was more than this in the letter. John Moyse, who hadn't written to them in six months, was now in full flow and his pen didn't seem to want to stop. He was at that stage in a writer's career when quantity of words suddenly becomes the most effortless thing in the world. But the important point had already been made. If Christopher were to take up his place this year he would find both Angelo and John alongside him among the autumn's intake of freshers and each of them living a couple of hundred yards away, although in different directions, from his own college, which was Oriel. The prospect made him inhale deeply several times. It seemed unreal.

They were reading John's letter together, standing side by side, in Sabine's salon. This too had become a hallowed familiar routine over the years. 'Well?' Christopher queried, turning to Tom, eyebrows raised. 'Do you fancy laying tables or sweeping floors?'

'Neither,' said Tom seriously. Then a grin came sheepishly. 'I've already applied to do a PGCE. At my old college. St Edmund's Hall. I've been accepted. I just have to accept the acceptance, if you see what I mean. A hundred yards from Oriel, on the other side of the road.'

His face became mock-severe again. 'I'll be there to keep an eye on you.'

Sabine's head appeared around the edge of the half-open door. 'Would pork tenderloin for dinner be OK?' The French language has a pretty translation for pork tenderloin. It's *filet mignon*. Cute fillet. Quite cute in itself.

A letter from Angelo arrived a few days after that. They hadn't really expected it. His letters were much rarer birds than John's. If John's came six-monthly, then Angelo's – except for those first weeks after the Christmas debacle five years ago – had tended to turn up just once a year. This one announced Angelo's pleasure at getting an Oxford place, and then: *I do hope you'll be taking up your place at Oriel this year – I'm talking to you now, Chris – because it would be really lovely to spend time with you again.*

Christopher wondered how he felt about that. He still had fond feelings for Angelo, despite not having seen him in the flesh for four and a half years, and part of him was thrilled and excited at the thought of renewing the contact in a new environment – and a heady one at that. Oxford. Starting out together as fellow students. Angelo no longer a child… Though he was not yet twenty-one, another part of Christopher warned sternly. And yet another piece of him was urgently reminding that Angelo had wreaked havoc with his life on two if not three occasions and that there was no very obvious reason why this should not happen once more if their paths became entangled yet again.

Tom and Christopher had seen John Moyse twice in the past five years. Twice John had been on a language exchange with a Parisian family and had asked to meet Christopher and Tom for a coffee on the Boulevard des Ternes. They had done a bit more than coffee, actually:

there had been a walk by the Seine on one of those occasions and a visit to Notre Dame on the other, but nothing remotely improper or untoward had occurred; John Moyse was not that sort of boy.

Angelo, of course, had proved himself to be very much that sort of boy, but they had had no contact with him except for letters in all the years since that seismic winter visit of his to Paris, and both Tom and Christopher had felt this was just as well. The repercussions of that December visit – Angelo dropping into their lives like a stone into a river, or like something falling out of space – had spread ripples far and wide. They had had to leave Gérard's house soon after their return from Boulogne in the New Year of 1963. Both Tom and Christopher had raised their fists against Charles and, however extenuating the circumstances might appear to the two of them, the whole business seemed murky when viewed by the rest of the household and it was agreed that for Christopher and Tom to leave the ménage would be the most appropriate thing to happen next.

It had been for the best, they thought, looking back. On balance. It had created difficulties at first. They'd had to find a find a flat. For that they'd had to find rent. That had necessitated a search for proper jobs. But in the end it had turned out well. Tom and Christopher found work teaching their own language to Parisian adults in a well equipped and well regarded language school in the 8th arrondissement, and they had found a flat nearby that they could afford. The area was known for good reason as the Quartier d'Europe. Street names included Rue de Florence, Rue de Rome and Rue de Berlin. Even Rue de Leningrad. In their own Rue de Turin they had a place of their own at last, and for the first time in their lives. After leaving the Rue St-Vincent they had stopped experimenting with threes and fours when it came to sex and for over four years had managed to satisfy each other's sexual needs entirely by themselves, inspired by the ongoing example set by Michel and Armand. Both of them now found themselves separately wondering what impact a move to England, and more particularly a re-encounter with Angelo, might have upon this happy status quo, but they didn't share this concern with each other. Instead they bottled it up within themselves.

In the five years that had passed since their escape to France they'd had visits from Tom's parents from time to time. These had included Christmases all together in Boulogne. Though Christopher's parents had remained, conspicuously and sadly, absent from all feasts. There had been exchanges of letters between the McGing parents and their son roughly every three months over the years but that had been as far as things had progressed. The letters had been friendly enough. Differences stated at the outset of the estrangement had not been restated or harped on. That was something, Christopher told himself. Better than nothing. (Although everything, anything, was.) A cheque would arrive, along with a card, each birthday and each Christmas, and that was lovely, and made Christopher's skin creep with love and wonder as well as pain. But it was a less than ideal situation to exist between a father and mother and their son. 'It'll get better now, surely,' Tom tried to reassure Christopher several times during those high summer weeks of 1967. 'Now the law has changed.' It wouldn't get better though: Christopher knew that full well. He knew that Tom, however loving, kind and encouraging he wanted to be, knew this too. They'd both lived all their lives in Catholic circles and they had no illusions about the way things were in that medieval world.

Sometimes the complications involved in organising a major change in life seem so overpowering that they prevent us from making the change at all. But experience eventually teaches us that when the desire to make the change is so strong as to make us decide to do it anyway, those complications magically disappear.

So it was for Christopher and Tom.

One thing that had changed over the years was the real cost of international telephone calls. It was no longer prohibitively expensive to phone Roger and Malcolm from time to time to discuss dates and arrangements for their shipping out. They could do this now without having to wait fortnights for letters to bring further questions among the replies. That first imagined problem of communication had disappeared like smoke as soon as they peered into it.

Another thing was the question of their travel documents. Since they had arrived in France both their passports had expired. Roger assured them this would be no problem. They had travelled to France five years ago without showing passports at either end, and they could do the same on their return. Once they were safely back in England, and when they next wanted to travel abroad, they could simply apply for new ones in the normal way. The chances of their being boarded by border control agents on the high sea between the French and English coasts were about a thousand to one against, Roger opined.

They gave notice to the school in Paris that they taught at and were told they would be welcome to return there and teach again if they found life brought them back to France another time. There was a *pot-d'adieu* – a farewell drink of champagne – in their honour on their final afternoon, and they parted with firm handshakes all round. They gave notice on their flat as well, and sent their five years' accumulation of belongings ahead of them by train to Boulogne. And they received a pleasant surprise. The returnable deposit they'd handed over on taking the flat on all those years ago was now returned to them – with interest. They had completely forgotten the sum. It made a handy leaving present now.

Gérard came to the station to see them off on the first stage of their journey: the stage that would take them to Boulogne. Tom and Christopher thought this was decent of him. Their friendship hadn't exactly soured after the incident involving Angelo, but it had grown more distant and more cautious over the years. Gérard had never painted them, separately or together, since those summer days at Audresselles in 1962. Tom and Christopher still considered themselves handsome. But at twenty-seven and twenty-four respectively they no longer stood among the ranks of the lithe teenagers that Gérard liked to paint and, in so doing, earn his bread.

Neither Tom nor Christopher said the following to each other: it would have been embarrassing. But as the train drew them out of Paris towards the coast and their journey back to England's mist-encircled shore they found themselves separately wondering if they would ever be painted, ever be models for a work of art, again.

TWELVE

Roger and Malcolm had shown their passports that September morning when they checked in with the harbour master to pay their mooring fees. They said they would be slipping away very early the next day and were told that was fine: there would be no need to show their passports again. They said nothing about taking extra passengers away with them and nobody asked.

It was fortunate that Michel and Armand now had a car. They drove it right up to the Orca in broad daylight, choosing a moment when a ferry was steaming past and momentarily obscuring the view from the harbour watch tower, to throw Tom's and Christopher's suitcases onto the deck, from where Roger and Malcolm very swiftly dropped them through the hatchway into the hold. Then Michel drove on a few yards and pointedly stopped at a fish stall where, nonchalantly and unhurriedly, he made a purchase of one large monkfish and four spider crabs.

There was a farewell dinner cooked by Sabine. It involved the fish and crustaceans that Michel had earlier bought on the quay. The crabs were simply boiled and cooled, and cut into halves. While the monkfish was cooked Brittany-style in a sauce of tomatoes, white wine, and onions, a pinch of curry spice, and flamed in Cognac. As well as Tom and Christopher and their hostess, Michel and Armand, and Roger and Malcolm of course shared the meal. Afterwards Sabine actually walked down with them to the Chat qui Pêche – it was something she had never done before – and there Benoît and René, and Thierry and Robert, joined them for one more final farewell.

Tom and Christopher passed a few brief hours in bed – with Roger and Malcolm snoring beside them on the floor – and then it was time to walk down the hill to the harbour in the dark hour just before dawn. They had discussed the option of Tom and Christopher's staying shut up in the hold with the luggage until they were out of the watch tower's view but decided against it. In the unlikely event that they were stopped and boarded they would say simply that they'd gone out for an early morning sail. It would have been more difficult to explain things had two stowaways been discovered in the hold.

It was strange, Tom thought. Five years ago they had escaped secretly from England under the cloak of night. Now it seemed that they were escaping in a similar fashion from France. They were not, Tom told himself. This time the only problem was the fact that their passports were out of date. Though a part of him wondered whether an atavistic thirst for adventure and mystery, shared by all of them but not admitted to by any, was playing a part in their plans. As it had done – Tom was sure of this – that other time.

They lit the oil lamps, cast off and set the sails. Out of consideration for people sleeping nearby they didn't use the engine to start them on their way, so their initial progress was slow. But after a few moments the night's land breeze caught the dark sails and blew the Orca down the river between the two harbour moles and cast her loose upon the sea.

Light was in the sky now. It silvered the crests of the wavelets in the open water in front of them and made a silhouette of the land-mass to their right. Where that shape came to an end the light of Cap Gris Nez calmly winked. Every fifteen seconds. On the dot.

An hour passed and then the sun rose. Gris Nez was nearly abeam by now but the sun came up over the open sea that stretched northward beyond the tip of land. It bubbled up through a shallow trough of mist, then poured red light into the Orca's tan sails, and lit the faces of the four young men. Then the coast of England came out of the misted waves ahead of them like a crescent moon.

How much easier this all was by daylight, Christopher thought, taking his mid-Channel turn at the helm. Their day-lit route was clear to see. The Calais-Dover ferries passed them at intervals a couple of miles to starboard, while the Boulogne to Folkestone ones overtook them a few miles to port. Christopher aimed the bow towards the easternmost tip of the South Foreland, twenty miles ahead of them, constantly adjusting their heading in response to the wind. Slowly but surely he was steering them towards... His mind balked at the thought of the word that would complete that sentence. But in the end he had to think it, had to say it in his mind. The word was home. He turned the word over in his head the way a chicken turns a nest-egg, and wondered what it meant.

They crossed the shipping lanes, prudently zigzagging as required, then chose a moment to turn across the Dover-Calais ferry route when no ferry was close enough to send them lurching with its wake. Dover itself came close to them – castle, harbour walls and blocks of flats all razor-sharp in the clear air – then slipped away to port as they rounded the South Foreland's cliffs. Ahead of them now the low cliffs of Thanet came in sight as the curvaceous chalky rim of *home* shape-shifted at their approach. As did the meaning of the word...

The cliffs of Thanet were almost on top of them, and the front of Roger's pub the Admiral Digby could be clearly seen, when they turned left and entered the winding estuary of the Stour. You were never there until you were there though, and that last bit, threading between pastures on the winding river, seemed to take an age. At last they reached the mooring just outside Sandwich where the Orca had her home among a forest of other masts and hulls. A car was parked nearby. 'Our new one,' said Malcolm. 'Do you like it?'

They did rather. It was old and battered but not short on breeding. Malcolm identified it for them in case their knowledge of English cars had rusted after so many years. 'Mark Two Jaguar. Eats fuel like crazy, obviously.'

Roger looked at his watch. 'Gone twelve o'clock English time,' he said. 'Anyone fancy driving into Sandwich for a pint and one of those?'

'One of those…?' Tom queried hesitantly.

'He means a sandwich,' said Malcolm deadpan. 'It's what the English call a play on words.'

Being back. The shock of return. The shock of discovering how little had changed in over five years. The shock of feeling that they'd never really been away. The shock of finding that a few small things had changed. The price of beer was one such. That somebody had invented the Ploughman's Lunch was another.

Malcolm drove them back to the Admiral Digby rather too fast to Tom's mind, showing off the Jaguar's turn of speed along the country roads. Then there they were. The buildings, especially the chapel, of Star of the Sea glowered down at them from its windswept hill. Its playing fields were un-peopled: term wouldn't begin for another week or so. To Christopher's dismay he felt that sinking feeling in his stomach that he'd always had when returning to the place. That this could happen now after so long away! He had no ties with the prep school now, it had no power over him… And yet it did, apparently. His innards were telling him that was so.

They parked outside the Admiral Digby. Suitcases came out from the boot; they were taken up to the room that had been got ready for the returning exiles. 'Why don't we meet again at teatime?' Roger said. He and Malcolm disappeared into their bedroom and Tom and

Christopher went into theirs. They lay on the bed fully
clothed, only kicking off their shoes. They embraced
briefly on top of the covers. Within seconds they were
both asleep.

There was a major new change at The Admiral Digby.
It now served food. Roger had told them this already. It
was the way the market was going, he said. The days of
pubs that sold only beer and crisps and pickled eggs
were numbered. And so the little kitchen that he and
Malcolm used had been extended. Deep-freezes and
deep-fryers had been installed. The food, cheap,
cheerful, and mostly either breaded or battered, went
from one to the other, then out onto hot plates with
lettuce, cucumber and tomatoes for garnish. Once they
had got used to it, Malcolm said, it really wasn't difficult
to do. Which was just as well. From the day after
tomorrow Tom and Christopher would be working as bar
and kitchen staff, covering a fortnight of staff holidays.

But this first evening Tom and Christopher simply sat
in the bar for most of the four and a half hours during
which the pub was open, trying not to drink too much or
too fast. They chatted with Roger and Malcolm from
time to time, when those two found themselves able to
take a break. They talked about parents, among other
things, and the trouble that species could cause. In
Christopher's case certainly. In Malcolm's, though... At
some point in the six years since he'd moved out of his
parents' home and gone to share Roger's bed at the
Admiral Digby full time he had told his parents he was
homosexual. (Nobody had though to call it coming out
back then.) The parents had been fine with it, just as
Tom's were. Malcolm had wondered why he'd ever
imagined it would be a difficult thing to do. It was
easier, in the end, he'd found, to be straight with them
than to go on trying for ever to pull the wool over their

eyes. Christopher wished he'd been half so lucky with his own family, but as he'd expressed this wish countless times already he contented himself now with saying, 'Hmm.'

He and Tom took a break from the pub when dusk came and walked a little way along the cliff. And then a strange thing happened, though it was strange only because it was something they'd forgotten about. Far across the water the lights of the French coast began to twinkle into life. There was nothing strange about it at all; it was very normal. It was the feeling that it gave them both that was weird.

In the morning Christopher got up early – it wasn't difficult, because of the hour's time difference: this morning's eight o'clock was yesterday's nine – and wrote a letter to his parents. He said that he was back in England and working in a pub before taking up his place at Oxford in a few weeks' time. He posted the letter in the box on Goodwin Road – it was the equivalent of lighting the blue touch-paper – and, as the instructions on the fireworks always said, retired. He would not have to wait long for a reply, he guessed. No longer in France, he could expect a reply at any time after an initial forty-eight hours.

Once that heavy task was out of the way thoughts of the beach enticed them and they asked Roger if he would mind letting them go down there. Roger said, of course there was no question of his minding, and told them there was still a torch hanging by the door in the cellar wall.

They made their way down the once-familiar tunnel through the chalk, the torchlight picking out the shining dark flints in the wall, and at last they came to a halt at the old iron door. Tom unbolted it and swung it open. The claustrophobic darkness of the tunnel was at once dispelled by brilliant sunshine and the briny open air of the little cove. Inaccessible except by means of the tunnel from the pub's cellar, the cove was rarely overlooked from above, and even then only by cats that hunted among the fennel fronds that grew on the cliff edge. This secret cove was a place of memories. Of happy ones: bathing naked with Malcolm and Roger, setting sail aboard the Orca on mackerel-fishing jaunts... But also it had been their sanctuary on that last day before their escape from England, their prison too, in a way, as they'd hidden out here, leaving Roger and Malcolm to deal with the policeman's knock at the door of the pub above, if it ever came (happily it had not come) and waiting for the darkness and the full tide. They had spent their last full day in England in this protected spot, beside the water, among rocks and sand. It seemed fitting somehow that their first full day back in their home country, or at least a part of it, should be spent here too. They stripped naked in the sunshine now, and made the most of it, lying on the sand together and swimming together by turns.

The following day they would not be working in the pub until the evening They decided to amuse themselves by taking a walk into the town. They set out along the familiar though five-year-forgotten suburban pavements that were overhung with miniature elm trees. After half a mile they saw a female figure walking towards them. From a distance the figure looked curiously familiar, like a character remembered from an ancient dream. Both had that thought. They didn't share it. There wasn't time. The female figure closed on them; they closed on her. All three of them stopped. Tom and Christopher found themselves looking into the lined and careworn face of a woman well on in middle age. Dark lashes still haloed her pale blue eyes, though. Those eyes of hers peered at them intently. The eyes are the windows of the soul, it's said. Now Tom and Christopher found themselves gazing into the soul of Molly O'Deere.

'Verlaine and Rimbaud,' she said. 'Verlaine and Rimbaud, two poets wandering the world.'

'We've come back, Molly,' Tom said, and rather timidly held out his hand.

Molly took it, to Tom's relief, and gave it a rather absent-minded shake. 'So many years,' she said.

'We've come back because the law's changed,' Christopher blurted suddenly. 'I can take up my place at Oxford now.'

'That's good to hear.' Molly's head was nodding rapidly, nervously; it seemed outside her control. 'The Oxford news, I mean.'

'Of course,' Tom said, wanting to skate past the difficulty. 'And I'm going back there to do my PGCE.'

'You'll be together then.' This was said neutrally, as if Molly couldn't decide whether the news was good or bad.

'Yes,' said Tom. 'And John Moyse is going up too.' He hoped desperately that Christopher wouldn't mention Angelo.

He didn't. Molly spoke. 'I heard so. So I heard.' There was an awkward pause. They all faced each other on the narrow strip of pavement between mown grass verge and road, like car drivers confronting each other in a lane and wondering who will reverse. Then Molly said, 'I'm sure you're wondering what happened to the picture.' Actually it had been nowhere near the forefront of their minds. A bizarre thought struck Tom as he looked at Molly's startlingly aged face. He imagined the picture of David and Jonathan also grown prematurely old while Christopher and he remained ever-youthful, as with the picture of Dorian Gray. 'It's hanging in the Convent of St Gilda's in Broadstairs,' Molly announced. 'It's in their refectory.'

'My Goodness,' was all that Tom could manage to say. After all the trouble it had caused, that the painting of the two of them, stripped to the waist and ostensibly at a cricket game, should be adorning the wall of a communal dining-room for the edification of nuns...

'It was the best solution I could think of,' Molly went on, evidently conscious that the painting's new circumstances required explaining. 'Nuns are very innocent, thank heaven. Thank heaven that some people are. They won't have a problem with it; they don't know its history.'

And Molly was very innocent too, Tom caught himself thinking, if she thought the picture would have no impact at all on a community of virgin females as they contemplated it at every silent meal.

Then Molly found something else to say. 'I'm sorry I never replied to your friend. The French painter who wanted to buy it...'

'Don't worry, Molly,' Christopher said. 'It was a whim of his. He has those. After a time he forgot about it. He hasn't mentioned it for years.'

'Well, I really have to make a move now.' Molly began to take her leave. 'Term starts tomorrow and there's so much to be done. As you both know.'

Tom and Christopher stood aside to let her pass them. 'Perhaps we could meet for a coffee some time in town?' Tom said.

Perhaps,' said Molly, extricating herself from their unexpected company. She half turned back as she moved away. 'It was good to see you both anyway.'

'You too,' said Christopher. He found that he didn't want Molly to walk away. But she did walk away, and he half wanted to cry.

When they arrived back at The Admiral Digby some time later that afternoon Roger had news for them. 'Christopher, your mother phoned.'

'My mother?!' Christopher almost lost his balance, quite literally, and put a hand on Tom's shoulder while he recovered from his surprise.

'She said not to phone back but that she would phone here again just after six. I told her you'd definitely be in then.'

About half an hour later Christopher found he was developing a headache. It seemed to be revving up, ready to be at full throttle just in time for six o'clock, the moment when (a) he would be starting his new job as a bar tender (for the first time on the English side of the Channel) and when (b) at approximately the same moment his mother would phone. Tom made him take three aspirin tablets with his afternoon cup of tea.

The bar opened at six, but food was not served before six-thirty, which was something. It meant that Tom could be behind the bar with Roger when Christopher's phone-call came. Which it did, at eight and a half minutes past. Christopher's head was pounding. Aspirin or no aspirin.

'The Admiral Digby,' Christopher said when he'd lifted the receiver. 'Christopher here.'

'Oh Christopher, it's Mummy.'

'It's nice to hear your voice again.' Christopher didn't know how he was going to be able to go on.

'It's good to hear your voice too,' came from the other end. It sounded as though the mother was having the same difficulty as the son.

'I'm going to Oxford in three weeks,' said Christopher, repeating what he'd put in his letter yesterday.

'I know,' said his mother. 'I'm so pleased. Will you have a room in college, or…?'

'Mature students usually don't get rooms in college. They're expected to live out. The college is looking for a flat for me to share to share. With another chap. He's at another college, apparently, doing a PGCE.' It wasn't exactly a lie direct – except perhaps for the word apparently. But Christopher had been well trained in moral nuance. He knew a lie by omission when he told one.

And perhaps his mother knew. Perhaps she was grateful not to have to hear Tom's name. She said, 'I'd like us to meet before you go up. Just you and me.' There was a second's pause. Then, 'I have needed to see you.'

'London,' said Christopher a bit wildly. 'We could meet at the National Gallery. I've heard they do lunches there.' Neutral territory, he was thinking. Perhaps his mother was thinking that too; she agreed to Christopher's proposal quite willingly. They talked a minute longer, making arrangements to meet at Charing Cross station, then Christopher said that he was at work and needed to get back to the bar. They said a polite goodbye, and Christopher put down the phone.

'I'm meeting her on Monday in London,' Christopher told Tom. 'Hope Roger will give me the day off in the circs.'

'I'm sure he will,' said Tom gently. He wanted to put his arms round Christopher and hold him tightly, but he didn't dare. The pub was full and they were in a very public position behind the bar together. The law had changed but public attitudes might take another generation to catch up. Instead Tom asked, 'How's the headache now?'

One night as Tom and Christopher were lying in bed, a minute or two away from sleep, Christopher said suddenly, 'It would be nice to see that picture again, don't you think?'

'What picture are you talking about?' Tom asked. His brain was already fuzzy with sleep.

'You know what picture.'

'Oh for God's sake! It's hanging in a convent. We can't very easily just go and look at it. And actually, do we really want to?'

'Probably yes,' answered Christopher calmly. 'Anyway, St Gilda's doesn't belong to an enclosed order. It's not as though it was the Poor Clares.'

'You still can't just walk into a convent and demand to see a painting,' Tom said patiently.

'I don't know,' said Christopher. 'We could pretend to be electricians, come to inspect the wiring or something.'

'Darling, don't be ridiculous. Electricians come when they're booked to do a job, they don't just turn up at convent doors on the off-chance.'

'Bet they do sometimes,' said Christopher and giggled sleepily. 'We could say we were inspectors. From the department of conventual safety. Come to carry out...'

'Now you're being ridiculous. Look, turn over. We're going to sleep.'

No mention was made of this late-night exchange in the morning and Tom was rather glad of that. All the same, Molly's mention of the painting, and Christopher's saying that he wanted to go and see it, had stirred something up for Tom. He had a very clear image of the David and Jonathan in his mind's eye. The traumas it had unleashed had etched it deeply into his retina. There returned to him now the idea he'd had of it when talking to Molly those few days ago: his face and Christopher's etched with the lines of age and worry, self-doubt and conscience, as Molly's face now seemed to be. He wondered, a bit more seriously, what

impression the painting would make on him now were
he to see it again after all these years. All the same, he
wasn't going to don an electrician's boiler-suit and forge
an identity card.

Christopher got his day off work on Monday. Roger
and Malcolm were more than understanding and wished
him luck with what would inevitably be a momentous
day. Tom walked to the station with him in the morning
and saw him onto the London train, even buying a
platform ticket so that he could stay with him till the last
possible second. Christopher wasn't sure what train he'd
be getting back, he said, but it wouldn't be late.

He walked into the bar of the Admiral Digby at seven
o'clock. Tom thought he saw mixed feelings written on
his face. 'How did it go?' he asked him, instinctively
pulling him a pint. Knowing what the customer wants
before the customer has even thought about it has
become a mantra in more recent times but Tom seemed
to have known about it even way back then.

'She looked older, somehow,' Christopher said. 'Like
Molly did. She was very smartly dressed.'

'I think perhaps,' said Tom, 'though this may surprise
you, she had made an effort for her son. Go on.'

'Well, there were pluses and minuses. The meal was
good, for one thing. We had chicken and chips, then
autumn fruit with cream.'

'Yes,' said Tom. 'When I said go on...'

'She wants me to go home and see her and my father
before I go to Oxford. Then she wants to come and visit
me there.'

'I think that's excellent,' said Tom.

'Hmm,' said Christopher and his face pulled itself into
a doubtful frown. 'The thing is, though, that like
drowning people clutching at straws she's chosen to tell
herself I'm no longer with you. I should have been

strong and told her we were still together. She's pulled the wool over her own eyes. I should have had the courage and the honesty to remove it.'

'No, you shouldn't have,' said Tom gently. 'You did right not to mention me. It's not about lying to her. It's about not hurting her more than she can bear.'

'But when she comes to Oxford and finds I'm living with you...'

'We'll cross that bridge when we come to it,' said Tom. 'Don't worry. I can always move out of the flat for the day. Assuming we've got a flat by then.' He grinned mischievously. 'We could find a friend to impersonate your flat-mate if it comes to it.' The grin broadened even more. 'I could turn up dressed as an electrician. Read the meter or inspect the wiring while she's there.'

THIRTEEN

Although the law had changed in their favour, when it came to looking for a student flat to share it was not yet the case that a homosexual couple would be offered the same automatic consideration that would have been accorded a married pair. Yet Tom and Christopher were in no worse a situation than any heterosexual couple of the time who hadn't tied the official knot. They wrote a carefully worded letter to the university's accommodation office, signed jointly, in which they said they were old friends who had shared flats together for five years and, although they were going to be in different colleges, would like to be housed together. With other mature students if necessary but for preference without. They could only hope that the person in whose in-tray this landed would read between the lines and be sympathetic, not hostile, to their case. In 1967 that was still quite a big thing to hope for.

They were luckier than they had dared to imagine. There was a small house available for them in the area of the town known as Jericho. It was owned by a professor of paleontology who was taking a sabbatical year. He wanted the house well looked after by responsible adults. If Tom and Christopher felt this might suit them... But the professor would want to meet them before finalising the arrangement.

They went up to Oxford by train, travelling through London on the top of a bus. It was the first time they'd done this together, the first time they'd seen London through their double pair of eyes rather than just a single pair. The moment was surprisingly big. Then Oxford itself. Jericho turned out to be handily near the station. They walked there past the imposing classical front of Worcester College. This would be Angelo's college a few weeks hence. This thought came sharply to both their minds. Neither of them volunteered to share the thought.

The house in Jericho was a treat. Two up, two down, a late Georgian cottage with big sash windows at the front. Inside all was impeccably kept. And there were fossils everywhere they looked.

They had rather imagined the professor would be a fossil too, but he was anything but. A small, wiry, energetic man, he was probably less than ten years older than they were. His complexion was wonderfully tanned. He was off to Africa, he explained. (To top the tan up, Tom thought facetiously, though didn't say so.) 'Parties are fine,' the professor said. 'But not wild parties. Things in glass cases that can smash.' He waved a hand in the direction of the nearest one. 'That's why I wanted a pair of adults.' He looked at them beadily for a second. 'You are a pair, I take it? No need to explain. I understand these things.' He snickered nervily. 'As a bachelor boy myself.' It was probably as close as he could let himself come to saying that he was of the same kind as Christopher and Tom.

It was clear to all three of them that there would be no ifs or buts or need to think about it. The professor ('Professor Hollis, call me Mike,') had decided with the alacrity of the experienced interviewer, within seconds of their walking through the door and introducing themselves, that Tom and Christopher were his ideal tenants. He spent a short time showing them stop-cocks and fuse-boxes and how the boiler worked. Then he set to and spent much longer showing off his cases of trilobites and ammonites, and various other things with less familiar handles, and some – um – human stuff. 'I might return a couple of times during the year,' Mike said, 'and want to camp out in the spare bedroom.' Tom and Christopher nodded vigorously, to indicate that his unspoken assumption that they'd be sharing a sleeping-place was not wide of the mark. 'That might well be in vacation time. When you might or might not be here…'

'It won't be a problem either way,' said Tom, unexpectedly finding himself beaming as he said it.

Tom and Christopher might not have chosen to share their ideal home with quite so many reminders of the distant past. Nothing was ever completely perfect, but overall the house, its prettiness, its size and its location, and the wonderfully low rent Mike was prepared to charge them in return for their being responsible and looking after the coprolites made it perfect enough.

They were sitting in the garden at the Admiral Digby, enjoying the melancholy sunshine of late September among the autumn flowers – rudbeckia, golden rod – when a figure walked past in the lane beyond the low wall … and turned out to be Molly O'Deere. They could hardly ignore one another: she was only six feet away.

'Oh,' said Molly, surprised. 'I didn't think pubs opened in the afternoons.'

'They don't,' said Tom. 'But we're staying here before we go to Oxford. Doing a bit of work behind the bar in lieu of rent.'

'Well,' said Molly a little breathlessly, 'It's good to know you're…'

Christopher was already on his feet, had sprung towards the low gate and was opening it. 'Look, come in for a moment. Sit with us.'

Too startled perhaps to find an excuse Molly was sitting at their rustic table with them a moment later. 'Can I get you a cup of tea?' Christopher asked solicitously. 'A lemonade, perhaps?'

Sometimes a single, simple word can have magic in it. With Molly the mention of lemonade seemed to do the trick. She softened visibly. 'Lemonade would be lovely,' she said. 'If you're sure…'

'Of course,' said Christopher. 'We live here. We're on our home turf.' He went up the path towards the door to organise the lemonade.

Molly sighed and looked at Tom across the table. 'Extraordinary,' she said. 'I've walked past this garden time and again these past ten years and never been through the gate. Well, a singe woman. Pubs...'

'Of course,' Tom said.

Molly looked around her. 'The garden is really lovely,' she said. 'Who keeps it up?'

'The owners,' said Tom. 'Roger and Malcolm. They're friends of ours.' He paused before saying the next bit. 'Over the years they've been very good to us.'

Molly had registered the two male names. Tom saw her register them. 'I can imagine they would have done,' she said thoughtfully, and Tom heard a wisp of understanding in her voice. Then suddenly, 'I was thinking about that picture again...' but at that moment Christopher arrived with a tray on which a jug and three glasses sat. The jug had lemonade in it, with curls of real lemon zest, and ice cubes that chinked. 'How lovely,' Molly said.

'You were saying about the picture...' Conversation had moved to other, inconsequential things. Tom found an unexpected need to wrest it back again before it was too late.'

'Oh yes, of course,' said Molly. 'It struck me after we last spoke that you might have wanted to take a look at it for yourselves. I'm sure the nuns would have no objection once they knew you were the sitters...' She looked away and down for a moment. 'For all the trouble it caused... But it's water under the bridge.' Her gaze came back to them. 'I can write you a little note of introduction, if you like, which you could hand to the sisters if you called round when you're next in Broadstairs. That is, if you would like me to.'

Christopher said enthusiastically, 'We'd like that ever so much. That's a wonderful thought.'

Molly pulled her cardigan together at the top with her two hands as if they at any rate didn't think the thought quite as wonderful as that.

'Can I ask,' said Tom, doing exactly that, 'what has become of Father Louis, Father Matthew and the others?'

Miss O'Deere's face tightened suddenly and she drew a breath. 'Father Louis died,' she said. 'Within six months of being taken away. It was as if the school had been his life and once he was separated from it he had no reason for existing any more. So very sad. He was a good man.' She paused a second. 'Then Angela Coyle returned to Ireland two years ago.' She gave a barely perceptible sigh. 'She's much missed, of course. As for Father Matthew, he went back to his old monastery in the West Country. We've never heard anything from him...'

'Who took over as headmaster after Father Louis was...?' A vivid memory came back to Tom of the bonfire of belongings and bed-sheets the old headmaster had built in the courtyard on his last night in office, and of the car coming to take him away the following morning... 'After Father Louis retired.'

Molly's face tightened yet further. 'Father Claude took over. It wasn't a happy time. He had a... He had a breakdown in his second year would be the most diplomatic way of putting it.'

'And now?' asked Christopher.

He had meant, who ran the school now, but Molly took the question to be a follow-up about Father Claude. 'In prison, I'm afraid.'

'Whoooo!' Tom expelled a gust of breath in his surprise. 'I see.'

'And the new headmaster?' Christopher tried not to be derailed by the startling news.

'Not a headmaster exactly,' said Molly. 'A headmistress' She managed to smile very faintly, self-deprecatingly. 'It's me.'

'I think that's wonderful,' said Tom, and recharged all their glasses with lemonade.

After Molly had gone, Tom and Christopher moved on from lemonade to beer. 'I'm sorry that Father Claude ended up in prison,' Tom said. 'All the same...'

'All he ever did was brush his hands against boys' penises when he took their pants down to spank them,' said Christopher. 'At least that's what you told me.'

'And that's what I was told by the boy who replaced Angelo as house-captain: Edward Abelard, if I've remembered the right name. But that was probably quite enough considering that he was in a position of authority over the boys. And that was before we left. Who knows what might have happened after he was in full charge?'

'Perhaps we should have questioned Molly further,' said Christopher.

'No,' said Tom, who was still three years older than Christopher was and always would be. 'I don't think we should.'

In the days that followed, the world inhabited by Molly O'Deere, by memories of Father Louis, Father Claude and by their own past selves became smaller and more distant, despite the fact that the building that housed that world of ghosts and memories stood just a few hundred yards away from the Admiral Digby and glowered wrathfully down at them every day from the top of its grassy hill. The Star of the Sea, which had loomed large again in their consciousness since their return to England's shores was now fading astern once again as they re-packed their suitcases and their expectations in readiness for the Oxford experience that lay just ahead and increasingly filled their minds.

Roger and Malcolm drove them and their luggage to the station. The four had had a low-key, private send-off meal the night before. The world was not ready for a public celebration among a public house's customers of the fact that two male members of the staff were setting off to Oxford together as a couple and forming a queer household there.

It was one thing to travel to Oxford by train on a September day to inspect a house in which you might one day live. It was quite different to repeat the journey a few weeks later in the knowledge that you were voyaging to the place in which you were actually going to live, and knowing that you would have to sink or swim there. It was a less dangerous journey than the one they had made across the water to France five years earlier, and a less physically demanding one. And it was a less exhilarating journey than the one they'd made a month ago, in the same sailing smack, the Orca, returning home after their long exile in France. But this one-more-time journey into a new life for them felt just as fraught.

The railway line from London to Oxford hugged the River Thames for most of its journey. But only at intervals was this apparent to travellers on the train. There was the blink and miss it moment when the railway crossed a swinging loop of the river at Maidenhead; there was the longer period of proximity, willow-bonded, between Pangbourne and the Goring Gap, and then the final few miles from Radley, during which the dreaming spires began to assemble in the distant view, to group and regroup themselves amidst a confusing parallax of trees and other buildings before finally standing to the salute, tall and honey-coloured, as the train slowed and pulled in to platform two.

Mike, their landlord, had shown them a short cut between the station and the house in Jericho. It ran alongside the canal, past the bottom end of Worcester College gardens, then cut away into the little streets of Jericho. Straining their arms with a suitcase apiece, they took this short cut now. Mike greeted them at the door. He would be setting out on his African travels in the morning. Tonight he would be camping, with their agreement, in the spare room.

'I'm dining with a few chums at The Randolph,' Mike told them. 'A sort of au-revoir meal. I don't know if you'd care to join…'

Tom shook his head vigorously enough for both of them before Christopher could accept. The Randolph was the best hotel in Oxford and was priced accordingly. Tom the Oxford graduate knew this already but thought that Christopher might not.

Mike registered the shake of the head, understood what it meant and carried on seamlessly, '…As my guests, obviously.'

Tom pretended his headshake was some sort of nervous tic, a response perhaps to the alighting of a tiny insect on his ear. 'We'd be … er … delighted,' he said and turned to Christopher. 'Wouldn't we?'

'It's just a ten-minute walk,' said Mike. 'I'll let you sort yourselves out now. Suppose we meet downstairs in an hour?'

'Well, Mike, how very nice. You take yourself away but in return…' The don whom Mike had introduced to them as Sidney beamed at Christopher and Tom. '…In return you give us this delectable pair for the duration.'

Three friends of Mike's had been waiting for them in the Randolph's dining-room. Two fellow paleontologists, of whom Sidney was one, and a lecturer in chemistry. They all sat down together. Sherry was served and a chilled soup called Vichyssoise.

We could have guessed but we didn't, Tom was thinking. Mike's little coterie of academic friends... Well they're all queer. For want of a better word. Time someone invented a better one...

On the short walk from Jericho to The Randolph via Walton and Beaumont Streets they had observed – they couldn't not do – some of the new intake of students, the freshmen, or freshers as they were starting to be called, beginning to explore the streets of Oxford in twos or threes. They were like baby rabbits that had dared to leave their maternal burrows for the first time. They would be looking for the safety of a pub to dive into (they were exclusively male) and partake of their first reassuring pint of ale in Oxford. The first of many, many pints, you could suppose. The matter of Tom and Christopher's freshmen status came up now. It was raised by Tom.

'I'm not sure how we should handle freshers' week,' he said to the table at large. 'We're both mature students. Me twenty-seven, Christopher twenty-four. Don't know whether to mingle or stay aloof. Eighteen-year-olds... Besides, I've been a freshman here before. I came up nine years ago.'

'What did you read?' asked the other paleontlogist, whose name was Simon.

'History,' said Tom. 'As Christopher is about to do.'

'Ah, the world of the arts!' said Simon theatrically and the other scientists all laughed as though the joke had been one of the funnier ones in the history of the world.

'I understand your concern,' said Sidney, becoming serious again. 'It's a difficulty all mature students face.'

'Not only students,' said Mike. 'Dons too. How close do we allow ourselves to get to our students? In social contexts, I mean.'

There was a bit of a snigger from the others. Mike turned to Tom and Christopher. 'Some dons have been known to be quite naughty in this respect, as I'm sure you both know. And I'm not talking about student parties or visits to pubs, obviously. There are official penalties, though, if things go too far.'

'You mean, if people break the eleventh commandment,' said Simon. 'Thou shalt not be found out.'

'Quite so,' agreed Sidney, and Christopher found himself suddenly thinking of Father Claude again, and wondering exactly what he'd gone to prison for.

'You need to remember,' said Mike, 'that although it's sixteen for women, it's still twenty-one for men.'

'Thank you,' said Tom. 'I don't think we were going to forget that, but thank you for reminding us.'

'It wouldn't be unreasonable to join a drama group, like the OUDS,' said Nicholas, the chemist at the table, a quietish don with greying hair. 'Assuming you can act, or would want to. Though Mike introduced you as having some experience as teachers. A profession closely allied to the actor's one in many ways.'

'Ah,' said Tom, wresting his thoughts away from the law and the age thing. 'I was in the OUDS when I studied here before.' He made an effort to sound modest about it.

'I'm sure they'd have you back with open arms,' said Nicholas. 'Though it might be diplomatic not to insist on playing all the leading roles.'

'Quite,' said Tom, and Christopher added, 'I agree.'

The empty plates of Vichyssoise were cleared away and the party refilled its wine-glasses and prepared mentally for the dish to follow, which was going to be roast lamb.

When dinner was finished the party sat for some time over port and coffee in the Randolph's lounge. It was quite late by the time goodnights were said, and au revoirs were made to Mike by his older friends: goodnights that looked as though they wanted to turn themselves into embraces but, on the door-step of the Randolph, didn't quite dare. By now the streets were full of freshers who were no longer in twos and threes but in eights and tens, as groups had welded themselves to other groups in the pubs in the intervening hours. They were also noisier and more boisterous and in most of the groups there had surfaced a natural leader or else simply a loudmouth who had become, however momentarily, in charge. Still there were no girls to be seen. Presumably the female freshers had spent their first evening demurely in their rooms, or in their college JCRs. A Freshers' Ball was scheduled two days from now. No doubt that would be the moment at which the new young women of Oxford would unleash themselves, in full panoply of war-paint and terror, upon the rabbit boys.

Suddenly, in the midst of one group of them, which was filling the pavement outside the gate of Worcester College, there was Angelo. He was taller now than Christopher, taller than Tom even, but he was quite unmistakeable. His dark hair was longer than it had been kept at school. It curled almost to his collar, and touched the tops of his ears. His nose had grown somewhat: it was on the way to converting his profile from a snub-featured child's to something more resembling that of an Italian man. But his eyes were the same deep luscious brown ones they knew all too well, and unchanged was his glorious pearl-toothed smile. This last was deployed at once, for he saw them both as soon as they came upon the group that filled the pavement, and hailed them immediately and unselfconsciously.

'Tom! Chris! How absolutely fab!' Wildly Angelo began to introduce everybody. 'Peter, David, you must meet Chris. One of my oldest friends. An ex-teacher at my prep school. Tom. This is Barney, and this is Phil.' There was a mumble of demur. 'Sorry. Not Phil: Bill. And this is…?'

'Mike,' said Tom.

'A don, I'm afraid,' said Mike in a self-deprecating tone. 'But you won't have to meet me again this year. I'm off to Africa in the morning.'

'The kind of things dons do,' said Christopher, laughing unnecessarily loudly and making an extravagant gesture with his hands. He was already high on wine and port; this encounter had propelled him into the stratosphere. 'We're living in his house while he's away.'

'Oh wow,' said Angelo. 'You've got a house here? A whole house to yourselves…?'

'Just round the corner from here,' Christopher said before Tom had had time to stop him. 'One of the nice old cottages in Jericho.'

'And the walls came tumbling down,' sang two members of Angelo's group in loud rough tenor voices in two different keys.

'You'll have to invite me round,' said Angelo. 'My friends too,' he added in an undertone that he probably hoped not too many of them would hear. 'I live just here.' He jerked his head towards the college entrance that towered just inside the gate, with the lit-up clock above the round-arched door. 'I'm in the Nuffield Building.' He pointed along the road beside the wall of the college grounds. 'Just there. Room twenty-six. Come and find me there anytime. Tomorrow, say. It's two rooms actually: bedroom and study-sitting-room, with an oak to sport when I don't want to be disturbed.'

'Angelo,' Tom said, falling back into a schoolmasterly tone he hadn't heard himself use for years, 'We're going to leave you now. But we will see you soon. As well as John Moyse, I hope. Good-night now. Enjoy the rest of your evening with your friends.' He began to move off, shepherding Christopher ahead of him, while Mike seemed quite relieved to be able to move off with them, tagging alongside. Christopher kept thinking to himself, twenty-six, twenty-six, and wondering how he could manage to remember the number without having to write it down before he got back to his new home.

'Well,' said Mike as soon as they were out of the pavement group's antenna range, 'he's a handsome young man and no mistake. And you were both his teachers at school? I must say he seems awfully fond of the pair of you. Though I can't help feeling he might be trouble.'

'Indeed,' said Tom. 'And thereby hangs a tale. Though I'm not sure I ought to be sharing it with you.'

'Oh go on,' said Mike. 'I'll pour us a nightcap before we all go up the wooden hill. My train tomorrow's not till ten.'

They continued along the last hundred yards of the road towards Jericho.

FOURTEEN

'What did Angelo mean when he said he had an oak to sport?' Christopher asked. He waited till Tom and he were undressing for bed before asking this. He hadn't wanted to look ignorant in front of Mike.

'OK,' said Tom, pulling off his new flared trousers. It wasn't the easiest of tasks: they clung rather tight around his buttocks and thighs. 'At Oxford and Cambridge colleges many student rooms have a second outer door which is called the oak. Shutting this outer door is a sign you don't want to be disturbed. If you're working hard or have a woman round. Or a chap. "Sporting the oak" is simply the old-fashioned expression for shutting your outer door.'

'You're a mine of information,' said Christopher, now standing naked, having more easily pulled off his baggier leg-wear. 'Do you want me to give those flares a pull from the bottom?'

'Maybe,' said Tom.

'OK. Just lie back on the bed.' Christopher knelt, and tugged and pulled, and a moment later Tom had joined Christopher among the ranks of the great un-clad.

In the morning Tom wondered momentarily whether he had been unwise in spilling the whole story of Angelo to Mike over a whisky nightcap. But he promptly dismissed his concern. Mike would be away for a whole year. The Angelo story was hardly going to be in the forefront of his mind when he got back. They parted finally with smiles and handshakes after breakfast: Mike to catch his train to Africa, Tom and Christopher to sign in at their respective colleges, St Edmund's Hall and Oriel..

The events of freshers' week were packed tightly into the schedule. Some were formal, official and obligatory, others merely social, some a mixture of the two. Some concerned the university at large, others were internal to the individual colleges. For this reason and because they were going to different colleges Tom and Christopher coincided only once or twice during that first day; for most of the time they were in separate bits of space. Christopher had lunch in the college hall at Oriel, he would be eating at home in their Jericho cottage in the evening.

In fact Christopher found himself wending his way homeward at four in the afternoon, his mind a whirl of information – there had been a tour of the college buildings and a familiarisation with the workings of its handsome library among much else – and with a huge bundle of papers under his arm, administrative stuff that would all need reading and digesting.

There were different routes that threaded the streets between Oriel College and Jericho. One lay past Worcester College. It was not the shortest but Christopher chose it this afternoon nevertheless. At the corner of Beaumont and Walton Streets he didn't turn right but walked straight into Worcester. He made his way unchallenged past the porter's lodge inside the gate and, turning left, found his way along a cloister towards the Nuffield Building. Twenty-six, he remembered. He found the room on a landing of a staircase. Outside its shut door another, oak-panelled, door was open, flat against the wall. If Angelo was in, at least he hadn't put his heavyweight do-not-disturb sign up. Christopher knocked but there was no answer. He waited a minute, then knocked again. After a further minute he walked away down the stairs, feeling slightly disappointed. He wondered whether he would tell Tom about this little non-adventure but in the end decided not to.

Tom, meanwhile, had had his own lunch in his own college, St Edmund's Hall – Teddy Hall as it was affectionately known. It was the college in which he had lived and studied, and occasionally loved, getting on for ten years ago. It was a shock to be back. As when revisiting one's prep school in later years, it was curious to see how much smaller everything looked. The more curious for the fact that Tom hadn't grown much in the meantime. Not physically at any rate. Not between the ages of twenty-one and twenty-six. Unlike between the ages of thirteen and twenty-one... At the earlier of those two ages Tom had left the Star of the Sea as a pupil; at twenty-one he had become a teacher there. Here at Teddy Hall, though, the odd change of apparent scale could only be explained, Tom supposed, by the fact that he had grown as a person – and had nothing to prove any more. At least, not to the extent that an eighteen-year-old has things to prove. St Edmund's Hall back then had had the reputation of a hearties' college; prowess on the Rugby field had been the hallmark of its alumni rather than academic excellence. Tom wasn't sure if that still held good now. But all those years ago he'd found the heartiness of the college's ethos a godsend. He hadn't been bad at Rugby himself, not bad at cricket either, and thanks to his ability to shine on the sports field had managed to hide the softer side of his nature, the homosexual side, from the prying thoughts of suspicious, or simply perceptive, minds. But something else had changed for him in the intervening years. Walking out through the main quadrangle, leaving home in Jericho mid-afternoon he was aware, as he had never been before, among the autumn flowers and mullioned windows, of the exquisite, cocooning beauty of the place to which he had returned.

He zigzagged his way from the High Street, past the Radcliffe Camera and along Brasenose Lane into the Broad. He had just rounded the corner of the Sheldonian Theatre and the astonishing line of busts that decorated the railings outside when he almost literally bumped into someone he knew. 'John,' he said.

'Tom,' said John Moyse. They had seen each other in Paris just two years ago but John, who had then been in the very middle of his adolescence was now practically a full-grown man. Tom had to make a real effort to stop himself from unnecessarily pointing this out to him.

Unlike Angelo John had not been an obviously pretty child. He'd had a pleasant, well-made face and a pleasing figure and form. All this remained true today. He was perfectly well-proportioned, and had nice smiling eyes, but it would have been difficult to describe him as handsome. His looks lacked something. Tom tried not to think about what it was that Angelo had and John hadn't. But there was no getting away from it. It was that most indefinable of qualities: the one that was these days labelled sex-appeal.

'How very good to see you,' Tom said, and heartily pumped John's hand. 'We ran into Angelo last night...'

'He said you had,' John interrupted. 'We ran into each other this morning. We're meeting up this evening for a drink.' A thought then obviously struck him; it pinched up his brow. He said cautiously, 'I don't suppose...'

'I'm not sure you'd want us,' Tom said gently, to let him off the hook. 'Old codgers like Chris and me. I'm sure you've got catching up to do that's quite unfit for our ears.'

'Don't worry,' said John. 'We actually met in London just two weeks ago and got all that out of the way then. So ... but only if you want to ... we've arranged to meet in the Lamb and Flag at half past eight. The Lamb and Flag being roughly midway between his college and mine.' He paused a second then added, 'And not too far from your home in Jericho.'

'He told you that, did he?' Tom said, remembering in a flash how news travelled here and that if you didn't want everyone to know absolutely everything about you, how careful you had to be.

'You've got a house of your own,' John said approvingly. 'You'll have to ask us over one day.'

'Of course,' said Tom. 'But this evening. Lamb and Flag, eight-thirty. You may see us or you may not. I'll see what Chris has got planned.'

Tom relayed this conversation to Christopher as soon as he got back home. And if Chris had had any tentative plans for the evening then he was prepared to shed them now. He certainly didn't mention any other plans. As far as he was concerned an evening drink with John and Angelo seemed a heaven-sent ending to his first university day.

The Lamb and Flag was one of those Oxford hostelries that go back centuries. When Tom and Christopher arrived Angelo and John were already there, though they hadn't been there long. They were standing at the bar and in a very adult way, deciding which bitter to drink. Tom did what was expected of him as the senior person present. 'I'll get those.' He delved in his wallet and pulled out a one-pound note.

'It's incredible how many societies there are,' John said when the four of them were sitting around a table. 'Poetry society, steam train society, you name it – as well as one for every subject in the system, each religious denomination and every political party.'

'Including the Communists,' said Angelo.

'You're not going to join that one, are you?' Christopher asked him.

'Why not?' Angelo shot back with a straight face. 'I'm also joining the Conservatives, but they meet on different nights so there wouldn't be a problem.'

'Seriously,' John said, 'I'd like to join the OUDS. But you have to audition and I don't suppose I'd be good enough.'

'If music be the food of love,' said Angelo, 'I'll have a second helping.' Everyone laughed, but Christopher couldn't help noticing that Angelo looked him very challengingly in the face as he said it.

Christopher had been dreaming of auditioning for the OUDS without telling Tom in advance, and then surprising him with the news that he'd bagged a major role in something. Even after five years he still wanted to do things that would make Tom admire him. Not a day had passed during those years during which Christopher hadn't thought through the terrible scenario: the one in which Tom would turn to him, perhaps on waking one morning, perhaps after a goodnight kiss, perhaps on a bus or in a train, and say, smiling through a shared pain, 'It's been wonderful, Chris darling, all these years. I wouldn't have missed a minute of it. But it's time to say it's over. I need to move on.' The thought of this made Christopher shudder some dozen times every day.

But now he thought that perhaps they couldn't all four of them join the OUDS. There were thousands of people at the university and the OUDS only did two or three shows each term. It was unrealistic to think of them all ending up in the cast of the same production of, say, Julius Caesar.

Conversation turned to other things. Neither Tom nor Christopher was insensitive enough to ask the younger pair if they'd met any girls yet, but Angelo had no reason not to put the question to John, albeit teasingly. To the others' surprise John answered very seriously, absently fingering the lapel of his sports jacket, 'One or two prospects actually. And a particularly nice girl I met on the tour of the Bodleian. Brunette. Lucy.'

'Well,' said Tom, and neither of the others could think of a response that sounded more appropriate or interesting.

Of course, they realised the next morning – societies morning – you didn't have to audition for the Oxford University Dramatic Society merely to become a member. You simply joined the society today, signing up at the stall. Tom had known that once but had forgotten over the years. Though you would have to audition, obviously, if you wanted a role in a particular production. Tom and Christopher asked to be kept informed of future audition calls. It had occurred to Tom that he might go and audition for something without telling Christopher in advance, and then surprise him with the news that he'd bagged a really good part in something. He now saw that the chance of surprising Christopher in this way was unlikely. Living together, receiving the same audition calls, they would end up going to the same auditions. They might even find themselves competing for the same parts. And that wouldn't do at all, Tom realised. He had been young when he'd embarked on his life adventure with Christopher. Luckily he had been blessed with an innate understanding that competing for things could sound the death knell for any homosexual love-relationship. It wasn't such a big issue with heterosexual couples, he guessed. Partners of opposite sexes began from a starting point of difference. There were differences of gender, physical, emotional, mental. Whereas the difficulty for a homosexual couple was that you were already too much alike to start with. Especially if you were close in age. You had the same ambitions, the same needs and wants. And, not to put too fine a point on it, the same things made your cocks twitch.

Presumably Angelo and John were also at societies morning. But Tom and Christopher didn't cross paths with them. The occasion, with a multitude of stalls laid out in the vast space of the Sheldonian, was attended by thousands, so this non-encounter was not surprising.

That afternoon Christopher had an introductory meeting with his college history group and their tutors, while Tom was free. He wandered around the covered market for a while, smiling, as he could never help doing, every time he encountered the pillar box that incongruously stood in the centre of the glass-roofed hall, and bought some things for supper. Then, in no hurry to go home and start cooking, he called in at The Cross-Keys and bought himself a half pint. The Cross-Keys had been a favourite haunt of his during his undergraduate days. But back then he had come here to meet friends, or come here with friends, not as a solitary drinker. He looked around him now. There were a few students among the mid-day drinkers but he knew none of them. All were nearly ten years younger than he was. He felt a sudden stab of loneliness and wondered for a moment if he had done the right thing in accompanying Christopher to Oxford. Perhaps he should simply have got a job somewhere nearby and, while supporting Christopher from a prudent distance, let his lover get on with the business of being an undergraduate.

Someone walked in from the courtyard and looked straight towards him. The face broke into a grin and Tom realised with a shock that this was Angelo. He walked up to the table where Tom was sitting. 'I thought I might find you here,' he said. 'I mean, I thought I might find one of you, or both of you.'

'How on earth...?'

'Easy as anything. You talked about your plans for the day in the pub last night. One of you was going to go shopping at lunchtime in the market. So you said, and so

I remembered.' He paused a second and the expression on his face altered, infinitesimally but, Tom thought, very charmingly. 'Actually I forgot all about it. Only I happened to be taking a short cut through the market just now… It's an amazing place, isn't it? And the weirdest thing is there's a red post-box right in the middle. Wonder if it's the only indoor pillar box on the planet.'

'I doubt it,' said Tom.

'And it was then I remembered. But I didn't see either of you. Passed this pub on the way out, though, and – well, I know the two of you have an enamoration for pubs and so…'

'I'd better get you a drink,' said Tom. 'Now you're here.' He thought, it wasn't me he came looking for; it was Christopher. He said, 'By the way, I don't think there's such a word as enamoration.'

'Better be half a pint, then,' said Angelo. 'As it's the middle of the day. And as that's what you're having.'

'Mmm,' said Tom. 'Though now you're here I think I shall have another.' He fished two half-crowns from the pocket of his jacket. 'You go and get them. Save my old legs. Practise your social skills. I'll keep your seat at the table.' Angelo took the half-crowns and went off to the bar.

'So tell me about this house you live in,' Angelo said brightly as soon as he was back, was seated, and they'd said cheers to each other. 'Somewhere along Walton Street?'

'Walton Street leads towards it,' said Tom a bit unsteadily. He was having a vision of one way this afternoon might turn out, but refusing to let himself believe it. He willed himself back into the conversation. 'Walton Street leads to Jericho. Which used to be workers' cottages. These days they've been bijou-ised. Well, we live in one of them.'

'I don't think there's such a word as bijou-ised,' said Angelo.

They walked together up the Corn, and Magdalen Street. Down Beaumont Street, turned right at the front entrance of Worcester into Walton Street... And am I imagining all this? thought Tom.

'It's sweet,' said Angelo, looking up at the front of the cottage as Tom unlocked the door.

'Attached on both sides, as you see,' said Tom, 'so there's a limit to how much noise you can make, but apart from that it's about as perfect as things come.'

'Mmm,' said Angelo. They were both inside now. They moved from hall to living-room.

'You met Mike,' said Tom. 'He's a palaeontologist.' He gestured towards the glass cases, feeling they needed explaining. 'We didn't install those.'

'Interesting though,' said Angelo, inspecting ammonites and the imprint of a feather from one of the world's earlier birds.

'There's tea or coffee,' said Tom. 'Though actually Mike did leave behind the remains of a bottle of whisky. He wasn't going to take that to Africa, obviously. Not that I should be suggesting whisky in the middle of the afternoon...'

'Whisky sounds fine to me,' said Angelo. Alarmingly eagerly. 'Tell me,' he said, plonking himself down on the sofa while Tom went to the sideboard in search of glasses and the bottle, 'has the change in the law made any practical difference to you?'

'Which law?' asked Tom absently. He was concentrating on the whisky and the two glasses and trying to estimate what the correct dose would be.

'The homosexuality bill. I mean...'

'It brought us back to England,' Tom said. 'That was a pretty major thing.'

'Yes,' said Angelo, 'but in practice people go on having sex anyway and always have done, whatever the law might say. I mean, look at me.' Tom turned away from the sideboard and did so. 'Any kind of sex I've ever had has always been illegal, and – unless it's with a girl – will remain so for the next three years.'

'Maybe you should take a leaf out of John Moyse's book, then. Try it with a girl.' Tom carried the two small tumblers back to where Angelo sat on the sofa, handed one glass to Angelo, then sat down next to him.

'John talks about girls. But it is just talk. He's never done anything with one. Never will.'

'How can you be sure? Men like John are the dependable types we rely on to bring children into the world. Someone has to pay for our pensions one day after all.' Tom realised that with that flippant remark he had bracketed Angelo, or might seem to have done, with the type of men to which Christopher and he belonged. He wondered if Angelo had realised.

'I suppose I might grow out of it,' said Angelo. He took a sip of whisky, then sprawled backwards a bit dreamily. He spread his legs a little, as if unthinkingly. Tom hadn't kept his very tidily together when he'd sat down. Suddenly he and Angelo were touching knee to knee. 'But right now I don't particularly want to.'

'Want to what?' asked Tom, unsure if he was being cautious or just pretending to be.

'Stop preferring boys.'

'Meaning…?' Tom found himself pushing his knee a little harder against Angelo's. He felt Angelo pressing his own knee a little harder into him in return. He thought there was something cosmic about that mutual squeeze.

'Meaning that I like doing it with boys. Not particularly interested in girls.' Angelo shrugged. That is, the top half of him did. The bottom half of him remained unmoved, pressing tightly against Tom.

'Boys?' Tom queried. His voice had quietened now. 'Up to what sort of age? How would you…? How would someone of your age define a boy?'

'Up to about thirty, I suppose,' said Angelo in a very matter-of-fact way. 'I never really thought about it. But certainly not excluding Christopher or you.'

At that moment Tom found it not only the easiest thing in the world but also the most natural thing to place a hand on Angelo's nearest thigh.

FIFTEEN

'Perhaps we'd better not tell Chris about this, eh?' said
Tom when they were putting their clothes back on.

'No. Obviously,' said Angelo, hopping about, getting
into his cords. Tom inspected the bed-sheets carefully,
though trying not to let the inspection appear too
obvious to Angelo. There were no wet patches or
splashes; they'd both been careful, thankfully, to avoid
those. If Tom were obliged to change the sheets
Christopher would certainly wonder why, as they had
only been on three days. But would the bed, or maybe
the whole room, be scented with Angelo's healthy
boyish musk? Tom decided that once Angelo was on his
way he could hang the sheets out in the yard for an hour.
The bedroom window could be left open during that
time. When Christopher arrived home for his supper all
would be well.

'Well, now you've found the place...' Tom left the
sentence dangling while they walked downstairs. There
didn't seem to be much to hang about for. Neither of
them could find very much to say. They gave each
other's lips a peck while Tom's hand was on the latch of
the door.

'And you must come and visit me sometime,' said
Angelo. 'Nuffield Building, twenty-six.'

Tom opened the door. 'I hadn't forgotten the number
of your room,' he said. He failed to keep a thoughtful
half-smile from his lips.

Angelo hopped out onto the pavement. 'See you soon,'
he said, then turned and walked away. Tom closed the
door behind him. The house felt very claustrophobic,
very changed. Practical things, he told himself and,
thinking about the sheets, went upstairs.

Christopher found Tom almost startlingly bright and
cheerful when he came home at the end of that

afternoon. But there was a tension about his eyes and lips that caused him to ask, 'Have you had a hectic day?'

A few days later, when freshers' week was over and the academic term had properly started for them both, a Roneo-ed note appeared in their individual pigeon-holes at their two colleges. The OUDS was going to present a production of Romeo and Juliet, for which open auditions would be held in a couple of days. The idea that both of them had had, of going to audition secretly, had to be abandoned. Both had joined the Dramatic Society, and each would know that the other had received an identical audition call. Instead they discussed it together that evening. 'Well, do we or don't we?' said Christopher.

'I say we do,' said Tom without hesitation. 'So long as we agree not to mind if one of us gets cast and the other doesn't, or if neither of us gets cast at all.'

'Fair enough,' said Christopher. 'I agree.' Christopher had a funny, rather formal and old-mannish way sometimes of saying *I agree*. It made Tom smile affectionately to himself. It had done all these years.

They arrived for the auditions separately. They were unsure to what extent they could flagrantly behave as a homosexual couple and to what extent they should simply allow others to surmise. They shared an address: they let anyone who asked know that. But beyond that they didn't go out of their way to flaunt their coupledom. They didn't kiss or hug in public, nor even stand too close when they talked together among others. Queer couples were still very much the object of ridicule. There were Julian and Sandy on the radio, and people with silly names in bawdy jokes. Claude and Cecil. Or Ben Doone and Phil McCavity among the less refined. So when they came, three minutes apart, to the audition room at the Playhouse they greeted each other but not effusively. And the same went for Angelo who, with a couple of friends of his own age, was also there.

The director, who rejoiced in the name of Basil, was a few years younger even than Christopher and he looked slightly taken aback by the arrival of the two senior men, but thoughtfully found them speeches of the older characters to read – The Prince, the Chorus, Old Capulet, Old Montague – when their turns came. Both thought they did rather well. They also thought, though neither of them mentioned this immediately, that Angelo read splendidly. He was given speeches of Romeo, Mercutio and Benvolio to do. But so were all the other male hopefuls of his age, and there were an awful lot of those. Tom offered Christopher a word of caution. 'It's one thing to do well, and to know that you have. But that doesn't clinch anything. It depends entirely on what the chap is looking for.'

When the proceedings were finished Basil thanked everyone for coming, and for being so talented. He had a few more people to see later, he said, but decisions would be made no later than by teatime the following day. There would be a note in everybody's pigeon-hole, he told them, whether they had secured a part or not. He dismissed the assembly with an authoritative nod. Everyone stood up. At that point Angelo came towards Christopher and Tom. Tom could see no sign of awkwardness in his manner and was highly impressed. He would not have been able to behave with such aplomb had he been in Angelo's situation at Angelo's age. He was only just about able to muster the sang-froid required for his own situation vis-à-vis Angelo now.

'No sign of John, though,' Christopher was saying to Angelo. They were walking out into Beaumont Street with a gaggle of others. 'I was sure he'd show up for something like this. Right up his street.'

'Oh, haven't you heard?' Angelo answered brightly. 'He got snapped up for something else. Pretty major. He won't have time for this as well.'

'A part in something else? I didn't know…'

'Well, sort of,' said Angelo. 'Yes and no. They're doing a revue later in the term. John told them – you know that list we filled in of special abilities? – well, he put piano playing and they immediately got him to sight-read stuff for them. He's landed the job of pianist and musical director for the revue.'

'Wow,' said Tom. But then he reflected that he – and Christopher – had last heard John play when he was thirteen. He'd been pretty assured and technically competent even then. There was no reason to suppose his skills would have failed to develop further over the past five years.

Christopher said, 'Good for him.'

The following evening Tom and Christopher compared notes in the most literal of senses. Tom's note had been deposited in his pigeon-hole at Teddy Hall, Christopher's in his pigeon-hole at Oriel. Christopher's note informed him he'd been cast in the role of old Montague, father of Romeo. His first rehearsal would be tomorrow evening. He was delighted, elated even, but anxious as he walked home to Jericho that Tom might not be too willing to share his excitement if he himself had not been given a part.

But he had been given a part. 'Friar Lawrence.' Tom showed him the note he'd had. 'No rehearsal tomorrow, though. I don't appear until Act Two. Wearing a monk's habit. So I won't get to show off my lovely legs in tights.' Christopher wasn't sure if Tom was joking or being serious. Neither was Tom himself.

'I probably won't get to show my legs off either,' said Christopher in a spirit of solidarity and support.

'Montague's got to be forty. In those days men went into long gowns in middle-age, I think.' An unspoken but happy thought lay beneath the surface of this exchange: that even after five years together Tom and Christopher still admired the contours of each other's limbs. And all the rest.

They had an early supper the next day. Tom had some work to do in his college library while Christopher was rehearsing; they arranged to meet at The Turf at ten o'clock. They walked together as far as the Playhouse and parted on the pavement outside. When Christopher arrived in the rehearsal room a large crowd of student actors was gathered in readiness for the first run-through of Act One. For while professional productions of Shakespeare cut characters and scenes ruthlessly, the first for reasons of economic necessity, the second out of consideration for the audiences' patience, no such concerns affect productions mounted by students. Where number of cast is concerned it's the more the merrier, and time is not an issue for people whose evenings stretch infinitely ahead, just like their lives.

So the play began with an untrimmed first scene, Samson and Gregory struggling to make their wordplay on collier, choler and collar laughter-worthy four hundred years after Shakespeare penned it, before struggling with drawn swords against Abraham and Balthasar, the next pair of characters to make an appearance. Except that there weren't any swords this evening.

'OK,' said Basil. 'We'll go to Benvolio's entrance. A friend I know who does fencing will set all the fight sequences when he comes up next week.'

'What about swords?' the lad playing Sampson queried disappointedly.

'They'll be coming in due course,' said Basil, just managing to be suave. 'They just need sorting out from the store. Don't worry. OK now. Enter Benvolio, closely followed by Tybalt…'

Benvolio entered. *'Part, fools! Put up your swords; you know not what you do.'* Benvolio was Angelo.

There was a bit of a muddle next as some half dozen further characters entered, bumping into each other because they had their scripts in front of them and were peering into them, trying to follow the dialogue and not miss their own cues, while scuffling a bit with each other in between the lines. Basil stopped the proceedings and worked out the moves for them. 'Never mind the words for a moment…' Now Capulet arrived with his wife, then Christopher strode onto the stage as Montague, alongside his own wife: father and mother to Romeo. The actor playing Capulet, who was big and burly, promptly sprang on Christopher and knocked him to the floor, where he lay pinned beneath Capulet.

'Hey,' said Christopher, suddenly angered. 'Not as hard as that. It's a play we're in. Not a real fight!'

Those were not the words that Shakespeare had written for Montague. Basil didn't need to point this out. 'Stand up both of you.' He managed a voice of authority here. 'Montague's right, Capulet. Don't fight him. Act it.'

'Sorry,' said Capulet. 'I got a bit carried away.' He took hold of Christopher now by the elbows, as gently as if he was going to give him a kiss.

'Thou villain, Capulet!' said Christopher. *'Hold me not. Let me go.'*

His wife piped up, completing the rhyme. *'Thou shalt not stir one foot to seek a foe.'*

The Prince of Verona swanned in at that moment and dispersed the considerable crowd with the most beautifully composed speech that ever did duty as a riot act. With everyone else now gone Christopher found himself alone on stage with Angelo. Christopher spoke first. *'Who set this ancient quarrel new abroach? Speak, nephew, were you by when it began?'* Until this moment Christopher hadn't recalled, if he'd ever known, that Benvolio was Montague's nephew. It came to him as a very poignant discovery now.

Angelo shone his dark brown eyes into Christopher's blue ones.. He was taller than Christopher by an inch, they both now realised.

'Here were the servants of your adversary
And yours fighting ere I did approach:
I drew to part them; in the instant came
The fiery Tybalt, with his sword prepar'd,
Which, as he breathed defiance to my ears,
He swung about his head, and cut the winds,
Who, nothing hurt withal, hiss'd him in scorn.
While we were interchanging thrusts and blows,
Came more and more, and fought on part and part,
Till the prince came, who parted either part.'

Angelo did the speech beautifully, Christopher thought. But there was something else. He held his script – the Arden Edition paperback – low and barely glanced at it. His eyes were fixed almost all the time on Christopher.

He's learnt it already, Christopher thought. The idea flashed through his mind, most flatteringly, that Angelo had known in advance who would be playing Montague, but he dismissed it quickly. He'd had no information to the effect that Angelo would be Benvolio. So there was no reason to imagine that Angelo would have known Christopher was to play Montague.

The scene went on. They talked about Romeo, who was Benvolio's cousin and Montague's son.

'Away from light steals home my heavy son,' said Christopher.

'And private in his chamber pens himself,
Shuts up his windows, locks fair daylight out,

And makes himself an artificial night.
Black and portentous must this humour prove
Unless good counsel may the cause remove.'

'*My noble uncle,*' said Angelo, '*do you know the cause?*' A second later he glanced rather theatrically towards the wings, then said, '*See where he comes: so please you, step aside;*

I'll know his grievance or be much denied.'

A second later it was time for Christopher to leave the stage. They were only doing Act One this evening. Christopher had no more left to do in it. But Angelo did. So Christopher stayed to watch.

When Angelo was off-stage they sat together and passed whispered comments on the performances of the actors who were on-stage. They couldn't comment together on one of the highlights of Act One: Mercutio's Queen Mab speech. Christopher thought the boy playing Mercutio had done it rather well. He looked forward to asking Angelo – to whose character the speech had been delivered, and who had listened to it on stage – if he had thought the same. But the chance wouldn't come yet. The last scene of the act was the Capulets' ball, to which Montague had understandably not been invited. But Angelo, alias Benvolio, was there, although he had only one line in it. *(Away, be gone; the sort is at the best.)* For the rest of the scene he simply had to react. Rather a lot, Christopher thought. He would need to tell him tactfully about that.

They worked on to the end of the scene and then Basil sat everyone down and read out, and elaborated on, his notes. There were none for Christopher and none for Angelo, to their combined astonishment. Then they were dismissed. Probably, thought Christopher, there would be a general wildebeest-type migration towards the nearest pub, the Gloucester Arms. He didn't have time to pursue this thought or act on it, though, because Angelo said to him, sweetly, simply, 'What are you doing now?'

'I'm meeting Tom in the Turf at ten,' he said. The unplanned alliteration gave him a jolt.

'Hey,' said Angelo. 'I said I'd meet people in The Turf at ten o'clock. We can go together.' He looked at his watch. 'It's not quite nine yet…' Angelo looked Christopher very steadily in the eye as he let this thought float.

'I came up to your room one day last week,' Christopher said. 'You weren't in.' He hadn't meant to say that. He just heard the words sliding out.

'Pity,' said Angelo. 'But it's only two hundred yards away. Want to…?'

'Yes,' said Chris.

They extricated themselves from the wildebeest herd that was making for the Gloucester Arms and headed down Beaumont Street. Ahead of them the moon-like clock face above the gate of Worcester College beckoned them, while immediately above it, by coincidence, a real full moon, apparently the same size as the clock face, peered down and shone on the twin roofs of Worcester's frontage: one block the chapel, the other the dining-hall. 'Well,' said Angelo as they walked, 'ain't that nice.'

'You know you're not supposed to say ain't,' said Christopher facetiously, then found that he'd clasped Angelo's hand for a split second as he spoke. Neither of them reacted to that.

They walked together through the vaulted arch, nodding to the duty porter in his cubby-hole as they passed. 'Turn left,' said Angelo when they got into the cloister. 'Though, silly me, of course you know that.' They emerged from the Georgian arcade and went down the steps. On the pathway of twenty or thirty yards that led to the Nuffield Building across the grass Christopher took Angelo's hand again. This time he was bolder as well as deliberate. He didn't unclasp it, and nor did Angelo attempt to shake the handclasp off.

Up the staircase, hands unlocked now although a bit reluctantly, Angelo opened his door, put lights on and showed Christopher in. Then he threw himself backwards into one of the two armchairs, and Christopher, taking his cue, threw himself into the other one. Now was when the choreography grew difficult, Christopher realised. It would have been easier in Jericho, where there was a sofa at least. Angelo said, 'Want a coffee?' not very confidently and Christopher said, 'Maybe not. We're having a beer in forty-five minutes.' What he meant, as they both fully realised, was that they needed to get on with it. Whatever it was.

'Would you think me a bit brash if I asked you to come next door and see my bedroom?' Angelo asked.

'I wouldn't think that brash at all,' said Christopher, thinking how conveniently brave Angelo was. They both stood up.

The bedroom was neither large nor luxurious. But it had a bed in it. That was the big thing going for it. Now they stood together, carefully not looking at the bed but at each other. I have to take the lead here, Christopher thought, with a sudden flutter of nerves inside him. I've never done this before, he thought. It's always been the other boy who's started it. As if planning to adjust Angelo's shirt he put his two hands out and primly grasped him just above each hip.

'You've seen me with my shirt off,' said Angelo, managing to keep his voice steady, though only just. 'But I've never seen you with yours off.'

Christopher didn't rise to the bait immediately. Let Angelo wait for once. 'I saw you with your shirt off that time in Paris. When the odious Charles was starting to strip you off. But I've seen you with the whole lot off, don't forget. On bath nights. When you stood up in the tub with a full erection and flirted with me outrageously.'

'Did I?' asked Angelo, as if he'd forgotten the incidents. Perhaps he had. A lot happens to people between the ages of thirteen and eighteen; there's enough there for some of it to be forgotten without being missed.

'All right,' said Christopher. 'But I don't have any hair on my chest. I have to warn you.'

'That's all right,' said Angelo. 'These days I've probably got enough for both of us.'

That gave Christopher a jolt. When he'd seen Angelo naked all those years ago the boy had sported a proud little pubic bush but his chest had been hairless. As had still been the case when he'd seen Angelo shirtless six months later in Paris. A lightning bolt of lust shot through Christopher at that moment. As swiftly as the thunder that follows the flash he pulled his shirt off.

Angelo's hands were all over Christopher's chest at once, quickly homing in on his pale pink nipples. 'Yours off too,' Christopher murmured. He started to unbutton Angelo from the collar downwards. That brought his lips very close to Angelo's. They began, brushingly, to kiss each other.

Angelo hadn't been boasting when he'd said he had enough chest hair for the two of them. Christopher thought you could have stuffed an armchair with it.

What they both did next came automatically, as perhaps it does to all members of the male sex when they are feeling relaxed and uninhibited. They felt each other's dicks through their trousers. Christopher's first reaction, once he'd grasped the thing and got a feel for its dimensions, was that Angelo's was now quite a bit bigger than his own. Bigger than Tom's too, perhaps, though he would need to subject it to a proper, trouserless examination to be sure of that. Meanwhile Angelo was now running his fingertips up and down Christopher's own erection in his trousers and the feeling this was giving Christopher was sublime. He said, 'Perhaps we should get horizontal.'

Where had that line come to him from? He'd never before used it or even heard it. Because most of his sexual experience to date had taken place in Paris his unfamiliarity with the language used in sexual encounters on his home side of the Channel was understandable.

They pulled their own trousers, shoes and socks off swiftly, discarding them on the floor, before leaping onto the bed and onto each other. 'What do you want to do?' Christopher asked as, by way of a warm-up, they cuddled and tussled and pressed and twisted their stiff cocks together.

'Do you want to fuck me?' Angelo offered. His sense of the natural order of things convinced him that Christopher, six years his senior, should have first choice when it came to what would happen next.

'Yes,' said Christopher without hesitation. His own upbringing had been similar. 'Turn over.'

Angelo had apparently had some practice and there wasn't much showing or explaining for Christopher to do. Angelo turned onto his front, then drew his knees beneath him till his buttocks rose helpfully towards Christopher, and cradled his forehead in his folded arms atop the pillow.

There was a minor confusion as to whose hand would deal with Angelo's cock, unseen beneath his belly, while Christopher fucked him. After a minute's fumbling Christopher withdrew his hand from there and let Angelo get on with it. At least he'd offered. A couple of minutes later Angelo ejaculated unmistakeably, with a good deal of squirming and gasping. That uncapped

Christopher's well almost immediately, and he felt himself pouring spurt after spurt deep into Angelo. Five years this had been pending, he thought. Bizarrely he imagined himself giving away a long-hoarded necklace – pearl after pearl after pearl.

SIXTEEN

Christopher had been introduced to The Turf Tavern by
Tom, who'd known and frequented it when he was an
undergraduate years ago. It was unlike any other pub
that Christopher had encountered before. Whereas most
pubs have an interior, surrounded by walls, with the
streets and alleyways kept firmly at bay outside, The
Turf had a conjuncture of alleyways at the heart of it,
from which its various bars led off in different
directions. Its walls were the outside walls of the
colleges that hemmed it in and created the alleyways. It
was difficult to find if you went looking for it. But when
you weren't looking for it you somehow found yourself
there. As Alice discovered in Through the Looking-
Glass. Christopher wondered if Carroll had got his idea
for the kernel conceit of that book from a difficulty he
might himself have experienced, a century earlier, in
locating The Turf.

But experience is a great teacher and Christopher,
having visited the place with Tom three times in the last
fortnight, had no difficulty in finding the place tonight
with Angelo. They spotted Tom at once, standing under
a floodlight in the centre of the little twisting courtyard
with a trim-figured grey-haired man whom Christopher
recognized but for the moment couldn't place.

'Nicholas. Christopher.' Tom promptly reintroduced
them. 'We had dinner together with our landlord on our
first night here.'

'Of course,' said Christopher, recalling clearly now the
urbane chemistry don with whom they'd sat at table at
The Randolph with Mike and two others. That evening
seemed an aeon ago.

'It was Nicholas who suggested we join the OUDS,'
Tom reminded Christopher. 'I've just been telling him

how we took his advice, and about Romeo and Juliet…'
He broke off. 'Nicholas, this is Angelo.'

Christopher added, 'Who is giving a very creditable portrayal of Benvolio.'

'I'm sure you are,' Nicholas said, shaking Angelo's hand with the unmaskable pleasure of any homosexual man of fifty who's being introduced to a handsome eighteen-year-old.

'We've just run through Act One,' said Angelo with a degree of composure that Christopher thought was, in the circumstances, enviable. 'It went quite well.'

'It'll go even better,' said Christopher in a senior-statesman tone, 'when the boys have got proper swords.'

'The boys, are we?' said Angelo coquettishly. 'Back to boarding school? And what does that make you?' He turned to Nicholas and said very deliberately, 'These two used to teach me at my prep school.'

To the others' astonishment Nicholas said, 'Ah, so you're the one. I had a letter from Mike this morning. He's in Nairobi. He mentioned meeting you.' Even Angelo, who was remarkably unflappable these days, seemed awed by the news that he'd got a mention in despatches sent from Kenya by someone he'd met for a mere second or two.

But he pulled himself together quickly and said, 'Christopher, what are you having? My turn. You two've been buying me drinks for weeks now.'

Neither Tom nor Christopher took any notice of that last sentence right then. But it would return to them in the days to come, written in letters of fire.

They gave each other conducted tours of their different colleges. Tom proudly showed off Teddy Hall – having spent three years there previously he knew the place extremely well – while Christopher took Tom round Oriel less knowledgeably and a bit more timidly. He didn't live in college, he had tutorials and occasional lunches there; he didn't know many of the other students except for those in his History cohort. Walking around the rooms and courtyards, the chapel and the great hall he still felt a bit of an outsider, anxious that he might be challenged, in front of Tom, by some official who would call out, 'What are you doing here?'

Of that little local difficulty Tom had no inkling. He had just returned from his second Romeo and Juliet rehearsal and had difficulties of his own. 'Basil's a total idiot,' he told Christopher as they passed beneath the statues of Edward II and Charles I standing in their niches like a barometer's weather-men. 'He hasn't read it properly and what he has read he hasn't understood. It's the blind leading the blind.'

'It's because they're mostly eighteen- and nineteen-year-olds,' Christopher said patiently. 'You knew that before you joined. You happen to be twenty-seven and they happen not to be. That's all it is. If you were going to have trouble with it you shouldn't have signed up. Anyway, most successful student productions succeed in spite of the director, not because of him.'

There was no need to say *because of him or her*. Directors of student drama were ipso facto male. Although women students were allowed these days to have a crack at female roles, they found themselves more often involved with make-up and costumes and the necessary but unexciting task of sewing buttons on.

'You're right, of course,' Tom allowed. 'It's just that it gets a bit frustrating at times.' Tom got frustrated in the day-to-day course of his studies too, Christopher knew. It couldn't be easy for him, Christopher guessed: being taught how to teach from the very beginning when he'd already been doing it for years. All right, so he'd been teaching English as a foreign language and now he was being trained to teach history; but presumably the classroom management skills required were much the same. Christopher wondered about himself. Would he be on a post-grad teaching course himself in three years' time? By then he'd be the age that Tom was now. It was impossible to look so far ahead. It made his head swim. Even looking a little way ahead, say just as far as Christmas, was fraught with difficult ideas.

'We need to talk about Christmas,' he said now. They were climbing the steps towards the shade of the portico. If they were airing problem subjects, he thought, they might as well get this one out in the open now.

'We're still in October,' Tom said.

'Our parents will have been thinking about it for months now. Just because they haven't said anything... Well, you know that perfectly well.'

'By which you mean,' began Tom heavily, 'that your parents will expect you to spend the Christmas vacation with them. Without me.'

'Not the whole vacation,' said Christopher placatingly. 'But a few days over Christmas itself, yes.'

'And the New Year?'

'That may be get-out-of-able. Negotiable. To be discussed.'

'And me?' asked Tom. 'Where am I supposed to be?'

'Oh come off it. Your parents will want to see you too.' An idea came to him. 'You could take them to Boulogne. We've spent the last few Christmases there.'

'On the money I'm not earning now that I'm a student again?' said Tom.

'Well, they'd pay, obviously.' Christopher reflected a second on what he'd just said. 'Sorry, Tom.' He paused again, looked round to check that no-one could see them in the dark shelter of the portico, then leaned forward and kissed Tom quickly on the lips. He went on. 'The thing is, I had a letter from my mother today. She wants to come up and see me – see the college and the place where I live – next Saturday.'

'Ah,' said Tom. 'Now I see.'

'Well yes. And obviously she'll bring up the subject of Christmas. She's only human. She can't not do.' Christopher had paid his planned visit to his parents in the days before the start of term. Although he'd entered his parental home – for the first time in five years – with his stomach clenched in a knot of fear the day had actually gone very well. His father had been genial and gentle with him, and no mention had been made of sin or aberrant behaviour. But no mention had been made, by any of them, of Tom. Christopher had felt quite uncomfortable about this: dishonest, cowardly and disloyal, Even so, the tight knot of his entrails had come unpicked loop by loop as the day wore on and he'd returned to Tom at the Admiral Digby that night with a spring in his step and in his heart a feeling of great relief.

'You did know she'd show up here,' Christopher reminded Tom. 'We talked about getting someone else to stand in as my house-mate for the day. You said jokingly that you'd turn up as a pretend electrician and read the meter or something.'

'The people who read meters aren't electricians.'

'No, of course. You know what I mean.' They opened the great door and entered the hall. 'Hammerbeam roof,' said Christopher, pointing upwards to the graceful cantilevered construction of king posts and queen posts, purlins and collar beams. 'You can still see the louvres where they used to let the smoke out – in the days when the fire was in the centre of the hall.' He introduced Tom to some of the portraits on the walls. The ones he could remember. 'Edward the Second. Sir Walter Raleigh. Matthew Arnold. Cecil Rhodes.' Tom murmured appreciatively. Eight years ago he'd had a fling with a student from Oriel. He'd given Tom this identical tour. But now was not the moment to tell Christopher so.

'It's fine,' Tom said. 'I mean having your mother come up on Saturday. I'll find things to do.' One thing he might do, he thought, would be to seek out Angelo. Nuffield Building. Room twenty-six. It was not an address he would forget easily.

Christopher met his mother at the station. The day was warm and sunny, a little October bonus, and he took her first, by means of the canal towing-path, to the house in Jericho. His mother was more than pleased with it. 'It's wonderful,' she said. 'I'd pictured it as much smaller, shabbier. More studenty, if you like. More run-down.'

'Well, it isn't studenty because, as I've told you, it's owned, and usually lived in, by a don. We were very lucky to get it.'

'We?' queried Mrs McGing.

'Charlie and me,' invented Christopher hastily.

'Of course,' said his mother. 'Though surely, *Charlie and I*. How many years did you teach English for?'

'Or even, *For how many years did you teach English?*' They laughed together. It seemed they'd both decided to be friends for the day.

Out of politeness Mrs McGing inspected the objects in the glass cases. She didn't ask her son to name or explain them. They were not what she had come to Oxford to see. 'Let's go and see the college,' said Christopher over-brightly. 'Then we can find some lunch somewhere.' If he had a game plan of any sort at all it was to keep his mother on the move constantly, not give her time to ask difficult questions, and send her home tired to the point of speechlessness, like a dog that's been walked all day.

Christopher was ten days bolder than he'd been when he'd given Tom his hesitant conducted tour of Oriel and now did a very good job of it. 'I can't help noticing the oriel windows all around the place,' Mrs McGing said at one point. 'Did the window get its name from the college, or was it the other way around?'

'The jury's still out on that one,' said Christopher with the confident authority of someone answering a question to which no-one really knows the answer. 'It's a bit of a chicken and egg thing. There was a Sir Somebody Oriole involved in the founding of the college, I think. But then the windows were always there…' He shrugged. 'At any rate the connection between the college and the windows was so strong that even the newer buildings have oriel windows in them. Right up to 1911. None of the original oriel windows survive.'

'Interesting,' said Mrs McGing.

'Let's go and have some lunch,' said Christopher.

They went to The Mitre, on the corner of Turl Street and The High. 'It's actually owned by Lincoln College just down there,' Christopher said, pointing along narrow Turl Street, shadowy even at midday.

'Lucky old Lincoln,' said Mrs McGing.

The Mitre went in for immaculate white table-cloths and napkins in rings. It also had large plate-glass windows like a shop's. Passers-by who were interested could peer in easily and see who was lunching or dining there, while those within had an excellent view of whoever might be passing by on the outside. Christopher found his composure mildly disturbed while they were eating their prawn cocktail starter (it was still something of a novelty back then) by the sight of Tom walking past in cheerful discussion with Nicholas the chemistry don. They looked like two people who were on their way to have lunch together somewhere. Nicholas didn't glance in through the window, but Tom did. Christopher had told him that his plans might include lunch there. Tom saw Christopher evidently, for his eyes widened slightly and he began instinctively to raise one hand to give a wave, but then let it fall back again as he passed on. Christopher was able to offer only a flinch of surprise by way of a reply. The thought of Tom lunching with Nicholas startled him a bit. Tom hadn't said he was going to. But then, why should he have done? He had very sportingly agreed to keep away from the house at Jericho for the best part of a day. That gave him a day at a loose end. Christopher wasn't going to criticise him for what he chose to do with the day, or enquire too deeply into it.

'Charlie,' his mother was saying. 'What does he do?'

'Who?'

'Your house-mate.'

'Of course. He's doing a PGCE at St Edmund's Hall.' Provided names were changed to protect the guilty it was safe enough to tell the truth about most of everything else.

'I hope I'll meet him,' said Mrs McGing.

'That would be nice,' said Christopher. 'But it's a bit unlikely today. He's out to lunch with a friend. Oxford lunches can go on a very long time.'

'I hope you don't mean he drinks,' said his mother primly. Christopher saw her take a sudden narrow interest in his half-empty glass of white wine.

'No more than anybody else. I just meant that life here's pretty sociable. But if you don't meet him today, then – well, probably next time.' Dear God, thought Christopher, what have I said? What have I sentenced myself to? Three more years of this? Three more years at Oxford pretending I live with someone who isn't Tom? With someone who doesn't even exist? And then what? A whole lifetime of pretence unrolled ahead of Christopher just then. Oh what a tangled web… If dishes of fine crisp gammon and chips hadn't arrived just then

– with fried eggs on top of the gammon – Christopher would have tasted something like despair.

Tom had run into Nicholas in the covered market. A casual inquiry as to where Christopher was this morning had prompted Tom to spill the whole story of Christopher and his parents. He was surprised to hear himself pouring it all out: it wasn't the kind of thing he did usually. The result of this bout of candour was that Nicholas, in a spirit of combined kindness and opportunism, said, 'Then why don't you come and have lunch with me?' They were on their way to the White Horse when they passed The Mitre and Tom glanced in.

'I should have taken you to the Jolly Farmers, really,' said Nicholas, when they had got their pints, ordered sandwiches and sat down at a cosy table beneath the beams. 'It's quite well patronised by … by men of our kind. Though perhaps you knew it when you were up here before.'

'I didn't,' said Tom. 'I knew of the place and of its reputation. But I was far too shy to actually set foot through the door. And I hadn't admitted to myself back then that I was … of the kind I am.'

'Of course. It takes most of us a few years to work it out.' Nicholas paused a second. 'Tell me, you and Christopher. How did that come about? Or am I prying? Tell me to mind my own business if you like.'

'No,' said Tom. 'It's fine.' He told the story of how the two of them, he twenty-one and Christopher still just eighteen, had started new jobs together at Star of the Sea and had fallen in love within the first few days. 'Once you've actually fallen in love with a person of your own sex, and it's also the person you're sleeping with, it's difficult to go on pretending to yourself that you're other than who you are.'

'Yes, indeed,' said Nicholas, sounding wistful, and took a glug of beer. 'And your young friend Angelo...?'

So that story came out too. Tom had told Mike all about Angelo, believing that with Mike in Africa it was unlikely to be passed on. Yet Mike had mentioned Angelo in a letter from Kenya... Better than the story coming out in dribs and drabs from Mike in correspondence, Tom thought, that Nicholas should hear the whole story told by him now.

'My goodness,' said Nicholas, when Tom had finished. 'He does sound quite a lad. And have you ever... You and Chris, I mean...?'

'With Angelo? No, never,' said Tom firmly. There were times when the only possible thing to do was lie.

When the beer was drunk and the sandwiches eaten Tom thanked Nicholas profusely for buying him lunch, said he hoped they'd meet again soon, and got up to go. He wanted to be polite about it but he'd needed to make it clear to the older man that he hadn't been bought for the whole afternoon. He walked away along The Broad, then on towards Worcester College via George Street and Gloucester Green. He thought there was less chance of running into Christopher and his mother on this route than on the more direct way up Magdalen Street and down Beaumont.

Though Tom had never before set foot in Worcester's college grounds, Angelo had pointed out the Nuffield Building from the street outside and it wasn't difficult to find the place once you were on the inside. Tom climbed the stairs and found room twenty-six easily. The oak was open, but there was an envelope pinned to the inner door. Tom peered at it. Written on the outside was the single word *Tom*.

Tom tore the envelope open and pulled out the flimsy leaf, torn from a note-book, that nestled inside. Angelo had written, *I know Christopher has gone out with his mother, so I've gone to look for you at your house in Jericho. This note is just in case you decided to come and call on me!*

Tom let out a tiny sigh of disappointment. But then anxiety set quickly in. Christopher wouldn't be at lunch all afternoon. He might be out sightseeing with his mother now, but it was just as likely he'd have taken her back to Jericho for coffee or tea. If Angelo were to turn up on the doorstep... Quite apart from anything else Christopher would wonder how Angelo knew which house was theirs.

He hurried down the stairs. There was no knowing how long Angelo had been gone. If he'd left just minutes before... Tom ran all the way along Walton Street and into Jericho.

He met Angelo on the corner of two small streets, almost literally bumping into him. The most obvious thing to notice was that Angelo was not on his way to where Tom and Christopher lived but coming back again. The next thing was the expression on Angelo's face. He looked shocked and upset. The third thing was that when Tom tried to speak he found he couldn't. He'd been running so hard that he'd completely lost his breath.

'Tom, are you all right?' Angelo enquired anxiously. 'Have you been running? You're all puffed out.'

'I found your note,' said Tom eventually. 'Tell me, did you...?'

'It wasn't good,' said Angelo.

'You'd better tell me, then,' said Tom. He felt something sinking like a lead weight inside him.

'Do you want to sit down?'

'I'm fine,' panted Tom. 'Anyway, there isn't anywhere.' So they continued to stand on the pavement corner, facing each other, next to the wall of an anonymous house.

'I think I've done something stupid,' said Angelo.

Tom said, 'Join the club.'

'You've read my note so you know where I've just come from. I was about to knock at the door. I had my hand raised. But the door opened of its own accord and a woman – Chris's mother, I presumed – was standing there. I had to say something. I said, "I'm looking for Tom." The woman said, "Tom who?" I said, "Tom Sanders." I couldn't think fast enough. Of course I should have said I was looking for Chris.'

That might have helped, or it might not, Tom thought.

'She looked shocked. I saw her face go white. At that second Chris appeared behind her shoulder. You've read the expression *his face was a mask of horror*. Well, that's exactly how it was. He said very quickly, "You've come to the wrong house. He doesn't live here." I said I was sorry, that I'd made a mistake. I turned away quickly and walked away. I guessed they were coming out of the house anyway. To go to the station perhaps…'

Tom said, 'Fucking hell!' quietly. Then, looking past Angelo's shoulder, round the corner, 'Are they coming this way?'

'No. They took the little path that goes down to the canal bank. I saw them go. Look, Tom, I'm terribly sorry if I've opened my mouth and put my foot in it. I guessed from the look on her face that Chris's mother isn't OK about him and you. I should have thought, I suppose.'

'Perhaps,' said Tom. 'But there's another thing. How am I going to explain to Chris how you knew where our house is? You might have thought about that too.'

'Sorry, Tom.' Angelo looked even more discomfited than he'd done a minute ago. Then, after a second's pause for thought, he said, 'I don't know if it would make things easier if you both knew I've had sex with both of you…'

If this was going to make things easier that wasn't going to happen straightaway. Tom's breath, and his voice, came back to him. 'You what?' he practically shouted. 'You had sex with Chris? At our house?'

'Keep your hair on. I only did what I did with you. But it was in my room. And only the once. Same as with you.'

A window opened above them. A male voice called out, 'Keep your noise down. And keep your filthy little secrets to yourselves.' The window shut again very smartly. Not that either of them could think of anything very clever to shout back in reply.

'Oh shit, Angelo,' Tom said, more quietly. He found he was trembling all over. The expression *trembling like a leaf* came to his mind. To his great surprise he discovered that that was exactly how it felt.

'Do you want to come up to my room now?' Angelo asked. But the idea, which had been so alluring until just half an hour ago, was now about the least desirable prospect Tom could imagine.

SEVENTEEN

When Christopher returned home from seeing his mother onto the train he found Tom sitting on the sofa in the least relaxed state he could remember seeing him in.

'Well?' said Tom, still sitting.

'Well?' said Christopher, still standing.

'Your mother,' said Tom. 'I met Angelo in the street just after he'd called on you. He told me there was a bit of a disaster.'

'It was pretty awful,' said Christopher. 'I've had to lie and lie to her. It wasn't easy, and I don't think she believed me. I said that your being at the University was a coincidence. That we'd finished some years ago and that apart from passing each other in the street we had no contact.'

'You said all that?'

Christopher looked thoroughly miserable. 'I don't like lying but what else could I do? Angelo completely landed me in it. My mother and her bloody religion. I'm coming to think she's as mad as a hatter and so is every other practising Catholic. When she got on the train she turned back to me and said, "Be courageous," as if she'd been saving the phrase all day like a sweet in a handbag. I said, "See you at Christmas?" She sort of shuddered and said, "Yes. See you at Christmas."'

'I don't know,' said Tom, 'whether on balance you think that's a good outcome.'

'Nor do I,' said Christopher uncomfortably.

'Which brings us to the other thing,' Tom said.

'What?' said Christopher.

'Angelo.'

'What about Angelo?'

Tom said in a rather tense voice, 'We've both had sex with him.'

'What?!' said Christopher in a tone of astonishment.

'You already know that *you* have, so don't do the surprised bit. You say you don't like lying, but you're still doing it, if only in your tone of voice. I know what happened because Angelo told me. In the street outside. Half an hour ago.' He shrugged bitterly. 'Well, now I'm telling you that I've had the same intimacy.'

Christopher, still standing, nevertheless managed to give the impression of a punctured balloon. 'Here, of course,' he said flatly. 'That's how Angelo knew the way here. I sort of guessed that.' He paused and his eyes travelled involuntarily towards the ceiling. 'Upstairs? In our bed?' Tom nodded. You could imagine the movement hurt him. 'Which side was he on?'

'Your side,' said Tom without expression. Christopher winced and tried to disguise it. Tom still saw it. 'And you? In his room?'

Christopher said, 'He's only got a single.'

'For God's sake,' said Tom. 'As though the side or the size of the bed matters. Look... All those years ago, when we moved from Boulogne to Paris, we agreed we'd only have sex with other people when we were both together. Now we know that's changed.'

'Only with Angelo,' said Christopher hoarsely.

'There may have been others,' said Tom. 'On your side, I mean. That I haven't known about.'

'There haven't been, I swear it.'

'What's that worth now?' said Tom wearily. 'We've both blown it. There haven't been any others on my side either. But why should you believe that either? Neither of us will ever again be able to believe the other about anything.'

Christopher stood in the centre of the room motionless. Tom saw the tears start from his eyes and glisten down his cheeks.

'What's in a name? that which we call a rose

By any other name would smell as sweet;
So Romeo would were he not Romeo called,
Retain that dear perfection which he owes…

The boy playing Romeo answered, *'I take thee at thy word.*

Call me but love and I'll be new baptiz'd;
Henceforth I never will be Romeo.'

Above him, from the construction of scaffolding poles that swayed, Juliet asked,

'What man art thou that, thus bescreen'd in night,
So stumblest on my counsel?
My ears have not yet drunk a hundred words
Of that tongue's uttering, yet I know the sound.
How cam'st thou hither, and wherefore?
The orchard walls are high and hard to climb,
And the place death, considering who thou art…'

Romeo said, *'Thy kinsmen are no stop to me.'*

From above, *'If they do see thee they will murder thee.'*

And Romeo answered, *'Alack! There lies more peril in thine eye*

Than twenty of their swords: look thou but sweet,
And I am proof against their enmity.'

Tom watched and listened to all this while waiting for his entry in Act Two, Scene Three. Had things been like that for Christopher and him when they had started out? The death-defying bravery. The adrenalin-laced intensity of young love. He cast his mind back and tried to remember. The awful thing was that he couldn't quite. He hadn't scaled orchard walls in fear of swords and bayonets. He hadn't declaimed reams of the greatest poetry under heaven inside a double bed. And yet… And yet he had. He'd set off across the Channel in a sailing boat. They'd risked their lives together as they faced a mountain wave. Soaked and destitute they'd started a new shared life. Their love, naked on the beach at Audresselles, was immortalised in works of art that now hung in gilded frames, who knew where, in salons dotted around France. Yes, they had done the Romeo and Juliet thing. But now they'd reached this point, what were they? A cheap and tacky pair who had betrayed each other for a fistful, or an arseful, of boy's spunk.

They had actually talked about the possibility of repairing the damage by having three-way sex with Angelo. Christopher, younger and more optimistic as a general rule, thought this might work out well, provided Angelo was agreeable. Tom, three years older, was less sanguine though he agreed, if a bit reluctantly, to give the idea a try if the moment seemed right one future day.

Tom wondered how it would have gone with Juliet and Romeo had they not poisoned themselves. Fleeing Verona and the wrath of their parents, as they would have had to, they would have been obliged to beg for jobs as servants in some other great house, far from Verona. Padua, Mantua, Venice, or Milan. Their prodigious talent for writing and declaiming rhyming couplets might have been discovered and allowed to flower, or it might not. Perhaps Romeo would have taught in the great university at Bologna, Juliet ironing his ruffs and cuffs. But would the early intensity of their first loving have survived as the years passed?

Juliet had said at one point in the play,

I wish but for the thing I have:
My bounty is as boundless as the sea,
My love as deep; the more I give to thee,
The more I have, for both are infinite.

If they had lived on into their sixties, could they have sustained that? Could anyone? Had anyone in the history of the world done that? Scene Two came to an end. The hapless couple exited separately. *Parting is such sweet sorrow.* Tom strode into the centre of the rehearsal room, with a basket of imaginary herbs, as Friar Lawrence.

> *'Now, ere the sun advance his burning eye,*
> *The day to cheer and night's dank dew to dry,*
> *I must up-fill this osier cage of ours*
> *With baleful weeds and precious-juiced flowers.'*

You could say what you liked about Shakespeare, Tom thought, spouting the lines from memory, now "off the book", but he certainly knew how to spin a good verse.

Tom's role and Christopher's kept them rehearsing separately for most of their evenings, just as their different courses kept them at different lectures in different colleges for part of most days. Friar Lawrence and Old Montague only shared the stage during the final scene of the play. When that ended they came off stage and sat together while Basil gave his notes to the cast. 'Be very careful with that final couplet,' he warned the young man playing the Prince. *'For never was a story of more woe Than that of Juliet and her Romeo.* It's only too easy to find yourself saying, *For never was a story of more woe than that of Romeo and...* And then you're stuffed, of course.'

'I'm hardly likely to get that wrong,' said the Prince a bit tartly. Basil's criticisms and suggestions did not always go unchallenged.

'You'd be surprised,' said Basil. 'Others have.'

Tom and Christopher turned to each other and exchanged a look that nobody else could see. The shock and hurt they'd each suffered on discovering the other had had sex with Angelo had abated somewhat with the passing of the days.

'I've been meaning to ask,' said Christopher as, dismissed, they strolled towards the pub with all the others, 'what you were doing with that Nicholas chap that day.'

'Which day?' asked Tom.

'You mean there were other days?'

Tom sighed. 'No. Yes, I mean, I remember. The day your mother was here.' He didn't say, the day of the Angelo bombshell. 'I met him in the market, quite by chance. He asked where you were and I told him. So he invited me to have lunch with him. We had a pint and a ham sandwich at the White Horse. But that was all. Well, it's conceivable that he might have wanted more. But it was't on offer. He paid, I thanked him and left the pub.'

'Left him sitting there?'

'We parted on the pavement. He went one way, I went the other. And in case you don't believe me, I'll remind you where I was going. As you already know, I was going to see Angelo.'

'I see,' said Christopher. He drew breath to say something more but was prevented by the arrival beside them in the street of Angelo himself.

'We're being joined in the pub by John,' he said cheerfully. His chirpy manner with the pair of them was exactly the same as it had been before bombshell day. Neither of them had had a private conversation with him since that day, or found themselves alone with him. Certainly, neither of them had called on him in his room. Neither of them was that bold now. And there had been no further talk of plans for three-way sex.

Christoper said, 'Joined by John? John Moyse?' They hadn't seen him for a couple of weeks now. A minute later they were all piling into the Lamb and Flag, and there was John already ensconced, sharing a table with a rather pretty girl. Her presence seemed to have done wonders for his self-esteem: he greeted them in a very self-assured and grownup way. He even seemed to have put on a bit of flesh. The three of them now joined him at his table. It was usually the last table to be occupied, as the dartboard was on the wall above it, and the players' missiles flew right over the heads of the people who sat there. You took your life in your hands rather, or at least you risked a head wound, while hoping that the players were all good shots. Another member of the cast of Romeo squeezed in amongst them. It was the young undergraduate who played Mercutio. He was in the same college as John was, and also got on well with Angelo. Piers was his name.

'Don't forget to come to the revue next week,' John told them all. He said that almost as soon as he'd introduced his girlfriend, who was called Celia. (He'd talked of someone called Lucy at the start of term, Christopher remembered. Presumably that was in the past now.) The revue would be presented at the Playhouse every night of the following week at nine-thirty, John said. 'When everyone's had the chance to down a few beers – which helps with the laughter. Everyone, that is, except me.' There were some things you could do on stage after drinking a beer or two, John opined. Declaiming Shakespeare, Being funny. But playing the piano, both hands together, was not one of them. 'Even so,' John said, 'Two beers is probably about the maximum. Three or four might tip the scales the other way. The revue's called The Right Box, by the way.'

'I know,' said Christopher. 'I've seen the posters. But, The Right Box? Why?'

'After Robert Louis Stephenson,' said Celia, speaking for the first time. 'He wrote a comic novel called The Wrong Box...'

'Of course,' said Piers. 'It was turned into a film...'

Angelo said, 'Though not in Stephenson's day,' and everybody groaned.

'He didn't write a lot of comedy,' said Celia. Unless you count Travels With A Donkey. Most critics say...'

'We'll all be there,' said Tom. Older than the others he knew better than they did that that was what John was waiting for somebody to say.

Christopher remembered to ask, 'John, are you still keeping your diary these days?' but immediately regretted it. It sounded exactly the kind of question that gormless adults asked people much younger than themselves.

But John replied with alacrity, 'Yes, I am. I'm writing other stuff as well.' And then he gave a smile that neither Christopher nor Tom had seen him give before. 'I've actually written some of the material for the revue.' Tom and Christopher both found themselves somehow alarmed by this last piece of news, though neither of them could think of any good reason why this might be so.

A letter came for Tom and Christopher in an envelope that was surprisingly large. It was from the Admiral Digby and was signed jointly by Roger and Malcolm. The need for the large envelope became apparent when they saw that another letter nestled inside it, like a Russian doll within another Russian doll. They read Roger and Malcolm's missive first. It was clear from a glance at the two signatures that it was actually Roger who had written it.

Dear Tom and Christopher
How are you both? A lady came into the bar today with the enclosed. She said she taught at your old school and needed to send you something but had no address for you. She wouldn't give her name but we couldn't help wondering if she was the art teacher who had taken such a shine to you and painted that picture that caused such a rumpus all those years ago.

Life goes on here much as usual. We are going to get a dog, a collie, probably, because they need a lot of exercise and it will help us both to keep our weights down a bit. In your forties these things creep up on you.

Don't know what your plans for Christmas are. If you'd like to spend some of the 'vacation' as you university types like to call it, with us at the Digby please feel free. We'd love to see you. Hell! Some of the vacation? That was mealy-mouthed. Spend all of it here if you want to, though we appreciate you may get better offers and have other plans.

Anyway, we'll stop now, to allow you to read the mysterious enclosure. Hoping for your sakes a cheque may be inside...

Best wishes and love
Roger and Malcolm

Tom slit the other envelope. A third envelope lay inside. That discovery made them both giggle. They read Molly's letter first.

Dear Christopher and Tom

I remembered the other day that I had promised you something and not delivered it. Please find enclosed a letter of introduction to the sisters of St Gilda's in Broadstairs. In case you decide one day to visit them and ask to see the picture of yourselves.

Should you find yourselves in the area over Christmas do please call on me. I shall be at the Star of the Sea for part of the Christmas holiday at least. The phone number, which you are unlikely to remember after all this time, is above.

With my best wishes
Molly O'Deere

The final Russian-doll envelope was addressed to the
Sisters of St Gilda. Tom and Christopher toyed with the
idea of steaming it open, reading what was written inside
and then sealing it up again but decided not to. If it
should happen that they found themselves at the convent
they would hand over the envelope unsullied and intact.
And they certainly had no intention of slitting the
envelope with a forefinger and handing the thing over in
a state like that...

The audience had got quite well tanked-up in the
Playhouse bar before piling in through the doors for The
Right Box revue. Tom and Christopher found
themselves sitting next to two other members of
Christopher's college. Christopher knew them slightly
and introduced Tom. The younger members of the
Romeo cast were mostly sitting a couple of rows in
front. Angelo, Christopher noticed, was sitting next to
Piers. The musicians, John Moyse and two others,
entered the pit in front of the stage, in dark trousers,
white shirts, and red braces and bow ties. They turned
and waved in response to boisterous applause, then they
sat down, and struck up something equally boisterous on
piano, double bass and drums. The curtain rose.

There was a sketch called Chekov in which three
women, one of whom was Celia, mournfully and
repeatedly observed that *Nahthing eeverr haappens*
while servants kept entering with ever-worsening news.
Someone sang a song to the tune of Percy Grainger's In
an English Country Garden, the last line of whose every
gory verse was *In a Transylvanian Graveyard*. Another
sketch consisted of a very long shaggy dog story told by
a tramp, the punch line being, 'Oi reckon oi could have
'ad that woman if oi'd 'ad a moind to.'

Then two young men appeared who were clearly
meant to be schoolmasters, since they wore gowns and

mortar-boards and carried curved-handled canes. In response to a knock on a door they called together, 'Come in.' A third young man entered, dressed as a young schoolboy in shorts. 'Aha, so what have you been up to, then?' asked one of the schoolmasters.

'Please sir,' said the boy, 'I was sent up because I broke a window with one of my balls...' There was some ribald laughter at that.

'Well, well,' said the schoolmaster. Then to his colleague, 'Shall this one be mine or yours?'

'Oh, mine, I think,' said the other one, and gave the audience a leer.

'Oh what a shame,' said the first schoolmaster. 'I'd rather hoped...'

'I tell you what,' said schoolmaster two. 'We could take him in turns. Bend over, boy...'

The audience's laughter had changed gear by now. No longer free and easy, beer-oiled, it grew embarrassed. Then, as the double entendres became ever less subtle and the subtext ever more clear it died away. Tom felt his face flush, while Christopher's neighbour whispered to him, 'This isn't right, you know.'

The sketch limped on for a few more lines, though the actors' delivery was faltering now. They had taken fright as the laughter died. Then someone in the audience got to his feet and shouted, 'Shame, shame!' Another voice called, 'Get them off. Pull them off the stage.' Tom thought that if anyone had brought eggs or tomatoes with them, at this point the missiles would have been thrown.

But the actors gave up anyway. They turned to the audience for a bare second, raising hands in surrender, then ran off into the wings dodging a hail of jeers and boos. After a second, during which the three musicians sat motionless, thunderstruck, John launched into a jolly medley of tunes at the piano, the bassist and percussionist quickly joined in, and then the next act arrived a little breathlessly on stage.

Neither Tom nor Christopher could pay attention to the sketch that followed. They sat rigid with shock, clammy with the horror of what they'd seen. Had John Moyse written it? Was it meant to be a parody, obscene and grotesque, of what had happened between the two of them and Angelo? Had they just seen themselves portrayed, guyed, caricatured, on stage?

Christopher looked ahead of him, peering between heads to see Angelo. How had he taken this? The back of his head was perfectly still. But what was going on inside? The expression on his face couldn't even be guessed at. Had he exchanged a corner-of-the-mouth remark with Piers?

Tom thought of getting up and leaving. Heading for the bar. Or somewhere further afield. Anything to get away. But he remembered the scene in Hamlet: the one in which Claudius rushes out of the room when his own crime is presented in a play. *Give me some lights! Away!* Tom decided that he and Christopher could do without the attention this would bring. Not daring to touch each other in the imperfect darkness, isolated in their separate misery, Tom and Christopher sat unhappily through the rest of the revue.

EIGHTEEN

Tom and Christopher were waiting for John as he slipped out of the stage door. All the revue cast were slipping out, trying to look invisible. There would be no meeting the audience in the Playhouse bar this night, or celebration in the Gloucester Arms. Tom laid a hand on John's shoulder to get his attention as he tried to walk past. He had been trying to adopt that most wrong-headed of beliefs, said to be widely held among ostriches: that if he looked at no-one then no-one would see him. 'John,' Tom said. 'Was that you? Did you write that…?' He stopped, unable to find a word.

John turned eyes of anguish on him. 'No! How could you think such a thing?' He looked ready to burst into tears. 'Celia left already. She went even before the show finished. Didn't wait for the applause. What little of it there was.'

Tom sighed. 'Come for a drink. Just the three of us. Somewhere the others won't be.' He looked around. The other members of the revue cast had melted into the night. So had the rest of the audience. There was no sign of Angelo and Piers. They were alone on the pavement. Just the three of them.

They went to The Welsh Pony. It wasn't far away, but it was mainly the haunt of workers at the bus station; dons and undergraduates were rare birds inside. It was a good place for the three of them to disappear.

It seemed late for beer; it would soon be closing time. Tom bought the three of them a whisky each. 'I don't know how it happened,' John said. They were standing near the bar, a bit squashed up in the middle of a beery crowd. All the tables were already taken. 'The three of them said they had something up their sleeves, but wouldn't show it to us in advance. They said it was something they'd done at school and it had gone down well. Phil, our director, didn't ask to see it. It was a bit foolish of him.' John took a sip of whisky. 'Of me too, I suppose. I am the M.D. I should have said something. Made Phil take a look at it in rehearsal instead of simply trusting them.'

'I suppose it could all have been perfectly innocent,' suggested Tom. He was beginning to feel relief now. The sketch hadn't been written by John. It had been concocted by total strangers, and they'd done it at their old school. Or so they'd said. But in any case it now seemed fairly certain that it hadn't been aimed at them.

'You mean the double meanings were something we all imagined?' said Christopher. 'They must have all been very innocent at those chaps' school.'

Up until this moment John had felt comforted by the attention bestowed on him by his two former teachers. They'd plucked him from the crowd, taken him aside to buy him a drink and smooth his ruffled feathers following the disaster in which he'd been involved. Now suddenly he realised that this meeting, this drink, this conversation, were not all centred on him. The unpleasant shock of this discovery was both audible and visible. He flinched and said, 'Oh!'

'Oh, what?' asked Christopher.

'This isn't about me,' John said. 'You didn't bring me here out of concern for my feelings, did you? It's about you. You thought it was the two of you being portrayed on the stage back there. You thought it might have been written by me.'

'It crossed my mind,' said Tom.

'Mine too,' said Christopher sheepishly.

'Oh, bloody hell,' said John. 'How could you think I'd do a shitty thing like that. To you two. After what we all went through all those years ago. When Angelo…'

His own mention of Angelo prompted another startled thought. 'Angelo let something slip the other day, talking to Piers and me. About the two of you. I thought he was joking… Oh shit. Oh fuck it. I can see it on your faces. You've been doing stuff with Angelo. Bloody hell!' John regarded them in silence for a second. His face had turned pale. Then he said, 'Thank you for the drink, Tom.' He downed the last of his whisky in a quick gulp and, reaching between crammed bodies, placed the empty glass back on the counter. Then he turned and barged his way towards the door.

The term seemed hardly to have started, but now they were looking towards its end. The weekly essays continued to be written, tutorials to be attended, and Romeo and Juliet to be rehearsed; but all these things could now be numbered like the days. Three more essays for Christopher on Anglo-Saxon England, then two, then one… The Right Box revue had limped through its one-week run, shorn of the sketch that had caused the outrage, but attendance had been poorer than hoped for; reviews were less than enthusiastic, and the performances that followed the first night had been lack-lustre, the cast subdued and rendered nervous by the experience of the opening night. Attention was now turned in hope to Romeo and Juliet, whose own first night was approaching fast. The production had a lot of expectations to fulfil.

Real swords arrived from Berman's and Nathan's. Costumes were tried on, altered and tried again. In Friar Lawrence's osier basket there were now real herbs. Rehearsals moved from the room above the foyer to the theatre's actual stage. A set was built of scaffolding, faced with painted flats. There was a belief-defying staircase which shook as you walked down. You had to be very careful with it. Dress rehearsal succeeded technical rehearsal. The dress was succeeded by the first night with scarcely thirty minutes in between.

The opening scene went well. People even tittered at the collier, collar, choler joke. And when, in the heat of the first fight sequence, the tip of Balthasar's sword broke, sliced off by an energetic swipe from Gregory's, and went flying out into the audience, the excitement of the spectators was palpable, their attention rapt. The girl in whose lap the sword-blade landed would talk about it long afterwards.

Angelo really was a good little actor, Christopher thought, sharing the stage with him later in the long first scene, listening to him speaking the verse that interleaved with his own speeches. He wondered for a moment whether Angelo was thinking of making the theatre his career. But then he had to stop wondering and concentrate on his cue and lines.

Both he and Tom had been very careful of Angelo in recent days. They met him in rehearsals only. All idea of having three-way sex together had been abandoned in the wake of the Right Box revue. Tom and Christopher hadn't even mentioned it between themselves. As for the tasteless sketch itself, that subject had not been broached at all with Angelo. And because Tom and Christopher knew that Angelo had been in the audience and he knew that they had, the three-way silence about the matter was an unpleasantly telling one.

The storms of love and death raged around them. The five acts followed on from each other, each more quickly than the last, it seemed to Christopher. So many lifetimes, so much love, begun and ended in two short hours. One day, Christopher thought with a sudden shock, his own life, viewed in retrospect, might seem to have passed just as quickly away.

All was wrapped up. Tom and Christopher were among the last few left on stage, among the few left still alive. The Prince declaimed,

'A glooming peace this morning with it brings;

The sun for sorrow shall not show his head:
Go hence, to have more talk of these sad things;
Some shall be pardon'd, and some punished:
For never was a story of more woe…'

Hearts were in mouths. Would the Prince get the two names in the right order?

'…Than that of Juliet and her Romeo.'

A feeling of relief swept through the whole cast. The Prince permitted a ghostly smile of triumph to flit across his face.

There were mutual congratulations in the dressing-rooms. Make-up, 5 and 9, was removed with cold-cream. Then all trooped out of the stage door and into the Gloucester Arms.

Everyone was there already. The buzz – there was literally a buzz, almost like electricity – was good. Everyone was there. Including John Moyse. Without Celia. John saw Christopher and came up to him. Christopher thought that brave of him. He said, to make it easier for them both, 'Hi John. Good to see you.'

'You were great,' said John. 'I really do mean that. And so was Tom. I'd never seen that side of either of you. So I didn't know.' He thought for a split-second. 'Though perhaps being a teacher is the biggest acting job in the world.'

Christopher said, 'It certainly is at boarding school.'

John moved inside his clothes a bit uncomfortably. Then he said, 'I'm sorry about the last time we met. The way I behaved, I mean.'

'There wasn't anything very good about our behaviour either,' said Christopher. 'I mean mine and Tom's.' He felt something welling up and hoped he wouldn't start to cry in front of this child.

'It's just that we're not supposed to be shocked by anything these days,' said John. 'But sometimes, in spite of ourselves, we are. We shouldn't be.'

'It's good to see you here anyway,' said Christopher gently. 'Tom'll be over in a second. He's just getting a drink at the bar… Hey, what would you like…?'

'Angelo's getting me one,' said John. 'Him and Piers. Oops, sorry. I meant he and Piers.'

'Or even Piers and he,' said Christopher, smiling his relief at John. And remembering he'd once corrected this young man's letters home. Tom arrived at that moment with two pints of beer. A second later so did Angelo. He was carrying two drinks. Piers, beside him, was carrying the third. Piers's free hand was laid lazily, familiarly, around Angelo's shoulder. Both boys wore comfortable, easy smiles. Christopher remembered the smiles that had looked out at them from the David and Jonathan portrait of himself with Tom, as if from a mirror, all those years ago.

A letter arrived from Mike. He would like to make use of his house for at least a part of the Christmas vacation, if that was all right with them. If they were staying up in Oxford, then he would cheerfully use the spare room.

They wrote back, saying that of course he was welcome to use his own house during the Christmas vac, they named the date on which they would be going away and added that there would still be no problem should he want to turn up before then.

Mike phoned from London a couple of days before the end of term. He wanted to arrive the next day. If they were still agreeable to having him sleep that one night in the spare room he would stand them dinner again at the Randolph Hotel.

The term spooled down towards its end. The final night of Romeo and Juliet came and went. The production was considered a success and at the party afterwards, in someone's house in North Oxford, several of the youngest members of the cast became extremely drunk. Two of the young lads (they were not Piers and Angelo) were discovered in flagrante in a broom-cupboard under the stairs. 'What happened?' Tom asked the young woman who'd made the discovery when she told him about it a few days later.

'I simply shut the door again and let them get on with it. Some people seem to be made that way. We're all different I suppose.'

'Indeed,' said Tom.

Tom, Christopher and Mike – his skin by now the colour of a conker – walked to the Randolph from the house in Jericho. Ten weeks had passed since the three of them had done this walk together but it seemed eerily as though it had been just the day before. Passing the front of Worcester College Tom and Christopher hoped that Mike wasn't going to mention Angelo and were relieved that he hadn't done when they turned away from the college's classical frontage into Beaumont Street..

The same little group was gathered at dinner, to welcome Mike back and celebrate his safe return from Africa. Tom and Christopher had had no contact with either Simon or Sidney since that first night, except for an occasional wave across a crowded street. Nicholas they hadn't seen since the day Tom had had lunch with him.

'We saw Romeo,' said Simon, 'and thought how good you both were.'

'Of course they were,' said Sidney. 'Artists to the core.' And everyone laughed politely.

'You should have come backstage and said hallo,' said Christopher.

'Ah,' said Sidney. 'We might have looked a bit grownup, don't you think?'

'Also,' said Nicholas, 'we couldn't help noticing your young friend Angelo. He's a nice little actor.'

'Yes, Angelo,' said Mike, alert suddenly. 'Did anything more happen there?'

'Not as far as we were concerned,' said Tom very quickly, before Christopher could jump in.

Christopher said, imitating the accent employed by the three girls in the Chekov revue sketch, 'Nahthing eeverr haappens.'

'He's got a boyfriend now,' said Tom. 'Chap called Piers.'

From across the table Sidney said rather quietly, 'Yes, I know.'

It was good to be back at the Admiral Digby. Christmas decorations, paper chains and twists of aluminium foil, were hung in both the bars. Tom and Christopher even served behind the counter and helped in the kitchen from time to time during the pre-Christmas days. Over Christmas itself they would be separated, to do their filial duty at their respective parents' homes. This would not be difficult for Tom, except in the matter of being apart from Christopher. It was Christopher who would find himself treading on egg-shells, or walking over hot coals, whichever metaphor one preferred.

'Thank you for forwarding that letter,' Tom remembered to say to Roger one day. 'You guessed correctly about its author. That was the lady who painted us. Molly O'Deere.'

'An unfortunate name,' said Malcolm.

'An unfortunate painting too,' said Roger.

'Actually that was what her letter was about,' said Tom. 'She's sent us an introduction – though God knows why it couldn't have been done by phone – to a convent of nuns in Broadstairs. Apparently that's where the picture is now. We thought we'd go over and take a look one day. Tomorrow, maybe.'

Roger frowned thoughtfully. 'Are you sure that's wise? Re-visiting the past, I mean. Some people say it's a thing you should never do.'

'Oh, I don't know,' said Malcolm. 'They both looked very cute in it, I seem to remember. How long is it now?'

'Five and a half years,' said Tom. 'Five and a half years we've been together.' He paused a second, then added, 'And ... I knew, but can't remember... What about you?'

'Eighteen,' said Roger at once. The tally was evidently lodged quite near the front of his mind.

'So however many years we manage to notch up, you'll always be thirteen ahead.'

Malcolm looked at Christopher then quite sharply. 'And have you always been...? You know. As a couple, I mean.'

'Mostly,' said Tom.

'More or less,' said Christopher.

'Same here,' said Malcolm, nodding thoughtfully.

Roger said, 'More or less.'

They caught the bus to Broadstairs. It was only a few miles. 'Do you think,' Christopher asked facetiously as they oriented themselves in the little town, 'that the picture will have aged, like in The Picture of Dorian Grey, while we've stayed young?'

Tom said, 'We shall see.' He was a bit tight about the lips.

St Gilda's convent was tucked away in a little winding street that led down to the sea. The last time they'd been here, they both remembered, had been the night of their shared birthday, June 21st, in 1962. They couldn't remember the dishes they'd had, at Marchesi Bros' restaurant on that momentous night – it was the night on which Angelo had been discovered in bed with his fellow house captain, Simon Rickman, the fallout from which H-bomb moment had sent them off to France – but they rremembered the wine. It had been Beaujolais.

Christopher knocked at the door. A very long time passed and then an eye-level grille was opened in the door. 'The Lord be with you,' said a voice from inside.

Tom said, 'And also with you.' *Dominus vobiscum,* it would have been back then. And *Et cum spiritu tuo.* 'We carry a letter of introduction. From Miss Molly O'Deere.'

'Oh dear,' said the nun inside. 'How very awkward.'

'Would you like to see the letter?' Tom enquired. The grille was opened inwards, a hand stretched out. The letter, still in its unopened envelope, disappeared inside.

A long half-minute later there came the sound of big bolts being withdrawn. The door opened inwards and a small thin nun beckoned them carefully inside. She looked them up and down most searchingly. Tom realised after a second that their appearance, their two faces and physiognomies, were being compared minutely with the picture than hung in the refectory here.

'Oh dear,' the nun said again. This time they could see that she was shaking her head. 'I can well understand that you might want to see the picture again all these years later. But I'm sorry to have to tell you that you've arrived just three days late.'

'Oh,' said Christopher. He stopped. A silence that was as heavy as an altar-cloth hung in the air. He went on. 'May we ask…?'

'The picture has gone, I'm afraid. It hung in pride of place in our refectory, as you no doubt know, for five whole years. A very fine portrayal of innocent friendship it was.' The nun drew breath significantly. 'We have a new Abbess Visitor in the Order. One result of her first visit here last week was that the picture has had to be removed. Her predecessor could see nothing wrong with the picture but... Well, that's all I am at liberty to say.'

'So where has it gone?' Tom asked. 'Was Miss O'Deere consulted? Does she still own the picture or...?'

'The picture was gifted to us by Miss O'Deere. Had she simply lent it, well, it could have gone back to her. But as it is...' She gave a little shrug. 'I'm afraid the portrait was taken away. No doubt it will be sold by the Order and that is the last any of us will ever hear or see of it. I'm so sorry you've had a wasted journey.'

'I don't know,' said Christopher. 'Part of the journey of life, I suppose.' He wasn't sure why he'd come out with that, or what he was trying to say.

'Well, I won't detain you,' said the nun, in the tone of voice of someone saying, *You won't detain me*. Her hand went to the handle of the door. 'I must say, though,' she said as the closing door began to sweep them out towards the pavement, 'you both look a great deal older than you did when Miss O'Deere painted you.'

Part Three

1978

NINETEEN

Fucking wasn't really Michel's thing. He would do Tom occasionally if Tom asked him to and, happily for Tom, would let Tom penetrate him whenever Tom wanted to. But what he liked best was to grip something tightly between his knees while he rode to a climax and as often as not that would be one of Tom's legs, while he thrust his long cock up and down, rubbing against Tom's hip or belly until he shed his load. The friction would give Tom an incidental massage as well, so that he would be well on the way towards his own climax by the time Michel, drained out, could focus his entire attention on Tom and finish him off. Tom was quite happy with this, Michel's way of doing things. And they did other things too, of course.

They'd been together eight years now. The current state of affairs had come about quite gradually, not abruptly as was more usually the case. Things had begun in the Oxford days, though they had hardly realised it. Though Tom asked himself, when did anything begin? Had it in fact started with that kiss on the doorstep, on the corner of the Rue Faidherbe and the Rue Hamy, back in 1962, two mornings after they had first met? Had seeds been sown at that moment that had lain dormant for years afterwards? He still remembered the chain of events clearly. So did Michel. They sometimes reminded each other of it.

They had met in the Chat qui Pêche while waiting for Armand to join them that first night. Tom recalled vividly how Michel's appearance had struck him at once. A young man of Tom's age (at that time twenty-one), with a ruddy complexion and thick, curly, dark brown hair. His eyes had been dark and lustrous as damson plums. (Sixteen years on, they still were.) Michel had been wearing a one-piece workman's overall of blue denim and as far as one could see – and one could see quite a long way – he had nothing on underneath it. No shirt or vest, certainly, and as the dungarees were cut so low at the sides that his naked hips were visible, Tom had assumed there were no underpants either. His feet were clad in sandals and bright mauve socks. He carried the ensemble off with great assurance. (Even now Michel still dressed in dungarees with nothing underneath them when he was painting, though he would not wish to be seen dead in sandals with mauve socks. White socks and white tennis shoes were his trademark footwear these days.)

It was the night after that, after supper – the four of them eating at Sabine's house – that the drama had occurred. Back in the Chat qui Pêche, Tom had caught sight of Christopher drunkenly feeling Michel up. Tom had flown into a temper, directed some invective at both of them, then dragged Christopher out of the place and back to the Hôtel Faidherbe. There he had vented his anger on Christopher by giving him his first fuck, thereby providing a silver lining to the evening's little dark cloud.

In the morning Tom had felt contrite and had walked up the hill to Michel's place to apologise. There had occurred the famous kiss in the street. Which, if it had had repercussions in the years ahead, had not been without them in the weeks that immediately followed, back in England.

For, while still locked in Tom's embrace Michel had seen something over his shoulder. He'd said, 'Somebody waved to me just now. Or waved to you, to your back. A kid or young teenager in the back of a car. A British car heading down to the port. Do you know anyone like that here?'

Tom had said, *'Merde, merde, merde!'* The kid in the back of the car had been Angelo, of course.

But it was in the Oxford days, during those long summer vacations, that things really took off.

'Pendant la grève,' were the words on everyone's lips in the summer of '68. At least that was the case in France. *Pendant la grève.* During the strike. By the time Tom and Christopher arrived in Boulogne for that summer's vacation the government was back in control. The events of May seemed unreal in retrospect. It no longer seemed quite believable that France had been on the brink of its third or fourth or fifth revolution – it depended which ones you counted and which you did not – and a revolution brought about by student protest at that, Daniel Cohn-Bendit kick-starting things at the University of Nanterre back in March. It no longer seemed believable at the Channel seaside in July.

Sous le trottoir est la plage – beneath the pavement is the beach – had been one of the more anarchic slogans of the spring disturbances. Probably because, when protesters lifted cobbles from the Paris streets to hurl at police, they found them to be bedded in golden sand. But here at Boulogne the sand had been deposited by nature and it stretched for miles.

'I feel very mixed about it,' Michel admitted. 'I ought to have been on the side of the students. In principle, I mean.' His shoulders did an uncomfortable little dance. 'I don't mean manning the barricades in Paris. Age twenty-seven, I'd have been a bit old for that. And of course you two actually are students…'

'Mature ones,' Tom helped him off his hook.

'I'm an artist. That's what the revolution was supposed to have been all about. Well, up to a point. But I'm also a businessman in my own small way. I wouldn't have wanted a mob of revolutionaries looting the shop.'

'Of course,' said Christopher. 'Of course that's the case.'

Michel and Armand no longer lived in the studio above the shop, living among easels with a gas-ring and a single bed. This conversation was taking place on the balcony of their sea-front flat at Wimereux, the stylish resort just three miles up the coast from Boulogne harbour. Michel and Armand each had their own car now and, every morning, drove to work.

Michel un-crossed, then re-crossed, his shorts-clad legs. It was rare for young men to wear shorts in the late sixties. The memory of having to wear them as schoolboys, the indignity and the chafed knees that went with that… those things were too recent, the memory too raw. The only people who wore shorts for anything other than football or tennis were retired rear-admirals who wore them in their gardens and didn't care what they looked like. And Michel, who also perhaps didn't care what he looked like. With his dark-haired, lean and muscular long legs… Tom for one was admiring of Michel's disdain for fashion, and thought that he looked good.

They'd arrived that morning on the ferry from Folkestone, exchanging one set of white cliffs for their cross-Channel counterpart. Sitting in the evening sunshine now, and with sunlight ricocheting around them from off the water, with the coast of England comfortingly just visible on the horizon, occupying a little corner on the right, it felt good to be back in France.

'Michel has an idea,' said Armand. 'He's probably too shy to tell you, so I'll have to do it.' Michel snickered faintly but didn't intervene. Armand got on with it. 'He wants to paint the pair of you. Naked, of course. Title… David and Jonathan reunited. Or something like that.' They did laugh, of course.

Tom felt very flattered by the proposal and would have said so … except that Christopher suddenly pitched in with the story of how they had gone in search of the first David and Jonathan picture at a convent only to find…

'We'll have to tell Gérard that,' said Armand.

Tom snorted. 'Don't say he's still in pursuit of the picture!'

'I wouldn't go so far,' said Armand. 'But he does still talk about it.'

'Heavens,' said Tom.

'You'll be able to discuss it with him tomorrow,' said Michel. He moved one of his bare legs minutely, and Tom found himself fascinated by that. 'He's coming to Boulogne for a few days.'

'The place is becoming a colony of artists,' said Christopher. 'Like St Ives.'

'Go on about this picture Armand mentioned,' Tom prompted Michel.

Michel smiled. On a scale between shy and proud it was difficult to say exactly where that smile lay. 'I don't know about it being called David and Jonathan. Armand may have made that bit up…'

'I did not!' said Armand, and tweaked Michel's leg.

'But I had a hankering to paint the two of you,' Michel resumed. 'It started… Oh, I don't know… A few months ago. Now here the two of you are. I thought, full frontal, standing, arms round shoulders, on the beach at Audresselles.'

'Naked?' Christopher asked innocently.

Armand guffawed. 'Of course naked. You've been there before. All four of us, if I'm allowed to remind you.'

'For some reason,' said Michel, apparently seriously, 'the two of you have sold very well. Those paintings by Gérard, at Audresselles and the studio ones in Paris. Gérard made serious money out of them. Some have been sold on. For even bigger sums.' He paused and added more cautiously, 'Or so we're told.'

'I can't think why,' said Christopher. 'It's not as though we've got the biggest dicks in the world.' He was on his second glass of champagne; it had loosened his tongue and was making him bold.

'Yours always seemed plenty big enough to me,' said Armand.

'Anyway,' said Michel in the tone of someone drawing a line under the last exchange, 'I thought I'd see if I could capture the fugitive essence of the pair of you as well as Gérard did – and,' he laughed at himself, 'make as much money out of you as Gérard.' His face became serious. 'I'd pay you of course.'

'We'd be more than honoured,' said Tom.

'The weather's set fair for the next few days,' said Michel as though casually.

'So…' said Tom. 'Do I take it that tomorrow we're off to Audresselles?'

Michel's car was a Renault 4L, just as Gérard's had been ten years ago. But the marque had been developed over the decade. Michel's car had upholstered seats where those in Gérard's had been covered simply with deck-chair canvas. Arguably that had been appropriate for an artist. Michel's was painted fire-engine red. That seemed appropriate for an artist too. Wimereux was almost halfway along the road from Boulogne to Audresselles. Getting there took no time at all.

Gone were the days of the pink lotion applied to sunburn after the damage was already done. By 1968 you were rubbing a protective cream all over yourself before you could burn. Or you got a friend to do it for you.

Tom and Christopher got naked on the shore, beside the little river mouth. Armand applied the cream to Christopher while Michel, still clothed in dungarees though nothing else, did Tom. They didn't try to hide the erotic nature of the moment, as they had done that morning years ago when Tom and Christopher had arrived dripping wet at Michel's door and they'd had to be kitted out with fresh clothes. 'Better do you here as well,' said Armand, and briskly applied the cream to Christopher's dick and balls.

'Careful,' warned Michel, though he immediately did the same thing to Tom. 'We might be seen.'

'Who by?' Armand asked, looking around them at the empty waste of rocks and sand.

'Fishermen in their huts?' Michel suggested though he didn't sound as though he'd entirely convinced even himself. A minute later he had a new idea: he now thought Armand should be in the picture too. He should sit on the sand, a little way behind the standing pair and to the side. 'Might as well make use of you while you're here,' said Michel.

That meant Armand taking his clothes off and Christopher slathering sun-cream all over him. And then, inevitably, Armand demanded that Michel too should take his dungarees off so as to equalise things. Which meant Tom applying the cream to him... It wasn't the first time Tom had seen Michel's long penis but it was the first time he'd held it in his hand. It was all right, he decided, because Christopher and Armand were there. All four of them were together, and had done the same thing. So was this the moment, Tom sometimes wondered, that had begun it all? But then, when did anything that changed your life ever actually begin?

The inevitable happened. Not out on the beach during the day. But the very fact that it couldn't happen there had the effect of increasing the sexual tension hour by hour. As soon as they got back to the flat in Wimereux, though... There wasn't room for the four of them in either of the two double beds. They got it together in a sun-warmed naked huddle on the living-room floor.

In the evening they met Gérard in the Chat qui Pêche. Nobody referred to what had happened earlier that day. They talked about paintings – the one that Michel was working on, of course, and the disappeared David and Jonathan too. But Gérard could read the sexual situation clearly; the air was electric with it; and the others could read Gérard's knowledge of it quite clearly from his face. That night, though, Tom went to bed with Christopher as was fitting, and Armand slept, as usual, with Michel. And that was how things continued for the rest of that summer, the rest of that year.

Michel made his first mini-fortune from that picture. It was sold to a collector in New York and so was removed for the foreseeable future from the gaze of European eyes. He made his second mini-fortune by selling the ironmongery business, buoyed and confident now in the wake of his success and new-found celebrity. Between them Sabine and her son had owned not just the business but also the building it was housed in. Even with half the proceeds going to his mother Michel found himself sitting on a very comfortable cushion of capital. He only used a very small part of it to buy a rickety little studio around the corner from his apartment in Wimereux.

By the time the next summer came round Michel was a full-time painter, and had had two more exhibitions of his work at the gallery in the Rue de Seine. He had had respectable sales from there over the years but now things had changed so dramatically that he could look at the prices he had charged two years ago and simply add a nought onto the end.

'I feel I owe a lot of this to you,' Michel said to Christopher and Tom as they walked together that summer of '69 on the promenade at Wimereux. Michel's face had filled out slightly since they'd last been together the year before. He was talking now about his wealth and status but because of where they were it did sound rather as though he'd bought the whole town.

'Don't feel guilty,' said Tom. 'You paid us handsomely when you sold the painting. And Armand was in the picture too.'

'I've been in a lot of his pictures,' Armand piped up. 'Nude and solo. They've never sold like that one of you two.'

'Us three,' Christopher insisted.

'It was just a happy accident,' said Michel. 'These things always are. Just one particular buyer in the world who was prepared to pay over the odds.'

'Perhaps we should find him and alert him to the existence of the David and Jonathan,' said Christopher. 'He might find he wants to buy that too.'

'Perhaps he already has,' said Tom mischievously.

Over the next few days Michel painted a further two pictures of Tom, Christopher and Armand, naked on the beach at Audresselles. This was done only partly in the hope that lightning might strike twice in the same place. They did it mainly for the sheer fun of it. They did other things too, for the sheer fun of them. One of those was to repeat the four-way sex adventures they'd enjoyed the previous year on the carpet in the living-room. (In the intervening eleven months both couples had kept themselves strictly to themselves, having sex only with each other.) What was new this year was that afterwards – to see what it would be like – Tom and Michel curled up in bed together, while Christopher slept wrapped round Armand.

In the morning the four of them breakfasted together on coffee and fresh croissants from the baker's just below. 'Your boyfriend's very lovely in bed,' said Armand to Tom.

'So's yours,' said Tom. It was the only possible reply. And then, for the rest of that holiday they rang the changes night by night. Sometimes Tom would sleep with Michel, and Christopher with Armand, and sometimes they'd all return to their regular partners for the night. Tom and Christopher had enjoyed a certain amount of bed-hopping between friends all those years ago in Paris. Nothing much along those lines had happened since that time. Now this new holiday arrangement at Wimereux did seem a logical development. All four of them thought that. They made sure to check.

Armand was no longer a full a full-time waiter at La Chope. He did an occasional shift there, helping out in times of need for friendship's sake. He also did a stint on the reception desk at the Hotel Faidherbe from time to time: again for friendship's sake, when Thierry and Robert were short-staffed and needed him. But for the most part he worked now for Michel. He did his invoices and other paperwork, kept track of tax-allowable expenses, liaised with galleries and purchasers, kept the studio stocked with brushes and paint. It was hardly a full-time job, and certainly not an onerous one. Michel paid him generously; he could afford to; and it was a wonderful thing to be able to do. In addition, Armand was an excellent cook – thanks to all those years at La Chope he was even better than Michel – and he kept the apartment immaculately clean.

Sabine had confidence, which was not misplaced, in Armand's ability to manage her son's financial affairs and was happy to keep out of them. Wealthy enough to retire, she nevertheless did a couple of shifts a week, book-keeping for the ironmonger's business that had once been hers, still poring over ledgers in the windowless little cubby-hole. No, she didn't need the money, she said. But it gave her something to do, and kept her brain in gear. Michel and Armand still went to dinner with her twice a week in the big house at the top of old Boulogne, and when Tom and Christopher were staying in the summer they went too. They would drive the couple of miles into Boulogne in Michel's new Citroën DS, which they would park swankily outside the town hall. Sabine knew nothing about the new sleeping arrangements over at Wimereux. It was hardly a mother's business who her son slept with after all.

By now things had changed in Oxford too. Tom came to the end of his PGCE course when Christopher's degree course had two more years to run. At the same time Mike the paleontologist returned from his African sabbatical and re-established himself in his house in Jericho. Tom got himself a job teaching in a preparatory school on the outskirts of Oxford, and now that he was earning money again, was able to set Christopher and himself up in a reasonably spacious first-floor flat in North Oxford. If it wasn't quite as pretty as the Jericho cottage, well, it could be theirs for as long as they wanted it. With the money that Michel sent them when he had his stroke of luck with the painting they were able to buy a second-hand Morris Minor 1000 Traveller that had been built just down the road.

It did strike Tom as rather grimly ironic that after all these years of doing other things, and laboriously acquiring his PGCE he should find himself doing exactly the same job that he'd been doing at Star of the Sea. But he had told himself at the beginning though that it was only for two years. Then Christopher would have his degree and they could move on to better things. They would see. At least prep-school masters' pay had gone up considerably since the Star of the Sea days, which was something. But then so had the cost of everything too.

Those two years came to an end in the summer of 1970, when Christopher got his degree. This involved an elaborate ceremony in the Sheldonian Theatre. Christopher and all his contemporaries hired gowns, mortar-boards and hoods for the occasion, collecting their scrolls of parchment one by one in front of a sea of proud parenthood. Christopher's parents were there, his sister too. Tom also attended, just as proud of Christopher as his family were. But he stood at the back, anonymous in the crowd, and wasn't introduced to them.

This year Roger and Malcolm brought Tom and Christopher over to Boulogne on the Orca. They travelled in daylight on a summer-calm sea. By now Christopher was finding it difficult to recall the terror he'd experienced during that first night-time crossing eight years ago. Roger and Malcolm stayed the next few days at the Wimereux apartment. There were three bedrooms. Malcolm and Roger stayed in one and, so as not to open up cans of difficult questions, Tom and Christopher had the second bedroom and Michel and Armand had the third.

When Roger and Malcolm departed, with the other four waving them off from the quayside at Boulogne, and when that other four had turned away to go and get the car, Christopher said suddenly, 'Armand wants to go and spend a few days with his grandmother in La Rochelle, He wants me to go with him.' He looked uncertain for a moment. 'Would that be OK with the two of you?'

Sometimes the right thing gets said at exactly the right moment. 'That's fine,' said Michel, and Tom said, *'Oui, d'accord,'*

The next morning Tom and Michel saw their two partners off on the train towards Paris and beyond. They drove back from Boulogne station to Wimereux. For both of them it was an extraordinary moment. They found themselves in a newly emptied space in which the future echoed and the silence boomed.

'So what would you like to do today?' Michel asked, when they reached home.

'I think,' said Tom, doing the thinking bit carefully, 'I'd like to share a bottle of champagne with you and fuck you senseless.'

So they did both those things, although in the reverse order. It was a surprise to both of them. Everybody knew that you could have a few drinks and then have sex afterwards and that was the normal way of things. But when you did it the other way round...

With Armand and Christopher three hundred miles away in La Rochelle the world spilled open for Tom and Michel over the next few days. They went to Audresselles. They didn't paint each other; they just frolicked there. They spent a day in Calais, doing shopping. There was a new thing in Calais: a shop where you could buy almost everything. It was called a *supermarché*. They bought several days' supply of food there, and very reasonably priced wine.

Another day they went to Paris and had an extravagantly expensive meal in the Quartier Latin, paid for by Michel. They didn't tell Gérard they were there. 'We should have done,' said Michel afterwards, mugging an expression of mock-shame.

'Too complicated,' said Tom complicitly.

The rest of the time they simply lazed on the beaches of Boulogne and Wimereux. The July sun soaked into them and when they went to bed at night they were almost too hot to hold each other comfortably. 'You're like a fire,' said Tom to Michel.

'I am?' said Michel. 'And what about you?'

It was July, and barely dark as the two of them lay in bed, with the last glimmer of the dusk coming at them through the curtains, reflected off the sea.

It just slipped out, as Michel cradled Tom in his arms. 'I love you,' one of them said. 'I love you too,' said the other. Neither of them would ever remember which of them had gone first.

'Merde,' said one of them, and the other, 'Now where do we go from here?'

TWENTY

'Does she dress in black?' Christopher asked Armand. They were waiting for their connection at Poitiers, standing on the platform in the sun.

'No,' said Armand. 'You're thinking of Brittany. They still do it there. Widows wearing long black dresses, I mean. From the day of their husbands' deaths until the day of their own.'

'It sounds a bit medieval,' said Christopher. It was hard to reconcile such customs with the social and sexual revolution that had occurred in the last few years. 'Anyway, I'm glad your grandmother doesn't go round in widow's weeds.' Their train, blue- and grey-liveried, pulled in then and they climbed aboard.

'We'll have to have separate rooms,' Armand explained a bit apologetically. *'Grand-mère* is quite with-it for someone of her age, but she's not so up-to-date that she'll let me share a bed with you. She sort of knows about Michel and me but even that's not something she'd ever talk about. Actually it's probably something she doesn't even like to think about.'

'I'll be careful with her,' said Christopher. The years of having to treat his own mother's sensibilities with kid gloves had given him plenty of practice.

Grand-mère did not run a car; she wasn't expected to meet them at the station. They walked from there, in a wide arc around the inner harbour, their rucksacks on their backs, to the house where she lived. The house was big. It was also situated most gloriously, right on the harbour-side, and its front windows had spectacular views across the mast-tops of the fishing boats tied up at the quays and of the two massive medieval guard towers that formed the entrance to the inner port. Like many people in her elderly widow's situation Grand-mère owned a building that was worth half a gold mine while considering herself as poor as a church mouse.

Happily for Armand and Christopher, Grand-mère's thinking of herself as poor did not prevent her from cooking Armand and Christopher a lavish meal on the evening of their arrival; she was French after all. She brought to the table fish soup, which was followed by an *omelette aux fines herbes*, then veal cutlets breaded and oven-baked, a selection of local cheeses, and finally a tart of mirabelle plums.

Armand said to her, when they had consumed all this and said thank-yous that were not just fulsome but sincere, 'Christopher and I will need a walk now.' To Christopher, who looked a bit startled by the idea, he said quietly, 'It's all right. I know a place we can go.'

'Well, take a key if you're going to be late,' his grandmother said placidly. 'Just don't come back drunk, please.'

'It's all right, Grand-mère,' said Armand sweetly. 'We won't do that.'

They did something nicer instead.

They turned right along the quayside and passed the northern guard tower. Hugging the edge of the outer harbour they found their way into a public seaside park at the far end of the Allée du Mail, which was dotted with umbrella pines and tall clumps of rhododendron and broom. In the middle of the day it was an area favoured by dog-walkers and families out for a stroll. By night it provided a convenient setting for other pursuits. When Christopher and Armand reached the spot the day was just fading from light to dark. Dusk. A magical state that the French call *entre chien et loup*. Between dog and wolf.

They hadn't gone far before they found themselves walking hand in hand. There were few people to see them and those few didn't seem to care.

Armand brought them to a halt in a little space beside the pathway that was shielded on all sides by high-growing broom. They turned and faced each other, kissed each other, and it seemed the rightest thing to be doing in the world. They felt each other's erections through their trousers, then very soon were undoing buttons and zips.

There was a lazy assumption, prevalent among men of Christopher's kind, and usually unchallenged, that you were expected to prefer big cocks; to hanker after and aspire to handle the ones that were bigger than your own. Well, Christopher thought now as he prised Armand's cock and ball set out of his underpants, scooping it all out with the cup of his hand, that wasn't necessarily so. In Tom he had a partner who was slightly bigger in all respects than he was. He had lived with the slight sense of inferiority that gave him for years. He found Armand's lively little number, prettily tapered and with an attractive, rather short, foreskin, a charming change. He reached in, groped behind Armand's balls with his middle finger and rubbed that finger against the spot that tickles all men most of all.

'Vilain,' said Armand softly. You naughty boy. Then promptly did the same to Christopher. 'Get naked,' he whispered throatily.

'Dare we?' queried Christopher, his voice also a whisper. 'Out here?'

'It's not against the law,' Armand said, beginning to massage Christopher's dick experimentally. 'We did it often enough at Audresselles.'

'At Audresselles we didn't actually…'

'Come here,' said Armand and pulled Christopher gently by his dick, using it as a leading-rein, into a deeper thicket of broom bushes where crickets chirped in the oncoming dark.

They took off everything, except socks and shoes. Then they stood together a moment, fondling, cuddling, rubbing, for the first time without the sanctioning company of Tom and Michel. A moment of generosity was given to Christopher. 'You can fuck me if you want to,' he offered. 'Tomorrow I'll do you.' He lay down on his back at that point. He wasn't going to go tummy-down on the bare earth and twigs, his cockhead and his navel a prey to earwigs and ants. Armand lay on top of him, lifting Christopher's legs and wrapping them around his shoulders like a stole. He lubricated himself with spittle and, without any exploratory moves with fingers, entered Christopher gently and with ease. His deep blue eyes gazed calmly into Christopher's paler ones, though it was too late to make out their colour in the deepening gloom. He gave a couple of experimental thrusts and grinned at Christopher. He said, 'Sometimes it pays to be relatively small.'

'Everything is relative,' said Christopher, then, since Armand was making no attempt to do so, started work on his own cock with his right hand.

On the way back, once again fully dressed, they stopped at a quayside bar that was just metres away from the door of Grand-mère's house. They sat out on the quayside drinking a nightcap of Pineau de Charentes. The sound of a boat's engine began to thrum in the distance. And then, between the two great fortress towers that guarded the harbour, there appeared a small white light. The boat came chugging onwards, invisible save for its masthead light. 'How beautiful,' said Christopher.

'Yes,' agreed Armand. Christopher felt his hand alight softly on his knee. Armand said, 'Tonight everything is. Just look at that. It's like a star. A moving star. Star of the Sea.'

Words Christopher hadn't remembered in years came flooding back to him.

Dark night hath come down on us, Mother, and we
Look out for thy shining, sweet star of the sea.

Armand looked sideways at him suddenly. 'You're crying, Christopher. Why is that?'

'Crying?' said Christopher. 'I didn't think I was.'

Sleeping in separate rooms was not the greatest of hardships. Not after they'd fulfilled their urges and each other's in a pine-scented glade under the sky. Not when they knew they would be breakfasting together in a few hours' time. And would be returning to their trysting place the following day at some point. And there were several more days ahead of them.

There were boat trips around the bay. Armand and Christopher took one on their third afternoon. The sea was calm and a sparkling blue. They paid their money and hopped down onto the deck which, because of the state of the tide, was a metre or two below the level of the quay. It rocked as they touched down. It seemed a very familiar thing, Christopher thought. He had many sailing trips behind him now. On the Orca over the years and, on more recent summers in Boulogne, on other boats besides.

They puttered out between the not-quite-identical twin towers. The outer harbour broadened in front of them. Their outbound route lay close in to the pine- and broom-clad promontory where they'd had sex together the past two nights. They caught each other's eyes and exchanged intimate smiles.

Above them a plane was circling. A flying boat. Its colour was flame yellow. 'They do trips round the bay in that too,' said Armand. 'Though not quite like that. Not so brief. I think someone's having a flying lesson this afternoon. It's a training flight.' The plane was flying in a pattern that was the shape of a race track or a paper-clip; it was disappearing towards La Rochelle airfield every few minutes and then zooming back. It would dip low towards the water, almost brushing it with its belly and wing-floats, then with a roar of opened throttles, rise steeply up.

'It's doing circuits and bumps,' said Christopher authoritatively. 'We used to see them doing that from an airfield near Star of the Sea. Teaching landing and take-off technique.'

'Aren't you the knowledgeable one?' said Armand archly. By now the whole expanse of the sea had opened out ahead of them. They passed beyond the limit of the flying-boat's circuit; its noise faded behind them and they forgot about it. The Ile d'Oléron came in sight, heaving round a corner of the mainland, and then the Ile de Ré appeared on the other side. Eventually a third island appeared above the horizon. 'What's that one?' Christopher asked.

'The Ile d'Aix,' said Armand. 'Very small. No cars allowed.'

'Like Sark,' said Christopher.

'Ah,' said Armand. 'Among the Anglo-Norman Islands. The ones the king of France forgot about when some treaty or other was signed.'

'I see,' said Christopher. 'Was that how we came to keep the Channel Islands? I've sometimes wondered that. There's a few things they still don't teach English students about the history of our two countries.'

The islands shifted shape, and exchanged their positions in the sea as their boat made its leisurely circuit of the bay. Ré, Aix and Oléron came closer, one by one, so that you could make out trees and houses; then they receded again across the flat expanse of the sea. At last the boat had turned full circle and was heading eastward back to La Rochelle. The sun-silvered Atlantic lay behind them now and the two towers of the inner harbour entrance could be made out distantly ahead beyond the wave-crested blue.

They came back once more beneath the race-track circuit of the flying-boat. It flew towards them, down, down, down, and this time it actually brushed the water about a mile in front – they could see the plumes of spray – before it rose up steeply, banked and turned away. Less than ten minutes later it was back again, a small but growing speck above the town, heading towards them and the sea. The next thing seemed to happen very slowly. At least it seemed slow at the beginning. Calmly a fishing boat started to cross their path about half a mile ahead. Calmly, inexorably, the flying-boat, flame-lit by the declining sun, came towards them, down, down, down.

They will have seen each other, Christopher thought, quite calmly. They know what they're about. He went on thinking this, not even bothering to say anything to Armand, until, with shocking acceleration, events proved him wrong. Debris was in the air. The fishing boat must have lost part of its mast. It was rocking wildly but still afloat. The flying-boat had lost half a wing. From a height of twenty feet or so it toppled sideways into the sea.

The skipper of the boat they were travelling on reacted instantly. That was evident from the changed note of the engine as the throttle was opened to its fullest and they started to charge ahead towards the downed plane, their speed increasing till they seemed to bounce across the waves like a skimming stone.

In front of them, three hundred metres away, then two, then one, the plane lay low and tilted in the waveleted sea. One float had gone missing along with the shorn-off wing. The other float was doing some service for the moment, lifting the port wing high, but the hull was more than half submerged. A hatch above the cockpit was thrown open. A moment later a human form appeared.

Fifty metres. There was a loud splash. It was the noise of that that alerted Christopher to what he had just done. Thrown himself into the water, fully clothed and in his shoes. That and the shock of the cold. He started to swim, breast-stroke, towards the plane.

Behind him he heard yells. Another splash. And then a hand was grabbing him, pulling him back to the boat from which he'd leapt so unthinkingly. Christopher didn't have to see the face, or hear the voice. It was Armand, of course. Armand, the stronger swimmer of the two. It was Christopher who had plunged into the water to go to the rescue of whoever had survived the disaster on the plane. But it was Armand who had now plunged into the water to rescue him.

'What were you thinking of?' Armand kept asking. He was almost in tears. 'You could have died.' Christopher had no answer. For the moment he had no idea. He was in shock. So was Armand. And so were the other three: the captain, the co-pilot and the trainee pilot from the plane. They sat huddled in the boat, blankets wrapped around them on top of their soaked clothes. The boat's small engine roared and the craft's frame shook with the unaccustomed strain that was being placed on it as they powered their way full-speed towards the shore, heading for the harbour entrance between the two ancient towers that had stood for centuries and had seen everything before.

The rescue had gone perfectly. The text-book ease of it had left everyone almost stunned with surprise. First, a forest of strong arms had pulled Christopher, then Armand out of the water and hauled them on board, the boat slowing but not actually stopping while this was done. And then they were alongside the hull of the plane. It still lay slantwise in the water, showing no sign of going under just yet. The boat's second man – boatswain, mate, or whatever he was called in French – reached forward with a grappling hook and collared a handily jutting piece of plane – radio antenna perhaps, or Pitot tube. The pilots, who had been sitting on the cockpit roof, now slid down the side of the hull into the arms of passengers on the boat and were pulled on board. By this time the dis-masted fishing-boat had arrived at the scene. But the rescue was already complete and there was nothing for it to do. It followed them lamely into port, lagging a little way behind.

'I think perhaps I know,' said Christopher finally. It was late evening and, following their usual activity among the broom thickets they were drinking a final Pineau de Charentes outside the little bar on the quayside. Armand had been asking him again and again, 'What made you do it?' To which Christopher had kept replying, 'What made you jump in after me?' And Armand had said each time, 'Because you can barely swim. I've seen you often enough at Boulogne and Audresselles.' And Christopher had countered, 'I was doing fine in the water back there. I'd have got to the plane fine.'

'To drag three grown men down into the water with you seconds before the boat arrived…?!'

But now Christopher had said he thought he knew.

'Remember us talking about that first crossing, the morning we came to you? When we'd been soaked by the sea? An enormous wave. I wasn't brave on that occasion. I've thought of myself as a coward ever since that day.'

'You've never been a coward,' Armand said gently, and under the table he equally gently rubbed his knee.

'But if you had been… well, you more than made up for it today. I know that what you did was crazy, stupid… It was also incredibly brave.'

'I didn't think before I jumped,' said Christopher. 'I think my mind made itself up unconsciously.' He paused. They were sitting side by side both facing the harbour. Now Christopher turned his head and looked searchingly at Armand. 'But why did you jump after me? I'm not that bad a swimmer…'

Now Armand returned his serious gaze. 'In my case too it was pure instinct. But also … I think … perhaps … I wanted to impress you.'

Christopher breathed deeply. Then he said, 'That too. That also went for me.' Then they both looked out across the fishing-boat dotted harbour again, each felt the other's hand steal slowly up his thigh, and for the moment neither of them could think of anything more to say.

'I don't want to go back.' That was the sentence that Christopher had kept repeating and repeating during their remaining days in La Rochelle. He'd meant, go back to England. He was supposed to be going back to Oxford, to do what Tom had done three years before: his PGCE in teaching history. 'I just can't,' he would say. 'I don't want to teach any more. My parents will say I've wasted my degree…'

'Then stay,' Armand had said. 'Stay with me.'

'It's what I want,' said Christopher. 'But how? With no money. Nowhere to live…'

There was a good deal of going back to do, Christopher thought, as a succession of trains carried them from La Rochelle to Poitiers, from Poitiers to Paris, from Paris to Boulogne. There was not only the return to England to deal with, and the separation from Armand. Before that there was the return to Boulogne.

The terrifying moment to face, when he would have to explain to Tom that he had fallen in love with Armand. And when Armand would have to explain to Michel that it wasn't a one-way thing.

'Qu'est-ce que nous allons dire?' Armand kept saying as the bus bounced them back from Boulogne station to Wimereux. What are we going to say? They climbed the stairs of the apartment building as if mounting the scaffold steps to the guillotine.

Tom and Michel were both in, evidently. They'd heard them climbing the stairs and came out of the apartment onto the landing. Both pairs of men then froze. They looked at each other, Armand and Christopher peering up a flight of stairs, Tom and Michel peering down. Abject terror was only one of the flickering emotions that each pair read in the other's eyes. The silence lasted a long time. It felt never-ending. Then at last it was broken. It was Michel who spoke. Michel, as usual, who managed to say the un-sayable. He said it in French, of course. *'Paraît que nous sommes tous dans le même bain.'* That is, *Seems we're all in the same bath.* Same bath, same boat. Same difference.

After that moment things had happened astonishingly quickly. Christopher telephoned the authorities at Oxford and told them he would not be taking up his place on the PGCE course in October. Tom phoned the prep school at Wolvercote and said that he wouldn't be returning to teach in the coming term. 'A term's notice is required,' protested the headmaster in a very firm tone.

'Sorry,' said Tom. 'There just isn't time.'

'That is outrageous,' said the head. 'No way for a responsible Christian to behave.'

'I'm not a Christian,' said Tom.

'The worse for you, then. I…' The man sighed, finding no further suitable words. 'I can only say, then, do not come to us for a reference – ever – because you won't get one. And your name and your behaviour will be mentioned among prep school headmasters, by me in person, everywhere from John O'Groats to Land's End.'

'Sorry about that,' said Tom. 'But I can't do much about it now.'

'What did they say?' the others asked when Tom, looking a little shaken, had put down the phone.

Tom screwed up his face. 'It wasn't very pleasant,' he said. 'Not that I expected it would be.'

With their parents they took the cowards' way. They did it by letter. Although, as generation after generation had discovered, it was easier to present your parents with an unpalatable *fait accompli* than an unpalatable action plan. Tom actually told his parents about his change of partner. Christopher stopped well short of that.

For a time they had all lived together in the apartment at Wimereux. Then an opportunity had presented itself that allowed the newly configured couples a little more space to themselves. At the Café La Chope – where Tom and Christopher had first clapped eyes on Armand, where Christopher had worked for a summer some eight years ago, where Armand still helped out from time to time – the *patron* retired. His single son didn't want to run the business – he had a career in the French navy – and asked Armand and Christopher, a bit diffidently, if they would manage the place for him. There would be accommodation for them.

The offer came as a major surprise. Christopher in particular had to search quite deep inside himself for his response to it. How did he feel about it? He had never imagined himself turning into a French innkeeper in his early twenties. But the free accommodation was tempting, and there would be the bonus of working with Armand. They talked it over, consulted Tom and Michel – they all still remained close friends – and in the end said yes. They moved into the flat above the café: the retired patron and his wife had bought a bungalow a little way up the coast at Ambleteuse. Christopher used to say that they lived above the *Chope*. Only Tom found this at all amusing. You had to be English-speaking and know the French pronunciation. It wasn't funny otherwise.

Tom took over Armand's job as well as his place in Michel's apartment, bed and heart. He became Michel's manager and agent. As Armand had already found, the task was not an arduous one. In the abundant spare time they shared together Michel would teach him to paint.

TWENTY-ONE

'Good heavens,' said Roger. He hadn't finished reading
the letter. He still sat with it on the table in front of him,
next to his toast and marmalade. They always had a
proper sit-down breakfast together. It was one of their
customs that was almost a rule.

'Good heavens what?' asked Malcolm, looking up.
Usually Roger would read Tom and Christopher's letter
first then, without comment, pass it over to Malcolm.
Only after that would they discuss the letter's contents –
if there was anything to discuss. It was another custom
that was almost a rule. Broken though, that August
morning in 1970.

'Tom and Christopher have swapped boyfriends.
Christopher's gone off with Armand, and Tom's living
with Michel…'

'Jesus Christ!' said Malcolm.

'They're not coming back to England but staying on in
France.'

'Bloody hell!' said Malcolm. 'How did that come
about? Did the younger two get it together and Tom and
Michel were left with each other as a consolation prize?
I mean, how…?' He shook his head, unable to express
his incomprehension in any other way.

'It doesn't say. You could hardly go into all that in a
letter.' Roger paused and thought for a second. 'You
know, it's funny and I've never thought of this before,
but when people change their relationships, their
circumstances in this way – or any other way – like
announcing a marriage or something – they never say,
we hope you approve. And yet the very fact of
announcing it actually says exactly that. By writing this
letter Tom is actually saying, we hope you approve.'

'And do we?' asked Malcolm. He genuinely wanted to
know the answer. If Roger approved, then so would he.

'I don't know,' said Roger. 'We'd need to see them face to face, wouldn't we? Look into all their eyes and see what kind of light is there?'

'So long as they're all happy, I suppose,' said Malcolm, sounding uncertain. He bit off a piece of toast and chewed it thoughtfully.

'But I mean...' Roger steered onto a slightly different tack. 'Supposing we had done it. Not that we ever would. Would we expect to be happy?' He looked across at Malcolm very searchingly and with a frown.

'Who would we ever have done that with?' Malcolm asked, apparently artlessly. 'A partner swap, I mean.'

'Tom and Christopher?' suggested Roger. 'For example, I mean. No other couple springs immediately to mind.'

'Hmm,' said Malcolm. Doing precisely that swap with Tom and Christopher – with himself getting the younger boy – had been a fantasy which he had entertained at odd moments over the years. It was not a thought he'd ever shared with Roger, and he wasn't going to announce it now.

Roger's eyes had wandered down to the letter in front of him again. 'Good God!' he exclaimed.

'What now?'

'It says Armand and Christopher rescued three pilots from the sea following a crash in a sea-plane.'

'Bloody hell...'

'I'll let you read it in a second, I promise,' said Roger.

'Who's written this letter?' Malcolm asked, bewildered. 'Whose is the signature?'

Roger turned over the pages to see. 'The hand-writing's Tom's,' he murmured. He exhaled audibly when he found the end of the letter. 'This is the weirdest thing of all. It's been signed by all four of them.'

It wasn't as if Tom and Christopher would never set foot in England again. Or as if they would never again cross the Channel together. They arrived just a week after their letter had. They had to go to Oxford. Vacate their flat. Collect belongings. Tie up loose ends. Sell the car. They sold it to John Moyse, now married to a girl called Maisie and staying up at Oxford to do a PhD, for ninety pounds.

They didn't have time to go to the Admiral Digby but spoke to Roger and Malcolm on the telephone. They hoped to see them in France again before too long. So a few weeks after Tom and Christopher had returned there the Orca made its annual journey to Boulogne. Her crew were undecided, though, about where they should stay when they got there. With Tom and Michel at Wimereux, or with Armand and Christopher above La Chope in Boulogne? Thinking it the most diplomatic solution, they had almost decided to spend their nights under the stars on the deck of the Orca when Sabine took the matter out of their hands by inviting them to stay with her. She gave them the room that had once been her son's, then later Christopher and Tom's.

'You seem to have taken it very calmly,' Roger said to Sabine. They were drinking tea from dainty bone china in Sabine's salon before the men went out to join their friends for dinner down in the town.

'Children are not like servants,' said Sabine. She had always spoken in a very assured manner, confident in her opinions and ideas. As the years passed and her hair became greyer the air of wisdom she carried about with her had become more marked. 'You only have one set of children in your life. In my case just a single child. They can't be sacked and replaced by more suitable or better ones. My son has known Tom for eight years now – and I have always liked Tom. If Tom is the person who can make him happiest... Well, who am I to know better than he does what is in my son's heart and mind?' She took a small sip of tea. 'I have to admit it caused me some *chagrin* when Michel first announced it. I couldn't see the point somehow. And if Christopher or Armand were going to be hurt and abandoned in the process ... well I would have argued against it very vehemently. But Armand and Christopher also are very happy. Though I wasn't prepared simply to take my son's word for that. I saw them together that very day. I looked carefully to see the light in their eyes.' Sabine smiled. It was a smile expressive of a deep relief. 'And it was there. That light.'

Roger and Malcolm exchanged glances. Roger said to Malcolm, 'What did I say when the letter first arrived?'

Later that evening, over a dinner for ten Chez Alfred – Benoît and René, Thierry and Robert joining the other six – Roger and Malcolm did look very carefully into Michel's and Armand's eyes. Perhaps without the deep insight of Michel's mother. Nevertheless, what Sabine had told them seemed to be true. Armand and Christopher seemed as happy with their new partnership as Tom was with Michel, Michel with Tom.

Malcolm's father would retire on his sixty-fifth birthday. Or so he had been saying for years. While his son and Roger suspected his plans might change as the time approached, the date itself would not. Like every birthday it was fixed among the stars until the universe came to an end. July 23rd 1973. His retirement, whenever it did happen, if it did happen, would have a major impact of Malcolm's and Roger's lives. Malcolm's father was a master shipwright, and a boat-repairer by trade. He owned a yard on the banks of the Stour on the outskirts of Sandwich, working mostly by himself but from time to time employing the odd casual labourer. Malcolm, who had worked with him before moving into the Admiral Digby with Roger (he too had his master shipwright's papers) was his only son. In the June of 1973, just a month before the fateful date there was still no sign that his father would change his mind about retiring on the dot, on the twenty-third of July.

'It'll leave me with two businesses to run.' Malcolm explained to Christopher and Armand.

'One and a half,' corrected Roger. He nodded, with eyes twinkling, towards Christopher and Armand. 'He doesn't have full charge of this one.' They were sitting in the garden of the Admiral Digby. Roger jerked his head towards the pub building as he said the words.

'They knew what I meant,' said Malcolm.

'Just sell it,' said Christopher. 'If you don't want to take it on.'

'Dad doesn't want it sold,' said Malcolm. 'He may be retiring in the sense that he'll no longer take a salary. But he'll still be on the board. I mean, at the moment he actually is the board.' (This puzzling English usage had to be explained to Armand.) 'It'll still be up to him whether the business is ever sold. I mean, sold before he dies.'

'So what'll you do?' Christopher asked. 'Commute between the pub and the boatyard?' The distance was about six miles.

'And work a twenty-nine hour day?' asked Malcolm a bit rhetorically. Then he said, 'I was thinking about your experience actually, the other day. I mean, at La Chope. Boss retires, kids don't want to take it on; he gets in two people he knows and trusts as managers. Is that still working out OK?'

'It's fine,' said Armand. 'As far as the arrangement goes. But three years we've been doing it…' He screwed up his still lovely face for a second. The expression was an easy one to read.

'Don't suppose,' said Malcolm, poker-faced, 'you'd like a change of scene. Come over to England and manage a boatyard...'

Christopher and Armand laughed, of course. 'Only problem is,' said Christopher, 'I've never repaired a boat.'

'I too,' said Armand.

'I'm sure you did some carpentry at school,' said Malcolm, evidently unwilling to let go.

'I once built a rabbit-hutch,' said Christopher.

Armand giggled and said, 'I too.'

'Changed spark-plugs on a car?' pursued Malcolm. 'Painted a wall?'

Christopher said he had. Armand too.

It was strange how things had reversed themselves with such pleasing symmetry. Armand with Christopher, Michel with Tom, and all four of them still happy with the arrangement after three years. During the Oxford days Tom and Christopher had lived in England but spent part of every summer in Boulogne. Now they lived in France but spent a summer holiday each year in Kent, at the Admiral Digby. Usually there were two separate visits these days: Tom and Michel's then Christopher and Armand's. It was easier that way because of the limited accommodation available upstairs. But it worked out nicely. All four of the occasional summer visitors helped out willingly behind the bar and in the kitchen. The bar ticked over much as it had always done but the kitchen work had been modified somewhat, or added to at any rate. A new concept had been invented, which had extended the pub's menu considerably. It was called Boil-in-the-Bag. Armand, with a French chef's credentials and French sensibilities, was mightily horrified but, out of the strong affection he bore Roger and Malcolm, set to and boiled the bags just the same.

In the boatyard Christopher and Armand started with the basics. Sanding and preparing metalwork and wood for painting. Applying anti-fouling. Laying on paint. Changing filters on engines. Changing oil. Cleaning blackened hands with Swarfega when work finished for the day...

Malcolm was pleased, surprised, and relieved to discover capabilities in them that they hadn't even known about themselves. 'You were wasted on rabbit hutches,' he said. He reckoned that, under the careful supervision of himself (some of the time) and of his father (for rather more of it: out of enlightened self-interest he had agreed to teach the two young men unwaged) they would be on top of the whole operation, and the business, within about a year. They'd run a café-bar successfully for a few years: why not a boatyard too? They wouldn't yet be master shipwrights – if indeed they would ever achieve such exalted heights. Malcolm would continue to deal with any major repairs to hull planking or the rigging of masts. But it happened: the system gelled, the business worked.

Over in Boulogne, meanwhile, Benoît and René were persuaded to take over the running of La Chope, and Christopher and Armand moved to England, lock stock and barrel, in the New Year of '74. They moved in to their accustomed room upstairs in the Admiral Digby and drove the six miles to work every day in the hand-me-down Mark 2 Jaguar that had previously been Malcolm's and before that his father's. It was now sixteen years old. But its continued use proved very reassuring to the boatyard's regular customers: they liked to see a bit of continuity in a business.

There was unfinished business between Christopher and Malcolm. Both were conscious of it, but neither of them mentioned it, let alone did anything about it, during the first eighteen months of their living in the same building. They had adjacent bedrooms above the bars of the Admiral Digby, where Malcolm still slept every night with Roger, and Christopher with Armand.

Ten years earlier the fact that Malcolm sometimes slept at the pub was something of a secret, known only to a trusted few. But social attitudes were gradually changing. By now they were none of them bothering to conceal the fact that two male couples lived above the pub. If people didn't like it they could lump it. It wasn't against the law. People talked, of course they did. They surmised that the two pairs of men were... There was a new word for it these days. The word was *gay*. Christopher remembered a hymn they'd sung at school. One verse went – he thought he remembered it correctly –

Let me in season, Lord, be grave,
In season, gay;
Let me be faithful to thy grace,
Just for today.

He wondered if it was sung in the churches still.

Malcolm and Christopher's unfinished business went back some fourteen years. To that terrifying night-time crossing of the Channel when Christopher had thrown himself around Malcolm in terror, wailing childishly, 'Take me home.' And Malcolm had reminded the boy that he belonged to Tom. But why had Christopher thrown himself at Malcolm? A month earlier they had been driving together in Malcolm's car. Malcolm had taken the opportunity of their being alone together for the first time ever to say, 'Jesus Christ but you're a little beauty and no mistake.' Then they'd both run their hands up the other's shorts-clad legs as Malcolm drove, but had pulled back, aware that if they went any further they'd be unable to hide the state of things from the others when they rejoined them ten minutes later. And even that moment hadn't been the beginning of it. They'd seen each other naked in the cove, when swimming with Roger and Tom. They'd been mutually attracted right back then. And Malcolm had kissed Christopher lightly, in front of the other two, the night they'd all gone out in the Orca for the first time, fishing for mackerel. Who could ever say when anything began?

They'd swum naked together more times than they could count, since then. Descending the tunnel on fine afternoons, or on Sundays when the pub was closed for a longer time. With Roger and Tom in the old days. These days with Roger and Armand. They knew what each other's cocks looked like after swimming. They'd never seen them hard.

Malcolm and Christopher found themselves alone together at the Admiral Digby one August Sunday during the hot summer of 1975. Roger's parents, still alive and dwelling in a bungalow some fifteen miles away, had a French student staying at their home. Thinking that a little contact with a compatriot might be welcome in the middle of the student's stay they had asked Roger if he'd like to bring Armand over for Sunday lunch. Malcolm and Christopher did the lunchtime shift at the pub between them. When the doors closed at two the afternoon was pretty much their own.

Malcolm turned keys and shot bolts. He turned to Christopher. 'Fancy coming down for a swim?'

'Why not?' said Christopher. He knew exactly what was going to happen. Looking back later he thought he'd known what was going to happen even before Malcolm suggested the swim. He knew exactly what was going to happen? Perhaps exactly was too strong a word, but he had an idea of the general thrust of it.

They descended the tunnel together, Malcolm with the torch in his hand. Neither of them touched each other on the way down; they certainly did nothing as suggestive as hold hands.

Out through the iron door at the bottom and onto the beach of the little cove. They stripped off, then stood and faced each other on the sand. They were both hard.

'You're even bigger than I thought you were,' said Christopher. 'You're massive. Bigger than Tom is. Bigger even than Michel.' He felt intimidated by Malcolm's size. Malcolm was six feet tall and had just entered his forties. Christopher, now thirty-two, was still elf-slender. Still five foot eight.

'And yours is the cutest and loveliest under the sun,' said Malcolm gazing at it. 'There's nothing very important about size. Come on, let's get into the water.'

Still they hadn't touched each other. But when they'd waded out a little way and found themselves waist deep they suddenly did. Each embraced the other. Quite simultaneously, as if sharing a single will, a single thought. They couldn't see each other's privates through the water. A gentle swell rose about their navels then sank bubbling around their hips. But they felt each other under water. The first contact of hands with cocks made them snigger, but when they moved on and started pumping each other the expressions on their faces grew more serious. They peered into each other's eyes. 'I'd rather like to fuck you,' Malcolm said.

'You're far too big for me,' said Christopher.

'Then you fuck me,' said Malcolm simply. Christopher thought that was generous of him.

'What? Here, standing in the sea?'

'I think it would be difficult,' said Malcolm, continuing to masturbate Christopher's unseen cock beneath the waves, while Christopher continued to do the same to him. 'We'd fall over. Even if you managed to get it in.'

'On the beach?' Christopher suggested hopefully.

'Think about it,' said Malcolm. 'Neither of us are circumcised. All that sand.'

They waded ashore, though. Malcolm said, 'Up against the door?'

It turned out to be a non-starter. The ground was uneven. It was higher where Malcolm needed to plant his feet than it was where Christopher had to stand. Malcolm was four inches taller anyway… 'It's no good,' said Christopher. 'Even up on tiptoe I can't get it near.'

'Then let's go back up the tunnel and do it in bed,' said Malcolm. 'Like every sane person does.'

'We should have thought of that in the first place,' said Christopher. They walked away a few paces and started to pick up their abandoned clothes.

'Is that what we were going to do in the first place?' asked Malcolm. 'I though we were coming down to have a swim.' He winked at Christopher humorously.

They didn't put their clothes on but carried them, as they walked up the tunnel, on their arms. Naked they walked up from the cellar together and through the afternoon-empty, Sunday-silent pub. Upstairs they completed their unfinished business very satisfactorily (for both of them) on the bed that Christopher usually shared with Armand.

Nothing was said by either of the others: neither that day nor in the years that followed. Yet somehow Roger and Armand both knew. By instinct perhaps, or they read signs in their partners' faces that for all their best efforts they had failed to hide.

Malcolm and Christopher never attempted to repeat the events of that afternoon. The unfinished business had been successfully completed, it seemed. There was no need to re-open negotiations again in the years to come. And like their respective partners they never referred to it again. The only thing that changed was that from that day forward Malcolm, without asking permission, would address and refer to Christopher as Chris. And Christopher seemed to like that.

Occasionally Armand and Christopher would travel into Broadstairs. It was the same distance east of the Admiral Digby as the boatyard was to the west. About six miles in each case. There was a specialist ships' chandler there, which sold the kind of things that boat-builders needed but that couldn't easily be obtained elsewhere. Not, for instance, at Christopher's father's builders' merchant store, or at the ironmonger's in Boulogne that had once belonged to Michel. Things like fairleads, bottle-screws and pintles – as well as items with more ordinary names. Once or twice over the years they had found themselves parking near the convent where Christopher and Tom had gone to look for the David and Jonathan painting only to be told it had been taken away three days before. Armand had been told the story a few months after the event, but it was many years later that he first saw the outside of the convent where it had taken place.

'The sad thing is,' said Christopher as they were walking past that forbidding, highly polished, front door on one occasion, 'that we completely lost touch with Molly O'Deere as a result.'

'It's a funny expression you have,' said Armand, seemingly off at a tangent. 'Keeping in touch. Losing touch. But it's a very wonderful phrase. Very descriptive, Very deep.'

'Deep?' said Christopher.

'Every time I hear it I think of the Sistine Chapel ceiling.'

'What?!' said Christopher. It came back to him, suddenly and startlingly, that a comparison had been made – by some fool of a local journalist – between the David and Jonathan and the Sistine ceiling when the painting (the David and Jonathan, that is) had first been exhibited. 'Why? Whatever makes you think of that?' He felt ill at ease suddenly, discomfited.

'The touch between God and Adam?' suggested Armand. 'That electric spark? Getting in touch. Keeping in touch. Losing touch. The phrases are very descriptive, very apt and accurate. We don't have them in French. We use the word contact. As you know. *Contacte*. It's not quite the same, though. Not the same as *touch*.' He paused a second, planting his feet carefully as they walked down a steep and awkward bit of pavement. 'How do you mean, you lost touch with Miss O'Deere as a result?'

'She'd said to look in for coffee. Well, we would have done. But it would have been a bit awkward. Having to explain what had happened about the picture. Perhaps she wouldn't have heard about it yet... Well, that was in our first Christmas vacation at Oxford. Term started again and we rather forgot about it. The years passed. Well, when someone asks you to drop in for coffee they usually mean within the next few weeks. They don't expect you to wait a decade.'

'That's quite true,' said Armand. 'I understand that.'

'It's strange because there she still is – so far as we know – in charge of that school just five hundred metres from where we live and yet we never see her. She's not the sort of person to walk into the pub, obviously – although she did once, as you know,– and she'd have no reason to guess I was living there again unless she saw me. But we never do see each other. In all these years our paths have never crossed.'

They equipped themselves with their necessaries – their dollies, cleats and D-shackles – at the chandler's, then drove back towards Sandwich. Their route took them almost past the front entrance of the Star of the Sea. 'Where Molly hangs out still, so far as we know,'

Christopher reminded Armand. 'Unseen by human eye since 1967 or whenever it was. And never to be seen again.'

But he was wrong on that last count. For, as they passed the corner of Goodwin Road and its familiar red letterbox in the wall by the entrance arch of Star of the Sea, there she was.

Anthony McDonald

TWENTY-TWO

Christopher was driving. He stopped the car, jumped out of it and called across the road, 'Molly!'

For a second she gazed at him, startled. Then there was recognition on her face. She called back, 'Christopher.' Christopher immediately darted across the road and, to his own surprise as much as hers, gave her a hug.

A minute later the car was parked inside the entrance arch of the school grounds, on the gravel sweep. Christopher looked at the circular grass plot in the centre. The last time he'd seen it a fearsome bonfire had been blazing there. Of that extraordinary event no trace remained. The lawn grew peacefully over the spot as on some ancient battlefield.

Stepping inside the building Christopher had the feeling of returning to an old familiar dream. He had spent a mere six weeks of his life in this place, but in that time the most seismic events had occurred and his memory, unlike the grass plot outside, had been permanently seared. The entrance hall, with its polished, polish-smelling, floor of alternating red and yellow tiles; its bare white walls on which a plain crucifix hung above the inward door; the pointed-arch Gothic doorway that led into the main cloister... More tiles, more polish. Lancet windows that looked out into the garden court. Stillness. A striking absence of boys. They were all in class. When you adjusted your ears to the silence you could hear the restrained mumble of lessons being taught on the other side of closed doors. There was classroom 2A. And there, next door to it – Christopher's breath caught in his throat a moment – was the door to his own old classroom, 2B. What in the world would happen were he, on a crazy impulse, to push open that classroom door...? 'We can have coffee downstairs,' Molly said, cutting in, just in time, on his awe-struck reverie. 'To save them bringing it all the way up.'

'Down to the refectory,' Christopher said in an aside to Armand as they began to descend the mirror-polished stairs. Molly put her head in at the kitchen door as they passed it, ordered their coffee, and then sat them down on the end of one of the long tables that were clatteringly being laid for lunch in the high-ceilinged refectory.

Little had changed in Molly's life since they'd last met, except – as Christopher noticed, though he wasn't going to mention it – she was now completely grey. On Christopher's side so much had changed that he didn't know what to tell, and what to leave out, or where to begin. But begin he did, and then went on, while Armand interrupted just occasionally, when he thought Christopher had missed out something important or got a detail wrong.

Armand was himself the stumbling-block, though. Christopher had introduced him simply as 'my friend'. Molly didn't query his existence and accepted his status as Christopher's partner in the boatyard, and fellow lodger at the Admiral Digby, without comment or show of surprise. But Christopher doubted that this state of don't ask, don't tell would be allowed to persist till the end of the interview.

'The picture…' Christopher brought the matter up eventually. He'd thought it too difficult a subject to broach with Molly ten years ago. It now seemed by contrast a fairly easy one. He told the story of that visit to St Gilda's and the discovery that the painting had gone.

'Oh yes,' Molly said. 'I did know that. The nuns told me eventually. Also that you and Tom had gone to look for it, armed with my letter, and been turned away.'

'Do you – did the nuns – know who it was sold to?' Christopher asked.

Molly ducked her head and sipped her coffee. Then she said, 'I've no idea at all. Nor have the nuns. Yes, I must admit I asked them. But they didn't know. They didn't know then and I'm sure they don't know now.' She paused a moment, looked at Christopher and cautiously smiled. 'Perhaps that's as it should be. Perhaps for all of us... Perhaps it's time to draw a line under it.'

They had all finished their coffee, eaten the Osborne biscuits that went with it, and now Molly straightened in her chair. She said, 'Well, I must get back to work. It's been nice to see you again, Christopher ... and a pleasure to meet you, Armand.' They all stood up and as they filed out of the refectory their footsteps echoed faintly around the big room. It was on the stairs that Molly at last asked it. 'And where is Tom?'

'He's living very happily in France,' said Christopher bravely. He took a breath. Suddenly he felt less brave. 'He lives with Armand's former partner, Michel. It's turned out to be a very good arrangement. Though I do realise that you won't approve.'

'Oh Christopher! Oh no!' Molly had stopped climbing the stairs. A tremor ran through her face and Christopher feared for a moment that she was having a stroke. She put her hand on the baluster and held onto it lightly. Christopher was relieved to notice that she hadn't literally clutched at it. She looked him very painfully in the eye. 'Oh Christopher, dear Christopher, what can I say to you? These things aren't meant to be. I have to say this to you most sincerely: these things are not meant to be. Now I have something to confess to you. Over the years I've made some changes in my own heart, and in my mind, to accommodate ... if I can put it like that ... the idea of you and Tom. And even that has not been easy. It flies in the face of all that I believe, and it's an accommodation that I've kept as a very private, very difficult idea. Trying to imagine that perhaps the two of you – Tom and you – were like two married people. In spite of everything I'd been brought up to believe – in spite of everything that is taught in the penny catechism – I dared to think such a thought. But now… oh Christopher. Oh dear. You know Christ's words as well as I do. Whom God hath joined, let no man put asunder.' She reached out a hand and grasped Christopher's. He felt his own hand tremble, and hers shook too. 'I don't know, Christopher. Did God join Tom and you? I let myself believe that. I may have sinned in thinking so. And now I don't know. I really do not know. Oh Christopher! I'm so afraid. I'm so afraid for you. I fear things will go very ill for you. For Tom. For Armand here…'

Armand had stayed mute. His mouth had fallen open and he stood motionless on the stairs. He was standing two treads above them, facing them down the stairs. But now he said, 'Dear lady, it is not bad, it is not bad,' quite vehemently.

Molly turned to him. 'You do not know. You are too young. You can not know…'

Armand protested, 'I'm thirty-three…'

'There are other ways of being young,' Molly said. 'Other ways of being young than simply in years. For those like you… For those who live like you… I have to warn you. I have to warn you because I've seen it. It can be a very lonely old age.'

'But you, Molly,' Christopher countered. 'You are un-married. What about you?' He was surprised at how cool and reasonable he was managing to be.

Molly gave him a look in which calm acceptance joined with dignity. 'I have religion to sustain me. I shall trust in God.' She put one foot on the next tread of the staircase to signal that they should continue their climb. 'Now, if you don't mind, I shall see you to the door.'

Again the cloister was eerily quiet and empty of boys. It was twelve o'clock. In every classroom the Angelus would be being recited. Through one of the doors Christopher actually heard it suddenly. A male teacher's voice: *The Angel of the Lord declared unto Mary.* A susurration of childish voices in response: *And she conceived of the Holy Spirit.* That was Vatican Two, Christopher guessed. The last time he'd said, led, the prayer, in one of these very classrooms more than a dozen years ago it had been the Holy Ghost. The Holy Spirit was new. In silence Molly escorted the two younger people to the front door. The sunshine they walked into when they found themselves the other side of it seemed to come to them from another world.

Christopher and Armand got into the car and drove out through the archway, beneath the huge stone cross that crowned it. They turned out of Goodwin Road and headed back through the countryside to the boatyard. It was good that the sun was still shining. They both felt very shaken and found little to say.

It was a little time after that uncomfortable encounter with Molly O'Deere – how long Christopher couldn't say: weeks, months? Who could ever say when things began? – that Armand had started to say, whispering it quietly in the intimacy of night-time, that he was missing France. He had missed it after the first excitement of the move to England: that had kicked in after about two months; every expatriate knew about that. But that initial homesickness had subsided, as it usually does, after another few weeks. Only to resurface after the Molly experience. Which had been in the summer of '76. It had been a summer that everyone in Britain would remember. The hottest in living memory. 1975 had been a hot year, but 1976 was the one in which no rain fell in southern England between February 13th and the end of

August. The fields turned white, there were standpipes in the streets in Midland towns, and in an attempt to improve the situation the government created a new cabinet post: there was to be a minister of drought. It worked wonderfully. Days after his appointment the rains broke and the minister's job title changed. Denis Howell, for that was his name, became minister of flood.

Christopher didn't find it easy to reply to Armand's statement that he missed France. *Do you want to go back?* That would have been an obvious thing to say, but it would not have been easy to deal with Armand's answer had that been yes. They had jobs in England, managing a small boatyard business and helping Malcolm to build it up. Malcolm and his father paid them decently, and their bank balances were also building up. And if Armand had said yes, he did want to go back, the next questions would have rolled out as inexorably as in the penny catechism. *Why do you want to go back?* The answer to that question might well have been, *I miss Michel and want to get back with him.* Christopher would have been unable to handle that answer; he preferred not to let the situation arise in which he'd have to hear it said. So when Armand, relaxing towards sleep, would stir and murmur that he missed France, Christopher would whisper back that he too missed France. But they went there often on holiday, didn't they? Then Christopher would wrap Armand in his arms and cuddle him comfortingly and caress his familiar dick. 'We've got each other, at least, though, haven't we?' he'd say. 'Isn't that enough for us?' And to his relief Armand would each time move his head up and down a little against the side of Christopher's head, with a little scritch-scratch of hair, in a signal that approximated to a nod.

Extraordinarily it was Malcolm who found a possible answer to Armand's private admission that he missed his homeland – without, so far as Christopher knew, even having heard the admission expressed in the first place. But Malcolm was a sensitive man, and was perhaps aware of states of feelings, and of atmospheres, that hadn't actually been talked about.

Or perhaps it was just coincidence.

'The yard could expand now,' he told them all, one weekend at the beginning of 1977. 'My father's ready to put money into something like that.'

'Expand where it is?' Christopher asked. 'Or into additional premises somewhere else?'

'Somewhere else,' said Malcolm.

'What? Like somewhere further down the coast?'

'Not exactly down the coast. There's a small yard for sale in Boulogne…'

Christopher and Armand were visibly astonished. 'How the hell do you know that?' Christopher asked. 'Armand and I didn't.'

Malcolm said in that imperturbable way the others knew so well, 'There was an article in one of those boat-builder mags he takes and the rest of us are too busy to even look at. Yacht porn, I call it. There's a phone number in the article. Dad thought… Well, he wondered if one of you – Armand, I suppose – would like to ring them up.'

The United Kingdom had joined the European Common Market a few years before. It had become vastly easier to negotiate a property sale in a neighbouring country than it had been before. Within two weeks of that first phone-call Christopher, Armand and Malcolm had crossed the Channel to have a look at the Boulogne boatyard. It was January and spells of foggy calm in the Channel were alternating with squally snowstorms. They didn't travel on the Orca but opted for the comfort of the Folkestone ferry instead. They took a taxi when they disembarked, across the town and along the Boulevard de Châtillon to the Bassin Napoléon. It was in a distant corner of the harbour – a remote region into which, despite living in Boulogne for years, none of them had ventured before.

'Un coin paumé,' said Armand. Which translated approximately as the back of beyond. But there at last was the boatyard, its central building a small barn with sliding doors. They were met by the owners, the would-be vendors, a husband and wife pair. They looked a bit surprised by the appearance of the three visitors – who might or might not have come across, simply through weight of numbers, as being visibly gay. But Armand, introducing himself as a dyed-in-the-wool Boulogne boy, eventually managed to put them at their ease.

The yard was smaller than the one on the Stour at Sandwich. It was well equipped, though. There was a long slipway that sloped reassuringly gently and which, because the Bassin Napoléon was separated from the outer harbour by lock gates, could be used at all states of the tide. Indoors there were work-benches with massive vices attached, jigs and a lathe. There was even an old blacksmith's anvil in one corner of the floor. A half-finished small boat sat on a cradle just inside the door. Separate negotiations would be required to arrange how that particular job would be completed, and by whom. Back in England Armand had been discovered to have a talent for such discussions. He was even better when he found himself dong it in his native French.

A couple more cross-Channel trips were required – even Malcolm's father consented to be ferried across on one of them. A French *notaire* who spoke English got involved, and an English solicitor who spoke French; some awkward issues had to be resolved with a bit of head-scratching and extra payments but then, quite suddenly one day, the deal was done. Malcolm's family business had one foot now in England and one in France.

The commercial end of the thing might have been finalised; the personal aspect remained undecided for a little longer, though. Not that it hadn't been talked about, pussy-footed around, kicked in and out of touch. It was the matter of where everyone involved would work. Where everyone would live. And with whom.

But even that had all sorted itself out most naturally in the end. After a hectic few months of to-ing and fro-ing across the Channel the three people most involved – Malcolm, Christopher and Armand – had settled their living arrangements in the most logical and logistical way. Malcolm continued to live with Roger at the Admiral Digby, working part of the time at the boatyard and part of the time at the pub. Armand moved back to France, for most of the time at any rate, staying with Michel and Tom in the apartment at Wimereux. While Christopher was the moveable one. He'd spend a week or a fortnight in England, living at the Admiral Digby, followed by a week or two in France. There he too would stay at the Wimereux apartment. Where he shared Armand's bed. Only Armand's. Not Michel's. Not Tom's. Not that those last two were different beds.

As a business arrangement this worked wonderfully. The Boulogne boatyard began to prosper alongside its English counterpart. But from the point of view of Christopher's personal relationship with Armand it was rather less than perfect. At least that was what Christopher thought. There were things he had taken for granted during his seven years with Armand. The nightly good-night and *bonne nuit* exchanged across the pillow. The familiar head discovered comfortingly on that selfsame pillow every morning on waking. But now, out of work-related necessity, those privileges, among others, had been withdrawn. It was the same for millions of people all over the world, Christopher knew. It always had been and always would be. That knowledge didn't make it easier, though. That lack of a familiar head on the pillow during the weeks he slept without Armand mattered enormously. He felt it like an emptiness in his heart at night – on those nights when he slept by himself in the room next door to Roger and Malcolm's. Next door to the room in which the older pair spent their nights together companionably, and made love occasionally, though these days more often simply snored.

Sometimes at night, if the weather was clear, you could see the lights of the French coast, thirty miles distant. Calais, Sangatte and Wissant. The coast turned a sharp corner at Cap Gris Nez, though, and the lights of Audresselles, Boulogne and Wimereux were hidden. Christopher couldn't see the windows of the Wimereux apartment. But he would think about it often enough when he was absent from it. There a similar sleeping arrangement to the one at the Admiral Digby was in place, or would be until he next returned across the Channel. There would be Armand, sleeping alone in the room they shared when Christopher was in residence; there would be Tom and Michel sleeping together in the room next door to him. At least that was what Christopher presumed was the case during his absences. Though it was impossible to be sure. After all, he had had sex with Malcolm once. Only the once, it was true. But all the same…

The missing head on the pillow. Christopher wondered sometimes whether Armand missed him during his absences these days quite as much as he said he did. He wondered if Armand was also missing Michel's company at night, separated from him tantalisingly by just a wall and the presence of Tom. He fought shy of the next thought, though it would keep coming to him in the night if, as sometimes happened, he awoke with the cares of the world on his shoulders in the small hours. The thought that he tried not to think, but eventually found he couldn't help thinking was simply this: was it only Armand's head he missed on the pillow beside him when he awoke during a week or fortnight of mornings in England, or was it Tom's also?

TWENTY-THREE

'When are we going to see you exhibiting in the Rue de Seine?' Gérard asked Tom. It was a joke. At least Tom presumed it was.

'When hens have teeth,' he replied – the French equivalent of when pigs might fly.

'He's too modest,' said Michel. 'I mean, look. That's not half bad.'

The three of them were sitting in the big kitchen at Rue St-Vincent. Propped on an easel between the washing-machine and the fridge was Tom's latest effort in oils: a Montmartre streetscape. It was peopled with Lowry-esque figures. Tom did not attempt to capture the human form in a strictly representational way; he knew his limitations and had never attempted a portrait. This was in part due to the fact that he lived with an artist of Michel's stature and reputation, and had friends like Gérard. They cast intimidating shadows for him to sit painting in. But the other side of the living-with-Michel coin was that Tom had learnt a lot from him over the years, and his representations of buildings and urban scenes really were very competent now. 'Thank you,' he said. 'Not bad for an amateur perhaps.'

'Not bad, full stop,' said Gérard kindly.

Tom and Michel always stayed with Gérard and Henri when they were in Paris. That meant twice a year at least: on the occasions of Michel's spring and autumn exhibitions at the Gallerie Laval. Usually they were the only other occupants of the house; the likes of Charles, Alain, and Marcel had departed years ago. They were welcome guests; the events that had led to Tom and Christopher's abrupt departure from the household sixteen years before were deemed, it appeared, to have been expunged from the record.

Muffled noises announced the opening of the street door and a moment later Henri pottered into the kitchen from the hallway with a bag of shopping and a newspaper. He was long retired and at seventy-five pottering was his default mode. 'Shouldn't you be gone?' he queried. 'A short afternoon to hang pictures…'

'We'll have time,' said Michel. 'Three of us. The *vernissage* doesn't open till six.' Nevertheless they took Henri's warning to heart and, after taking Tom's latest creative effort down from its easel ('Very accomplished,' was Henri's verdict on it) they left the house and made for the metro station at Lamarck-Caulincourt. It still seemed to Tom to be a shame to travel underground through this beautiful city, even after all these years. But the buses and taxis could get horribly snarled in traffic on any route that crossed the Seine, causing problems to anyone who had somewhere to get to and a time to be there.

Michel was sharing the exhibition space with Gérard. People said that was very good of Michel, but he was simply returning the favour that Gérard had done him in years past – letting Michel exhibit alongside him when Gérard was famous and Michel an unknown. Now the boot was firmly on the other foot. Gérard's reputation and achievements could not be taken away from him, but he didn't sell as well as he had done twenty years before. His fascination with gilded naked boys was beginning to seem in questionable taste, and he had changed the subject matter of his work. In recent years his speciality had been busy sea- and harbour-scapes. He painted at Boulogne and Calais. And because the foci of his paintings were often relatively fast-moving ferries, catamarans and hovercraft, he had taken to snapping photographs and using those to help him complete his work. Years ago he had stood at the rail of a Folkestone-bound ferry and wondered how to capture the speed of its departure from Boulogne in the slow medium of oil-paint. The camera had provided the obvious answer.

As for Michel's work, that still featured gilded naked boys from time to time and the art world seemed to find that fine. For Gérard and him, it seemed, sauce for the goose was not sauce for the gander. Nothing was quite as strange as public taste, they all thought sometimes, unless it was critical opinion. Gérard might have been bitter about the quirk of fate that had reversed his standing and saleability with Michel's, but he was wonderfully sweet natured, and never gave any indication that he was galled by this turn of events. Not by deed or look or word.

As the three of them discussed, and occasionally disagreed over, the positioning of the various works of the two painters this afternoon Gérard remembered the circumstances of that cross-Channel trip – when he'd stood at the rail and thought he'd like to paint scenes like the one that was opening out before him as his ship pulled out into the bustle of the sea. He had been on his way to Canterbury to see the David and Jonathan painting. Now he said somewhat absently, and surprising the other two a little, 'What was the name of the organism that staged the exhibition at Canterbury? The one I went to look at?'

Michel might not have remembered; he'd never gone to Canterbury or seen the painting, but Tom brought it to his mind and lips at once. 'It was the East Kent Arts Society,' he said. 'An association of amateur painters.'

'Well,' said Gérard, looking at him, 'perhaps you should take your cue from that. I'm sure there must be such a society in the Boulogne area. You could seek them out and get your work hung at one of their exhibitions. You might sell a few. Earn yourself some cash and free up a bit of space in Michel's studio.'

Before Tom could answer Michel wrinkled up his nose and said, 'I don't think there is such a thing around Boulogne. I've lived there all my life and I think I'd have known about it if there was.'

'Well then,' said Gérard,' not at all deflected, 'why not try the East Kent Arts Society itself? You still have a foothold in East Kent. You could give the pub you used to work in – the Admiral Dogsby is it? – as a home address. Go over on the ferry with a few canvasses tucked under your arm.'

Tom laughed. He thought the effort and the distance were out of all proportion to his modest talent and any rewards he might expect to reap. But Michel jumped at the idea. Perhaps because of a vague unease that was due to his not being able to hang Tom's amateur work next to his own paintings in the Gallerie Laval that day. Or any day. 'I think Gérard's is a good idea, Tom,' he said. 'We can write to the Society and ask, at least.'

'I wouldn't know the address,' said Tom, attempting to dismiss the notion before it grew too substantial in the minds of the two Frenchmen. You couldn't simply Google things in those days; it was not easy to trace the address of a small organisation in England if you were based in France.

'Your Miss Oh-No would probably still have it,' said Gérard. He enjoyed getting Molly's surname wrong half by accident, half on purpose; he'd been doing it for years.

'I haven't seen her in ... well, not since my first term with Chris at Oxford. That's over ten years ago now. I remember Chris and Armand saying they ran into her a few years after that, but that the meeting didn't go all that well. Well, I think that's what I remember.' Tom shook his head. 'I'm a bit vague about what they actually said. It was a long time ago.'

Gérard lowered the painting he was holding and rested it on the floor. 'Because you haven't seen someone for ten years, and your former lover had an uncomfortable meeting with her... That is not a reason why you can't write her a letter requesting an address. Of course she may choose not to answer you ... but that decision is not yours.' He paused for a moment, then added, 'As she once chose to ignore two letters of mine.'

'Oh Gérard!' said Michel, a note of gentle teasing in his voice. 'You're not still sore because you couldn't buy that picture, are you? After all these years?'

'Of course not sore,' said Gérard. 'But all the same...' He shrugged and gave a grin that was almost impish. '...If I saw it up for sale somewhere and it was at a price I could afford...' He shrugged a second time, then he picked his own picture up from the floor and hung it very firmly on the wall in the place where he had wanted to put it but which Tom and Michel had been trying to persuade him wasn't suitable for it at all.

'Your mother phoned,' said Roger when Christopher returned from the boatyard at Sandwich.

'Oh no,' said Christopher. His mother rarely phoned him. He could think only of bad news: the sudden death of his father, or a serious illness diagnosed ...

'She said to tell you it's nothing to worry about,' Roger quickly reassured him, seeing the dismay in his face. 'She said, could you phone her back. She'd like to meet you sometime soon and have a chat.'

'That's quite enough to worry about,' said Christopher, though he smiled as he said it. It could have been worse.

Over the last dozen years Christopher's relations with his parents had thawed, then re-frozen, then started to thaw again. Christopher used to think gloomily about the end of the last Ice Age. It had happened very quickly on the geological and evolutionary timescales, but still not

quickly enough to fulfil itself within a human lifespan.
The last big freeze involving his parents and him had
occurred in 1969 or '70, Christopher reckoned. He'd still
been living with Tom at any rate. During his Christmas
visit to his parents' home that year – whichever year it
was – his mother had made a reference to Christopher's
living alone. Christopher found suddenly that this was
too big a piece of self-deception to allow his parents to
live under. 'I don't live alone,' he had blurted out. 'I live
with Tom.' No answer had been forthcoming from either
of his parents, except a dreadful silence. Happily his
sister or one of his brothers had broken the spell with a
change of subject. Thank God for his siblings,
Christopher often thought. They were there for their
parents during the long periods when Christopher was
being branded the black sheep. He hadn't seen his
parents for three whole years after that little moment of
candour – not even at Christmas. When at last the
contact was resumed no mention of the person he lived
with was made on either side. This time Christopher
found himself unable to volunteer the information that
he was no longer with Tom but lived with Armand.

Now Christopher found himself returning his mother's
call and arranging to meet her in London one day the
following week. Then he had to phone Armand at
Wimereux to explain that he would be two days late
returning to France.

Dutifully Christopher met his mother at Marylebone
station and they took a taxi to Piccadilly. There was an
exhibition at the Royal Academy they had both thought
they would enjoy. Christopher was glad his mother's
summons hadn't come a month or two before. The
previous exhibition had been of the Leonardo da Vinci
anatomical drawings from Windsor Castle. Beautiful
though these were, Christopher thought the sketches of
burgeoning wombs and other genitalia might have

proved an uncomfortable backdrop to the thorny conversations of a mother and the gay son with whom she had a difficult relationship and hadn't had a private chat for years.

It was easier by far to bask in the sensual delights of the Fabergé exhibition that was running currently. In near silence they paced slowly around hushed and darkened rooms. Warm spotlights shone on jewelled enamelled eggs, some garlanded with tiny wreaths of bright gold flowers, others on trivets of legs like lunar landing modules. Their colours leaped like flames into the darkness: rose, cerise, vermilion, turquoise, emerald green, primrose, cobalt blue... There were cloisonné cigarette boxes, models of state coaches just three inches long, with diamonds encrusting the exquisite spokes of their wheels. Miniature cathedrals. Vases of lily of the valley, or snowdrops, with green enamel leaves and silver flower baubles dangling from the thinnest of stems. Christopher's favourite was a single ear of oat-grass, from which each golden grain hung by a separate tiny hook and which shivered when anyone breathed nearby, glittering then as gloriously as a whole field of oats in sun and wind before harvest time.

'How beautiful,' and, 'Look at that,' and, 'Can you imagine the level of concentration, skill and care?' were the templates for most of the conversation they exchanged. It was afterwards, as they walked out into the shocking spring sunlight that his mother came out with her surprise. 'I suppose I have to accept the fact that you're... Oh dear, I have to say gay these days. I don't like it, but I can't change it now, I realise, after all these years. I can't now change my son.' Christopher remembered that Michel's mother had said something along those lines about sixteen years ago. Why couldn't his own mother have made life so much easier for them both by reaching the same conclusion right back then?

Still, he thought, late was better than never. He didn't say anything in reply to his mother's announcement. After a second's hiatus she went on. 'Even the word gay. The hi-jacking of a beautiful little word with a meaning which was quite special and unique... Now a no-go bit of language, unusable for its original purpose.'

'We do need some sort of word to describe ourselves,' Christopher protested in a measured tone. 'Would you prefer to hear your son described as queer, as in the old days? That's another word whose meaning got hi-jacked. Though in that case not by my kind.'

'Your kind?!' Mrs McGing sounded as though she was preparing to launch a frontal assault on her son and his sexual disposition but then, hearing herself, evidently changed her mind. 'Let's not argue,' she said and suddenly clutched at her son's hand as they walked out of the Academy's courtyard and into Piccadilly.

Christopher said, 'I agree,' in his occasional old-mannish way.

'The thing is,' his mother went on, 'the thing I wanted to say, was that I would be prepared to meet Tom. Just to say hallo. A brief chat over coffee or tea, perhaps. On neutral territory. Like this. Like today.'

Christopher tried not to smile too broadly as he thought of Tom, now living in France with Michel, being summoned from Wimereux or Paris all the way to London for a cup of tea. He wanted to keep things civil, to be placatory. 'I think that's a lovely idea,' he said. 'Thank you.' He leaned over as they walked and gave his mother a kiss on the cheek. It took her a little by surprise and she breathed out a little 'oh!' But Christopher's thoughts were whirling. He hadn't lived with Tom for eight years now. However this was the least propitious moment in all that time to apprise his mother of the fact that Armand was his partner now. The future of his relationship with his mother hung quivering like one of Faberge's golden oat grains. 'I'll talk to Tom,' he said. 'We'll find a date. I know that he'll be very pleased…'

On the train back to Kent Christopher pondered his new difficulty and thought about what he could do. His mother had never met Tom, though she'd seen his likeness captured by Molly in the David and Jonathan. But that had been sixteen years ago and she would only have a hazy recollection of his physiognomy. Which in any case could have been expected to change in such a time. The first solution that presented itself to Christopher was to have Armand stand in on the day and pretend to be Tom. Its advantage was that the deception could be replicated ad infinitum into the future should further meetings be proposed. The disadvantage was of course that Armand was French. He not only looked French but had the accent to prove it, while his by now excellent English was nevertheless sprinkled with occasional startling howlers the way a beautiful night sky is visited by shooting stars.

An alternative stand-in could be Malcolm. He would probably be more than willing. But he still had a strong Kentish burr of an accent – something Mrs McGing would not be expecting in a man who had studied at Oxford not just once but twice – and furthermore he was now forty-six. He had eleven years on Christopher, against Tom's three, and it showed. At last the possibilities had whittled themselves away to one: Christopher would have to enlist Tom's help and beg him to travel to England with him. Unlike Armand or Malcolm he would not have to pretend to be other than the person he was. He would have to pretend, though, to be Christopher's lover when he no longer was.

Instead of taking his usual train trip to Folkestone and then the ferry to Boulogne, Christopher returned to

France the following day by means of the hovercraft
from Pegwell Bay to Calais. The hoverport, built ten
years earlier, was only a walk away from the Admiral
Digby. They didn't use it often, though – the hovercraft
was no-one's favourite form of transport, and there was
a one-hour bus ride down to Wimereux at the other end.
However, the bus route switch-backed through
wonderful cliff-top fields and villages and that part of
the trip made a treat on fine days. While the hovercraft
had the saving grace of taking only thirty minutes to
cross the sea. Its less attractive features were the
perpetual curtain of spray that prevented you from
having much of a view and the sand-blasted windows
that almost prevented you from seeing even the spray;
also the hideous din of its four roof-mounted engines
and the vibrations they set up – they were more than
sufficient to cause a major tempest in anyone's cup of
tea, or glass of wine or beer.

Christopher arrived at the Wimereux apartment in the
late afternoon. Armand was still in Boulogne, at work in
the boatyard, but Tom and Michel were at home. The
three of them had coffee together on the balcony, which
trapped the late sun's warmth, even in early spring. A bit
diffidently Christopher outlined his difficulty, and asked
if Tom would be prepared to cross the Channel some
time soon and join Christopher, when he next saw his
mother, in the harmless pretence that he remained his
partner still.

Tom was more than willing. He would probably have
been agreeable anyway, but his readiness to play along
was sharpened by the fact that he wanted to ask
Christopher a favour in return. Would Christopher be
prepared to rattle Molly O'Deere's cage by calling on
her in person and asking for the East Kent Art Society's
contact details? Yes, he could easily write a letter, but
with Gérard's long-ago experience to draw on, he feared

that a letter to Molly on the subject of David and Jonathan would not fare very well.

Christopher pulled a face. 'I'd be very happy to,' he said. 'But I'm afraid I might not be the ideal messenger. If you remember, the last time I saw her – with Armand – she rather chewed our ears off about sexual constancy.'

'You could at least try,' said Tom, sounding disappointed.

'Of course I'll try,' said Christopher. 'It's just that I thought I ought to let you know I don't think it'll go very well. Is there someone else, someone less controversial…?'

'Controversial?' queried Michel.

'Less tainted in Molly's eyes, then… Someone else who could go there instead of me.'

'The obvious choice would be Roger or Malcolm,' said Michel unexpectedly. 'She called on them once, I remember you told me, to hand-deliver a letter for you two…'

'She won't remember them,' said Tom. 'It was ten years ago. They don't even look the same.'

'Then they can remind her of the occasion,' Michel persisted. 'A very good way to break the ice on the doorstep, I should think,'

Christopher said, 'I agree.'

An hour later Tom phoned across the Channel and spoke to Roger at the Admiral Digby. He made his odd request quite tentatively, explaining in some detail the circumstances that had made it necessary.

Roger didn't seem to find the request an odd one at all. He cheerfully accepted the commission. It would take him no more than five minutes to walk round the block to the front entrance of the school. The worst that could happen, he said, was that she would refuse to see him, or that she'd lost the address. 'She can't berate me for changing life-partners,' he said. 'As far as that detail's concerned I'm in the clear.' He chortled down the phone. Then he promised to carry out Tom's simple request within the next two days.

And he did. Two evenings later he phoned the flat at Wimereux and spoke to Tom.

'We went together, Malcolm and I.' Roger had been a school teacher thirty years before. There was no question of his saying, in this context, *Malcolm and me*. 'We thought that might help to jog her memory. The only time we met her we were together, after all.

'Anyway, we rang the bell and waited ages. Finally a cook or cleaner, female, came to the door. We asked for Miss O'Deere, explaining we were the landlords of the pub at the bottom of the hill. We were shown into a little bare parlour just off the entrance hall. Where we waited another age. At last Molly appeared. She can only be about my age, I think, but she hasn't worn very well.

'We explained what we'd come about and then it was all amazingly easy. She seemed to light up when we said you'd been painting pictures, and remembered a conversation she'd had with you once. You'd said you used to paint but hadn't kept in practice, apparently, and she told you that you should.'

'Good heavens,' said Tom. 'I don't remember that.'

'Anyway,' Roger went on, 'she said she thought she still had the address of the art society in her office, and we all trooped round there. Along about a hundred miles of cloister that smelt of floor-polish. Then there we were, while she looked through papers in a desk. It took very little time for her to find the address. She copied it down and gave it to us. Then ... and this is really the reason I'm waffling on so, she asked after you, Tom, and asked after Christopher. We trod on eggshells a bit, but we told her you were fine and doing well, that Christopher was often at the Admiral Digby, that he was still hitched up with Armand (not that that was the phrase we used) and that you were still with Michel. She looked almost relieved by that, somehow. Anyway, she sends you both her best wishes. She said that she'd spoken a bit harshly to Christopher and Armand once. She hoped they'd forgiven her that. Also that she often prayed for the four of you.

'Well, anyway, I've told you. You can make what you want to out of it. Now here's the address... Oh, and there's a phone number too...'

Tom telephoned the Society the next morning. While he was speaking Michel wrenched the phone away from him and explained that he was a professional painter who was well-known in France, that he could vouch for the quality of Tom's work, and had a high opinion of it. He did all this in English, which was brave of him – though he didn't actually use the word vouch. Tom took the phone back and explained that, despite the poor quality of the phone connection, and Michel's accent, he was actually resident in East Kent. He gave the address of the Admiral Digby. He was invited to bring one of his paintings – or two at the most, and they should be representative of his best work – to be entered for a possible place in the exhibition at Canterbury in June.

When Christopher returned to England a fortnight later he took two well-wrapped, framed oil-paintings of Tom's with him, carrying one under each arm.

Tom enjoyed the weeks, the sometimes fortnights, when Christopher was working in Boulogne and staying – sharing the room with Armand – in the apartment at Wimereux. They were a friendly four: they would dine all together Chez Alfred sometimes, or at Sabine's, and while away an evening at Le Chat qui Pêche, or chew the fat with Benoît and René at La Chope.

307

He sometimes though about suggesting a return to the arrangement of nine or ten years ago when they would have sex *à quatre,* or alternate bed partners night by night. He didn't dare suggest this: Armand was very proprietorial where Christopher was concerned. Tom was pretty sure Armand never had sex with Michel when Christopher wasn't at Wimereux. And Tom himself was still very contented in his partnerships – work partnership as well as bed partnership – with Michel. Yet he couldn't help wondering sometimes what would have happened if he hadn't fallen in love with Michel – and if Christopher hadn't fallen in love with Armand. If Christopher and he had stayed the course… Would Tom now be joint manager of two boatyards on opposite sides of the Channel, cleaning his hands with Swarfega every night? The hypotheses could stretch to infinity: there were what-ifs too numerous and too unlikely even to contemplate. But he did miss Christopher when he wasn't there. He couldn't deny it to himself. He missed waking up next to that still blond-haired head, missed the sight of Christopher's smile when he awoke and caught sight of Tom lying beside him. That had been a daily delight of his for years – years ago – but it was one he couldn't return to it. He had to make do with the memory.

TWENTY-FOUR

There were people you lost touch with as the years passed – it just happened like that. (Armand would have said, referring to his fond analogy with the Sistine Chapel ceiling, that the spark went out.) Then there were other people whom you realised you would never lose touch with as long as you both lived. Angelo Dexter came into the first category where Chris was concerned – and Tom for that matter – while John Moyse secured himself a place in the second. In both cases that was perhaps to be expected. The connection with John ran quite deep. It involved the theft by Christopher in 1962 of a cream-coloured exercise book from the stationery store at Star of the Sea – in order to give it to John so that he could write his diary as a more expansive, less cramped document than the three-days-per-page booklet that he'd been using up until then. It also involved the sale of the Morris Minor Traveller for the sum of ninety pounds in 1970… It was not too surprising that they should keep in touch.

As for Angelo, he'd never been much of a letter writer. Not that that mattered while they were all still at Oxford. He didn't disappear from Tom's and Christopher's lives after that first term in 1967, although the emotional and sexual tumult his company had engendered faded into the past. He remained friends with Tom and Christopher, and even appeared on stage with them in a couple of productions by the OUDS. The three of them brought the house down as the sinister trio in Pinter's The Caretaker in their third term, while the following year, by which time Tom was no longer a member of the OUDS or even of the university, Christopher and Angelo had a ball among a much larger cast in The Duchess of Malfi. Angelo played Duke Ferdinand while Christopher gave his evil all as the Machiavellian Bosola. But that was as far as it went. Angelo had lost his romantic and sexual taste for older men. He had his contemporary, Piers, for a boyfriend during his first year, then came Jason, Marco, Peter, Alex, Stuart...

It was after Oxford that Angelo lost contact with Tom and Christopher. It was hardly surprising, as they'd disappeared very quickly to France. Still, news of Angelo in the following years did keep coming, thanks to the letters of John Moyse, with whom Angelo did keep in touch. In this way Tom and Christopher learned that Angelo had tried to get into drama school after leaving Oxford. That he hadn't been accepted. He hadn't been put off, though. He had got himself a job sweeping floors in a repertory theatre on the south coast. His eagerness and his appetite for hard work in the right environment paid off. Soon he had been offered a job as assistant stage manager, which involved the playing of a few small roles from time to time. After a year he secured his Equity card and from then on travelled the country, taking smallish roles in other reps. But the roles got bigger as time passed. John had reported a couple of years later that Angelo was looking to move into the more lucrative world of television. It was just a matter of time, he thought, and that time was getting close. Meanwhile he was very happy in the world of rep. It was a world well populated with handsome young gay men; and that was a circumstance that suited Angelo as comfortably as a matador is suited by his *traje de luz*.

John's letters charting Angelo's progress arrived roughly six-monthly. They were addressed at first to Christopher and Tom then later to Christopher and Armand. They gave news of John's progress too, of course. John wrote about his marriage, the births of his three children, Anna, Nerissa and Tarquin, about his progress from local journalism to writing TV scripts, and in due course his purchase of a house in Godalming and the acquisition of one dog and two cats.

Christopher was pleased to hear of John's progress as a writer. So was Tom, to whom Christopher showed the later letters. They had taught him after all, and every teacher enjoys the reflected glow of a pupil's success. The letters were nicely written, as they might have expected: full of wry, understated humour and a willingness on the author's part occasionally to laugh at himself.

John's most recent letter had arrived around Easter, in that spring of 1978. He wrote entertainingly about his elder daughter's barnstorming romp through her first year at school, and shared the good news that he had been commissioned to write several episodes of a major new drama series for ITV. Then came an item of news that gave Christopher an almighty jolt, and it startled Tom no less when Christopher showed him the letter when he went back to France. For John wrote: *You may be interested to hear some news of Angelo. Some time after Christmas he had, he claims, a 'religious experience'. He told me this in a letter; I haven't had an opportunity to question him about it face to face. He has returned to the fold of the Roman Catholic Church, he says, has returned to the Sacraments, and apparently re-embraced the whole panoply of beliefs. (Does one embrace a panoply, by the way? I'm never sure about this.) But to be serious again, he says he's doing a lot of thinking, and considering trying his vocation as a Catholic priest...*

'Well,' said Tom to Christopher as he finished reading John's letter in the Wimereux flat. 'Of all the unlikely things to happen...'

'Of all the unlikely people for it to happen to,' said Christopher. Neither of them could think of anything to say to John in reply, and his letter still remained unanswered at the end of May, the time of Christopher's return to England with one of Tom's paintings tucked into each armpit.

It was fortuitous that Christopher had a return ticket for the hovercraft rather than the Boulogne-Folkestone boat. Fortuitous but fortunate. He didn't have to struggle from Folkestone to Canterbury by means of two trains, changing at Dover. Instead Roger met him at the English hoverport, a mere half mile from the Admiral Digby, and drove him to the door of the office of the East Kent Arts Society. The office was housed in a small cottage right in the centre of Canterbury, a stone's throw from the cathedral but in the middle of the most nightmarish maze of a one-way system that any planner had ever devised. 'We should have brought a ball of string,' observed Roger.

'It wouldn't help,' said Christopher, struggling out of the car with his parcels. 'Theseus was able to go back the way he had come after he'd killed the minotaur. He didn't have to contend with a one-way labyrinth.'

Christopher rang the bell, was let in, ushered up to a small room where he handed the pictures over and signed a couple of forms on Tom's behalf. He did this very quickly. From outside he could hear the impatient horn-blasts of the traffic that was trying to get past Roger in the narrow street. Roger had decided to stay where he was, unwilling to attempt to go around the block, in case he should never find his way back.

Christopher ran down the stairs, let himself out and leaped across the pavement into the car, through the passenger door that Roger was holding open for him. Then they sped away, at the head of a long queue of backed-up traffic. It turned out to be only marginally easier to escape from the centre of the Cantuarian labyrinth than it had been to penetrate it.

The mills of the East Kent Arts Society ground slowly. Several weeks passed. Then a letter arrived for Tom at the Admiral Digby. With Tom's advance permission Christopher opened it. Both of Tom's paintings had been accepted for the Society's annual exhibition. The paintings would be hung in the cloisters and chapter house of the cathedral from Friday June 16th until the middle of July. Inside the envelope were six invitation cards to the private view on the evening of the opening day. Christopher telephoned Tom at once with the news.

A few days later Christopher's mother phoned him. She wanted to invite Christopher to lunch in London, bringing Tom with him. The ideal date from her point of view would be Wednesday 14th. The venue she suggested, a bit grandly, was to be the Challoner Club in Pont Street in the vicinity of Harrods. It was a Catholic gentlemen's club, Christopher vaguely remembered. 'Don't you have to be a member?' Christopher asked.

'I am a member,' replied his mother. 'Membership has been open to women for some years now. Their lunches are good.' Christopher sometimes wondered if his mother thought she'd married beneath her, wife of a builder's merchant that she was. He said he would check the date with Tom and phone her back.

'It fits rather well,' Christopher told Tom on the phone. 'Lunch in London on the Wednesday, private view in Canterbury on the Friday. Come over for a few days.' He didn't mention the fact, though Tom must have been equally keenly conscious of it, that the Wednesday after that would be their shared birthday. Christopher would be thirty-five, Tom would turn thirty-eight. Tom agreed – Michel could manage without him for a few days, he said – and Christopher then phoned his mother to confirm their date.

Tom arrived the day before the planned lunch date with Christopher's mother. He was nervous about the encounter. That was clear to Christopher, and to Roger and Malcolm, even though, in the bar of the Admiral Digby that evening he said the exact opposite. 'It's not that I'm nervous. Don't think that. I'm just wondering what on earth we're expected to talk about.'

'If you're very busy eating you may not need to talk,' said Malcolm, poker-faced.

'Don't be ridiculous,' Roger told him; then, to the others, 'He still makes the sort of jokes he did when he was eight.'

'What does anybody talk about when they're introduced to their boyfriend's parents?' Christopher said. 'All over the world. All through history... The weather, the food, the décor... It'll be all right.'

'Except,' said Tom, 'I'm not your boyfriend. Armand is.'

There was a very sticky silence then, as there was nothing that could very easily be said to follow it. Perhaps it was as well that the telephone behind the bar rang at that moment. Roger went off to answer it while the others, thinking that anything was better than the current awkward silence, strained their ears to hear what was said.

They didn't strain them long. Roger looked towards them, his hand over the mouthpiece. He did something very expressive with his eyes. 'Christopher, it's your mother,' he said.

A moment or two later it was Christopher who had his hand over the mouthpiece. 'She's very sorry but she can't make tomorrow. She wonders if we can do it next week instead...'

'The Wednesday?' Tom asked.

'She knows it's my birthday,' said Christopher, his hand still over the mouthpiece. 'That's why she's suggesting it. She wasn't to know it's your birthday as well, of course.'

'Oh God...' said Tom. 'I don't know if Michel's got something planned for us over in France...'

'I'll tell her that it's complicated and we'll let her know tomorrow or the next day,' said Christopher. 'Best thing to do, don't you think?'

Tom nodded his agreement to that, and Malcolm nodded too, though the question hadn't been addressed to him and it was hardly his business.

Christopher spoke again to his mother, then put the phone down. He rejoined the others. 'So,' he said, 'Looks like I'm back at work tomorrow instead.'

'No you're not,' said Malcolm. 'You took the trouble to arrange a day off. Have your day off. You can't just abandon Tom. He'll think you dragged him here under false pretences.'

Christopher looked at Tom and Tom looked at Christopher. 'Are you OK with that?' asked Christopher. 'Spending a day with me? Just the two of us?'

'More than OK,' said Tom. 'Relieved to be spared your mother, if the truth be known. Though I've got to face it one day I suppose.'

'That could be your birthday treat,' said Malcolm mischievously, and Roger said to him, 'Cut that out,' then laughed.

'Just don't drag me up to meet Molly O'Deere tomorrow instead,' said Tom. 'That's all I ask.'

'I promise,' said Christopher. 'I won't.'

Before bedtime Tom phoned Michel in France. No, Michel hadn't made any special plans for Tom's birthday, nor – he immediately checked – had Armand made any for Christopher's. Neither of them had been looking that far ahead. They had made another plan, though. They had hatched it just that evening and would have phoned Tom shortly if Tom hadn't made his call first. The plan was for Michel and Armand to travel together to England on Friday and join Tom and Christopher at the private view in the cathedral. The Boulogne boatyard could be left for the one day in the hands of the current apprentice.

Tom relayed all this to Christopher when the call was ended. 'I just knew they were going to do that,' said Christopher. 'I somehow felt it. Just as well we've got those invitation tickets.' There had been six. Two for Tom and Christopher, naturally, and two, just as naturally, for Roger and Malcolm. That the remaining two had been unconsciously reserved for Tom and Christopher's respective French partners now seemed equally obvious.

In years gone by the Admiral Digby had offered accommodation as well as food and drink. That had been in the days when hotel guests willingly shared a bathroom with a dozen strangers and didn't mind queuing to use the lavatory. There was still only one upstairs bathroom at the Digby, but there was ample sleeping space. On the rare occasions that Tom and Michel, and Christopher and Armand, had all been there together it had been easy enough to find a separate room for each couple. And so it was tonight. There was one room for Christopher and another one for Tom.

In the morning Malcolm drove off to the boatyard, refusing Christopher's renewed offer to put in a day's work. Roger had some cellar work to do. He too spurned offers of assistance from Christopher and Tom. With nothing very obvious else to do they set out on a walk.

You could walk into the outskirts of the town and on into the centre, by the inland road or via the cliff-top promenade. Or you could walk away from the town's edge and into the countryside. It was a sparkling June morning and they chose the countryside. Leaving the pub they set off on the cliff-top path. Thorn bushes intermittently hid the view of the sea and the South Foreland on the edge side, while fields of ripening oats bordered the path on the other. Whitethroats, yellowhammers and linnets darted ahead of them. They crossed the approach road to the hoverport and came to the spot where a massive replica Viking ship stood behind railings. It was fully equipped with oars and shields these days. Years ago it had been starkly under-furnished. But the same dragon's head at the prow leered down at you, smacking its lips.

They cut inland, along a lane that wound through little-visited villages, full of knapped-flint cottages and rural charm. One of them was going to say it. Both of them knew that. In the end it was Tom. 'We came here that first time.'

'Of course,' said Christopher. 'Only then it was May. The hawthorn was out and there were cuckoos calling.'

'Oh yes,' said Tom, and tried not to make it sound like a sigh.

They came to the lovely farmhouse of Sevenscore, which had been built in the graceful reign of Queen Anne. Graceful in its architecture at least. Tom said, 'I remember you saying it was so lovely you wouldn't mind living there. That was the first inkling…'

'Tom,' said Christopher in a warning tone, 'we must not do this. We just mustn't.'

'Sorry,' said Tom.

Then they came to St. Augustine's Cross. It wasn't the most exciting of tourist attractions. The nineteenth century had seen fit to erect a monument, designed like an Anglo-Saxon cross some twenty feet high, beside the road. It marked the spot – very approximately, one supposed – where the saint had landed in 597 on his mission to bring Christianity to the benighted British kingdoms. But it commemorated something else as well.

On this spot, on the plot of mown grass around the monument Tom and Christopher had picnicked sixteen years before. They had taken their shirts off and lain down in the sun. Christopher had been wearing his cricket whites. The reason behind his odd choice of clothing for that country walk might have been subconscious. Only in hindsight did it become – almost absurdly – clear. Neither of them would need reminding what had happened next. Tom had tickled Christopher's bare tummy by blowing down a grass-stalk, and Christopher, to his infinitely deep embarrassment, had promptly and visibly ejaculated inside his pants.

Behind the tall cross a spinney of poplar and hawthorn grew. Looking towards this now Tom said, 'I think I need to pee.'

Christopher said, 'Think I do too.'

The spinney was not impenetrable. There were clearings in it, and in one of those, screened from the road, the two ex-lovers unzipped and did what they needed to do.

That wasn't enough, apparently. When the moment came for tucking away and re-zipping it was obvious that neither of them wanted to. Tom touched Christopher's now hard cock. 'We shouldn't,' Christopher said. He spoke in a tone of voice that is often used by people who are about to do exactly what they've said they shouldn't.

'We both want it,' said Tom. 'We've been wanting it since we set out. Maybe since last night… Look, I can't think either Michel or Armand would be upset if we simply gave each other a wank. For old time's sake.'

Christopher said, like someone bowing to fate, 'Then we'd better lie down on the grass. Though mind the wet bit.' Before doing so he gave his old lover a kiss.

They slept separately again that night. In part this was out of respect for their hosts. But also they were afraid, now that they'd opened the safety-valve a little, that an awful lot more – in emotional, not just physical terms – might come pouring out. Roger and Malcolm might well have guessed what had happened when they'd all met up again that evening; they may have seen it in their faces, or simply reasoned that it would be obvious. But they behaved politely, and nothing was said.

In the morning the four men breakfasted again together. It was all very usual. Except for one thing. A letter arrived, addressed – astonishingly – to both Christopher and Tom. The envelope was typed. They looked at it with something like trepidation, like primitive people confronting an omen. It was eight years since they had split up. 'Well, one of you had better open it,' Malcolm said.

Christopher slit it open with his forefinger. The address, equally unforeseeably, was that of a Franciscan friary just fifteen miles away. And the letter, too, was typed.

Dear Christopher and Tom

(The writer was using the new block style, recently introduced from America. There was no comma after the salutation.)

The wheel comes full circle. I find myself writing to you both at an address just metres from where we first met, at Star of the Sea. An address given to me by John M. He has also given me the address in Wimereux. I have sent a copy of this letter there also, in case neither of you are in England at the moment. (Or should it be, neither of you is?) I know that you, Christopher, live with someone called Armand these days, and Tom – you are with Michel: again someone I haven't met. But I'm addressing this letter to you jointly (forgive me) because something in it concerns you both.

I need to begin, though, by telling you how I came to be in the place I now am, because otherwise the end of this letter will make no sense.

We were all brought up Catholic. We've all heard vocations to the priesthood described as 'a tap on the shoulder' or 'a twitch upon the thread'.

In my case it was a tap on the shoulder. I'd had sex with a young man (very nice) and had seen him out of the door of my flat. I need to tell you that we'd had very little to drink, and no other drugs of any sort. I was washing in the bathroom, to get ready for bed and sleep, when I experienced exactly that. A shoulder-tap. I spun round. Of course there was no-one to be seen. I got my toothbrush and started to clean my teeth. The tap came again. And this time, with it, there was a voice. The voice was muffled. It was as if the speaker too had a toothbrush in his mouth. The voice said, 'My son, I have need of you.' Again I spun round. No-one to be seen, of course. Now I spoke. 'Who are you?' I said. And there was an answer. Again as if speaking through a flannel or a mouth full of toothbrush, 'I Am Who Am,' the voice said.

I don't need to tell you that I fell apart on hearing that.

So here I am, a postulant at Canterbury, queuing to join the Franciscan order as a monk, and being considered for training as a priest.

Now to the part that concerns you both. Joining a religious order is just like starting work in the theatre –

or perhaps any other job. They give you the nastiest tasks first, to see if you can stay the course. So I have been tidying up the cellars. Dusting things. Packing up rubbish in boxes and taking it out. I've even discovered two toads, one frog and one newt (sadly not pissed.)

I found a stack of pictures leaning against a wall. I pulled them apart to dust the frames. Dreary devotional pictures, most of them, devoid of any merit as works of art. But then amongst them I found something that sent me reeling. It was the David and Jonathan picture of the two of you that Miss O'Deere painted all those years ago.

Maybe the last thing in the world either of you would want is to be reminded of it. Though you did talk of it a bit at Oxford. I remember you went to look for it in Broadstairs but found it not. Anyway, it is here, and I am here. If you would like to see it again, let me know before it gets thrown out. Rubbish cart. Landfill next stop.

If I don't hear from you I shall understand.

I will keep you in my prayers (or should that be shall?) and hope you'll pray for me too some day if ever you find you get back into that sort of thing.

Yours affectionately in Christ

Angelo

Brother Michael O.F.M.C.
(Angelo Dexter in a previous life)

TWENTY-FIVE

They took the train to Canterbury. Nobody wanted to run the gauntlet of the drive through the one-way system again. From an embankment they looked down on St Augustine's Cross as they sped past, just minutes after leaving the station, and an instant later glimpsed the huddle of roofs that made up Sevenscore Farm: their epic journey of yesterday flashing before their eyes in the cheap currency of seconds.

At breakfast they had shown Angelo's letter to Roger and Malcolm and had tentatively suggested calling on Angelo the following day on their way to the evening's private view. Malcolm had overridden their cautious plan. 'Sod the boatyard,' he said. 'I can look after it for one more day. Wait till tomorrow and you'll have the complication of Armand and Michel with you. As well as Roger and me.' He tapped a forefinger against the side of his nose. 'Know what I mean?'

So they had dialled the number that was included in Angelo's new home's letterhead. Surprisingly he was quite easily found and brought to the phone. It was arranged that they should come to the friary and meet Angelo during the hour of recreation, at two o'clock that afternoon.

Their train arrived in Canterbury at half past one. To fortify themselves against the unknown complications of the encounters ahead of them they quaffed a pint in the medieval-timbered bar of the Falstaff Hotel, conveniently on the route from the west station. They invested in a packet of Polos too, not wanting to breathe alcoholic fumes into a meeting in a monastery in mid-afternoon.

'I'm not sure,' said Christopher as they drank, leaning against the bar, 'how to talk to a man I once had sex with now that he's had an encounter with God in his bathroom.'

'Same here,' said Tom. He looked searchingly at Christopher for a second, then downed the remains of his beer. 'Now drink up,' he said. 'It's time to go.'

They didn't need to knock or ring the bell. There was a small garden courtyard in front of the friary and rather to their surprise there was Angelo standing in it, all alone and looking a bit thoughtful, looking out for them, when they arrived.

He was changed. Changed by more then the mere passage of eight years. He was taller, he was thinner, he was dressed like a friar. Grey tunic and half-cape with thrown-back hood. White knotted cord for a belt. Sandals on his feet but no socks. His luxuriant curls had gone; his hair was as short as an American GI's. His face was gaunt, with lines and hollows that they were surprised to see on the face of a twenty-nine-year-old. But his dark brown eyes were as alive as ever. Only they were full of a different light from the one that had been there before. In years gone by those eyes had been lit by a sense of adventure, sexual excitement, and the idea of living life to the full. Today they shone with the light of other things. Contentment. Love. And joy.

Angelo extended a hand almost before they were close enough to shake it. The distance sent a signal that was very clear. There would be no embrace to celebrate this reunion; a handshake was all that was called for. Angelo said, 'Verlaine and Rimbaud. The wanderers return.'

'It's good to see you,' said Tom, sounding a bit awed by the encounter.

'Ditto,' said Christopher,' sounding the same.

'I've brought the picture up from the cellar,' said Angelo. 'It's in the parlour.'

Of course that was where it would be, thought Tom. The parlour would be just inside the front door. It always was, in any convent or monastery. A neutral spot that was not a part of the monastic enclosure. Women could be spoken to in there, so could Jews and Infidels, agnostics and homosexuals. They went inside.

Angelo or someone else had found an easel. The picture stood on it, placed so as to be lit from the natural light that came through the single plain window. They had forgotten quite how big it was: in its plain wood frame, about four foot by three. 'Oh gosh,' said Christopher. His voice was full of an emotion – perhaps a whole bouquet of emotions – that he hadn't expected to feel. Tom said nothing. Nor did Angelo. They stood and looked, in silence, for a long time.

There they were, an eighteen-year-old and a twenty-one-year-old, staring out from the canvas at the two men in their thirties, and at Angelo, who would soon be joining them there. For years Tom and Christopher had joked about the picture of Dorian Grey. They'd imagined the picture of them ageing while they themselves hung on to youth. How painfully clear it was now to both of them that things were exactly the reverse. They had grown old; the picture had remained forever young. Two boys in cricket whites, one shirtless, the other with his shirt buttons teasingly undone. An arm around a shoulder, another around a waist. A red cricket ball in a hand. Green grass beyond... Christopher felt – like an electric shock – the sensation of Tom's fingers stealing into, then clasping, his hand. Angelo broke the silence. Speaking French, surprisingly. Remembering a poem.

'Dans le vieux parc solitaire et glacé
Deux formes ont tout à l'heure passé.

Leurs yeux sont morts et leurs lèvres sont molles,
Et l'on entend à peine leurs paroles.

Dans le vieux parc solitaire et glacé

Deux spectres ont évoqué le passé.'

'Where did you learn that?' asked Christopher. 'The Colloque Sentimental.'

'Miss O'Deere taught it to us,' said Angelo. 'Verlaine's lament for the ephemeral nature of human love.'

Christopher, his hand still held by Tom, turned to Angelo. 'Molly O'Deere,' he said. 'The last we heard of her was that she'd been praying for us.' He'd expected to hear a chuckle in his voice as he said that but somehow it wasn't there. 'But that poem,' he went on. 'Why did you come out with that so suddenly? It's the most deeply tragic thing in the world.'

Angelo didn't get a chance to answer. For Tom spoke then, reciting softly, surprising Christopher as well as Angelo.

'In the old park, frozen, lonely,
Two figures walk, two figures only.

Their eyes are dead, their slack lips mutter;
We strain to hear the words they utter.

In the old park, frozen, lonely,
The past comes back to two ghosts only.'

'Heavens!' said Angelo, looking at Tom with respect as much as surprise. 'Was that off the cuff? You even rhymed it!'

'Sorry to disappoint,' said Tom. 'I had to turn it into English verses as a project in my sixth form. Only an attempt at verse, mind. And only an attempt to remember it.'

'It wasn't at all bad,' said Christopher, and he felt Tom squeeze his hand in an unspoken thank-you.

'I have to say the picture's beautiful,' said Tom. 'At least as good as I remember it.'

'Molly was very talented,' said Christopher. He said this with the authority of someone who had spent years of living and working with painters. 'I thought so then; I know so now.' Then he stopped. Looking into this picture was like no other experience he'd ever had. It wasn't like looking at an old photograph of himself. He found that he was looking into the depths of his young heart. And into Tom's. Deep, deep, deep ran this painting; like a hologram or a mirrored candle-flame. And in the deepest depth of it he saw his love. He saw the love he had for Tom, and the love Tom had for him.

Quietly Angelo asked, 'Do you remember how the poem goes on, Tom?'

'Unhappily,' said Tom. 'I remember my own poor attempt at a translation. Not sure if I can get through it.' He drew breath and had a try, though.

' *"Do you remember our ancient rapture?"*
"Why do you want me to recapture...?"

"Your heart still beats at the thought of my name?
Is my soul in your dreams?" "It's not the same."

"Beyond words was our joy that day
When our lips first met." "If that's what you say..."

"The sky was so blue, our hopes were so high..."
"Hope has fled, vanquished, along the night sky." '

'Hope hasn't gone,' said Christopher suddenly. His words came as a cry of pain. 'It's still here. I'm still here. Tom, I want you still.'

Tom squeezed Christopher's hand as tightly as a vice. His voice was a low growl. 'I still want you. I want you again.'

'What the fuck are you going to say to Armand and Michel when they turn up tomorrow?' Malcolm asked.

They were sitting in the pub garden, talking over a much needed early evening beer.

Tom shook his head slowly. 'God only knows.'

'Tomorrow, and tomorrow, and tomorrow,' said Christopher. 'Remember the way old Father Louis used to pronounce the word tomorrow? That frightening drum-roll on the double R…'

'Only too well,' said Tom. 'With Father Louis tomorrow was a thing to dread.'

'Not with you two,' though,' said Malcolm. They looked at him, puzzled. He said, 'Tomorrow life begins again. It always does.'

'Of course,' said Tom. 'Only we haven't quite dealt with today yet.'

'You may find,' said Malcolm, 'that Armand and Michel have news for you.'

'What?' said Tom. 'You think they might want to… Wow, you're hopeful!

Malcolm moved his head from side to side. His face was suddenly inscrutable. He said, 'You never know.'

Christopher said, 'We'll know tomorrow.'

Tom thought back to earlier that afternoon. How Angelo had allowed the emotional static to dissipate before saying quietly, 'Well? Do you want it?'

'Want it?' Tom had said, unclasping his hand from Christopher's. 'Of course. To give to Gérard. He said he'd pay a good sum for it. Tell us how much…'

'It was going to be thrown out,' said Angelo. 'There's no question of money changing hands.'

'But…' Christopher tried to protest.

'All right, then,' said Angelo. 'Next time you find yourselves in the vicinity of a charity box, give generously. And when you give the painting to Gérard you can pass that message on to him too.'

'Angelo,' Christopher had asked suddenly, though a bit uncertainly. 'Do you know if it's possible to fall in love with the same person twice?'

Angelo grinned. 'Heavens! Why ask me? People see other people dressed in a tunic and sandals and expect them to know the secrets of the universe. Like Friar Lawrence in Romeo and Juliet. But I honestly don't know.' He thought for a second and during that time managed to look like his old cherubic self again. 'Though if Richard Burton and Liz Taylor are anything to go by – well, it may be possible.' He shrugged. 'I guess you can only find out by experiment.' He looked back at the painting. 'Come. I'll find us some sacking and brown paper and you can help me wrap it up.'

'We'll be in Canterbury again tomorrow night,' Christopher had said as they began to swaddle the picture in hessian. It would be a big thing to carry through Canterbury's streets. He explained about Tom's paintings and the private view. 'Want to come along?'

'Not sure,' said Angelo. 'The last time I went to a private view in Canterbury cathedral...' He tapped the parcel they were wrapping... 'To see this very picture... All hell was unleashed afterwards. As you two remember better than anyone. Not a very happy precedent.' He paused. Then he said, 'Don't worry, Tom. I'll go and have a look while the exhibition is still on. Admire your work. Never fear. Only tomorrow...'

'Understood,' said Christopher. 'Roger and Malcolm will be coming. So will Armand and Michel. It might become a bit...'

'Exactly,' had said Angelo.

Five nights later came the shortest one of the year. Even when the pub shut it was barely dusk. 'Come walk with me,' Tom said. They took the path that led from the lane beside the pub, along the cliff edge. To one side the oat field rustled in the night breeze. To the other lay the sea. They sat, squashing a patch of flowering fennel, on the very edge of the cliff. Below them the bay was turning dark as pewter in the sudden onrush of night. On the other side the South Foreland gloomed on the horizon towards the west, a charcoal stick; then the lights of Deal and Sandwich bravely sparked into life, while Venus pricked the deep blue canopy overhead. Pointing up, Tom quoted, 'Look, how the floor of heaven is thick inlaid with patines of bright gold.' And Christopher wormed his hand into the clasp of Tom's.

The last few days had been extraordinary. Twenty-four hours after Angelo had shown them the David and Jonathan portrait of themselves they had had to confront Michel and Armand. They met them at Folkestone as they came off the Boulogne boat. The looks on all four of their faces indicated things that were waiting to be said. In the car, driving back to the Admiral Digby, they had said them. Christopher was at the wheel of the ancient Jaguar, beside him sat his partner Armand. Tom, with his partner Michel, had sat behind them. 'We slept together,' said Armand suddenly, staring straight ahead at the windscreen.

'We didn't,' said Christopher, behind him. There was a moment's frisson.

'Come on, Chris,' Tom said. 'Don't confuse the issue. Don't make it more difficult. Look – Michel, Armand – Chris and I did do something. In the open air, and it was fairly basic, but it did happen. What Chris meant, I think, was that it didn't involve bed or sleeping.'

'I'm not sure…' began Michel, then stopped as though unsure what he was unsure about.

Armand said, 'Where does that leave the four of us?'

'Still friends, I hope,' said Tom. The others made murmurs of agreement.

'It was Malcolm,' said Michel. 'When we spoke on the phone a few days back. Something he said … or maybe he didn't quite say it. I just got the feeling from him that the two of you had become … how to say it? … very close again.'

'The truth is,' said Armand in a sudden rush of candour, 'that it was rather a relief to us. Because we had, also.'

No-one had been able to find any appropriate words to follow that with and, after a moment's thoughtful silence they'd talked of other things for the rest of the journey.

At the Admiral Digby Michel and Armand had admired the David and Jonathan. It was propped against the wall of Christopher's bedroom awaiting its despatch, in the hands of Michel and Armand, to France and Gérard. Gérard was going to hang it in the house in the Rue St-Vincent. 'It's beautifully executed,' said Michel. It was the first time either Armand or he had seen it.

'Very moving,' said Armand. 'You two in touch together. Like the Sistine ceiling.'

The private view at the cathedral that evening had almost been an anti-climax. The six of them had armed themselves with a glass of wine each and then gone in search of Tom's paintings. They were hanging together, not in the chapter house but in the cloister. And though they were eliciting kind comments nobody had yet rushed to buy them. Tom found himself comparing those paintings of his, of which he'd been quite proud, unfavourably with the powerful, luminous David and Jonathan that he'd seen so recently and so life-changingly.

Then suddenly, unexpectedly, Molly O'Deere was with them, thin and angular in a dove-grey dress, and Tom's sense of anticlimax went away. Molly greeted Tom and Christopher warmly, Roger and Malcolm also, and was cautiously polite with Michel and Armand. No mention was made by any of them of the current configuration of the couples. To the shared relief of all.

'Tom, you have a talent,' Molly said. 'I think your two pictures are rather splendid. They give a real sense of Paris. You can almost smell Montmartre.'

And Tom, who had felt despondent about his work just two minutes earlier, now felt wonderfully boosted and took a slurp of wine. 'Thank you, Molly,' he'd said with feeling, and he'd almost kissed her. But instead he changed the subject. 'We have news,' he said, and told her about Angelo and the David and Jonathan.

Molly was astonished but also delighted to hear of the re-conversion of Angelo and his plan to try his vocation. The re-discovery of the David and Jonathan here in Canterbury in a cellar caused her, in comparison, a smaller amount of surprise. 'I'm glad it's going to a good home at last,' she said when Tom had finished his tale.

'It's at the Admiral Digby till Sunday,' Christopher told her. 'You're welcome to come and see it there.'

Molly hesitated for a second, undecided. Then she said, 'I probably won't.' Her half-frown became a half-smile. 'I'm sure you'll understand. But – Tom and Christopher – it's very good to see the two of you together.' Another pause. Then, 'But I'll say goodbye now.' She looked around her a little anxiously. 'I'm here with some of the boys. I'd better get back to them before they try to persuade the bar-tenders to give them glasses of wine.'

At the Admiral Digby that night Armand and Christopher had slept together while Tom had shared a bed with Michel. But the following night, at the end of a day in the countryside, roaming the banks of the Great and Little Stours, exploring the pretty riverside villages of Fordwich and Wickhambreaux – a day during which not much was said but a great deal was thought, felt and wordlessly negotiated, Tom and Christopher had gone to bed together and so had Armand and Michel. The next day Michel and Armand had departed for France, taking with them the David and Jonathan painting to give to Gérard.

'See that?' said Tom, pointing up again at Venus, shining like a lamp in the increasingly gold-painted sky. He lay back crushing the tall fennel flowers behind him. 'Verlaine's poem goes, *"L'espoir a fui, vaincu, vers le ciel noir."* Only it hasn't. Hope hasn't fled, vanquished. As you said when we saw the picture. And you were right. It's up there. There hope sits.'

'Hope for us?' said Christopher. He looked up, then down again and further out to sea. Looking due south now. Slim as a pencil stroke there was the coast of France. Lights moved along it. Headlights of cars that travelled the road from Calais to places round the corner of Grey Nose Cape: places out of sight. Audresselles, Boulogne, Wimereux… 'Hope for Michel and Armand?'

'I wonder,' said Tom, 'if they're sleeping together tonight.'

'I guess they are,' said Christopher. 'I hope they are.'

'Seconded,' said Tom.

'Other hopes?' Christopher probed. He too lay back now, then reached out and held Tom's hand again.

Tom said, 'Hope that we can sort things out with Michel and Armand?' He wondered if Armand would want his old job back, being Michel's personal assistant: the job that was now Tom's. Tom couldn't easily see himself working in a boatyard with oily hands. But those were concerns for another day. Tomorrow… Which thought prompted another hope. 'Hope that your mother will like me when we meet tomorrow?' he said.

'Hope that we won't be pretending we're a couple tomorrow?' said Christopher. 'Because we'll be the real thing?'

'Maybe,' said Tom. He heard himself and relented. 'No, not maybe. Make that a yes. Yes, I hope so.' He peered at his watch, twisting his wrist slightly, trying to trap the final light of the dying day in its glass. 'Hey, Chris,' he said quietly. 'What do you know? It's now tomorrow.' He pulled Christopher to his feet and kissed him. 'Happy Birthday, Chris,' he said.

Christopher said, 'Happy Birthday, Tom.'

Tom said, 'The night's cooling down now. Time to go home, I think.'

Chris said, 'I agree,' in that old-man way he sometimes had. They began to walk home.

Tels ils marchaient dans les avoines folles,
Et la nuit seule entendit leurs paroles.

So saying, they walk through the wild oat-grass.
While the night alone hears them as they pass.

The translation is Tom's, of course.

****

This is the second book in the Dog In The Chapel series. The third is Dog Roses.

About the Author

Anthony McDonald is the author of thirty-one books. He studied modern history at Durham University, then worked briefly as a musical instrument maker and as a farmhand before moving into the theatre, where he has worked in every capacity except director and electrician. He has also spent several years teaching English in Paris and London. He now lives in rural East Sussex.

Novels by Anthony McDonald

TENERIFE
THE DOG IN THE CHAPEL
TOM & CHRISTOPHER AND THEIR KIND
DOG ROSES
THE RAVEN AND THE JACKDAW
SILVER CITY
IVOR'S GHOSTS
ADAM
BLUE SKY ADAM
GETTING ORLANDO
ORANGE BITTER, ORANGE SWEET
ALONG THE STARS
WOODCOCK FLIGHT

Short stories

MATCHES IN THE DARK:
13 Tales of Gay Men

———

Diary

RALPH: DIARY OF A GAY TEEN

Comedy

THE GULLIVER MOB

Gay Romance Series:

Sweet Nineteen
Gay Romance on Garda
Gay Romance in Majorca
Gay Tartan
Cocker and I
Cam Cox
The Paris Novel
The Van Gogh Window
Tibidabo
Spring Sonata
Touching Fifty
Romance on the Orient Express

———

And, writing as 'Adam Wye'

Boy Next Door
Love in Venice
Gay in Moscow

All titles are available as Kindle ebooks and as paperbacks from Amazon.

www.anthonymcdonald.co.uk

Made in the USA
Las Vegas, NV
30 May 2022

49556086R00193